SIMPLY HEAVEN

Serena Mackesy is a novelist, journalist and travel writer. Both her bestselling first novel, *The Temp*, and her second novel, *Virtue*, were published by Arrow to great critical acclaim. She lives in London.

Praise for Serena Mackesy

'Brilliantly observed... a gripping read' *The Times*

'Mackesy's 400-odd pages whip by in a sitting... Say no more, except – more!' *Independent*

'A very funny novel about love, friendship, revenge and finding yourself' *Daily Express*

'Clever, witty and original' *Company*

'A thrilling, funny but very thoughtful caper' *Daily Mirror*

'A lively romance' *Guardian*

'Fresh, sparky, funny and sadly poignant' *Big Issue*

Also by Serena Mackesy

The Temp
Virtue

SIMPLY HEAVEN

Serena Mackesy

arrow books

Published by Arrow Books in 2006

1 3 5 7 9 10 8 6 4 2

First published in the United Kingdom in 2005 by Century

Arrow Books
The Random House Group Limited
20 Vauxhall Bridge Road, London, SW1V 2SA

Random House Australia (Pty) Limited
20 Alfred Street, Milsons Point, Sydney,
New South Wales 2061, Australia

Random House New Zealand Limited
18 Poland Road, Glenfield
Auckland 10, New Zealand

Random House (Pty) Limited
Isle of Houghton, Corner of Boundary Road & Carse O'Gowrie,
Houghton 2198, South Africa

The Random House Group Limited Reg. No. 954009

www.randomhouse.co.uk

A CIP catalogue record for this book
is available from the British Library

Papers used by Random House are natural, recyclable products made
from wood grown in sustainable forests. The manufacturing processes
conform to the environmental regulations of the country of origin

ISBN 978 0 09 941476 6 (from Jan 2007)
ISBN 0 09 941476 7

Printed and bound in Great Britain by
Bookmarque Ltd, Croydon, Surrey

For Anne Shore. Thank you, sweetheart.

Acknowledgements

The period of writing this book hasn't been the easiest time and has left me critically aware of just how much of a team effort both writing and life are. As ever, I am indebted to Jane Conway-Gordon, who has yet again gone way beyond the remit of an agent in terms of support, encouragement, friendship and patience in the face of rampant self-pity: I honestly don't know what I'd do without her. As I am, too, to each individual at Century and Arrow who has contributed their knowledge, skill and professionalism to the final product and beyond, but particularly to Kate Elton, whose judgement is unerring even if my acceptance of that is sometimes grudging. And to Henry Wickham and Sakis Tsikas for their Greek translation services, ancient and modern. And to Antonia Willis, Steve Delia, and Joe and Janet Camilleri for showing me the joys of Malta and the ecstatic weirdness that is the Birzebuggia Festa. The kids on the Block – you are crucial, and brilliant: may the froth on your cappuccino be always dusted with chocolate. To the following people: Ali M, Anne S, Beverley L, Bottomley (M), Brian D, Cathy F, Charlie H, Charlie S, Chloe S, Chris M, Claire G, Daddy, Diana B, Dido P, James O'B, Jo J-S, Joce M, Jonny L, Lucy McD, Mum, Matt W, Nik D, Venetia P, Will M: thank you, each of you, from the bottom of my heart. Finally, to Evil Princess Fifi: boing!

Acknowledgements

Chapter One
The Proverbial Thunderbolt

People always ask us how we got together, and I suppose you *would* wonder, him being so conspicuously equipped with silver spoons and me your average ockerina – all thighs and vowels – and we always make a joke of it, say: 'Oh, you know: I fished him out of the sea and he swept me off my feet.' But you know? That was what actually happened. Only, you can't describe that sudden rush of *knowing* in cocktail language. You can't say to people: I was ripping my knees apart on this pockmarked limestone beach and I'd just given this guy mouth-to-mouth and, once he'd thrown up a couple of gallons of seawater, he touched me on the arm, just a gesture of gratitude, a simple touch, and it was like someone had attached electrodes to us and switched them on at the mains. It would have knocked me off my feet, for sure, if I'd been on them: I've never felt anything like it before, and I doubt I'll ever feel it again. Not with anyone else, anyway.

It was the same for him. We leaped apart like scalded sea-monkeys and crouched – well, huddled in his case – five or six feet apart, trying to make sense of what had just happened. And after a bit, once he'd done with the panting and the looking lean and glisteny with his dark hair dripping down over his suntan, he said: 'Jesus. What the hell was that?'

I said: 'I think I just saved your life, mate?' trying, you know, to make light of the situation, and he said: 'No, I know. But what was *that*?'

And I was doing a bit of panting of my own, I'll tell you, and I wasn't concentrating too well, because I was getting a rush similar to the one you get when you're hanging over the edge of an extremely high cliff without a safety rope, so I said: 'I don't know.

It's got *me* beat. You mean you . . .?' And he said: 'Yes.'

And then we looked a bit longer.

I saw a man somewhere around my age and maybe a couple of inches shorter, which is pretty tall for the male population. And he had these deep brown eyes flecked with gold, and fringed with heavy, wet lashes that were so long they brushed his full, black eyebrows as he looked up. And he had a beaky nose and sharp cheekbones and a mouth that – I don't know – looked brave. Like he'd been hurt a lot, but wasn't going to give up, you know?

Right now, those lips were slightly parted, revealing flashes of the even, not-so-white-you-don't-believe-it teeth behind, the lower one starting to jut forward in the manner of one who wants to be kissed, and I knew it was an unconscious imitation of my own expression. I know. Crazy, isn't it? But of course, I already had a pretty clear memory of what those lips felt like, having had my own pressed pretty firmly against them, and believe me, they'd felt pretty good. And, Jesus, the guy wasn't even what you'd exactly call awake at the time, either.

Eventually, he spoke.

'Shall we try it again?' he asked.

'OK,' I said. I reckoned that if we set off some sort of spontaneous human combustion scenario, at least we had the Med to jump into. And besides, now I'd got over the surprise, that electrical thing was something I wanted to feel again. Possibly for ever.

'OK,' he said, and sat up. I was suddenly, painfully, aware of just how, well, *naked* we both were – me in a bikini (I'd thrown my sundress and hat off sometime between dropping my sketchpad and diving headlong into the briny) and him in those baggy shorts English guys think of as swimming gear – and how surprisingly *alone* we seemed to be. You'd have thought that, Gozo being an island twelve kilometres one way and six the other, that maybe *someone* would have been around to witness it, but the golden desert landscape remained empty. And we each reached out and grasped the other by the upper arm, and – kablamm! – it happened again.

Only, this time, we didn't let go. The surge of electricity ran from his fingertips, up my arm – bang! – through my brain, down – wham! – through my torso, over the old Mappa Tassie, sizzled down my thighs and calves to the very ends of my toes and – zap! – straight back up and out through my fingers into him. And he was kneeling bolt upright, eyes half closed, and shaking as he felt it too. And I swear, each of us had developed those anti-gravity hairstyles you see on people walking past a supercomputer.

Eventually, he opened his eyes and reached forward with his spare hand and cupped my face – *crackle* – and the back of my neck, and pulled me towards him. And my skin fizzed with pleasure at the touch, and I swear, if you'd been there you'd have seen St Elmo's fire dance up and down our spines when our mouths touched.

The next time I remember seeing beyond our bubble, the sun had dropped to almost the edge of the horizon, flushing the foreshore a thousand shades of scarlet, and the sea had turned to quicksilver. And there was the two of us, caked in sweat and salt and crumbled sandstone, each gazing with shock at the other and touching the other's skin as though it was precious silk. This was way more than lust. I know about lust – I'm from Queensland, after all – and this was something else. The erotic charge of the near-death experience? Maybe. Or perhaps the proverbial thunderbolt.

'Come home with me,' he said, 'please. You must come.'

I followed him in a dream. Left everything on the beach, damnit – clothes, paints, sketchbook, hat, sarong, towel, everything. I barely remembered to snatch up my purse before I trailed in his wake, one hand still clasped loosely in another, up rough steps hacked into great sandstone breakers carved by the sea, across the wind-bleached tarmac to his 4WD, parked immediately in front of my own battered little hire car.

We didn't talk much. I think we were both still in shock. And speechless at the discovery that such urgent change can come upon you out of a blue summer day. I was thinking: either this is the craziest thing that's ever happened to me, or the most romantic, or maybe both – and despite the heat pumping off the darkening landscape, I shivered and wrapped my arms around myself.

He drove quickly and surely, brown arms and strong hands caressing the steering wheel, eyes fixed on the road. There was a sort of shyness between us – not embarrassment, not awkwardness – an unwillingness to look at each other. I put my heels up on the seat, stared at mellow stone walls, at stone-carved, shuttered balconies, at red plaster onion domes and grand carved doorways, at caper bushes and great trees of prickly pear. I must remember this, I thought, for ever: this is the night I found love. Love, or an unmarked grave. Only time will tell.

'Where are you staying?' he asked.

'Xlendi,' I replied. 'You?'

'Xewkija,' he said. And took his hand off the gear stick and put it on my leg. Stroked the sensitive skin at the top of my thigh with his thumb and set off another paroxysm of shivering. He smiled, said: 'There's a jacket on the back seat.'

I found it, pulled it on. Dirty cream linen with a gold silk lining and that peculiar smell that Englishmen's jackets have: sort of sheep and rain and Granddad's pipe tobacco. The lining felt good against my naked back. I hugged it round myself as we passed through Victoria, wound up through newly active evening streets. Hole-in-the-wall shops spilled tiny figures, dwarfed by the meat-fed tourists around them.

Xewkija was quiet and cool, front doors thrown open to the evening air. He pulled in, creaked on the handbrake and turned to me. And the electricity jumped the gap between us.

'You can turn back now,' he said. 'It's OK. I'll take you back . . .'

I shook my head, no, ran a thumb down his cheek. He closed his eyes for a moment, butted against my hand.

'Oh Jesus,' he said, 'if I don't . . . I'll . . .'

I was out of the car like a scalded cat, leaning against the bonnet, jutting my hips, with my hands in the jacket pockets. And he was after me like a fox. Grabbed me round the waist and pulled me up an alleyway: blank sandstone walls and weeds growing bravely up

4

from dusty cart-ruts. And he got me up against a wall, grinding into me, both of us all hands and mouths and fast, hot breaths, and I had my leg wrapped round his backside and he had a grip on my buttocks like a sheep-shearer on a ram. And I was going, 'No, look, we can't do it here, someone might . . .' and thinking: 'oh, God, this is . . . will you just FUCK ME NOW, YOU BASTARD? Can't you see I'm DYING here?'

And eventually, in a voice that was choked and hoarse, he said, come on, come on, and hauled me to a rough, studded wooden door in the wall. And he's fumbling with keys and fumbling with me all at once, and I'm tearing at the tie on his shorts with my fingernails, and then the door suddenly falls open and we burst through it and I briefly catch sight of a courtyard and a couple of glass doors and some pots of bougainvillaea and geraniums, and a stone staircase leading up to the purple sky, and a huge stone table surrounded by large teak chairs, and then to be honest, I don't see anything much but stars for a while.

Chapter Two

Rufus

I come to in the small hours because someone somewhere has let off a firework. Which is fairly much par for the course. Making things explode is the Maltese national pastime. Peer in through a few garage doors here of a summer evening, and you'll find at least one set of men huddled over a tub of gunpowder, cigs dangling from lower lips, scratching hairy backs in off-white vests as they plan some *festa* mayhem.

I find myself curled up under a sheet in a huge room with a barrel-vaulted stone ceiling and a dozen niches, some the size of cupboards, some the size of shoeboxes, in the walls, the only bits of the room that have been plastered. And there's this stranger, Rufus – I know that much – sleeping beside me, back pressed against my side and feet entangled with my own, breathing softly against his pillow.

And my first thought is: strewth, Melody, girl, what have you got yourself into this time? He could have been an axe murderer for all you knew. And my next thought is: is this for *real*? Because, obviously, the backpacking experience has to involve some level of promiscuity if you like your naughties and have set out without a playmate, but this was way beyond naughties. This was, like, supersex. I feel stretched and pummelled and blissfully, dreamily washed over with satisfaction like someone's come along and given me a lovely big shot of morphine.

So my next thought is: I wonder how long it's polite to leave him to sleep before I wake him up and see if he's up for a spot more universe-expansion? But he looks so happy snuffling away there, and I suddenly feel shy. I mean. It makes you think, when you've spent half an hour with your ankles wrapped around someone's

6

neck before you've even learned their name.

So then I realise that the inside of my mouth is as dry as a bone. Because, though we took time out for a 'swim' in the emerald-painted pool in the walled garden at the back of the house, and swallowed a fair amount of water in the process, neither of us has actually thought to rehydrate in any serious way since we got back. And in 40 degrees of heat, at that.

My stranger-lover shifts slightly in his sleep, presses his face closer into the pillow and unwinds his leg from mine where the contact is making the both of us sweat like brumbies. I decide to take advantage of the opportunity, and very slowly, very quietly, lift my side of the sheet off my body and swing my feet to the floor.

Barefoot and naked, I search for something to cover up with. The linen jacket lies, as far as I can remember, just inside the alley door, and my bikini is most probably hanging in separate parts from the frames of a couple of the living-room pictures. Whatever, I don't fancy wandering about this unfamiliar house without a stitch. I sidestep a big heap of clothes on the floor and head for the armchair that stands in the shadows in the corner of the room, root around among the could-go-another-wear pile tangled up on the seat. From the feel of it, the chair is made of leather. Nice. Eventually, my hand lights on the reassurance of brushed cotton, and I extract a long-sleeved shirt and pull it on. Tiptoe back to the open door and out on to the stone staircase.

There's a church looming over me, lit by one of those flash Arab moons, as I emerge from the bedroom, the roof soaring above the slabby little houses like a rising sun, clad in a thousand hundred-watt lightbulbs. The Maltese islands would be a good few degrees cooler if they'd only leave the lights off. And I have one of those God-is-everywhere moments. Swiftly followed by one of those yeah-and-he's-watching-you-right-now-you-scrubber moments. So I pull my purloined shirt over my breasts and shoot down the stairs in a vain attempt to get out of sight of the Almighty.

In the kitchen, one of those huge old 1950s fridges that looks like a spaceship grumbles by the French windows leading to the pool. Smooth stone tiles, cool under my feet. I throw the light switch, flip on the fan standing in the corner and hunt through the wall cupboards for a glass.

The interior of the cupboards is pretty impressive, in a mad sort of way. I know he said it was a family house, but it looks like this is one of those families that buys a house so they've got storage for all the junk they're too mean to throw out. There must be six dozen glasses in here, none, as far as I can see, matching. The same with crockery. Soup plates the size of cattle troughs and teacups the size of sherry glasses, piles and piles of dinner plates and side plates, dessert bowls and sauce boats, each with a different pattern, each one bearing a chip, or a crack, or a glaze that has run to a million crazy-paving crackles. On the top of the cupboards, lined up like urns in a crematorium, half a dozen lidless soup tureens. My yaya had one of those, which she bought in an insolvency sale. She used it to grow hyacinths in. She had a chamber pot she used for the same thing.

I help myself to a large cut-glass tumbler and fill it with fridge-water. Help myself to a couple of fat purple figs from the blue glass bowl in the middle of the long, scuffed pine kitchen table and go through to the lounge to eat them.

More of the same in here. The maroon leather Chesterfield settee must have been gorgeous, ooh, say a hundred years ago. It's certainly well made, but you're not talking cutting-edge design here. The leather has been polished black in places by years of contact with the human body, and has worn through in others to the point where the rough hessian backing shows through. The two armchairs are in roughly similar states. Apart from that, the room contains two wine tables (chipped), a standard lamp whose shade has been eaten away by time and moths until it is little more than lace, and a couple of truly baleful old folk in 1930s gear glooming from heavy gold frames on the bare stone walls. A low bookshelf runs the length of one side of the room, crammed two layers deep with paperbacks that have obviously been building up for decades. Dozens of original Penguins in the stripy covers; a complete collection, as far as I can see, of Dashiel Hammett, the usual copies of *Valley of the Dolls*, *Riders* and *Jaws*, scotched and battered copies of Hardy, Eliot, Woolf, Dickens, King, du Maurier, Richardson, Rendell, Shelley (M., not P.B.), Crichton, Franklin M., Maupin, Manby: all hotched and potched together as they've been read and discarded.

The top surface of the bookcase is covered in dozens and dozens of household goddesses: rough miniature terracotta reproductions of the crazy Neolithic statuary from the great temples scattered across the islands. Fat ladies, long since decapitated, stand and recline by the score, flesh dripping downward like moulded lard, on chipped white gloss paint, watched over by a *mater dolorosa* printed on to knobbly cardboard and fadged into a brass frame so lightly plated with silver that a couple of rubs of a duster has taken the surface away.

'Mad, aren't they?' Rufus has come into the room without my noticing.

I pick up a goddess – a she-walrus who lies on her side on a primitive ottoman in a knee-length A-line skirt, like she's just got in from a twelve-hour shift mopping the floors at a discount supermarket – turn her over in my hands.

'Yes. Are you sure you've got enough there? Couldn't you cram a few more in if you put your mind to it?'

'People keep giving them to us,' says Rufus. I'm not sure if I like this 'us' business, but I let it ride. 'It's some sort of running joke. Would you like one? A souvenir of Gozo? Although, of course, she comes from Tarxien, which is over on Malta, but . . .'

He approaches, closes my hand over the statuette and squeezes. And smiles into my eyes. Which somehow manages to make both my heart leap and my nether regions contract, all in one go.

I wriggle out of his grasp. 'Nao-ouh!' I reply. 'I couldn't take something as obviously unique as that. It must be worth a mint!'

He's wearing boxers and a white T-shirt that's obviously come off the pile on the floor. He smells – well, *manly*. His beard's grown in and his hair stands up in tufts on the side of his head where he's been sleeping. He looks good enough to . . .

'Melody,' he says, and, spoken with those long English vowels that come from the back of the throat, my name sounds classy, romantic, sexy, even. I've spent most of my life being called 'Millerdee', and all it takes is one Englishman to turn me into a princess. I smile back at him because it's fairly obvious that he's not actually after an answer.

'I'm so sorry,' he says. 'I'm appalled I didn't at least give you some water. Would you like something to eat?'

'What time is it?'

He glances at his watch. 'Half four.'

More than fourteen hours since I last ate, and that was just a couple of pea *pastizzi* and a glug of water.

'What've you got in the house?'

We go over to the fridge and I replenish my water as he delves about inside.

'Eggs,' he says. 'Tomatoes, olives. And some of that disgusting cheese. And some – yes. I thought so. There's still some ham left.'

'Aah Jeez,' I say. 'The ham here's terrible. Reminds me of rinsing at the dentist.'

'Ah, no,' says Rufus, 'we get ours from Twanny Mifsud. He cures it himself. Well, I say cures. He covers it in salt and leaves it out in the sun, as far as I can work out.'

There he goes again with the 'we'. I don't like this 'we' stuff. It's the sort of word that's calculated to make you feel unsure of yourself.

I know. It's a bit late to be asking questions now.

He emerges from the fridge with a waxed paper bag in his hand, grins with pleasure. 'See? A totally different animal.'

Unwrapping the bag, he brings out a lump of maroon meat, an inch of white fat around the edge, marbled and stippled and perfect. 'It's almost like biltong,' he tells me. 'Totally illegal, of course. Well, it soon will be now they're in the EC, anyway. Have a taste.'

I peel off a flake, pop on to my tongue. It's like chewing pig-flavoured car tyre. Beautiful.

'Beautiful,' I say.

Rufus throws it on to the table, goes back into the fridge. 'I told you so. We've been getting it from him for ever. Well, his dad—'

I've got to know. It's not just the disappointment factor, though I know already that I'm riding for a severe disappointment, because this man is something different from anything I've encountered before. I don't do that sort of thing: just chuck myself into the love-thang without a single doubt. I've never done before and I'm not going to start now. So I say: 'Rufus, hold on a minute.'

He reappears. 'Uh-huh?'

'Look, I'm sorry to give you the third degree, but who's this "we"?'

He looks blank. 'Huh?'

Well, either he's a good actor, or he's lacking a few sandwiches in the old picnic department. Or he's going 'huh?' because I've caught him out and he's stalling for time.

'You know. You've done it about ten times. Said 'we' instead of 'I'.'

'Well, I . . .' He frowns.

Oh God. He's thinking up a story.

'Well, I did say it was a *family* house.'

'Oh God.' I sit down, heavily, in a wooden chair at the kitchen table. 'Oh, God. How stupid am I?'

Rufus is frowning some more. Puts the tomatoes and the olives on the table and sits down facing me. 'What's up, captain? You've lost me.'

'Well, shit, I might as well have known, but . . . Jeez. You could have told me. I mean, you can't be *that* desperate . . .'

He shakes his head. That's right, you low-down ratfink. Shake away. That's a lot less than I'm doing.

'So,' I ask, 'have you got kids as well?'

'Have I got . . .? What are you . . .? Oh God! Melody, no! You've so got the wrong end of the stick. You think I'm married, don't you?'

I look up. To my shame, I can feel that my nose has already started to puff up and go pink. 'Well, aren't you?'

He starts to laugh, which doesn't please me. Reaches over and bashes me on the shoulder, which, given the fact that I'm making

11

it so clear that I don't like what he's got me into, seems a bit inappropriate.

'You think I'm some kind of moustache-twirling lothario preying on innocent sunbathers while the Ball and Chain slaves away at home? Is that what you think?'

'Well, that's about the size of it, isn't it?'

He wipes his eyes. Collapses into another gust of giggles. 'And I threw myself into the sea as part of my cunning plan to get your pants off? Gawd, blimey, darling. There's a couple of hundred chicks who'll probably put out for a couple of glasses of Lachryma Vitis staying in Marsalforn alone. I really didn't need to . . . Bit of a high-risk strategy, isn't it? What if you couldn't swim?'

'I'm Australian, aren't I?' I snap. 'Of course I can swim.'

'Didn't check your accent. Sorry. Have an olive.'

He unties a plastic bag full of purple kalamata olives, pushes it across the table towards me. Starts to laugh again.

'OK, OK,' I say, embarrassed now, 'that's enough.'

'I can't wait to tell the wife about this,' he says, then, catching my expression, points and cackles. 'I'll tell you what,' he says, 'even if I was married, I don't think I'd *dare* try something like that on with you. Seriously, Melody, you look like you could come over Sicilian at the drop of a hat. You'd probably leave a horse's head in my bed or something.'

'Cypriot, actually,' I say. 'I've inherited my father's hair and skintone, but, fortunately, not my yaya's capacity to grow a beard. 'And it would be a goat, if I could get my hands on one.'

'I'm not married,' he says. 'Melody, I'm not married. I've been waiting for you to come along, honestly.'

'Don't overdo it, mate.'

Rufus stretches over and tucks my hair behind one ear. 'Will you have an olive, now?'

Sulkily, I pop a couple of kalamata in my mouth. Yum. Fat as a goose.

'I mean it, though,' says Rufus, and he hasn't taken his hand away. Caresses my ear and my jawline, and I can feel another shiver coming on. 'I know Englishmen aren't meant to be romantic, but

12

I swear I've been waiting for you. You're different. You're different from the kind of girls I know at home, but you're just – different too. Melody?'

'What?'

And a bit later, he says: 'You feel it too, don't you?'

And I say, 'I don't know. There's something. You're . . .'

And later still I say: 'Yeah, OK. This is totally . . .'

And at five thirty or so, dawn beginning to make itself known in a serious way through the French windows, I say: 'Rufus?'

'Melody,' he says.

'Did you really say that that ham was made by someone called Twanny Mifsud?'

Chapter Three
Truth Game

'I was head boy of my school,' he says. 'Well, they didn't call it that, but . . .'

Well, I can't do that. I wasn't a delinquent or anything, but most of my year twelve ambition was geared more towards popularity with first Liam Costello and then Troy Carver than it was to popularity with the faculty. Our piles of stones seem to be evening out again. Five minutes ago, I had only one stone left, was *that* close to whupping his backside, but I'm already back up to six. I'm going to have to put some effort in.

Genius. I pick up a stone, put it on the heap between us. 'All my education was free on the state.'

Rufus waggles a finger at me. 'That's cheating. Prior knowledge.'

'Take it like a man.'

'OK.' Rufus picks up a stone of his own. 'Well, if you want to play it that way. I've *never* been the recipient of state education.'

'Now, that really *is* cheating.'

He shrugs. 'Your petard, my darling. Take the hoisting . . .'

An impasse. That's the trouble with the truth game. If you start playing tactically, it gets boring. I mean, obviously you don't want to be the idiot drunk who misreads the point and starts sharing intimate detail they're going to remember with sick horror in the morning, but you've got to keep it moving to keep it interesting. Especially if, like Rufus and I have been doing for the past five days, you're using it to share information without looking like you're getting heavy. I look away over the sea to give myself time to think of something. And for the gazillionth time, I'm hit by the blinding beauty of this place.

Ask me about Gozo, and I'll tell you: it's blue. Gold and blue. Huge azure skies, sea that dapples its way from whitest turquoise to near-black royal, stones soft and crumbly like Cheddar cheese, houses casually fronted with decorative sculpture of wedding-cake complexity. It's blue and gold, with the scarlet of *festa* banners hung across streets, pink-marbled plywood plinths that raise plaster saints above the heads of Christians. It's the place I found my love.

And I'm giddy with love. I never thought I'd feel like this again, after Andrew did his disappearing act. I'd thought this was it: me, alone, own two feet, travelling the world and looking after myself, and here I am now, rushing like a hippie. I feel like I've got vertigo. I feel like I'm standing on the highest cliff-top, all the splendour of creation spread out below me, and I feel exuberance and terror rolled into one lurching wave of elation. It is delirium, this love. It consumes my waking thoughts and seeps, mellifluous, into my dreams, so that, each time I surface, it is with a new shock of *my God, but you're real*. I didn't know. I didn't know.

He is – Oh Lord, I don't believe in all that love-at-first-sight, consuming passion, not being able to be happy when you're away from someone thing. I thought that the *Our Song, We Just Couldn't Help Ourselves, Our Place, I Just Knew, Do You Remember The Moment When* . . . stuff was the province of people who didn't have enough in their lives, who needed to add drama to their histories, and I've had enough drama already to last me a lifetime. I'd thought the love-at-first-sight thing was a justification for losing your self-control, an excuse for all those greedy little acts of adultery that shatter other people's hearts.

But Rufus. To me, he's all of humanity, and a creature set apart. This familiar stranger, this ordinary man: he's a hero in my eyes. I want to fight his enemies, embrace his friends, leaf through his baby photos, wash his back when he's tired.

And yet I know nothing about him. Not really. I feel I know everything, and yet I know nothing. And he knows nothing about me. Beyond the basics: his father and mother ('married longer than most of the county and very full of it') and heavily pregnant older sister, my Cypriot dad and beach-blonde mum, my gravelly yaya, and Costa, my big brother, the Kebab King. That he went to an English public school (didn't they all?) and on to Oxford, and I, largely educated on the state, got out at eighteen and didn't get back in till I was twenty-three. His job in the family business ('I suppose you'd call it property management, really') and the reflexology practice I had in Brisbane. He knows a bit about my fucked-up, fractured engagement, and I know scant details of the half-dozen averagely fucked-up relationships that make up his past. We've agreed our political agendas (left-central, appalled at the way psychopathic corporations are taking over the world), our attitude to animals (love the ones we live with, eat the ones we don't, nothing personal), favourite song ('Rock'n'roll Suicide', David Bowie, him, 'Natural Woman', Aretha Franklin, me), worst food (tripe); favourite place (right here, right now). But we are as innocent as Pledgers. We know nothing of night fears, of insecurity, of hatreds and jealousies and failures, of cowardice and ignorance and limitations, of childhood illness and family timebombs. What do we want to know about that for?

I'm living in a fantasy world of figs and honey, vines and prickly pear, hot afternoons making love in the blast of the fan, early mornings diving for sea urchins with a knife and a mesh bag tied round my waist, snoozing in the shadow of a rock overhang, eating fried rabbit and olives, spaghetti vongole, driving up to Victoria for *pastizzi* hot from the oven at two in the morning, building chemical hangovers on local wine and swimming them off to the sound of church bells. But it's not these things that make me love him. It's that I'm certain that when we are together, we are invincible.

And I look up, sometimes, and catch him looking at me, and I can see the same thoughts reflected in his eyes. We've been together a week, and I've forgotten all about my onward plans. I collected my bags from the aparthotel in Xlendi as soon as we left the bed on the first morning, and lost myself in his arms – such an easy thing to do – and now I'm scared stupid because I know that this will have to end. There is life outside, and one day we'll both have to go back to it, and the prospect fills me with dread.

16

And now we're on the rocks at the top of Mgarr ix-Xini creek, lying side by side as salt dries into healthy skin, handing out a caress here, a kiss there, throwing each other quick glances of complicity and playing another round of the truth game.

What you do is this: you each have a bunch of stones. You take it in turns to say something about yourself that's true. If it's also true about the other person, they put one of their stones on your pile. The person who wins is the person who gets rid of all their stones first. As a drinking game, it can be pretty cruel, but sometimes, the way we play it, you're just as happy to lose, as the forfeit always involves physical contact. And, baby, the physical contact.

I think some more. Then I ante up, say: 'OK. I once manipulated the feet of a cast member of *Neighbours*.'

'Got me there. Which one?'

'A blonde one. You're not going to tell me you've heard of her. She didn't go on to have a blistering pop career. But she had toenails like pork scratchings and skin like Emmenthal.'

Rufus's lower lip wiggles like a seismograph reading. 'Just my type,' he says. 'A lot of the girls where I come from spend the entire winter in riding boots and never change their popsocks.'

'That's attractive.'

'Well, you don't want to be downwind of the hunt ball. It's amazing they manage to catch any foxes at all, really.'

I've slowly started picking up that Rufus comes from a more elevated background than my own, that the accent is more than Hollywood English. It's the small things: the references to horses, the occasional rueful mention of the fact that he wore a tailcoat to school.

'So was that a truth, then?'

He shakes his head. 'True, but not a truth. Let's see . . .' He takes his own turn at staring over the azure water.

'OK,' says Rufus. 'If my grandfather was alive, he'd be over a hundred and forty years old.'

'Bollocks.'

'True. He had my father when he was seventy-three.'

I laugh. 'No. But that would make him old enough to be my yaya's grandfather. It's too weird. And this was by his first wife, was it?'

Rufus, for some reason, tweaks my nose. 'Cheeky. No, his first wife went down with the Titanic at the age of thirty-eight. He was twenty-five years older than her.'

'I'm sorry,' I say, not sure apropos what.

'I don't think the family were too upset. She was running off with some Canadian lard baron she'd met on Paddington station. Saved everyone the embarrassment of a divorce, and besides, I think they all probably felt it was a judgement from God. My family has always thought that God was on their side, one way or another.'

'So who was your grandmother?'

'The youngest daughter of one of his shooting buddies. She was well over forty years younger than him.'

'God! Poor cow!'

He shakes his head. 'I think it was probably a lucky escape. Youngest daughters were generally lined up to look after the old folk and then eke out their lives on tiny allowances from their brothers' whims at the time, and at twenty-five she was already heading over the hill for a normal marriage in those days. As it was, she had fourteen years of pandering to Grandfather, and she's had another sixty pottering about the place telling everyone what to do. Mummy's been a daughter-in-law since practically the ark.'

'Your grandmother's still alive?'

'She'll be a hundred next year,' he says proudly, 'and still has most of her marbles.'

'Impressive,' I say. We live, after all, in a world that sees vacant longevity as evidence of a life well lived. 'And you mean they've lived in the same house all that time?'

He gives me a funny look that I can't quite interpret. 'Urrr . . . yuh.'

'Holy Ada. That must have been tough.'

'Well, there's a fair amount of room,' he says, and, changing the subject: 'Go on, then. What's yours?'

18

'Oh. Right. Um. . . OK. I once danced so energetically I dislocated my knee.'

He curls up into a ball and makes ai-ai-ai noises. 'Jesus, Melody. Would you be accident prone, by any chance?'

'I guess. Hadn't really thought about it. Do you think I have a lot of accidents, then?'

'Let's see. Third-degree burns from an exploding cherry bomb. A broken arm falling out of a tree. Kangaroo scratches. Losing a fingernail by catching it in a rucksack strap. Two crowned molars from falling downstairs. A torn ear lobe . . .'

'Now, *that* wasn't an accident. I told you: that was Linda Ho.'

'I don't think *my* sister *ever* got into a cat fight.'

'She started it.'

'I don't suppose you just sat there and took it, though, did you?'

'Bitch.'

He laughs. Loudly. Slaps his thigh. 'I like a woman,' he says, 'who won't take any nonsense.'

'Is that your go, or are you just patronising me?'

He puts a stone in the middle. 'Go.'

'I like a man who knows his place.'

Looking sly, Rufus picks up a stone to add to the pile. I'm on him in a moment. Any excuse for a play fight. 'Don't you dare! Don't you even think about daring!'

I pin him down, gripping his wrists, and feel him buck beneath me, laughing. And then, because it feels good, I make him buck some more. And then he twists his wrists until they slip out of my grip, and grabs me by my shoulders, pulling me down until we are body to body, mouths an inch away from each other's.

'This is a good Catholic country,' he pants. 'We shouldn't be doing this. A priest might come along at any moment.'

'Do him good,' I reply, a little breathlessly. 'We're not breaking the law. Not even beginning.'

'Yes, but if we're not careful, we soon will be.'

'I'll be careful,' I whisper at him.

'I don't want to be careful.' Suddenly, his beautiful face is serious, shy eyes looking up at me through lowered lashes. 'I never want to be careful when it's you.'

So I kiss him. Tender and strong. 'No need,' I tell him. 'I trust you.'

He pushes me back upwards, sits up himself, so that we are sitting, pressed together, face-to-face, legs entwined like an illustration in the *Kama Sutra*. 'Do you? Do you really trust me?'

I nod because, to my surprise I've just realised that I do. Trace the smile lines around his mouth with my right thumb.

'I believe that,' he smiles. Puts an arm round my waist and pulls me closer. 'OK, then. Here goes nothing.'

With his spare hand, Rufus picks up a stone and lays it on the pile in the middle. 'I love you,' he says, 'and I want to marry you.'

And I don't even hesitate. I take my final pebble and add it to the heap.

'I win,' I say.

Chapter Four

Marry in Haste

Twanny Mifsud isn't even the half of it. Our marriage, six weeks later in the registry on Merchant Street, in Valletta (Las Vegas this ain't – they force you to sober up before the wedding here), is attended by Twanny (which is short for Antwan, by the way) and his wife Marija, Stiefnu Micallef and Pawl Zammit, representatives of the Marsalforn police who were called out to investigate my disappearance by Marija Boffa, whose husband, Jakbu, had found my clothes on his salt pans and my unlocked car on the road above it, put two and two together and failed to come to the conclusion that I'd suffered a sudden attack of lust. The Boffas are with us too, as well as Stiefnu and Pawl's wives, Marija and Rita. Half the female population here is called Marija. Which, considering the average family size, makes the mind boggle a bit.

Rita wears a heroic amount of lipstick and is the only one of the women who didn't produce a bundle of knitting whenever we paused for one of the infinite periods of waiting that characterise dealings with Maltese bureaucracy. It was Rita who brought the bunch of lilies grown in her own garden to go with my bridal attire, and Rita who shocks the assembled by gaily ordering two bottles of sweet pink local frizzante to accompany the nuptial feast we treat them all to on the balcony at Giannini, overlooking not only the great expanse of Marsamxett harbour and the dancing lights of Manoel island, but also, as luck would have it, the firework display at the Sliema *festa* on the far side of the water. I can't help it: infected by the superstitious Catholicism amidst which I've been living over the last couple of months, I can't see it as anything other than a good omen.

Of course, a more pessimistic soul might see it as an omen of fireworks to come, but this is my wedding night. I know they always say that and everything, but I am the happiest I have ever been. I didn't know it was possible to be this happy and not actually die. I've got this permanent lump in my throat, and every time I look up and catch sight of this man who is now my husband, I feel an urge to start blubbing, to punch my fists through the air and shout out my joy and to wrap my arms around his neck and sink into the oblivion of intimacy, all at once, all in one go.

The evening is still hot though it's late October, and on the balcony, where tiny breezes catch and cool, we breathe in lungsful of that heady, combined scent of shit and oleander that will always tip me into romantic nostalgia from now on.

We've drunk the disgusting wine, which the locals have consumed with a lip-smacking gusto that suggests to me that their tastebuds have been eroded by too much seawater, and eaten antipasti, fat shrimp with chillis and olive oil, chateaubriand and a chocolate wedding cake that Rufus has spirited up without my knowing. I'm in a slip dress of gold silk that I ordered for big bikkies from Rome at the internet café in Rabat, and Rufus, after three goes at the dry-cleaners, has got his grandfather's linen suit, the one whose jacket he gave me when we first met, presentable enough to wear.

Rufus has his hand between my thighs under the white tablecloth, and I'm thinking: my God, this is it. Every day, I shall wake and the first thing I see will be him. I'll go to sleep to the sound of his breathing. He will kiss my neck another twenty, thirty thousand times before I die. And I'm thinking: glorious, glorious, glorious! This is what I've waited for all these years, and it's so *easy*! And then Twanny, as if he's heard my thoughts, immediately sabotages everything with a question I simply don't understand.

'Aooh!' he calls to me down the table. 'How you gettin' on with Lady Mary, then?'

'Who?' I ask. Actually, I say something like 'Uh?'.

He raises his eyebrows, glances at my husband. 'Lady Mary,' he repeats. The name sounds more like a racehorse to me than anything else. 'Ay yexpekted to see her here.'

'She's at home,' Rufus interjects smoothly. 'Tilly's having a baby, you know, and she's come home for the duration.'

'But she'll be gutted,' Twanny persists, 'to have missed it.'

'I'm sure she will,' says Rufus.

Twanny turns back to me. 'So how you been getting on, then, the two of you?'

The table has fallen silent, and eight pairs of eyes regard me with the bushy-tailed glee of people who have finally got on to the subject they've been dying to broach all night. And I still don't know who the hell they're talking about.

'I,' I say, thinking fast, 'I haven't had the pleasure of meeting her yet. I can't wait . . .'

There's an almost imperceptible shift among them, the *frisson* of a shared joke. 'I'm sure she'll love *you*,' says Rita, and I'm not sure if she's giving me a compliment or not. The heat begins to rise in my cheeks.

'So you all know her, then?' I ask.

All four men raise their hands, and three of the women. Oh God. So it's only me, then. I attempt to flash glances at Rufus, but, his hand suddenly withdrawn, he seems to be intent on studying the innards of a fig and doesn't look up. Who is Lady Mary? Rufus? Help me out here? Husband, remember?

'She's an amazing lady,' says Twanny. 'Everyone around here knows her,' and again I feel that *frisson*, feel it blow over the hairs on my back.

'She likes to *support* things,' says Marija Mifsud, and Rufus suddenly looks up and gives her a sunny smile of amusement.

'Sure does,' he says. 'What's she supporting out here at the moment? I've rather lost track.'

'Animal sanctuary. Traditional crafts. The museum at Gharb.'

'And family planning,' says Rita in her old-fashioned subcontinental-style English. 'She's got Father Buttigieg in a proper two-and-two.'

Another smile. 'Sounds like my mother, all right,' he says.

Shit, so this Lady Mary is Rufus's mother. It's already come as a bit of a surprise to find that I've married a man called, not Watson, as I'd thought, but Callington-Warbeck-Wattestone. I guess you should always have a look at someone's passport before you throw your lot in with them.

'How is she?' Stiefnu sits back from the table, lights a red Rothman.

'She's well,' says Rufus.

'So how come's you haven't introduced her to your fiancée, then?' asks Stiefnu. The idea that there are no emotional in-laws at the table is a source of perplexity to them all: they share the Mediterranean love for family, and evidently can't imagine a world where people get married without the full complement of polyester lace bandages and weeping grandmas.

But not just that: he's hit the nail on the head. And that makes me the sort of person who marries a guy without asking that question myself. I mean, how can I have got hitched to someone and not even known that there was a title in the family?

'Oh, you know . . .' I can see that Rufus is trying to make a joke of it. 'I was afraid Mel would run for the hills if I let her get a whiff of the family before I'd got her firmly tied down with a contract.'

The whole table laughs, and there's something alarmingly knowing about the sound of their mirth. I co-operate, laugh along. It's probably nothing. It's probably my own paranoia.

But I do notice that Rufus still isn't meeting my eye.

Chapter Five
Cold Feet

'OK, mate. Time to come clean.'

We're huddled together on the viewing platform at the Cirkewwa Tower. I've got his jacket on, and he's wrapped himself in the shawl that came with my dress. We've got an open bottle of lukewarm Lanson at our feet and a scotched and water-stained pack of Marlboro in the jacket pocket. And at last I have a chance to pin him down.

'Oh, bugger,' he says, 'I'd hoped you'd forget about all that until tomorrow.'

'Not a hope, mate.'

'What do you want to know?'

'Well, for a start, there's the small matter of your name.'

'What about it?'

'What about it? Well, exc-*yuze* me, but do you really think that 'Charles Rufus Edmund Callington-Warbeck-Wattestone' is not an issue?'

'Watson,' he says faintly; 'it *is* actually pronounced Watson.'

'Straying off the point, mate. So how come's you didn't see fit to break the news to me before I was goggling like a gurnard in the registry?'

'Yuh,' he says, 'well, because sticking your hand out and introducing yourself by that handle is not a guaranteed ice-breaker.'

'Yeah, and I looked like a right tit when my jaw cracked on the floor. I'm surprised they didn't call a halt to the whole thing there and then on grounds of kidnap. Still, I don't suppose it's any harder to pronounce than Katsouris. How do you fit that lot into the boxes on a tax form?'

'You don't,' he says. 'That's one of the reasons I call myself Wattestone.'

'And the others?'

'People make assumptions,' he says.

'You don't say.'

'You'd have made assumptions.'

'Would they have been false assumptions?'

He bites his lip, concedes the point. 'Well, no. Probably not.'

'Oh hell.'

'Blimey, Melody,' he protests. 'It's not *that* bad! I'm not a mass murderer!'

'Got any in the family?'

Rufus laughs nervously. 'No. No. Well, not for a while, anyway. They're all eminently respectable. Eminent respectability has been the family byword for hundreds of years. It's practically a motto.'

'Hundreds of *years*? I can't trace my lot back more than three generations!'

'Well . . .' he shrugs. 'It's not something I exactly show off about . . .'

'But all the same.'

'Well, I'm not going to be *ashamed* of it.'

I overreact. It's been a long day. 'Oh, right. So it's that *I'm* not good enough, then?'

'No. *No*. Melody, no! Please. Don't twist my words. You're fine. No, you're more than fine, you're lovely. You're wonderful. You're my wife. I'm prouder of you than anything else in my life.'

But I'm on a roll now, and I'm not going to let him get away with it that easily. 'Well, if that's so, how come you haven't told them about me?'

Rufus takes a slug from the bottle, a drag on his cigarette. 'My darling, I could ask you the same question,' he says drily.

He has a point.

I endeavour to change the subject. I'm a woman, after all. Keeping the menfolk in the wrong is second nature.

'Yes, but,' I say, 'you haven't just gone to your own wedding

26

party and found out that you're the only person there who doesn't know your mother-in-law. And that what's more, there's obviously some big joke I've not been let in on.'

'I told you,' he says, throwing away his butt, 'the Xewkija house has been in the family for ages. Mummy's father was stationed over here before the war and this was their holiday house when it got too hot in Valletta. Mummy spent most of her childhood here.'

Mummy. I didn't actually think grown men called their mothers 'mummy'. Especially not in that 'mumm-eh' way you hear people say it in period dramas.

'*Mummy*?'

'Mmm.' He is oblivious to my tone. 'And her mother was one of those colonial charitable types. Always trying to save the Papists from themselves, you know? And I suppose Mummy's sort of taken on some of her mantle over the years.'

I'm already getting a picture of this woman. And I don't think I like it.

'Rufus?'

'Melody?'

'Is your mother a bit of a harridan?'

'No!' cries Rufus. 'God, no! No! Mummy's charming! Charm itself!'

Yipes.

'But?'

'No buts,' he says.

'I don't believe you.'

'Well, you have to. Honestly. You'll love her. And I know she'll love you.'

'What makes you think that?'

'She loves me,' he says simply, 'and she wants the best for me.'

Worser and worser. We all know about mummies who want the best for their sons. 'Where are the smokes?' I ask hurriedly.

'In my jacket pocket,' he replies.

I light two cigarettes and pass one to Rufus.

'So,' I say, 'fire ahead.'

'What with?'

'Tell me everything. Tell me what I've been stupid enough not to ask about. Tell me what I've married myself into.'

'You make it sound like a jail sentence.'

I shrug. Jesus, I'm a hypocrite.

'What do you want to know?'

'From the top. Everything.'

'Where do you want me to start?'

'Are you rich?'

'Sort of yes and sort of no,' he says.

'No, Rufus, that's not an answer.'

'Sorry.' Rufus goes quiet, looks out to sea for a bit.

'Please don't be cross with me, Melody,' he says.

'That's an unreasonable thing to ask,' I tell him, 'when I don't know what it is I've not to be cross about.'

'It's nothing bad,' he says, 'really. A lot of people would be pleased . . .'

I take him by the wrist, shut him up. 'Then how come you're behaving like there's some dark secret? What have I got myself into? Mad wife in the attic? History of catalepsy? Possessive housekeeper? Which closet are the skeletons in, Rufus?'

'We don't have closets,' he says, 'we have wardrobes and wall cupboards. And the skeletons are mainly in the churchyard down in the village. Although every now and then a bone pops up and bobs about on the surface of the moat and scares the tourists.'

I blink. 'Oooo-K. Backtrack. Moat? Tourists?'

I can feel his blush warming the night air. 'Ummm . . . yuh.'

'And you didn't think to tell me about this?'

'Ummm . . . no.'

'You didn't think it might affect me? Just a bit? That I thought I was mixed up with a nice guy who did something in property, and now I find out he's got a *moat*? What is that? Something to do with a castle?'

'Um, yes, but they demolished the fortifications after the revolution. It's more of a house now, really . . .'

'. . . with a moat.'

He's quiet. Not a lot to say, really. He's busted and he knows it.

I take a deep, deep lungful of smoke while I wait for him to come up with some sort of reply.

'Wouldn't it rot your socks,' I say reflectively.

His arm, which was draped round my shoulder, has dropped to his side.

'So if your mother's a lady,' I ask, 'does that make you a lord?'

'No.'

'How come?'

'She's a lady in her own right. Her father was an earl. The rest of us don't have any handles. The Wattestones have the distinguished record of living a thousand years in the same house without once collecting a title.'

'Good Lord,' I say. 'They must have been seriously mediocre to manage that.'

'Yuh,' he says lightly, 'there's a lot to be said for mediocrity if you're aiming at longevity. Doesn't do to put your head too far over the parapet.'

'A shame, really.' I try to make light of it, though to be honest my stomach's in my boots. 'I would have got a laugh out of being Milady Melody.'

'You'd have had to take my name for that,' he reminds me.

'Ah, well, can't have everything, eh?'

'Are you all right with this?'

'No, I'm bloody not, Rufus Wattestone. Jeez-us. What kind of drongo marries a girl and hides stuff like this from her?'

'Well, I don't know a lot about *your* family, it's got to be said.'

'You do, you know.'

Even as I say it I recoil at my own hypocrisy. Because I've not been entirely honest myself. But it wasn't me who started on the old assumptions. Rufus obviously thinks I'm as poor as an Indonesian pork butcher, and I never thought down about *him* like that. I hurry on. 'I mean, what's it all about, Rufus? Are you ashamed of me? Ashamed of your family? I mean, aren't you a bit old for this sort of thing?'

'Well, I thought – I thought it might make a difference.'

29

'Oh, don't tell me you're going to do the old pop star "I want someone to love me for *me*" line now, are you?'

'Well, it's true, Mel.'

'And that's how much you think of me, yeah? That you had to check I wasn't some sort of gold-digger? Thanks a bundle.'

'Mel, you've no idea. At home, I'm an eligible. All I ever meet is girls in headscarves whose eyes light up like lasers when they hear my name. All they can see when they look at me is stabling and a banqueting hall. I'm not a person. I'm a career option. Wouldn't you feel the same way?'

I stay silent, beaming murderous thoughts in his direction.

'And then I met you, and you didn't have the faintest idea who I was or what you'd be getting beyond just me, and it was amazing.'

If I were brutally honest, I'd have to admit that this particular appeal didn't only work in the one direction.

'I'm sorry. I'm sorry, Melody, but you've no idea what it felt like getting to make love with someone who was making love with *me* and not my acreage. And no-one's ever told me to shut up, before. Well, apart from my family and a few teachers at school . . .'

'Rufus?'

'Yes?'

'Shut up.'

'OK,' he says. And we both do some staring over the darkened sea. There's still a good hour until the ferry is due. I take a swig from the bottle, hold back a burp as the dying bubbles make a final break for freedom.

'Rufus?' I say eventually.

He takes my hand again, doesn't look at me. 'Yuh?'

'Some start to a honeymoon, eh?'

He allows a small, nervous sound of mirth to break loose. 'I suppose you would have found out sooner or later.'

'I don't have the *clothes*,' I say. Though I've no idea why.

'Sweetie, you don't *need* clothes,' he says. 'Well, no, obviously . . . but really, it's the last thing you need to worry about. The entire *village* is made up of people who wear jumpers. They've all got one long velvet A-line skirt each, which they trot out at New Year, and a white blouse, and—'

'Oh *Jesus*!'

'What?'

'You own a village?'

'Well, we—'

'What have I done?' I ask, in a voice that seems to be a lot louder and a lot higher than I'd thought it would be. 'What have I *done*?'

'Darling, darling, *darling*!' Rufus lets go my hand, puts his arms round my upper torso and squeezes. 'I'm sorry. I'm really sorry. I'm a total, witless spaz. I should have given you some warning. But look, it's a shock, that's all. It's nothing *like* as bad as you think. Honestly. Look, really. Darling, you'll see, you really will. None of it's as bad as you think it is. Why are you in such a state? It's not like I've married you and emptied your bank account, or turned out to be a passport hunter, or something.'

'Just so many lies.'

'What are you talking about?'

'Rufus, I can't deal with any more lies.'

'Darling, what are you *talking* about? I haven't lied to you. I know I didn't tell you the whole truth, but . . .'

Not altogether to my surprise, I've got tears on my cheeks. It's been an emotional day, after all, and despite everything I'm still an emotional person. I wipe under my eyes with the cuff of his jacket.

'Rufus, it hurts, you know? When you find out that everything's different from the way you thought it was? It's happened to me too often, and I still feel like my heart's been burned by the last time, and I can't *do* it any more. I thought, this time, you know, I'd got a fighting chance, that I'd met someone who was clean and clear and we'd live honestly, and we'd be true, and we'd get to live like real people . . .'

'But we are. We *are*. God, what's hurt you so much? Why do you think I made all those promises today? Do you think I didn't mean them? What do you think I said them for?'

I wipe my eyes again. 'Oh, yeah. Promises. I've had a few of those before.'

'We've all had promises broken on us, Melody,' he says. 'Everyone. It's part of life. You can't use that as a reason for suspecting everyone else . . .'

I shake my head, fluff my hair up. Sigh. 'I know. Rationally I know that, but . . .'

'What?'

'I never really told you the whole thing about Andy, did I?'

Chapter Six

The Vanishing

It's the wondering that's the worst. The not knowing. I know that this is the great cliché of the press conference and the tabloid interview, but the fact that it has become cliché doesn't detract from the veracity of a statement. It's the daily ritual of hopeful waking and numbing remembrance. The relentless wish-fear-expectation that today, after all these days, after fiery tears and wasted appetite and sick, sick self-loathing, will be the day they call, or break their silence with a letter, a postcard, an e-mail, or someone bumps into them in a shop, a bar, some far-flung tourist spot. For a while, you can ameliorate the pain by convincing yourself that they've not been in touch because they can't: because someone or something, some circumstance or infirmity or Hollywood-style total amnesia, is stopping them from doing so.

But that's no alternative. That sort of magical thinking is corrosive. To wake up one morning and realise you've spent six months hoping that someone you love is in a coma, kidnapped and tied up somewhere, slowly desiccating in a roadside ditch, because all of these scenarios are more bearable than the idea that they hate you so much that they'd rather cut off all ties with everyone than have anything to do with you again: that's bad.

I knew, from the moment I put my key in the lock, that he was gone. And there I go again: manipulating the past to fit with what I would like to be the truth. I knew long before I went home. Of course I did. I knew as I was telling my mother that I didn't know why he'd done it. I knew while my father was invoking the gods and my brother was talking about having a word. I knew from the sinking feeling in the pit of my stomach as I got into the car, long sleeves to hide the bruises from the neighbours, to drive from

Redcliffe to the South Bank. I knew from the weeping fits as I lay in my bikini by my parents' pool, oversized sun specs disguising the discoloration around my eye. I knew during the dry-eyed nights spent scrolling through the empty menus on my cellphone.

Four years in each other's pockets, living as a couple, talking as a couple, thinking as a couple, and then – nothing.

The door was double-locked: on the mortise, as well as the latch. In all the time we had lived together, Andy had never locked the mortise. It was all part of his surfie persona: jogging out of the house, letting the door swing behind him, joy-killer me trailing in his wake dangling keys and nagging reminders. If I hadn't had a feeling before, this would have been enough to raise my suspicions.

I knew for certain the moment I crossed the threshold. It wasn't that the lobby was bare as a crypt. It wasn't that posters had been ripped from the lounge walls. Or the missing boy-toys: computer, TV, PlayStation, hi-fi, all gone.

It was the silence.

The silence of desertion.

I laid the keys down on the lobby console and walked into the house. Knew it was pointless, but called out anyway: 'Andy?'

Nothing. The air soaked up the name like blotting paper.

Advancing into the lounge, I was aware of a strange mixture of emotions. Trepidation. A growing melancholy. And underneath it all, small and suppressed, but there, and familiar, a tiny, warm glow of relief.

Apart from the missing electricals, the lounge looked pretty much the same. My blood had been cleaned up from the door jamb and the tiles, but everything else – the suite, the coffee table, lamps and knick-knacks, aboriginal carvings, the ikats hanging on the wall, the jokey bottle-top chandelier – gathered dust undisturbed.

'Andy?'

In the bedroom, it looked as though he had gone through the closets with a combine harvester. Drawers hung open, doors ajar, a tumble of cloth on a chair. And for a moment, as I caught sight

34

of a pile of jeans and T-shirts at the foot of the bed, my heart executed an unenthusiastic somersault. God, maybe he's still around after all.

And the little voice said: *and then you'll have to talk about it, little Miss Victim. And you don't want to do that, do you?*

I sat down heavily on the bed.

Andy.

It was my fault.

Oh, Andy, I'm sorry. You didn't have to go. You coward. You fucking yellow-bellied responsibility-shunning runmeister.

Rolling on to my side, I wrapped my arms tight around my torso and drew my knees towards my breasts. It felt better, for a moment. Protected.

A sound downstairs. The front door. The familiar lurch – relief, terror, urgency. He's back. He didn't leave. He's just been – clearing up. Wanting to make things . . . Oh God, what do I do now?

I sat up and listened. He was walking about. Soft-sole shoes squeaking on the tiled floor. I could barely breathe. Tears on the edge of spilling from my eyes. I crossed the room and stood at the top of the stairs, waiting for him to let me know he was there. Waiting for him to come to me.

Then Costa's voice, calling from the kitchen. 'Sis? G'day?'

I deflated like a popped balloon. Gripped the newel post and called back, 'Hi. I'm up here.'

Costa enters the hallway, all big and dark and handsome, sunglasses perched on the top of his head, teeth and T-shirt stark white against his suntan.

'What are you doing here, Costa?'

'Came to see you were OK,' he says.

'Why shouldn't I be?'

'Can't a brother look out for his little sis? Ma told me you were coming home and I wanted to see that . . .'

My legs turn, suddenly, to jelly. Andy's gone. He's left me, and he hasn't even left a note. Four years and not even a goodbye. I slump heavily down on the top step and bury my face in my hands.

'He's left me, Costa,' I say. 'He's gone.'
'Ah God,' says Costa. 'Ah God, I'm sorry, sis.'
And he comes and sits next to me as I start to cry.

Chapter Seven

In at the Deep End

By the time I've had a proper night's – morning's – sleep, the person I wake up to is no longer an evasive mystery man, but is, instead, my Rufus, only a Rufus with a more solid background. The day before yesterday, all I saw was the man: himself, no context, no surrounding colour, just Rufus drifting in a gentle space that allowed me to project anything I wanted on to it. And now – well, it's still the same person, still the man I fell in love with, but now there's a background coming into focus. I see the smug green of Merrie England, I see a cross-hatching of half-timbered magnificence, I see black swans on a moat and a hideous old crone in a headscarf bossing the servants. But most of all, eyelashes brushing the sun-freckles on his cheeks, I see Rufus once again. The other stuff I can deal with.

It's just that I don't realise that I'm going to have to deal with it quite so soon.

In fact, reality intrudes in the middle of the afternoon when, after the traditional honeymoon lie-in and a leisurely lunch of bread and tomatoes, we're in the pool doing what honeymooners are wont to if they have a pool to themselves. Our bathers are on the floor and I'm up against the wall, arms braced over the edge to give us some traction, my legs round my husband's elegant hips, soles of my feet pressed firmly on to his lean brown buttocks. And Rufus has a strong grip with one hand on the drain edge and a stronger one with his other on my shoulder as he grinds the old throbbing member into the flower of my being. Whatever. We're both red in the face, and my hair is plastered over my cheeks and forehead, and we're doing a lot of kissing because the pool is, after all, attached to a town house and we don't want to upset the neighbours in this grimly, sentimentally, Catholic country by making a lot of noise. Well, not much, anyway. Pawl Borg next door didn't seem to mind what he did with his Rotovator at six this morning, so I'm not so overbothered. So we're panting, and splashing, and I'm just starting to get that first amazing wave of feeling that starts at the toes and works its way all the way up my body until it explodes out of the top of my head, and I'm going, you know, uh-uh-uh-uwooooah, like you do, and Rufus has a big, silly, pleased-with-himself grin on his face, and he's going, 'You like that? You like that?' like you do, when a voice suddenly rings out from the interior of the house.

'Huh-*lo!*' it cries. A woman's voice, plummy as a plum-duff, at the same time silver like a little tinkling bell and brassy like a hunting horn in the fog. I don't know how it's done. I think it's genetic, actually. 'Anybody home? Rufus? Darling? Where are you?'

Zzzzzip. Rufus's cock shrinks to vanishing point faster than Dennis Quaid in *Innerspace*. 'Oh, shit,' he says. Then: 'Oh shit, oh shit, oh shit.'

'What is it?'

'Oh shit,' says Rufus again, 'it's my *mother*.'

He does a duck-flip and swims to the bottom of the pool, grabs his bathers and my bikini top and surfaces in a rush, shoves them into my hand. 'Get these on, for God's sake.'

I don't need telling twice.

The voice approaches. 'Huh-looooo! Is anyone at home? Rufus? Huh-looo! It's Mah-meh!'

The crimson tinge to his face comes from fear and embarrassment, now, rather than passion. He looks absurd, struggling to get his feet through the legholes of his trunks, getting caught up in the net lining, spluttering and cursing. I, meanwhile, am hooking up my top and going: 'Where are my bottoms? Rufus, where are my *bottoms*?' Eventually, I spot them, right over on the far side of the pool where, I now vaguely remember, he threw them in one of those grandiose gestures you nearly always regret later. I've got no choice, really: Rufus is still tangled up and I can hear the click of heels on the lounge floor-tiles.

I dive beneath the surface, eyes stinging with salt and chlorine, and swim for the cossie, arse to the sun. And when I surface, I find myself face-to-face with my new mother-in-law.

Chapter Eight
How's It Going?

The first thing I see is a pair of elegant ankles, clad, despite the heat, in low-density tan stockings and a pair of medium-heeled patent-leather Gucci pumps. Then I work my way up and see a tailored skirt in lightweight pink-and-green tweed, cut off just above the knee to show off the fact that the legs are exceptionally toned and slim on a woman in her mid-fifties, a matching jacket with a little, tasteful flourish of self-coloured satin edging on cuffs and collar, a cream silk blouse slightly opened at the neck to show a single strand of pearls and just the faintest hint of well-trained cleavage. There's a tiny gold watch on the left wrist and, on the fingers, a plain gold band and a solitaire diamond the size of a milk tooth.

It takes me a while to force my eyes up to look at the face. I'm at something of a disadvantage and I have to get myself organised and decent before I can look up.

And when I do, it's a surprise. Lady Mary Callington-Warbeck-Wattestone, far from being the battle-axe I've had in my mind's eye ever since Rita Zammit and Marija Boffa exchanged knowing looks across the dinner table at Giannini, is the quintessential English rose. She has that slightly papery peaches-and-cream complexion you can only get from living in a permanently damp climate, blue, blue eyes like a china doll, surrounded by a slash of the long black eyelashes she's obviously passed on to her son. It's a well-preserved face, the face of a woman who's watched her weight throughout her life, who's never gone through any sag-inducing expansions or reductions but has stayed the same, maintaining her looks with cold cream and a solemn refusal to allow her emotions to register in her expression. She has well-defined eyebrows, mid-brown, a pinky mouth that curls up slightly

40

at the edges, neat little ears touched with a pair of screw-in gold-and-pearl studs, and a girlish bob in Light Ash Blonde. I guess I'd been imagining that reinforced-concrete look affected by someone like Margaret Thatcher. I'm taken aback.

'Mummy!' Rufus says, splashing on to his back into the middle of the pool, now that he's finally found his way into his trunks. 'We were just . . .'

She keeps her eyes averted from my indecency. 'Having a lovely swim,' she says, fanning herself with a hand, 'So I see. Very wise. Gosh, it's still so *hot*, darling, isn't it? I feel grimy after the helicopter. I do wish they'd sort out some better way of getting into the terminal than walking past the petrol pumps.'

There's not a fleck of grime on her whole person. She may as well have just walked out of a beauty salon.

'You look lovely,' says Rufus, hauling himself up the ladder in the corner of the deep end, 'and what a lovely surprise to see you! What are you doing here?'

Lady Mary squeaks like a flirty kitten, waves him away as he approaches and pokes a cheek as far from her body as possible to receive a kiss. 'Don't you *dare* touch me, you foul creature!' she cries. 'You're *dripping*! No! You *bad* child!'

The son bends to plant the salutation. 'Why didn't you call?' he asks. 'I would have come and got you from Luqa. And how did you get here from the heliport? There are *never* taxis.'

'Well, if you would *ever* pick up the phone,' she replies, with an edge of reproach, 'I could have done that. But who cares, darling? It's hardly beyond me to find my way half a mile from the heliport. Marija Boffa got her brother to collect me.'

'Marija Boffa?'

'Yes. Yes, feckless offspring.'

I've never heard anyone talk like they're in a Mitford novel before.

'After,' continues the mother, 'she rang me yesterday with some absurd story about you getting married and not telling a soul about it!'

'Bloody *hell*.' Rufus folds his arms across his stomach and looks

41

down as he traces a pattern with his toe on the flagstones. 'What did she do that for? I wanted to tell you myself.'

'And when was *that* going to be? Next year? After the hunt ball? On my deathbed?'

This is said with nothing but an edge of light teasing. It's a verbal nudge in the ribs. She's talking as though everything in life, including this, is some great big Girl Scout lark. It's weird. I know my parents won't react like this. That's another reason I've put off calling them.

'So is it true, then, perfidious creature? Have you run off and got married like a thief in the night?'

I'm in my bikini now, but I feel seriously awkward. I don't really know what to do. Do I get out of the pool and approach, dripping, without permission, or do I wait and look rude, splashing about in the shallow end like I don't give a damn? Eventually, I decide to make for the ladder, which is closer to where they're standing than the shallow-end steps. As I'm on it, belly sticking out with the strain of pulling myself out of the water, Rufus, typical bloody bloke, no sense of appropriate timing, turns, waves a hand towards me, and says: 'Ma, I want you to meet Melody Katsouris. My wife. Melody, this is my mother, Mary.'

Painfully aware of my half-naked state, of the fact that my hair's a mess, that my bikini has seen better days and that there's probably a tuft of hair escaping from the bottoms, I cross the courtyard, holding out a hand to the aged relly. 'How's it going, Lady Mary?' I say, 'It's nice to meet you.'

To my surprise, I find myself being bussed warmly on both cheeks, though a firm grip on each arm keeps my dripping body away from the immaculate ensemble. Then she steps back and examines me, thoughtfully, as you might a new artwork. And then a smile reblossoms on her lips.

'Well, my *deah*!' she cries, releasing me. 'You're a picture! I can see why my son's been swept away! And *Aw-stralian*, to boot! I *love* Awstralians. A breath of fresh air! I always say that, don't I darling?' She looks up at her son for confirmation, bats – I swear; I'm not imagining it – her eyelashes at him.

42

'You sure do,' says Rufus, looking pleased. She turns back to me. 'Well, *welcome*, Melody! Welcome to my family! I just *know* we're going to be the *best* of friends. And for heaven's sake, please don't call me Lady Mary! You're my daughter-in-law now, even if it *is* all rather sudden! I'm Mary. Just Mary.'

'OK,' I say, gratified, 'Mary.'

'Now – oh, gosh!' she says, and her hands fly to her face. 'I don't know what to say! I really don't! I have a daughter-in-law! My son – my *darling* son – has a wife!'

I apologise for the shock.

'No!' she says. 'No! No! No! I'm made up, *ruhr*-leh I am! But what *naughty, naughty* children you are! I would have *killed* to be there. I *s'mp*-leh can't *bear* it! Rufus, I've *ruhr*-leh got to register a protest! How could you marry this *chah*-ming gel and keep it a secret? I'm so sorry, my dear! My son behaves as though his family are the most *dreadful* embarrassment to him, when really all we are is simply country bumpkins! Can't think why you've taken him on, but I can only be grateful that someone has at last!'

I think I've got my mother-in-law's measure. She's the sort of woman whose every phrase, if it's not an interrogative, ends with an exclamation mark! She's one of those people who has been raised to inject positive sounds into every remark as though they will magically transform the situation to their liking. You went to the shops? How extraordinary! I went to the shops too! I'm surprised we didn't bump into each other! Cup of tea! *Mah*-vlous! Do you know? Talking like this makes me sound really, *really* witless!

I'm feeling increasingly vulnerable in front of this chic woman. I've left a sarong on the painted metal table in the corner of the courtyard, decide that it would be better to risk insult by breaking away to cover myself up than it would be to stand here dripping like a model on a peanut display card.

I can feel both of their eyes on my back as I cross the flags. And just for a moment, I feel as though the Death Star is beaming a destructaray directly at planet Melody. But when I wrap up, turn and look at them again, all I see is beaming smiles. Funny. I guess I'm a bit paranoid, what with the abnormality of the circs.

'Do come here,' she says, 'and let me have a look at you.'

I smile and try to stand there looking relaxed.

'But, my dear,' she repeats, 'she's *chah*-ming! Nothing like I would have expected, but utterly *chah*-ming!'

'Thank you,' says Rufus complacently, as if I'm some personal possession picked out from the shelves of a design shop. 'Can I get you something to drink, Mummy? You must be dry as a bone.'

An exaggerated, languorous sigh. 'Why, darling, I thought you'd never ask!' she proclaims to the world. 'Is it unconscionably early for a G and T?'

He is already heading for the kitchen door, laughing over his shoulder. 'You must have been in transit for a good seven hours already, haven't you? That makes it well past yardarm, in my book. Darling, do you want anything?'

'Yeah, I'll just have a glass of water, thanks,' I say, then, too late, realise that I am no longer a guest in this house, that I should be doing the hospitality thing myself. Especially if I'm not going to come a gutser in front of the new family. I scuttle over to the foot of the steps, say: 'Honey, I'll give you a hand.'

'No, no,' says Rufus, 'go and sit down. It'll only take me a minute.'

'Well, then,' I say in a loud voice, 'you sit down. I'll sort it out.'

The minute we're inside the door, he wraps me in a big warm hug and plants a kiss on my forehead. 'I told you!' he whispers. 'I told you it would be all right! She loves you!'

'She's great,' I reply, because, you know, I think she probably is. It'll take me a while to get used to the way she expresses herself, and maybe I think she's a little – well, silly – but she's nothing like the gorgon that had been materialising in my mind. 'I'm so relieved!'

'Didn't I tell you?' he asks. 'Didn't I? Oh, Melody, I love you *so much*!'

'We'd better get her drink, or she'll be in wanting to know what's happened. Go on, darl. You go out and keep her company. I'll get them.'

'You sure?'

44

'Too right, mate. She's *your* mother.'

'Well . . . OK,' he says. 'Go on.'

And he kisses me again.

'Go on yourself,' I say.

'In a minute.'

'*Now.*' I take hold of his shoulder, spin him on his heel. 'Get out of here. Go, you dill.'

'OK. Thank you, darling.' He walks away from me, raises his voice so he can be heard from outside, and something about the tone of his voice suggests indulgence of my whim to play house rather than gratitude for a chore taken over. 'That would be kind. Can I have a G and T as well?'

I do a small ironical forelock tug. 'Your wish is my command, oh lord and master,' I say. And, lower, 'Watch it, buster.'

He vanishes into the light, and I set about making drinks while I listen to the sound of the two of them settling down at the table. They are the kinds of voices that would be hard to avoid eavesdropping on. I should think that half of Xewkija is listening in right at this moment.

'So tell me everything, you wicked boy,' she says. 'Where did you meet this blissy creature? Where did she sweep you off your feet?'

Blissy creature? I'm not a fucking Pekinese. I feel my shoulders tense. Rufus's voice, less distinct, begins to tell her whatever the suitable story is. I hear the words 'salt pans' and 'drowning' and 'kiss of life', but precious little else. I don't suppose he'll be telling her about how we spent the first twenty minutes in this house screwing on the outer stairs because we lacked the self-control to get any further.

The limestone that makes up these islands soaks up and retains heat as though warmed by a million little underfoot furnaces. And though the nights have cooled enough now that you can turn the fan off between two and seven, the days are still blazingly hot. Not the tropical hot I'm used to, but a dusty, paper-dry hot that sucks the moisture off your skin. But nerves have made me break out into a sweat despite this and I take a moment, when I open the freezer to get out some ice, to stick my head inside and try to cool down. This isn't the way I had imagined spending the first day of my honeymoon. And I'm mortified about the sort of impression I must have made at first glance.

'But how *thrilling*!' Mary, I notice, has a very slight speech impediment, pronouncing her Rs as Ws in the middle of words. I have no idea how much this is going to put my teeth on edge in the future. I guess it'll depend how our relationship progresses.

I manage to find three vaguely similar highballs in the cupboard, sling half a dozen lumps of ice into each, slice a lemon, pour over the gin and polish off the tonic bottle in filling the glasses to the brim. A good thing I only wanted water. Then I take the tray out from under the coffee maker and carry all three out through the French doors to the sitting room.

'No, no, darling. You're completely wrong. I couldn't *be* more thrilled! I mean, obviously, we can't help feeling a little *excluded*, but . . .'

Oh, well. I suppose it's inevitable that this is going to be a theme for a while.

'That wasn't what we meant to do. I just . . . I couldn't wait, you know? Maybe you don't. I don't know, I just . . . It's hard to explain.'

Lady Mary looks up. She has put on a pair of dark glasses while I've been gone: the type that are darker at the top than at the bottom because they're supposed to be more flattering.

'Well. We'll just have to have a party when you get home. Introduce her to the county. Ah! There she is!'

I put the tray down, hand the drinks around. The mother-in-law takes her glass and lays it down on the table, looks at it for a moment and then turns her full-beam smile on me.

'So tell me something about yourself,' she says. 'What brought you to Gozo in the first place?'

I shrug. 'Oh, you know. Just travelling. It was going to be part of a bigger trip. I've already been to Cyprus, where my dad comes from, and I was going to catch the ferry to Sicily and do Europe when Rufus got in the way. I didn't,' I say, and laugh ruefully, 'exactly come here with a plan to snare myself a husband.'

I anticipate a laugh in response to the attempt at levity, receive instead a slight flicker of the eyebrows. 'I never understand,' she says, 'with you young people. This "just travelling" thing. *Finding* yourselves. We didn't really have time for *finding* ourselves in my day.'

I shrug again. 'Well, I think, you know, it's something a lot of Australians and Kiwis have to do. I mean, there we are, a Western culture stuck out on the tippy-tip of the other side of the world from everyone else like us, and most of us have at least one parent, often two, who've come from a background that's so completely alien to the one they've raised us in . . .'

'Yeee-sss,' she says. 'Is that so with you?'

'Uh-huh. I mean, my dad's a Greek Cypriot, and my mum's folks came from Scotland, originally, though via South Africa, but I don't really have the first idea about where I come from, as it were. I think a lot of us are like that. Plus, I think a lot of the children of emigrants have a stronger sense of *choosing* where they end up, even if where they end up is the one-pub beach town they grew up in.'

'Yes,' she says, and I'm surprised to detect what I think is a slightly sharp edge to the comment, 'but aren't you a little *old* for this sort of gallivanting?'

I can't tell if Rufus has picked up on the bitchiness in this remark.

'Not really,' I tell her. 'I'd got to one of those crossroads and it felt like a smart thing to do before I got committed to something else and never did it.'

'Yes, but. This hippy thing is the sort of thing that most people do before their first year at university.'

'I never went to university.'

I'm surprised to see a little twitch. You'd have thought she'd like this in a girl. I'd be willing to bet a few thousand dollars that Lady Mary Callington-Warbeck-Wattestone never graduated anything more than finishing school. Oh, and riding school.

'Oh,' she says faintly. 'So what do you do with your time?'

'I'm a reflexologist.'

The debutante staccato begins again. 'A reflex*olog*ist? How *fas*cinating!'

I waggle my head, take another mouthful of water. 'Yeah, it can be pretty good. You get to meet some pretty interesting people, and it's a portable skill, you know? I can take it pretty much anywhere in the world and it won't take all that long to build up a client base. I spent a couple of summers working the beaches in Bali and Thailand, and it was pretty cool.'

'I'd have thought it was jolly hot,' she says. D'oh. 'So tell me, what *is* a reflexologist?'

'It's sort of like – you know acupressure?'

'Well, we don't get much of that sort of thing in deepest Gloucestershire.'

Oh, really? I'd heard the British countryside was awash with yuppies gone feral. 'Oh, well OK: There's a theory that there's a point on each part of your outer covering – your pulse points, mostly – that corresponds with your internal organs, your bloodstream, your moods, the state of your health and so forth. Acupuncturists put needles into those points to treat people. Acupressure works on a similar theory, but with massagey sort of stuff.'

'So far so good,' she says.

I decide to make it as simple as possible. 'Reflexology is sort of like acupressure. I understand which parts of your feet and hands correspond to your kidneys, your liver, your lungs, your back and so forth, and I'm trained in diagnosing which parts of your body need treatment and stimulus.'

'*Stimulus*?' (She says this in the manner of Lady Bracknell saying 'a *hand*bag?'.)

'Uh-huh.'

Rufus jumps in. 'It's wonderful,' he tells her. 'She's done it for me a couple of times and it's extraordinary. I had a headache one time, and—'

'Well,' she interrupts, 'I've always enjoyed a good pedicure.'

'It's a bit more . . .' I begin to protest, then think: whoa! Melody girl! Humourless proselytiser alert!

She picks up her glass. Takes a sip, pulls a face and puts it down on the table.

'Oh dear,' she starts fishing about with her fingers to extract the ice cubes, 'I'm afraid this is completely drowned. I should have said. I'd forgotten how obsessed you Antipodeans are with ice. I'm frightfully sorry.'

Rufus is on his feet. 'I'll get you another one.'

'We're out of tonic,' I tell him. I'm a tad surprised, to be honest. Way I was raised, you say thank you if someone gives you food or a drink, and if it's not done precisely the way you like it, you shut your bunghole and take it anyway. 'There's some juice, or Kinnie, or Coke, but I'm afraid we're out of tonic. Maybe he can get you something else.'

'Oh.' Then, in a little don't-mind-me-I'll-be-noble voice, she says: 'No, no, it's fine.'

'I'll go and get some more,' offers Rufus. 'It'll only take a few mins.'

'It's the middle of the arvo,' I remind him. 'The shop'll be shut.'

'The supermarket in Victoria will still be open,' he replies.

'No, no, *darling*, don't be silly! I'm not having you driving up to Rabat just because I'm a silly fusspot! I won't *hear* of it!' she says in a do-it-or-I'll-be-sighing-all-afternoon voice.

'Don't be silly,' he says. 'I was going to have to go and get some anyway, wasn't I?'

'Well, if you really . . . well, thank you, darling. You *are* kind.'

'Bollocks,' says Rufus.

I would never dare say 'bollocks' to my mother. 'It'll take ten minutes at the most.'

'I'll go,' I offer. I'm still not sure if I've got the conversation in me yet to be left alone with Mary.

Rufus shakes his head. 'It'll be far quicker if I go.'

'I *know* where the supermarket is!'

'Yes, but you're hardly decent.'

'But it won't take a minute . . .'

'Don't worry about it.' He fails to grasp my meaning. And there was me thinking we were such soulmates we could finish each other's sentences.

Another little tinkle of laughter. 'Melody, dear, let him *go*! You have to let the men be useful for *something*! Heaven knows, they're not use for much!' she says in that giggly confidential tone that antifeminists always use with younger women. 'And besides,' she continues, 'I'm dying to have a little girlie chat with my new daughter-in-law. Go on, Rufus! Off you go, darling! Make yourself useful!'

He heads dutifully into the kitchen and I subside into my chair. And Mary sits back in hers, leans her elbows on the arms and steeples her fingers at me. 'Yes,' she repeats, 'I can't wait to have a proper chat.'

He reappears in the doorway, shirt on and car keys bouncing in his right hand. 'Do we need anything else while I'm there?'

Temazepam, I think. I just might need some before the evening's out. I smile, and shake my head.

'Some lovely olives,' says Mary, 'and perhaps some snacky bits. I couldn't face the Air Malta food, and Caviar House wasn't open when I went through Gatwick. I'll take you both out to a celebration dinner at the Ta'Cenc tonight, but I'll need *something* to keep me going.'

'Thanks, Ma,' says Rufus, 'that would be lovely.'

'Good-oh,' she says. 'So it's a date. Unless I'm interrupting your plans? Sorry! Sorry, Melody! I should have checked.'

'Naah, naah, she'll be right,' I say, and they both look puzzled for a moment, like I've just come out with a slew of Swahili. 'It's fine,' I correct myself. 'I'm cool.'

'Now, off you go! Woman talk!'

'Bye, then,' says Rufus, and goes into the house once more. Mary waits as the slop slop slop of his deck shoes crosses the outer courtyard and the big wooden door bangs shut.

And then she turns, and runs her eyes from the top of my head, down the length of my body and all the way back up again.

Chapter Nine

The Upstart

It's a full thirty seconds before she speaks, and by the time she's finished with her caustic inspection, I feel as though I've been given a going-over with a wire brush. There's no more silly coquettishness about her. And her expression, now that he's gone, is an interesting mixture of contempt and curiosity. Eventually, she unsteeples her fingers, aligns her forearms with the arms of her chair, hands dangling loosely by her thighs, and speaks.

'So. You've landed on your feet, haven't you?' she says, in a tone that allows me to harbour no doubts that I might have got the wrong end of the stick. Lady Mary Callington-Warbeck-Wattestone means business, and an upstart like me is not a foe who alarms her.

I take a long, slow drink of water to give myself some thinking time. It's always useful to have a prop or two to hand for these sorts of contingencies. I'm sure that's one of the reasons so many people still smoke. Then I put my glass back on the table, very carefully and deliberately, lining it up so that the edge is up against the flourish of the cast-iron vine that runs around its surface. And then I smile and say: 'Yip. I reckon I have.'

I don't say any more. Purposefully, I cross my hands on the table and sit in silence, waiting to see what comes next.

Lady Mary shows off her own black belt in prop usage. She reaches sideways and plucks from the ground by her left ankle the small, plain black clutch bag she was carrying when she entered my world. Opens it and produces a lipstick that is encased in one of those tampon-shaped compacts people give each other as stocking-fillers and then usually store in backs of drawers to pass on to someone else. Quietly and deliberately, she twists the base, producing an inch-long, immaculate stick of going-on-apricot pink greasepaint, which has been worn, I notice, on both sides. Holding up the tiny mirror built into the inside of the compact lid, she sweeps the stick once across her lower lip, twice across her upper, crushes the lips together to set the colour, then retracts the stick, replaces the lid, slips the whole into the compact, pops the popper, returns it to the clutch bag, closes the catch on the bag, leans sideways and replaces it upon the ground. 'Take that, whippersnapper!' each movement says. 'Did you think you could outmanoeuvre me with a water glass? Just wait till you see what I can do with a teaspoon!'

And still I wait. I'm glad I didn't do anything as foolish as smile when I started; the expression would be all over the place after such a lengthy performance.

Eventually, she says: 'There isn't any money, you know. Not for you, anyway.'

This brings me up with a jolt. This isn't a needling little prod like the last one, a small experiment to see how I will react. This is a direct accusation.

'Sorry?' I say.

'I'm sure you are,' she says. Then: 'Would it be too much of an imposition to ask you for a glass of water?'

I get to my feet. 'Fridge water?'

'Thank you.'

I'm surprised she's given me this much thinking time. Although, of course, I quickly realise that what she's trying to give me is stewing time. What she wants is for me to get so worked up that Rufus will come back to find me snarling. She's smart. I guess she's already figured that I might have a bit of a temper on me, and is hoping that she can needle me enough to show her son what I look like when something's got me going.

In the kitchen, pulse going like the clappers, I roll the water bottle over my forehead, my cheeks and the back of my neck, and concentrate for a moment on lowering my heart rate. I take half a dozen deep breaths, do a bit of counting, and, once the moment of panic has begun to subside, I return to my mother-in-law.

She accepts the glass without thanks, takes a sip.

'No,' she continues, as though this hiatus had never happened, 'Rufus hasn't got much more than a bean to rub together. It's all in trust, I'm afraid. Has been for years. Since the socialists started trying to get their hands on it.'

'I may be Australian,' I inform her, 'but I'm not totally wet behind the ears.'

'I'm sure you aren't,' she says drily. 'I just thought I should let you know. There are so many fortune-hunters in the world,' she says pointedly, 'and so many of them end up disappointed.'

I take another sip of water, glance down at my watch. He's only been gone five minutes. If he doesn't make it back quickly, I'm in deep, deep shtook. So I decide to take the bull by the horns. 'Mary,' I ask as pleasantly as I can manage, 'are you implying that I've married Rufus for his money? Because, you know, that's not the case.'

She sips in turn. 'It's not *always* money. Cachet. Social status. He's a very attractive man from many points of view.'

'He certainly is. It sort of struck me the first time I clapped eyes on him. But believe me, I didn't know anything about this landed gentry sh—' I catch myself, correct my language in a hurry '—ebang until yesterday afternoon. He kept very shtum about that. Seriously. As far as I was concerned, he was ordinary. Well, not ordinary. Obviously. I wouldn't have married an ordinary fella.'

Call-me-Mary lets out a laugh that's a million miles away from the men-in-the-room fairy tinkle she affected when we first met. A rooster-like explosion of disbelief and disdain.

'So how exactly was I supposed to tell? With my magical powers of perception?'

'Oh, don't give me that,' she snaps. 'As you said yourself, you're hardly wet behind the ears. Where did you think this house came from? And his accent? Surely you're not trying to tell me you couldn't tell something from his accent?'

I force myself to relax against the back of the chair. 'Mary,' I say, and allow just a little trickle of I'm-indulging-you into my voice, 'if your film industry is to be believed, ninety-five per cent of your population talks like Rufus, and anybody who doesn't is probably carrying a gun. And besides, just look at him! The guy dresses like a scarecrow! Jeez. If I saw him in a bar, I'd probably think he was the cleaner come early.'

She blinks. Well, I guess blinks is the right word for it. Her upper lashes snap down to meet the lower ones, like the eyelids on an old china doll. 'I don't have the first clue what you're talking about.'

'Oh, come on, Mary. That linen suit with the elbow patches? Those checked shirts with the holes in the cuffs that look like they ought to be dishcloths? The tweed jacket? The lining on that must have gone while he was still learning to tie his shoelaces.'

'It's a *hacking* jacket,' she replies icily, 'and it was his grand-father's.'

What in hell's name is a hacking jacket? Something you wear for coughing in?

'Well, exactly,' I say. 'I mean, what sort of rich fella wears hand-me-downs?'

The blink again. 'The sort,' she replies – and I think, yes, I've got her grinding her teeth – 'who has clothes to *inherit*.'

'Oh, right,' I reply, injecting as much airiness into the words as I can muster. 'My lot only ever have one suit at a time, and they tend to be buried in it.'

A long, frosty silence. I check my watch. Ten minutes now. Hopefully he will be queuing at the checkout, or at least at the deli counter.

'How's your water?' I ask.

'Fine,' she snaps again, 'Fine. It's water. How else would it be?'

'Just asking,' I say. I'm beginning to think that I might quite enjoy winding this woman up. I mean, if she's going to think I'm a peasant, I may as well take it all the way. I bury my face in my glass to hide the smile that has started to play across my lips.

Eventually she can't resist beginning to speak again. 'So. You do something that involves *feet*?'

54

I nod. Think: I must remember to ask her what *she* does later. Just give her a little time to get settled in, first.

'And how about the rest of the family?' she asks. 'Any more chiropodists in the family? Or are you the only one?'

I go for it, really go for it. Lay on the accent like peanut butter. 'Naooouw waaay!' I cry, hamming it up till her eardrums reverberate. 'OI'm the inder*lik*-chewull in *moy* fimmer–luy.'

There's a long pause, and I think that perhaps she might have realised that I'm jerking her chain. But the encrusted horror in the 'rii–ull–uh' that emerges from her mouth suggests that she hasn't picked up on it at all, but has merely adjusted her own accent to show the contrast with my own proletarian vowels. I've noticed this before, actually: the very grand rarely have what anyone else would call a sense of humour, especially about themselves. I suppose a sense of humour is hard to develop when you've got so many noses wedged up your butt.

'Aow, yih! They were happy as Larry when I went to college when I was twenty-three. An *ology* in the family!'

'Really,' she says again. 'And what does your father do?'

'Whaddya *think*? He's a Greek Cypriot, for crying out loud. Obviously, he bought a cab, like everybody else.'

'A *cab*?'

'Yih. Done pretty nicely out of it, as well.' Yeah. But I'm not going to tell you the half of it.

'Oh yes?'

'Yih. After he married my old girl he jumped over the wall and set up a firm of his own. My mum helped out in the office, you know? They're pretty much retired now, but life's treated them pretty good, all told.'

Mary, by this time, has the sort of ghastly smile on her face that you usually only see stuck to the corners of cathedrals. 'A taxi firm? How . . . Well. And weren't you tempted to follow in their footsteps?'

'Naaaoooouuuuw!' I give her a really long one, watch her recoil. 'My brother, Costa, did, though. Dad's more of a sleeping partner these days.'

'Costa?'

'Yes. Like the coffee.'

'Like the coffee,' she echoes, and it's evident that she's not got the first inkling as to what I'm on about.

'Yeah, yeah, but that's not him. Though he's in catering as well.'

'*In* catering?' The '*hand*bag' accent is right back. 'What sort of catering? A restaurant?'

'Ke*babs*,' I say, and almost squirm with pleasure at the look of abject misery that crosses her face.

This is great. She thought she was going to put the frighteners on me, and I've turned it right on its head. Let's face it: my mother-in-law may have had some fantasies about the unsuitability of my background, but what I'm telling her is all her wildest nightmares come true. I'm not going to let her off the hook.

'Kebabs?' Her voice is faint. 'As in *doner* kebabs?' She pronounces it 'dough-ner', as in blood.

'Oh, yih. Doner, shish, shawarma, kofte, iskender. Pretty much anything you want, really. They're pretty popular, and not just with the ethnic communities.'

I pronounce 'ethnic' 'ith-nikk', and watch my mother-in-law close her eyes and suppress a shudder. This is fun. This is really fun.

'He and Dad had this great idea, and it sort of mushroomed,' I tell her. 'Like, you know how a guy likes a few bevvies and a takeaway of an evening? And I don't know if you know this, but our police have been cracking down on drink-driving lately?'

Mary says nothing. I don't know if she thinks I'm extracting the Michael or not. Not, as it happens. Well, only with my delivery.

'Anyways, they thought up the solution. Got franchises across most of the eastern seaboard. You've probably heard of them. KebabCab?' I announce, keeping the relish (mild chilli, of course) out of my voice as best I can. 'Get your fast food while you wait. Hundred-dollar surcharge if you chunder on the ride home.'

Eventually, and in a voice that contains more than a hint of a tremor, she says: 'Well, you're certainly going to find your new life a bit of a contrast with what you're used to.'

'No worries, Lady M,' I quack, watching her jerk about like a marionette, 'my old girl's always kept a neat house, and if there's no money, we could always think about opening up a couple of franchises in the grounds, eh?'

This time, I think I've gone too far. The light flush that has been playing over Mary's complexion drains away, blanching her face. And, having begun to slump as I described my family history to her, she suddenly shoots erect as though she's just got back from her duchess masterclass.

'I didn't say,' she says, enunciating with vicious clarity, 'that there was no money. I said that there was no money for *you*.'

It's like having a bucket of cold water thrown over me. Once again I'm brought up short. My mother can be pretty scary, but this woman seems to have a built-in ice machine.

She raises her chin, the better to look down her nose at me, says: 'I've got your measure, young woman. My son may be behaving like a cunt-struck teenager –'

It's my turn to recoil. Cunt-struck? *Cunt-struck*? Where in the name of God did she learn a phrase like that?

'– and from the way you were splayed out like a five-bob whore when I arrived here, I can understand why, but believe me, it won't work with the rest of us.'

'You know what?' I retaliate. 'I've married *Rufus*. I've not married the rest of you.'

'Ah, my dear,' she says, in a voice dripping with syrup, 'if you believe that, you're very, very foolish.'

I shrug. 'No skin off my nose, Lady M. If you're going to be like this I'll just make sure I never see you.'

A fruity, perfumed laugh, this time from the back of the throat. I don't like it. It's got a triumphal edge.

'Oh, my dear,' she says, 'you *are* naïve. Where on earth do you think you're going to be living?'

Chapter Ten

Calling Home

Dad picks up, barks:. 'Hold on' into the receiver and, before I can say anything, concludes the call he's having on his cellphone.

'Fuck 'em,' he says. 'Fuck 'em. No, fuck the lot of 'em. Tell them, that. Tell them, if I don't hear from them by tomorrow then I'll come round and fuck every single one of them personally. Yeah. That's what I say. You tell them that. Fuck 'em.'

He listens for a moment.

'H'OK,' he says. 'All right. I gotta go. Got someone on the other line. Bye, Mum. I'll see you tomorrow.'

Then he clears his throat and comes back to me. 'Ghhello?'

My dad smokes cigars: big, fat stogies, the sort that smoulder slowly away for an hour at a time. He can generally be relied upon to chew his way through five or so of the things a day, blithely ignoring the Greek tragedy chorus that follows him around going: 'why do you smoke those things? You know how bad they are for you. You're going to die and leave me a widow, and your children orphans, and all because you can't stop smoking . . .'

But the thing is, they're so much more than the simple nicotine hit, though the amount of the drug he takes in every day would probably stop the heart of a water buffalo. They are a symbol of his success. Though, obviously, he was never in as dire a position as the wave of Cypriots who followed in his wake after 1974, it would still be fair to say that my father arrived in Oz with pretty much squat. His cigars are proof of the degree of his achievement, as my mother's forays down Queen Street Mall are hers, and it would be impossible to overestimate the amount of pleasure they give him.

'Hi, it's me.'

'Owa! Milloddy-girl!' he shouts from the throat. Then takes the phone away from his face. 'O! Colleen! It's Milloddy!'

A distant squeal.

'Melody! Where you been? We thought we were going to have to put the feelers out!'

'Yeah, I know, I'm sorry,' I say, 'I've been, well – some stuff's happened.'

'Oh, no, what? You in jail? You need I send you some money?'

'No, no . . . no, it's nothing like that, Dad.'

'Well, what is it, Melody? What can happen you don't call your family, you don't write, nothing for nearly two months? Last thing we hear, you're leaving Cyprus, and then nothing. We been worried!'

'I know, Dad, I know, and I'm really sorry.'

'So you forgotten all about your family?'

'Give it a rest. You're tattooed on my heart. You know that.'

'Well,' he clears his throat contemplatively, 's'long's you don't go gettin' laser treatment.'

'How are things, Dad?'

'H'OK,' says my father. 'Can't stop your mother shopping, though. Every morning, shop shop shop, afternoon, shop shop shop, and now she discover the internet, it's shop, shop, shop all night, too, you know? Guess what she bought the other day? Go on! Guess!'

'I don't know.' With my mother, it could be anything. She's the queen of impulse. I guess that's where I got it from.

'Stuffed – how you call it? – armadillo.'

'A what?'

I hear him shift his cigar from one side of his mouth to the other. 'I know. That's what I said. She go out to buy sunglass, and when she come back, she got an armadillo. All dusty, like, in a glass box. I said, Colleen, what we need one-a them for? And you know what she said?'

'I dread to think.'

He raises his voice in imitation of my mother. 'Oh, but, Adonis, I saw him in the shop window and he looked so lonely.'

Yes, that's right. My father's name is Adonis, all five foot six of his hairy-backed self. Most people call him Don, though. I don't suppose more than a fifth of them know what it's short for.

'Well, maybe she can put him with the spiny anteater in the hall.'

He sighs. 'Don't even joke about it.'

I realise that I am stalling. I may have given Rufus a hard time about not coming clean to his family, but now it comes down to brass tacks, I'm as much of a coward as he is. I think maybe I'll start with Mum. Mothers are always easiest when it comes to breaking surprise news. It's because they live their whole lives expecting the police to come round and tell them your school's collapsed. And besides, she's right there, now, wrestling with Dad over control of the handset. 'Give it,' she says. 'Go on. Give it. I want to talk to her. Give-it-to-me-Don. Now.'

I can see the dance in my mind's eye, the ritual they perform hourly over the telephone; Mum hopping about around the outside while my dad forms the hunch-shouldered, free-hand-waving totem around which the world circles.

'Ho-ho-hold on,' he says to me, then: 'I am talking to my daughter right now, if you don't mind.'

'She's my daughter too!' protests my mum.

'Yes, and you can speak to her when I'm finished.'

'Hello!' I bellow from the other side of the world. 'Would you mind saving it for when I'm not paying a million dollars a minute calling you from the airport? Just – just one of you get on the line, would you?'

The credit card reader informs me that I have already spent over £8 sterling, and I haven't even started on my confession.

A brief interlude, then Mum's voice breaks through.

'Hello, lovey! How *are* you? We'd just about given you up for dead!'

'I'm great, Ma. I'm really great.'

'Where are you?'

'Gatwick Airport.'

'Hellfire, Melody,' she says, 'what are you doing there? Last I heard you were going round the Med.'

'I know. I . . .' I've got to tell her. I gather my courage. 'Yeah, well, something's sort of come up . . .'

'Never mind,' she says. My mum's always been good at blocking things that make her uncomfortable. 'As long as you're enjoying yourself. Hey, Mel, did your father tell you Costa's bought a new car?'

'No. But he told me about the armadillo.'

'Oh, that,' she says. 'Way he goes on you'd have thought it was a diamond collar for the dog or summink.'

'Look, Ma!' I say. 'Shaddap a second. I've got something to tell you.'

Suddenly, she's all concern. 'What is it, lovey? Are you OK? Do you need some money?'

'No,' I say. I do wish they didn't always think everything can be sorted by throwing cash at it. 'No, I'm fine.'

'What is it, then? You're not – oh God – you're not. . .'

Another struggle at the end of the line, and Dad is back on, wheezing and chomping in equal measure.

'Melody!' he shouts. 'What did we teach you? Didn't we bring you up proper?'

'Oh Jeez, Dad—' I begin.

'No!' he cries. 'You don't make it better with profanities! How this happen? Who is it? How you coulda been so blood' stupid? Tell me his name, and I'll . . .'

Yeah, yeah. Keel him.

Rufus, standing next to me, picks up the buzz of threat and imprecation over the bustle of the concourse, turns and raises his eyebrows at me. I shake my head.

'I'm not telling you anything till you calm down.'

Dad tries another tack. 'Baby,' he says in the Understanding Father voice that always used to put the wind up Costa and me when we were kids, 'don't worry. We'll stand by you, whatever you decide. You know you've always got your family—'

I try to stop him. 'Dad!'

61

'. . . least your mother and me still got our strength, eh? You'll see, Baby. It won't be the end of the—'

I take a deep breath and bellow into the mouthpiece. 'DAD! I AM NOT BLOODY PREGNANT, OK? I GOT MARRIED!'

A clatter, then, sounding startled, my mum. 'Your father just burned a hole in the rug. Did you say what I think you just said?'

'If you think I just said I'd got married, then yuh-huh.'

She sounds dazed. 'But, Melody, you've not even been gone three months.'

'I know. It was just . . . that was all it took. I met Rufus and I just *knew* . . .'

'In England? You got married in England?'

'No, in Malta. But he's English, and I . . .'

To my shock, she bursts, loudly, into tears.

Dad comes back on the line. I'm appalled to hear him close to tears as well. I'd thought – you know – that there would be the odd gurgle and then a great gush of jubilation. But suddenly, my dad sounds old and confused. 'Why you no tell us, Melody?' he asks, and his voice catches in his throat.

'I . . .' I realise that I don't have the right vocabulary for this sort of situation. 'I'm sorry, Dad,' I say humbly. 'It's just – we did it so fast that there wasn't time.'

'No time? Your mother and father? Your own *family*? There is *always* time!' This last comes as a wail, and I find myself gulping in response. You're not supposed to cry. Not *cry*. I've got *married*.

Mum, back on the line and slightly more composed: 'Your father can't talk for a minute, sweetie. He's a bit upset right now. I know he's pleased for you really. It's just he's—'

I'm crying myself now. Partly surprise, partly because I've been saving up to go through this, and now it's here I'm liking it even less than I had expected. Rufus has his hand on my shoulder and looks confused. 'But why?' My words come out in a croak. 'Why's he upset?'

'Oh, Melody. Give us some credit. You spring something like this on us, you can't expect us not to react. You must know why he's upset. It's one of the biggest things he's ever looked forward to, giving you away. You know how he's always gone on about it. He's been waiting for it ever since you were born! We both – I can't believe I wasn't *there*!' A sob slips out.

I feel like I've just been laid out on a slab and gutted. No wonder I got the reaction I did from Mary if this is the way my own parents feel. Have we really been that selfish?

'Oh, Mum!' I'm all tears and snot myself, now, because it has suddenly become very clear to me that I've screwed up, that I'll never have another wedding day and my most precious people were cut out of the loop. I wish they'd been there and there's nothing I can do to make it so. One unrepeatable moment, and I threw it away like it was a birthday party or something.

My dad's back on the line, nobly trying his best to speak clearly. 'Baby,' he snuffles, 'we're not angry. Really. We are happy. I'm sorry. I'm really sorry. I didn't want to cry on your wedding day. Tell me who this man is? Who is your husband?'

'He's called Rufus,' I tell him, 'and, Daddy, he's the best!'

'I don't want nothin' else for my daughter,' he growls. 'Though I don't know what sort of man marries a woman without her family. So tell me – he looking after you OK?'

'Yeah. He's – oh, Daddy, I know you'll love him. I so want you to meet him!'

'H'OK,' says my dad, and blows his nose. Mum must have got some paper towels from the kitchen. 'So what he like? Is English, yes?'

'Yes. Daddy, he's right here beside me. Do you want to speak to him?'

Rufus looks faintly aghast. Dad sounds fairly much as aghast himself. This passing-the-phone-over thing isn't really part of the male canon. 'Oh. H'OK,' says Dad doubtfully. I hold the phone out to Rufus, point at it. He steps back, waves opened palms across themselves, eyes like soup plates.

I throw him a glare of pure venom. There's no way he's getting away with this. Not after he made me talk to his mother without even getting to put a dress on. He drops his protest, meekly, steps forward and puts the earpiece to his ear. My word. I would have made an excellent teacher.

'Hello, Mr Katsouris?' The look of rabbit-like terror softens to your normal pommy twitchiness.

'Thanks. Thank you. Yes, that's right. Wattestone. But I don't think she's taking it.'

He barks with sycophantic laughter. 'You're right there.'

Rufus is conducting a frenzied palpitation of his scalp as he speaks. 'I know. Yes, I know. And I'm so sorry. I just, Mr Katsouris – Don – I'm so in love with your daughter and I couldn't . . .'

Good man. The right thing to say. Daddies always need to know that their daughters are still theirs, even when those daughters *would* be grandmothers in the Yemen.

'Yes, I will. I swear I will. I know that. I think so too. She's – well, she's amazing. I really do appreciate that. I swear. I'll cherish her and love her for the rest of my life, I promise you that.'

A pause, then a smile. 'Yes, you can,' he says, 'but it will never happen.'

Ah. The threats have come out, then. He's nothing if not predictable, my dad.

'Yes. Soon. Yes, in England. In the Cotswolds, you know where that is? Well, yes, not so far from there. Nearer to Cheltenham, I suppose, but not that near there, even. Halfway between there and Oxford. It's sort of quite in the middle of the country. Well, not by Australian standards, of course . . .' another gust of slightly nervous laughter, '. . . Yes. Don't worry. I give you my word. Sorry? Yes, yes please. I'd love to. OK. Yes, absolutely. Yes, it's been lovely to talk to you too. Goodbye.'

Another pause. My mother has obviously been scrabbling for the handset.

I look away at the concourse as he launches into another round of pleasantries, try to get some hook on my new world. I can't say it looks much different from anywhere else yet, except that the people are, generally, paler, and they're making themselves sick gorging on sausage rolls rather than Chicky Sticks or rice birds or chicken-fried steak.

I turn back. Rufus is assuring my mother that he values me above rubies or something, and promising that we will all meet soon. I can picture her, already in her curlers – because if it's two o'clock here, that must make it midnight back home – standing next to her stuffed animals with my dad strutting about beside her, and I'm assailed by a wave of homesickness so strong I have for a moment to lean against the booth for support. God, I miss them. I may have run away from it all, but I really, really miss my mum. I even miss my stinky brother. There's another prick of tears behind my eyes. By the time Rufus hands me back, I'm totally bunged up.

'Oh, darling,' says my mum, 'he sounds lovely.'

'He is, Mum. He is,' I assure her, and start blubbing despite myself.

'Well, don't *cry* about it,' she says sensibly, then starts doing it herself. 'Look, I'm going to hang up now. You take care of yourself, all right?'

'I will, Mum, and you too.'

'We miss you,' she says.

'And I miss you.'

'And we'll see you soon.'

'Yes.'

'You'll let me know where you are, won't you?'

'Yes,' I tell her.

'Promise?'

'I promise.'

'I love you, Melody,' says my mum, 'and your dad does too. Very much.'

'I love you too,' I wail.

'Bye, lovey.'

'Bye.'

'Bye.'

'Bye.'

I put the phone back in its cradle, and take a few seconds to scrub at my face before I turn out to look at my husband.

'That wasn't *so* bad.' I try to sound cheerful.

'That was bloody awful,' he responds, with far more gusto than I could manage. 'But it's done now. You OK?'

I do a huge snort, nod. 'Yeah, I'm OK.'

'Come on, then, Mrs W. Let's go home.'

I grab the strap of my bag and follow him into my new life.

Chapter Eleven

Brave New World

They like their anoraks. They are everywhere I look. Every third person is wearing one, even though, despite a sky that looks like it's been cast from lead, I can't see any real signs of rain. I think that this is your actual sartorial choice.

Rufus has bought a copy of a broadsheet paper, the *Daily Telegraph*, and sits with his legs extended, heels to the floor, holding it open as he leafs through it. The main headline on the front page says something like 'New Labour further undermines business with childcare deal for single mothers. World to end'. The downpage headlines read: 'Russians "untrustworthy" says report' and 'Elizabeth Hurley attends society dentist'. We've been lucky to get a seat. Two minutes later, and we would have been lucky to get through the doors, especially as the stations don't seem to be equipped with professional pushers on the platforms like in Tokyo. There's obviously been some sort of screw-up, as there are only two cars making up this train, and a good four hundred people trying to ride it.

'Christ,' I say to Rufus, 'there will be heads rolling for this.'

He lowers his newspaper. 'What?'

'Well, either something's gone wrong with the rolling stock or someone's ordered up the wrong train.'

He looks blank. 'Huh?'

I jerk my chin at the red-faced hordes who cling grimly to handles and seat backs, muttering 'surr-eh' over and over in that open-vowelled British fashion as another jerk of carriage on points flings them into the solar plexuses of their neighbours. 'They've only got two cars to get this lot to Hereford.'

He looks vaguely about him, as if taking in for the first time that he is not alone. 'Mmm, yes . . .' he says. 'I suppose it *is* a bit crowded.'

A bit crowded? Well, yes, in a similar way to how the Black Death was a bit contagious. Or Norman Bates was a tad oedipal. All we need is a couple of uniformed guards with guns, and we've got a Spielberg movie.

'Is it always like this?'

The elbow in my face shifts a bit, and its owner says: 'Yes.'

I'm only three hours into the country, but I have already discovered that the celebrated British reserve is largely mythical. Between Gatwick and Kingham, I've had full and frank exchanges on the subject of non-working ticket machines, the advantages of the Post Office queuing system, the way the ashtrays have filled up with chewing gum since they banned smoking, someone called Jordan, the blandness of mozzarella and – four times – how disappointing the weather is. I kind of like it. They may have no taste in outerwear, but this is obviously related to the fact that most of these people are madder than a box of frogs.

'The thing is, right,' continues my new friend, 'that they continue to claim that they're running at a loss. I mean, four hundred people to a carriage and they still pretend they can't make a profit.'

'That,' a tall, businessy-looking woman in a charcoal wool suit and four-inch stilettos, glamorously topped off with a bright orange cagoule, joins in, unannounced, from beside Rufus's shoulder, 'is because no one ever buys tickets.'

'No point.' A man with a mobile phone clicks his mouthpiece closed. 'When the chances of seeing a conductor are something like ten to one.'

'Yes,' says anorak man, 'that's right.'

'Took me eight hours to get home from Birmingham last week,' says mobile.

'Tchuch,' says businesswoman, 'typical.'

And then they all do something else British, which is that, having concluded this enthusiastic exchange, they clam up like clams and behave as though they've just discovered that not only are they in a room full of hardened criminals, *they haven't even been introduced*.

Rufus folds his paper over and lifts it up once more so that I can see the headlines on the inside page. Well, headline. Page 3 seems to be entirely consumed with what looks like a gruesome murder case. 'Man cooked fiancée's liver with onions and mash, court hears', screams the banner over a huge block of text peppered with emboldened sub-heads reading 'Labour voter', 'Tony Blair' and 'Hunt saboteur'. Above an advertisement for some kind of chairlift that lets you carry your walking cane upstairs, another legend reads: 'Further detail, p. 13, 17'.

I finished my novel on the train to Reading – quite appropriate, I thought – and staring out of the window has, so far, not been the most rewarding of experiences. Of course, I know that neigh-bourhoods next to a railway are rarely associated with affluence in any country, but this introduction to the English landscape is depressing. Everything here seems somehow a bit, well, small, cramped, constricted. And *grey*. Hints of lives lived at half-cock, swept into hiding from the outside world behind net curtains and stone-clad, double-glazed porches, tragically optimistic barbecue-patio combos.

Between bodies, over heads, I peer up at the digital noticeboard above the door. Of the stations we've already passed, there was Didcot, a place that looks from the station as though it doesn't exist apart from the huge, waisted concrete towers of a power station and a railway museum where knots of people mill about, knee-deep in bindweed, hands in anorak pockets, and Oxford, City of Dreaming Spires: a city that's always held out a promise of medieval splendour, but didn't seem to consist of a lot more than the usual light engineering firms and red-brick terraces, with a railwayside graveyard for good measure.

And after that, the station list has degenerated into strings of syllables that sound to my ears – accustomed as they are to bastardisations of Aboriginal descriptions, or convict jokes – like they've been put together by an advertising focus group intent on conveying quintessential Englishness. Fantasies of what these places are like flash through my head as the names crawl across the screen. Hanborough: got to have a horse fair. Charlbury: geese. Kingham: must be near a palace. Moreton-in-Marsh: blokes with long sticks. Evesham: good for sinful chickies. Pershore: big white cotton handkerchiefs. Worcester Shrub Hill: wattles. Worcester Foregate Street: cobbles, and those diamond-patterned windows that look like they're made of liquorice. Malvern Link: steam trains; Jenny Agutter shouting, 'Daddy, my daddy.' Great Malvern: big hats, limp wrists. Colwall: sticks of pink and white confectioners' rock. Ledbury: small kids down coalmines. Hereford: enormous swinging testicles. Yeah, I know. Don't go there. So far, Hanborough has been little more than a platform by a big field, Charlbury a cute little station covered in flowers with something that looks like an old quarry next to it, and Kingham a set of sleepers in a birch wood. Good sky, though: big, grey, sort of Constable-ish. We'll be getting off at Moreton-in-Marsh.

Rufus folds up the *Telegraph* and jerks his chin doorwards. 'Right. Better get moving. Can't be more than five minutes.'

He leads the way, and I note how trail negotiations are conducted on my new turf: the stream of unfinished sentences – 'Can I just . . .?', 'Excuse . . .', 'Sorry . . .', 'Do you mind if I . . .?' – as if a completed request would somehow be an insult. The corridor is packed to bursting, yet they all look like they're taking an exam or something: the odd rolling eye stands out for a second or two, but most faces remain impassive, calm, even. They must all be cultivating enormous ulcers.

The train slows, stops, and everyone wobbles like bottles on a conveyor belt. And then nothing happens. There's an elderly couple standing by the door, and they're looking out of the window, going 'Moreton-in-Marsh? No, that's not us. Where's Pershore, dear? Two stops up? Well, then . . .'

Some shifting. A couple of people clear their throats. Eventually, someone three layers ahead of me says, politely, 'Excuse me.'

The old lady looks up. 'We're not getting off here,' she explains.

'Yes, but could you open the door, please?'

'We're not getting off here,' she repeats, very slowly, this time, as though her interlocutor must be foreign.

The engine revs. We're going to get carried all the way to Hereford.

Suddenly, a huge, booming voice bellows: 'Yes, dunderhead, BUT WE ARE!!!'

'Well, I never . . .' begins the old man.

'OPEN THE DOOR, YOU MORON!' booms the voice.

'I will *not*,' begins the old man, drawing himself up as far as he can go in the limited space, 'have you speak to my wife like—'

And suddenly, thirty voices shout as one: 'OPEN THE DOOR!'

Finally, he gets it, presses the button. 'There's no need to be *rude*,' he says.

'Can you get out and let other people off, please?'

'I already said, we're not getting off here,' he explains.

'YES! BUT WE ARE!'

'Well, really, I—'

The single voice again. 'GET OUT OF THE WAY, OR I'LL TAKE THAT FLAT CAP OFF YOUR HEAD AND SHOVE IT SO FAR UP YOUR ARSE YOU'LL NEVER FIND IT AGAIN! MOVE OR I'LL CLUB YOU TO DEATH WITH A BABY SEAL! HIT IT, OR YOU'LL NEVER SEE YOUR BOWLS CLUB AGAIN!'

This finally unpops them. Three dozen people pile out on to the platform, panting and cussing. The owner of the big voice turns out to be a man so large he could carry a combine single-handed, purple of face and clad in, of all things, Prince of Wales check plus fours. You have got to be kidding. His rage over, he stands pleasantly by the old couple, helping them back on to the train and handing them their luggage. But the volume is little diminished. 'BLOODY AWFUL, THESE TRAINS,' he yells. 'CAN'T BLAME YOU FOR GETTING A BIT CONFUSED.'

The doors slide to, and the train moves off. I look around. Another halt as desolate as the previous three: desultory planting, cracked, gravelly tarmac. Not as desolate, mind, as the sort of one-shack-and-a-blowfly hellholes you get in the Aussie desert, but not exactly the glamour centre of the universe. And while I'm picking up my bag again (Rufus seems to have forgotten the theory that gents carry things for ladies. I'll find out later that this is fairly much par for the course), I hear my husband's voice, itself several dozen decibels louder than when he last opened his mouth, hail the blustering man in the plus fours.

'Roly!' he shouts. 'I might have guessed that it was you making all that racket!'

Chapter Twelve
Dead Birds

The man-mountain swings round like a piñata, and a passing traveller flies off down the platform as he catches him a blinding blow with the duffel bag on his shoulder. Oblivious, he strides towards Rufus (well, takes two enormous steps, which is all he needs to get from one side of the platform to the other), one meaty hand extended in greeting.

Rufus's hand disappears within Roly's clasp, and, as he opens his mouth to speak, he is reduced, instead, to coughing like a consumptive as the man's other hand descends on to his shoulder in three hearty claps of the sort that would have removed Rufus's dentures if this had been taking place in a comic book.

'Well, bugger me sideways, Wattestone!' he shouts. 'Was just thinking about you! On m'way to your casa, as it happens.'

Rufus, recovering, says: 'Really? Excellent. You can give us a lift, then.'

I've chosen to stand over by the exit gate, mostly because I don't want to be knocked, accidentally, on to the tracks. People scuttle past, ducking as Roly's elbows fly.

'Aha!' he bellows. 'So there *is* a 'we'! Heard about this clandestine marriage nonsense. Which one is she, then?'

He glares about him, and I get my first full sight of his face. He looks how I have always imagined the Minotaur probably looked: if you spliced bull genes into the human body, this would be the result. I wouldn't have been surprised, to be honest, if he had a pair of neat little horns and a curtain ring through his nose. This Roly has all the charm of a Charolais: pinky-red, wrinkled skin, devoid of any sign of a suntan; flattened, flared nostrils, eyes too small for the head, six kilos of pure muscle in place of a neck and a tuft of

Tintin hair sticking upwards from a forehead that is just made for butting. The guy's no beauty.

I stick a finger in the air and say: 'I think that'd be me.'

'Hah!' he cries. 'Wife. Wattestone Mrs, Junior! Congratulations!'

I'd half-hoped that my female status might let me out of the more enthusiastic greeting rituals, but instead I drop my bag as a meaty paw bangs down upon my back with excruciating heartiness. The contents – passport, makeup, a couple of tampons, notebook, pens, Ibuprofen, contraceptive pills, handful of Maltese coinage – scatter across the ground and I'm temporarily too winded to do anything about it. Rufus starts chasing them as I gasp for breath.

'Remember your own strength, Cruikshank,' he says. What is it with Englishmen and surnames? 'Melody gave up rugger years ago.'

'Sorry, sorry, sorry,' says Roly. 'Roly Cruikshank. Old school friend. Pony Club too, till m'last horse collapsed underneath me at Badminton. Pity. Fine old chap. Wouldn't let me shoot him m'self. Went for carpaccio on th'continent, no doubt.'

'How ya goin', Roly?'

'So you really *are* Australian. Good news. Cats. Pigeons. Say g'day ever, do you?'

'G'day,' I say co-operatively, and am rewarded with an earsplitting explosion of mirth. 'Good for you! Good for you! Welcome to the Cotswolds!'

'Bonzer,' I say. 'Good on yer, mate.'

He's easily amused. Subjects me to a bit more assault and battery, then picks up my rucksack and leads us towards the car park.

Rufus catches me up, pushes my handbag into my arms. 'Roly Cruikshank,' he says. 'Mostly harmless.'

'Mostly?'

'Mostly,' he says, out of the side of his mouth. 'He has what they call a vibrant imagination. Read a lot of Alastair MacLean as a child and never really got over it. Sees himself as a sort of Wooster-at-arms.'

74

'OK. So that was how come he was playing badminton on a horse, yeah?'

Rufus laughs. 'No. It's a horse trials. Attached to a house. That they named the game after.'

'Ah. Good-oh. We live and learn.'

Roly Cruikshank waits beside a canvas-topped Land Rover that has recently been up to its axles in mud. 'Sorry,' he says. 'Car's in the shop. I'll sling yer bag in the back.'

'Thanks.'

'Heigh-ho. Anything for a pretty lady. Better jump in the front with me. Bit of blood in the back. No place for a newlywed. You don't mind, do you, R?'

Rufus peers gingerly beneath the canvas and clear plastic flap that constitutes a back door to the vehicle. 'No, no. It's fine. You don't mind if I shift the front ones to the back, do you?'

'Be m'guest.'

Curious as to the source of this exchange, I crane over my shoulder the second I'm settled with my handbag between my feet. It's full-on charnel-house back there. Rufus squats on a built-in bench running along the side of the truck, against a background of dead birds. Pheasants. White-kid faces on lolling heads, clouded eyes, leathery talons crooked in rigor mortis, they hang by tied-together necks from meat hooks suspended from the rollbars. Twenty of them, sleek and russet and green, tail feathers sweeping the head of a friendly looking black-and-white spaniel, which thumps its tail when it registers that my eyes are on it. Rufus gives it a scratch behind the ear, trails a cuff through a puddle of congealed blood that lies on the lid of a toolbox. 'Hello, Perkins, old bean,' he says. 'How're you doing?'

He notices the blood, pulls a face. 'Damn,' he says. 'That'll make the old girl happy. Where'd you shoot this lot, Roly?'

Roly, turning the ignition key, says: 'Hampshire. Last week. Kept Perkins busy, anyway. Be just about ready to eat by now, s'pose. Fancy a couple?'

Rufus shakes his head. 'I'm sure there are a million lurking in the freezer at Bourton. Whose?'

'Weatheralls'.'

'Ah. Well?'

'Fine. Arthriticky. Two hundred brace. Only six of us.'

'Mmm. Bulldozer?'

''Fraid so. Took as many as a'cd.'

'City fellahs?'

'Austrians.'

'Ah,' says Rufus again. 'W'dn't mind a b'da'that ourselves.'

'Agency. Hols people. Int'n't. Waddya give th'man who h'zev'r'th'ng? Find th'URL for you f'y'like.'

'Good one. Ta.'

I decide that it's time to intervene. I could cope with not understanding what they're talking about. I can even live with a deficit of pronouns. But if they're going to dispense with vowels as well, I'll be floundering without a lifebelt.

'Can you guys just recap a little bit of that conversation?'

'Sorry.' Rufus's head and shoulders pop through the gap between Roly and my seats. 'Roly's been shooting with some friends in Hampshire. They've got a huge shoot and bagged four hundred birds in a day, though most of them were ploughed under because it's almost impossible to sell the things in that sort of quantity, let alone eat them. But they keep the whole thing going by renting a day's sport at a time to foreign businessmen. Corporate entertainment, that sort of thing. I was just wondering if we couldn't get a bit of that sent the way of us.'

'Four hundred birds in one day?'

'I know,' says Roly. 'Bit obscene, s'pose.'

'Too right. And they don't get eaten?'

'The great British public,' says Rufus, 'don't like to gut and pluck their own food. And most of them wouldn't touch game even if it was pre-packaged with a lemon up its arse. I'm afraid it's not economical to do anything else.'

'But why kill them in the first place?'

''Fraid the German businessmen expect to get value for their two grand a day. Our City traders expect exactly the same thing when they go boar hunting in the Black Forest. There's not a lot left up to chance these days.'

'Oh Jeez.' I can't keep the disapproval out of my voice.

Roly laughs. 'I say, Roof, looks like you've married a hippie! Vegetarian? Labour voter?' These last questions are aimed at me.

'No,' I protest. 'No, I've got nothing against people killing things they're going to eat. Or culling pests and stuff. But seriously. They breed these things, right?'

'Uh-huh,' they concur.

'So they breed these things to be shot and buried? Don't you think that's a bit –'

'Townie,' says Roly, dismissing me with a single word.

'No. Hold on—'

'Trouble with townies,' he says, 'full of opinions about things they know nothing about. Interfering in country ways. We don't go up there and tell them not to mug each other, do we?'

I'm stunned; lapse into silence.

'That's a bit harsh,' says Rufus. 'Come on. It does look a *bit* foul from the outside.'

'Well, I think their sinkholes of debauchery look pretty foul,' says Roly, 'but I leave 'em to get on with it. Stringfellows, Spearmint Rhino – wouldn't catch *me* taking a young lady to those sorts of place, but live and let live. That's what I say.'

I start up again. 'Now, hold *on*—'

'So what're you going to ours for, anyway?' Rufus changes the subject in a pointed manner.

We're on a road that leads through a grungy-looking estate of two-storey prefabs whose occupants' taste in garden design is mostly influenced by the fridge-and-nettle school, circa 1976.

'Dunno,' says Roly. 'Got a call from th'mater and thought I'd better oblige. Thought there was probably a drink in it, at least. Something about you coming home.'

'Oh cripes,' says Rufus. 'She's not put together some grim gathering, has she?'

'Possibility. Wet the bridie's head, that sort of thing.'

'You what?' I tear my eyes away from a picturesque vista of rusting car bodies beneath a clump of elders and look at Roly in horror. 'You mean, they've . . . but look at me! I'm not dressed! We've been travelling since eight this morning!'

'Ne'mind,' says Roly, 'don't suppose anyone'll notice.'

'Oh good God,' says Rufus, 'she could have told us. How many people has she asked, do you know?'

'Not that many, I don't suppose. Not a lot of notice, after all. Hunt. Locals. You know.'

'Oh, well, it could be worse, I suppose,' he says.

'No it couldn't! I haven't washed my hair in three days! All my slap's at the bottom of my rucksack and there's a hole the size of Tasmania in my pants.'

'Don't bend over, then.'

'That's some help. Thanks. Can we stop so I can brush my hair, at least?'

Roly sucks air through his teeth. 'Think things kicked off an hour ago. Can't really be much later than we already are.'

'How far is it?'

'Not much further,' says Rufus. 'See? We're on the Stow road already. We'll get signs in another couple of minutes.'

I glance back out of the window and see that our surroundings have changed dramatically. We're driving fast along an undulating main road lined with majestic deciduous trees and a dry-stone wall that is so well-covered with lichen that it looks as though it's been standing there since neolithic times. A wide green verge is broken at regular intervals by neat ditches a foot wide and six inches deep. Side-roads are announced by tidy black-and-white-painted Dick Whittington signposts that break the mileages down to quarter-mile distances. And suddenly, the place names are really, really foreign: The Slaughters; Lower Swell; Guiting Power; Shipton-under-Wychwood; Stow-on-the-Wold. I catch glimpses of thatch, of smokestacks and tiles made from a peculiar golden stone I've never seen before: not the strong gold of Gozo, but a gentle, silvery gold: palomino gold. And, despite the fact that we're driving through a landscape I know to be early winter, it's so – green. It's like a kid's been let loose with a paintbox and tried to come up with as many versions of the same colour as he can in half an hour. There's lime

78

green and lemon green, rusty green and green so dark it's almost black. There's eight shades of khaki and a good dozen of emerald. There's pea and olive and grass (at least a score of grass), and gold and leaf, malachite and verdigris, bottle and sea, there's green that flashes bright yellow when the sun breaks through the clouds and green that's almost oily in the shadows.

'Wow,' I say.

'What?' says Rufus.

'This.'

They both look a bit puzzled. '*What?*'

'This! This view!'

'View?'

I jerk my head at the scene out of the window.

'Oh, *that*,' says Rufus. '*That's* not a view.'

'Looks like one to me,' I say.

'No, no,' says Rufus, as we swing off the main road on to a road signed Bourton Allhallows. '*This* is a view.'

As he speaks, the woodland comes to an abrupt end and I see that we are driving along the high back of a rolling hill some hundred and fifty metres high. And on either side, two river valleys meander broad and mellow under a sky so huge it feels as though you must be seeing beyond the horizon.

'Wow,' I say.

'Sheep country,' says Rufus.

'Heythrop country,' says Roly. 'Best hunting in the world.'

The man's obsessed. He's like a surfing bore. Less decorative, though.

'Wow,' I say, again. I'm really lost for words. 'So this is where you grew up?'

Rufus nods. 'Learned to fish down there,' he says, 'and had my first sexual experience over in that field.'

'Who was that, then?' asks Roly.

'Miranda Vaughan.'

'Ah, Miranda,' says Roly. 'She was everyone's first sexual experience, wasn't she?'

'You too?'

79

'Pony Club camp, 1988. Asked me if I wanted to help her stuff her haynet. 'f'ya know what I mean.'

'We hit a patch of stinging nettles,' says Rufus. 'Knees like blackberries for a week.'

'Worth it, though.'

'Oh, yes. Well worth it. I thought I was King Kong.'

'Whatever happened to Miranda?'

'London. Minor modelling career. Lucky escape from drugs hell. Welsh landowner. Tow-headed children. Ponies. Roofing problems.'

'The usual, then.'

'Mmm.'

'Guys,' I say, 'I'm delighted to hear these details, but I need some advice here. What should I know before I walk into this party? Who are these people? What do I talk to them about?'

'Don't worry, darling,' says Rufus unhelpfully. 'I love you, so they'll love you.'

'Steady on,' says Roly. 'PDA, old chap.'

'You *are* odd, Roly,' says Rufus affectionately. He reaches over from the back of the seat and takes my hand. Instantly, I begin to feel better. Not that I'm some sort of little girl who needs Daddy to hold her hand or anything, but the solidarity's good. 'No-one's going to expect you to sparkle, darl. Just be yourself.'

'If I wanted advice from *Cosmopolitan* I'd have bought a copy. Be myself? Which self is that, then? Bookish self? Dancing on the tables self? Kitten-cuddling self? Trust-me-I'm-a-professional self? Weeping-over-tax-forms self? Which one would you like?'

'Look: they'll be curious. And they'll probably suck up to you, at least for the time being.'

'Which means?'

'Uh?'

'That they'll stop, yes?'

'Can't expect people to suck up to you for ever,' he says cheerfully.

'Your mother's managed it,' Roly points out.

'My mother is a very special person,' says Rufus, and, thank God, I spot a note of irony in his voice.

'That she is, old boy,' says Roly. 'That she is. Front or back, Roof?'

'Back. Front'll be crammed.'

Roly, who's changed down to second, changes back up again and accelerates past a pair of monumental stone gateposts and another road sign that reads 'Bourton Allhallows: House Only'. The verge has turned into a miracle of mown sward, the sort of grass that looks like it's been woven rather than cultivated. It runs beneath a six-foot wall, which is, itself, topped by a magnificent topiary hedge in the shape of crenellated battlements, fortified, every fifty feet or so, by a circular turret. Oh my God. If this is what the hedge looks like, what the hell is behind it?

Actually, the hedge is, now I look more closely at it, a bit raggedy: the trees that constitute the topiary have got thinner with age and show skeletal branches through gaping holes. The wall, product of thousands of hours of high-level craftsmanship, bulges in places, and has even, at a couple of spots, fallen down altogether and been filled in with half-hearted concoctions of wooden stakes, chicken-wire and strands of barbed wire. Fair enough, I think, it's a good few miles long, and keeping it up must be a similar task to painting the Sydney Harbour Bridge.

The wall curves off to the right and Roly changes down to take the corner. Another road sign flashes past: 'Bourton Allhallows', it says, 'Please Drive Carefully'. And then, we're in the village.

I get a shock. I am slap in the centre of a picture postcard again. The road we're on cuts through the centre of a perfect triangular green, crosses a narrow little hump-backed bridge over one of those little duck-filled creeks you always fantasise you're going to see your perfect children playing in one day. And surrounding the perfect green is a perfect village: all thatch and eaves and mullioned windows, tiny little front yards filled with cottage flowers. A fantasy pub, wooden benches and stone millwheels against the walls, to the right. The sort of village shop with the thirty-pane display window that Franklin Mint sell in miniature by the thousand every year, to the left. A squat, comely church, complete with bell tower, straight ahead. Clumps of bulrushes grow out of the stream, a majestic naked oak spreads anciently, a tumble of late roses spilling over a wall.

And then I get another shock. Because, attractive though the initial impact is, it is quickly discernible that, like the boundary wall to the estate, the entire village of Bourton Allhallows is falling down. The thatch on most of the cottages is so bare that you can see the wire that holds it in place. The lich gate of the church lurches at an impossible angle. There are no cars in the pub car park or on the track leading to it, and, on closer inspection, it is pretty obvious that not only is the shop not open today – it never is. In a less peaceable part of the world, those windows would be covered in weatherboard. Paint peels on front doors and window frames. It's as though the people have simply upped and left. I shiver, but stay silent. I'll find out later. No doubt.

Past the green, the estate wall swings back up to meet the road: rougher here, the hedging barely trimmed at all, woodland behind. Roly turns the Land Rover up the drive, through slumped white gates that I would guess haven't been closed in fifty years, and we drive through the woods in silence. Rufus puts a friendly hand on my shoulder and I lean my cheek on it. I'm so nervous now my stomach is turning over and I can feel a twitch in my legs where all the muscles are telling me to turn tail and run. He kisses the top of my head.

'Stay cool, darling,' he whispers.

'I am cool,' I lie.

'I know you are,' he lies back. 'Don't worry. It's going to be great.'

I turn and kiss him, give him a smile. Which plummets from my face as we emerge from the woods and I see my new home.

Chapter Thirteen
Simply Heaven

The ravens are the first thing I notice. Well, ravens, rooks, crows – they could be some kind of funereal local galah for all I know. Black birds, anyway, and scores of them, flying in and out of a hole in the roof the size of a Daimler. But I'll call them ravens, because I feel a bit like Duncan approaching my doom, and for sure I have my very own Lady Macbeth waiting for me under those battlements.

Although the battlements are only metaphorical. My fantasies of drawbridges and fluttering pennants are dashed on the reality of a hotchpotch of roofs and windows spread out over a few acres of flat ground enclosed on three sides by the weedy arms of an oxbow lake. The fourth side is wall: four metres of flinted grey stone with a huge hole in the middle where the main drive sweeps into a gravelled courtyard. The wall, naturally enough, is on the south side of the house, and produces a deep patch of dank shade where a lawn ought to be. Several dozen cars have been crammed into the yard, and a couple of dozen more are strung out, tyres carving deep ruts in the damp grass, along the edges of the main drive.

'Hell,' says Rufus. 'How many people did you say she'd invited, again?'

'Looks like one or two,' says Roly. 'Glad to see you've got the moat filled up again, anyway.'

'Yes. It did get a bit stinky. Dead fish and stuff.'

'Did they ever work out what it was?'

'Bizarre,' he says. 'They found a couple of cracks at the bottom, but nothing much else. He said they were probably quite deep and the whole lot had drained into them. Sealed them up with a couple of tons of concrete and it seemed to do the trick. Probably just one of those freak occurrences. It's not like we're in the earthquake zone or anything. Just have to keep our fingers crossed.'

'Well, it's just good to see the old place back on form,' says Roly. 'Always been a tad envious of you, old boy. Not many people have got to grow up in heaven.'

Rufus sighs. 'It is, isn't it?' he says complacently. 'Simply heaven.'

And I'm looking at it, and thinking: please don't let them ask me to join in right now, because I'm not sure I have the self-control. Because if Bourton Allhallows is heaven, then God's got some sense of humour. Bourton Allhallows isn't heaven: it's Gormenghast. It's post-Danvers period Manderley.

Oh God. We're closer now, close enough for me to see the forests of broken drainpipes, the great green slashes where years of rainwater have worked themselves into the walls. And – my blood runs cold – as I watch, a raven flies over the moat, and lands on what I've been trying to deny my eyes were seeing: the branches of a small tree that's growing out of the hole in the roof. The branch bends beneath its weight, and the bird flaps its wings for balance, disturbing a handful of its roommates, which set off on a pivot of irritable flight.

A tree. There's a tree growing through the roof of my new home.

Roly shifts down a gear as the road gets steeper towards the bottom of the valley, and says: 'Seriously, Melody. You're a lucky girl. Used to come and stay here in the hols. Happiest days of m'life. You can't help but be happy in a place like this.'

I glimpse the stable block as we go past, behind another collapsed wooden gate. Unpainted doors hang off hinges, bits of dilapidated farm machinery lurking in the darkness beyond. Here's what I see as we get closer. Window lintels leaning at drunken angles over split and peeling sills. Buddleia sprouting from cracks in masonry, and straggly lavatera bushes, six feet high, sprouting unchecked from the drains at the bottoms of rusting downpipes.

I crane upwards. There are boards across some of the upper-floor windows, close to the hole in the roof. And of the whole, I can make no sense at all. It's as though every generation that's passed through this building has felt it necessary to add a bit. A grim jumble of architectural styles tacked one on to the other with the carelessness that only bonded labour can achieve. And hanging over it all, yew trees; the sort of trees you see in boneyards: black, dense and dripping.

'There we go,' says Roly, cranking on the handbrake. 'Roof, grab a couple of brace of those birds, will you? Seriously. You can hand them out to the poor or something if you can't eat them.'

I don't suppose the poor would be all that grateful for four rotting game birds with their feathers still on. I'd've thought they'd probably prefer a six-pack and some vouchers for Mickey D's. But maybe the English poor are different from our lot.

I unlatch my door, step down on to slippery flagstones. Perkins, tail going like the clappers, stands up to exit with us. Roly shouts at him to stay.

'God, let the poor chap have a pee, at least,' says Rufus. 'How long's he been locked up in there?'

'Suppose you've got a point,' says Roly. 'And he's not touched any of the pheasants. Good chap. You're a good old boy.'

The dog leaps down, trots off, tail pluming, in doggy fashion, to relieve himself against a yew tree.

Somewhere high above us, an overflow pipe trickles, the water arching out to splatter the widest possible area of the yard. Rufus looks up at it, sighs. 'Damn. No-one's sorted that out yet.'

'Where's it coming from?'

'One of the lavatory overflows, I think. Just never been able to work out which one.'

'How many are there?'

He shrugs. 'Thirty-six that I can think of. Could be a couple more people have forgotten about. Bit of a habit of changing interior walls. We lost the chapel for a hundred and fifty years.'

'Stop it. You're just showing off, now.'

'And there are at least three secret corridors.'

'Can it, Wattestone.'

'And a dungeon, though there's not much left of it, given that it's below the water table.'

I give him a look. He grins. 'Welcome home, Mrs W. Bourton Allhallows salutes you.'

Roly pulls the handle off the back door. 'Shit, sorry,' he says.

'N'e'mind,' says Rufus. Takes the handle from him, lays it down on a moss-covered stone toadstool and opens the door with a hefty kick. 'It's not like it's the first time.'

'Jeez,' I say.

'It's a family house,' says Rufus. 'They all have quirks.'

'Got any ghosts?' I ask.

'Only eight or nine,' he says dismissively. 'You hardly ever see them.'

'Well, which are the main ones?'

'Um . . . there's a nasty old bloke who wanders about in the main courtyard at night with a knife. He tends to give people a bit of a shock if they don't know about him. Otherwise it's just the usual run of nuns and monks and fever victims.'

'And Eloise,' says Roly.

'Oh, yes. Yes, you need to watch out for her. She can be a bit of a frightener.'

'Who's Eloise?'

'Well, we're not entirely sure. We call her Eloise after Heloise and Abelard, you know?'

All Greek to me so far. I nod, understandingly.

'You'll recognise her,' says Roly, 'from the long white night-dress and the fingernails.'

'Fingernails?'

'Sort of bloody stumps. The usual, in a walling-up.'

'Huh?'

'Nasty thing.' Rufus pauses in the doorway. 'Bit of a habit back there for a while. Probably four or five of them about the place: it's one of the reasons you keep coming up against dead ends.'

'What's walling-up?'

'Nasty sort of medieval murder. Punishment for recalcitrant brides, slutty daughters, that sort of thing. Family went in for it in a big way, apparently, though of course it was always a secret. Murder not being any more legal back then than it is now. They used to knock 'em out and stick 'em in a bit of corner, or cellar, whatever, and build a wall across them so they'd come to in the dark and starve to death.'

'Scratching feebly at the bricks,' says Roly, with more relish than I would say was strictly necessary.

'God, that's *terrible*.'

'I know,' says Rufus. 'Well, people *were* pretty horrid back then. Constantly impaling each other and so forth.'

'And your family made a *habit* of this?'

'So the story goes.'

Roly's big hand clamps heavily down on my shoulder. 'So you'd better watch yourself, young lady,' he leers into my face, and bellows with laughter as he sees me react.

We go inside. A long whitewashed corridor, patched with more damp. Off to our right, a huge furnace roars and burps, metal walls thundering as though there's someone inside hammering to get out.

'Christ,' says Rufus, 'she's turned the heating on. In November. She's *really* pushing the boat out.'

We go up the corridor. I glimpse rooms full of dust and junk: piles of mismatched china, three giant perambulators, a pantry full of evil-looking Kilner jars. It's the sort of place where spiders lurk, fat and shiny from generations of undisturbed gorging. It smells of mice.

Rufus is hurrying forward, and, in the voice of a suburban housewife, is going: 'It's my babies! My boys!'

Jeez. He's been living here so long, he's made pets out of the rats.

The door bursts open, and three solid shapes hurtle forward, grab him, just as I imagined, by the neck, with large, slobbering mouths, knock him to the floor. As I cast about for a stick to beat them off with, all I can see is a whirl of paws and tails and slobbering tongues. And I realise that Rufus is laughing, clutching them about the torsos, not, as I'd first thought, to fight them off, but with the sort of great big affectionate hugs I thought he reserved for me. And he's going: 'Ooozamyboooys! Wuzza wuzza idga *boy*-boys! Voo–voo boof! Boof!' and other noises I can barely interpret beyond the fact that they're obviously sounds of affection. And they're licking him over every piece of available skin and – horrors! – he's letting them. Not just letting them, but sticking his chin out to give them extra space. Fat, wet, dog tongues all over his face, and, with extra-special accuracy, all over his mouth as well. I make a mental note not to let him near me till he's had a wash.

Gradually, as the squirming and panting slows down, I separate the muddle into disparate shapes. Seems like Rufus is getting love from a bulldog, a black retriever and a pug. Eyes shining like a ten-year-old, he looks up at me and treats me to a huge grin.

'These are my babies,' he says.

'Uh-huh,' I tell him back. 'Glad to know you've not got any of the human type.'

He ignores me. 'Darling, meet Fifi, Buster and Django. Sit!'

It takes me a second to work out that the final command isn't aimed at me. It's only when the dogs obediently line up with their backsides on the ground, tongues lolling in huge smiles, that I'm completely certain.

'Which one's which?'

He ruffles the head of the retriever, which responds by offering a polite paw. Despite myself, I'm drawn downwards, take it in my hand and shake it. If Pops could see me now. 'This is Django,' says Rufus.

'How do you do, Django?'

Django rolls his eyes and broadens his grin. The pug, unable to contain himself, says 'fuff' and rubs his backside across the flags. Looks like someone needs their glands squeezing. Bags not me. Big brown pop-eyes moisten with emotion and one ear lops piteously. I take his paw and shake it in turn. 'Fifi, right?'

'Buster,' says Rufus. He throws an arm round the neck of the bulldog in that homoerotic I'm-going-to-strangle-you pose that men keep for their best mates after rugby. '*This* is Fifi.'

Fifi has little pink-rimmed eyes and great big vampire teeth. They'd be threatening if they didn't stick upwards from his lower jaw. Instead, they make him look like a goof.

'The face that launched a thousand quips,' I say, and can't resist pulling his ears. We follow him into a kitchen that's – well, medieval. Literally. The only thing that would make it more authentic would be a hunchback in the corner.

Roly peels off his Drizabone – well, shapeless waxed coat – and drops it on to the back of a wooden chair. Rufus does the same with his jacket on the one next to it. On the table, three platters and two copper baby baths stand, filled with the sort of canapés you used to see in the seventies: cheese-and-pineapple cocktail sticks, listless-looking, pale vol-au-vents filled with what looks like coronation chicken, cheese biscuits smeared with greyish-pink pâté and topped off with a little chip of green olive, potato chips that smell even from a metre away like ersatz bacon and some stick-like things that I'm not sure aren't some sort of practical joke. I pick one up, sniff it. Smells a bit like Vegemite. Only disgusting.

'Shall we take some of these?' I ask their retreating backs.

Rufus turns, says: 'Oh, yeah. Good idea. Mummy's always forgetting them because she barely eats herself. We'll be living on stale bacon snaps for a week if we don't get them down people's throats.'

He takes the stick things. Roly takes the vol-au-vents. I opt for the cheesy pineapples. I follow them through a large door covered in shreds of green baize on the far side of the room.

They lead me up some stairs. Dark, unventilated, lined with more black wood. As we near the top, I catch a low rumble from the far side of another green baize door at the top. The rumble of a distant tidal wave. The hairs prickle on the back of my neck. Rufus barges through the door, which swings back on Roly and, in turn, swings back on me. We're in a hallway – shiny wooden floors and wooden panelling, a white, arched ceiling covered in diamond-patterned plasterwork, a collection of high-backed oak chairs lining the walls. At the end, no more baize, but a panelled oak door in a frame carved with vine leaves. And from behind it, the sound, louder, now, and more ferocious, like the roar of baying bloodhounds.

'Hell,' says Rufus, 'how many people did you say?'

'Sounds like a few,' understates Roly.

Sounds like more than a few. It sounds like my mother-in-law has lined up the entire cast of *Braveheart* to jeer my arrival. I can envisage them, faces painted blue, banging on their shields in anticipation. The roar gets louder and louder as the door gets closer. Now it's the roar of the New York subway, the sound of labour riots.

Rufus puts his hand on the handle and pushes the door open. I glimpse, behind a mêlée of olive green and navy blue, a cavernous hall lined, like the passageway, with wooden panelling, a huge expanse of hanging hammer-beam overhead, flashes of tapestry and metal against stark white paint.

The noise level suddenly drops.

'Hello, everybody,' says Rufus.

And a hundred voices bellow his name.

Chapter Fourteen

Neighbours

Rufus is immediately consumed by a rugby scrum of people who all seem to want to hit him at once. I suppose I shouldn't be surprised by this trial-by-combat form of greeting after the pummelling he got at Moreton-in-Marsh, but the sight of all these hands rising into the air and slamming down on his back, his shoulders, his head – whatever spare bit of body is available – is a bit alarming. Maybe it's just the crazy-mad surroundings, the collection of armour and weaponry hanging on the walls, the head-high wooden panelling that lines the cricket-pitch-sized space, the fireplace the size of a Soweto shanty, but I feel that these people aren't just touching him through affection, but because they believe that the physical contact will miraculously cure them of leprosy.

I've barely made it through the door, and the flailing elbows haven't let me get much further. Eventually, my canapés and I fetch up against the wall, hemmed in between a suit of armour and a high-backed wooden chair whose low, embroidered seat has caved in so far that it almost rests on the floor. Roly has pushed his own tray into the hands of a sabre-toothed blonde and battered his way to the other side of the room, standing under what looks remarkably, even to my untrained eye, like a Caravaggio, and is already replacing an empty champagne glass on a tray with his left hand while lifting another off with his right. I peer around to see if I can identify any of the rest of the family. A woman who must be Tilly – she has Rufus's slightly almond, slightly oriental-looking eyes – sits on one of those couches with the boxy frames you can open up by undoing the ropes at the top, in a huge bay window. Apart from the eyes, there's not a whole lot of obvious family resemblance — Tilly is short and ginger, her hair curly where his is straight and floppy — but she's the only woman in the room who's stuffed a cantaloupe up her dress so I guess this must be her. She is drinking fizzy water and shoving the contents of another bowl of the stick things into her mouth like she thinks someone will take them away if she doesn't get on with it. Beside her is a tiny little old woman, maybe the size of my thumb, who wears a hat and seems to have something wrong with her neck: her head tilts to the left, pointy chin jutting from powdered dewlaps beneath a smile of practised sweetness. She must be about a hundred. I guess this must be Granny Wattestone. I've never spoken to someone that old before. I don't think I've ever *seen* someone that old before in the flesh.

At the far end of the room, on wide steps that lead through a partially curtained arch into what looks like another sitting room beyond, I catch sight of Mary. Elegant as ever, in black-and-white houndstooth check, she twiddles her champagne flute by the stem and cranes to catch sight of Rufus. She's talking with a thin man who's a good head taller than she is, dimpling up at him like a fine-vintage Doris Day as he dips his head to share a pleasantry. There are no women around them, surprise surprise.

Our eyes lock, and the dimples drop, momentarily, from the sides of her mouth. Mary's eyes turn dark, like a shark's: they shine at me, beam something not altogether pleasant in my direction. Then she slaps the smile back on, touches his sleeve with a light and intimate hand and points me out. Raises her glass at me, says something that makes him laugh. He imitates her gesture.

With my spare hand, I raise an imaginary glass in return. They make no effort to come over. Just stand there, the two of them, and talk about me.

A thickset man in a kilt walks past, reaches out and takes half a dozen pineapple sticks from the tray, says something about being starving, moves on without once looking at my face. Hastily, I stoop and lay my tray down on the chair. I figure that being mistaken for staff isn't the best way to enter the fold. Clever old Mary. She's set it up so that the first impression everyone gets of me will be of a travel-raddled, grimy oik, a fish out of water. I'd expected a couple of days' grace, a chance to settle in. I guess she knew that. I can feel stirrings of respect deep in my breast. Clever old Mary.

I could murder a drink. There's no-one within hailing distance, though: just a hundred chinless, big-nosed, straight-haired, bellowing humanoids with vowels like drill-bits. No-one seems to have noticed me. They're all too intent on congratulating my husband. I guess it wouldn't be the thing to shove my way past them and grab a glass. Rufus's new wife, the dipsomaniac.

He calls me. Well, I assume it's me, though everyone here seems to be calling everyone else 'darling' without discrimination. I look over to check, and he's got a grin on his face and holds out a hand. 'Come on, darling,' he calls. 'Come and meet everyone! Don't be shy!'

There was a turkey farm down the road from where we lived when we were kids – a farm that made a smashing once-a-year profit from all the lunatics who insist on turning out a full 'traditional' roast dinner complete with spuds and stuffing in fifty degrees of heat because that's what their grandparents used to do. My friend Tina and I whiled away a lot of spring afternoons, before we discovered boys, by whistling at them. The thing is with turkeys, they tend to make no noise at all, or they all gobble at once. Not an individual thought between them. And the sound of someone whistling drives them into a frenzy of indignation. Tina and I used to sneak up on the barn and, when they caught sight of us, there'd be a moment's deathly hush as four hundred pea-sized brains tried to work out what the hell we were doing there. And then one of us – usually me; I've got the most raucous wolf whistle in the southern hemisphere – would let fly with a builder's special, and the whole lot would let fly with a shriek of *obbleobbleobbleobbleobble*, every one of them goggling at us in astonishment like we'd farted in church.

It's a bit like that now, only I'm not laughing. When Rufus began calling me, the entire room fell, bit by bit, silent. As a body, they turned in the direction of his reaching hand, stared, lips

93

slightly ajar, at me. And now, as I unpeel myself from the wall and step into the aisle that has opened up before me, the crowd bursts into comment.

'*Obbleobbleobbleobbleobble*,' they go. '*Obbleobbleobbleobbleobble*.'

And once again, the room goes quiet.

Feeling the blush rise in my cheeks, I cross the space to reach him, feel scrutiny of my gait, my crumpled travelling clothes, my shiny nose, my grubby trainers. And then I'm in the middle of it, hand pumped, clothes tweaked, air kisses flying about my ears. I don't stand a chance. There are a hundred-odd strangers in the room, and I'm the only one they have to take in. This is Rupert, says Rufus, this is Miranda. I nod, smile, fail to memorise the faces, grin inanely as the names fly past: this is Charlie, this is Jimbo, this is Ginny. This is LuluNessaTrinnyCaro and EddyReggieBertieSam. Mel, meet EmmaTobyLaviniaAndrew PoppyJamieSophieHugo. PippaDaddySusieTom . . .

Backtrack. I swing round to see the daddy.

He's fairly obvious: an older version of the son. A little shorter, and run to thinness in that way that some older men have, and the hair's gone salt-and-pepper and is cut with the sort of forced side parting that always makes you wonder about wigs, but it's all pretty good, considering.

He sticks a hand out. 'Edmund Wattestone,' he says. 'Shocked father-in-law. How do you do?'

I take the hand, return the greeting. 'Melody Katsouris,' I say. 'Horrified daughter-in-law. Good to make your acquaintance.'

And then, thank God, we both burst out laughing. 'How was your trip?' he asks. 'You haven't got a drink.'

'It was fine. Interesting to get a fix on your so-called public transport. I think Rufus is trying to keep me sober. Doesn't want me hoisting up my skirts and dancing on the tables on my first day.'

'Well, *he* may not,' says Edmund, 'but this is something I've *got* to see. Champagne do you?'

'No way. Makes me chunder.'

'Good girl,' he says, pats me amicably on the shoulder. 'Roly!'

he bellows across the room. 'Stop filling your own boots and get the girl a glass of plonk.'

Roly, face buried in his third flute of the fizzy stuff, looks up, calls 'Right-oh!' and heads in the direction of a woman with a tray.

'Sorry,' says Edmund, 'no-one came and picked you up. We weren't sure what flight you were getting in on, and then Mary wanted to put on this ghastly shindig. I wanted to give you a chance to get settled before you had to face this lot, but once she gets the bit between her teeth. . .'

'It's OK,' I lie, 'might as well jump in at the deep end.'

'Hmm,' muses Edmund, 'I'm not sure if *deep* is exactly the word you're grasping for. Still. Nice to have an excuse to turn on the heating, I suppose. Have you met the neighbours?'

'Sort of,' I say. 'Haven't seen this many pearl necklaces since my last trip to Pat Pong.' And then I think perhaps this isn't the most appropriate first impression to make on your father-in-law.

He laughs nervously. Hell. My only hope was that it might have gone over his head. Now I'll never know. 'So,' he says, the subject change as clunky as a learner driver's first move up to third, 'what do you think of Bourton Allhallows, then?'

It's probably a bit early in the day to tell him the truth. 'Amazing,' I say. 'I couldn't have imagined it in a million years.'

It works. A huge simpleton's grin covers his face. 'Well, you'll find there are one or two drawbacks,' he says.

'So have you lived here all your life?' A stupid question, I know.

'Well, yes,' he replies. 'Apart from school and Oxford, of course.'

What on earth have you done with yourself in all that time? is the next question that runs through my head. 'Wow,' I say. 'I guess it's pretty much a full-time job.'

'Not so bad now Rufus is on board,' he says complaisantly. 'And anyway, one has one's duty.'

We're standing side-by-side now, facing the room like old buddies. I squint at him out of the corner of my eye. Edmund doesn't look like a man who's spent his life burdened by duty. The lines on his face look like they've been earned by exposure to the elements, rather than to care. Like his son, he has the look of a man whose price has been put above pearls all his life. He's got the mild, open face of someone who has never, ever questioned his own position in the world, because he's never, ever had it challenged. I see it, sometimes, in Rufus. It's an attractive quality, especially to someone like me, eaten up as I am with social insecurity. Unquestioning confidence: it's what we all long for, isn't it?

Roly pants up, new glass of champagne in one hand, jaded-looking glass of red in the other. 'How you getting on, Mrs W?' he asks. 'See you've met the pa-in-law, then.'

I accept the glass, take a slug to steady my nerves. Old socks, car parts, tinfoil. Someone to our left is eyeing someone on the other side of the room. 'Fryful social climber,' she says. 'Family made its money in breweries.'

'Great,' I say. 'Though I wish I'd had some chance to look halfway respectable.'

'You look marvellous, m'dear,' says Edmund, and I think he means it. 'Such a relief to see something that's not navy blue for a change.'

Looking around the room, I see that he's right. Well over half the women here are wearing navy blue. Boxy jackets, businesslike skirts, Alice bands, silk blouses, all the same light-sucking shade.

'You'll find,' confides Edmund, 'that a large number of British women base their style on their school uniform.'

'Seriously? Why would you do that?' We didn't have uniforms at Redcliffe State High, but the thought of trying to recreate the look in adult life makes my spine turn cold. I mean, there's daggy, and there's *really* daggy.

'Saves them having to think about what they're going to wear, I think. If everything goes together.'

'And the small retailers,' adds Roly, 'you know, in towns like Stow and Moreton. It's a lot more convenient if they know what they need to stock, and as most of them belong to people's ex-wives . . .'

'. . . Empty nesters . . .'

'. . . younger sons . . .'

'So tell me, Melody,' says Edmund, 'Mary says you're something medical.'

'Not really. Strictly alternative.'

'Ah. You'll not find a lot of call for that sort of thing around here, I'm afraid. It's mostly shotgun wounds and broken limbs in Heythrop country.'

'Dog bites,' Roly interjects.

'The odd bull-goring.'

'Not a lot of use for the laying-on of hands. Mostly stitches and tetanus boosters.'

'Well, I can speed up the healing process, at least.'

A familiar voice speaks up at my elbow. 'Healing process? Melody, I hadn't taken you for a *psychobabbler*.'

Oh hell. Mother-in-law alert. I slap a smile on, turn to face her. 'Mary. Not psychobabble. Physical healing.'

She's wreathed in smiles herself. Gives me a perfumy, powdery kiss on the cheek and a squeeze on the upper arm. 'Well, thank heaven for that! I had visions of myself stumbling over pro-lesbian meditation encounters every time I went into the drawing room.'

Rufus seems to be having a boxing match with a couple of blokes who look like they might originally have been constructed out of modelling putty for a kiddies' show on TV. They are being cheered on by a young woman with front teeth you could cut logs with.

'Don't worry, Mary,' I attempt a joke, 'I'll just start things off slowly with the Wednesday-night know-your-vagina group.'

I really don't know my own mouth, sometimes. The smile congeals on Mary's face, and Edmund titters.

'Oops,' I say. 'Maybe I should have kept quiet about that until you'd got used to the naturism.'

Mary recovers, and gestures to the thin man, who's accompanied her over from the steps. 'Hilary Crawshaw,' she says. 'Melody Wattestone.'

'Katsouris,' I correct her. There's a visible gulp. Hilary, who wears an elegant grey suit with a tiny peak of spotted handkerchief sticking out of the top pocket, brushes my fingers with his. 'How do you do?' he says. 'And congratulations.'

This one's going to have to go straight on to my avoid list.

'I say,' says Roly, 'aren't you supposed to wish the bride good luck? I thought it was the chap who got congratulated.'

Hilary ignores him. 'Many, many congratulations,' he repeats. I've heard about the bitchy queens that aristocratic ladies gather around them to take them to art galleries. I think I've just met my first one.

'Hilary,' I say. 'Hey, isn't that a sheila's name?'

The fingers freeze against my palm. 'In Awstralia, perhaps,' he bats back.

'Yeah, maybe.'

'I wouldn't know,' he says. 'I always holiday in Florence, myself.'

'Hilary is an authority on fine art, aren't you, darling?' says Mary. Like I wouldn't have guessed. 'He used to stay with Harold Acton all the time.'

Well, that went straight over my head.

'Wonderful parties,' says Hilary. 'The thought of the Villa La Pietra overrun with American students . . .'

'Never mind,' says Mary.

'Never mind,' I say.

'I heard he was a frightful old poof,' says Edmund. 'Always jumping on Wykehamists.'

'Oh, but the *collections*,' says Mary. Then: 'How was your trip? I'm *so* sorry there was no-one there to meet you. If you'd *rung*, we'd have been *queuing* up to come and get you.'

'That's so sweet.'

'*Non*-sense,' she says. 'I wouldn't *dream* of leaving family hanging about at airports. Isn't that so, Edmund, darling?'

'Well, no, darling,' says the husband, 'except that you were knee-deep in sausage rolls all morning.'

'It was fine. We bumped into Roly on the train, so there wasn't a problem getting here.'

She slips an arm through mine. Pats me on the forearm. It must look great from the outside: it's only me that can feel the stiffness in the gesture, the way she holds herself so that as little of her body is touching me as possible. 'Well, *wel*come, my dear. It's *so* good to have my boy home at last. Have you met the rest of the family, yet? Have you met our neighbour, Cressy Lambton?'

I find myself facing a tall woman with a weatherbeaten face. She wears her hair short and shapeless, fringe hanging in her eyes like a Shetland pony's, and not a scrap of makeup. Her party clothes consist of green slacks with a puffed-sleeved white shirt over which she sports a padded jerkin of the sort people usually wear to shoot things in. I don't mind telling you, Cressy's as ugly as a hatful of arseholes.

'How do you do?' she says, and wrings my hand like it's the neck of a wounded rabbit.

'How's it going?'

She looks a bit nonplussed at this enquiry. 'All right,' she says, after considerable thought.

'Good,' I say.

We stand there awkwardly, both of us trying to think up a topic of conversation.

Eventually, Cressy begins: 'So do you hunt?'

'I – no. I'm afraid not. I've never had the opportunity.'

'Oh,' she says.

I've never seen anyone lose interest in anyone else so quickly. Her eyes, literally, glaze. She starts to goggle about the room. Looks at her watch.

'Good God,' she says, 'is that the time? Dogs need feeding.'

'OK,' I say.

'Sorry,' says Edmund, looking at her retreating back, 'Cressy's rather limited on the conversation front, I'm afraid. Still. You must meet the rest of the family. Tilly and Beatrice are waiting with bated breath.'

I glance back over at the sofa. Tilly doesn't look like she's waiting for anything much except maybe another bowl of those twig things. I know she's pregnant and all, but she does look alarmingly like a milch cow, unhurriedly chewing cud and gazing

99

off into the middle distance. Of Granny Beatrice all I can see is a bobbling confection of pale blue netting and silk flowers. I look around for support, but Rufus is occupied, looking at the diary of a woman so blonde that I suspect that there might be a small collection of leather lampshades in her attic. There's no way I'm going to go and meet a woman in a hat while I'm wearing cheesecloth.

'I'd love to meet them,' I say. 'Would it be a lot of hassle if I just popped off and changed my clothes, first, though? I wasn't expecting a party.'

'Nonsense,' says Mary, eyeing my unbrushed hair and the coffee stain on my jeans. 'You look perfect.'

'I'm sure,' says Edmund, 'they'd much rather meet you sooner than later. Come over.'

I realise that the only way I'm going to get out of this is by appealing directly to him. 'Your mother,' I say, and give it heaps with the old eyelashes, 'looks so elegant. I can't turn up to meet her like this. She'll think Rufus has married a hoyden.'

'Well, *I* don't,' says Edmund, 'and I don't suppose for a moment that mummy would, either, but if you really . . .'

'Do you mind?'

'Not in the least,' says Edmund.

'*Darling*,' protests Mary, 'we're in the middle of a *party* . . .'

'Well, it's hardly going to break things up, *darling*,' he says back, slightly sharply. 'I don't suppose the poor girl's expecting anyone to come and *watch* her.'

'I won't be long,' I say.

'Rufus!' shouts Edmund over the hubbub.

My husband looks up. 'Daddy.'

'Wife needs showing to your quarters.'

'On my way.'

'It's OK,' I protest. 'I can have a wash and brush-up in the kitchen.'

'Balderdash.'

'Well, just tell me which way to go and I . . .'

Everyone standing within ten feet bursts out laughing.

Rufus comes over and takes me by the hand. 'I think we'd like to see you again before Christmas. Come on.'

I follow him out of the room.

Chapter Fifteen

The Maze

It can't be more than a minute since we took the back route out of the kitchen, but I'm as disorientated as an evangelist in a barful of blondes. I don't even know which direction we're facing in. I'm sure we've turned enough corners that we should have passed through the Great Hall at least twice already. Black floor boards, worn Persian runners, and doors, doors, doors. I feel like I could go a week here and never see a window.

'I'm totally lost,' I tell Rufus.

'That's why I came with you. You'll pick it up eventually.'

'But I thought we were only popping up to the second floor.'

'We are.'

'Well, how come we've gone up two flights of stairs and down one?'

'This is the shortcut.'

'Err . . .'

'Think of it like an Escher etching,' he explains. 'Just because it looks like a staircase is going down doesn't actually mean it is.'

We push open a door at what seems like random, and enter my third lounge of the expedition. Like in the last two, most of the furniture is covered by dustsheets. Like in the last two, the drapes are drawn, and rugs are folded back from the windows to stop, Rufus tells me, any stray sunlight getting in and fading them. In the gloom, I make out pale grey wallpaper covered in bougainvillaea, flimsy scarlet belvederes and heavily stylised, smiling mandarins. Two huge, ceiling-height mirrors are fixed to the far wall, behind gilt tables scattered with junk and framed photos of dogs and horses.

'Which room is this?'

'Chinese music room.'

'Period?'

'Georgian. Pianos are newer, harpsichords are older.'

'Anybody play?' There must be sixty, seventy thousand pounds' worth of musical instruments mouldering under those sheets.

'Haven't been tuned in years. Costs a bomb, with five of them. I think Tilly used to plunk out the first movement of the Moonlight Sonata from time to time with the loud pedal down, but that was on the upright in the schoolroom.'

'*Schoolroom?*'

'Third floor. Victorian wing. Proper space heater and a doll's house.'

He's crossing the room as he speaks, stops in front of the left-hand mirror. 'Now pay attention,' he says. 'You'll need to know this.'

The table is scattered with bric-a-brac. A lamp. A small cloisonné vase. A leather-bound Bible, an ivory-handled whip. Rufus lays a hand on a ceramic King Charles spaniel, which merely tips forward rather than lifting up. There's a clunk somewhere in the wall.

'Important thing to remember in the Wattestone household,' says Rufus, 'is that anything secret is probably disguised as a dog or a horse.'

The mirror, complete with the table, which I see now is attached to its frame, legs hanging a couple of centimetres above the floor, swings back.

'That's the coolest thing I've ever seen,' I tell him. And, apart from a few score other things I've seen that were cooler, I sort of mean it too.

'It *is* pretty cool, isn't it? They didn't want to spoil the look of the room when they built the Victorian wing, so that was the solution.'

'Brilliant. This must have been great when you were kids.'

'Fabulous. There's half a dozen more scattered about the place. Hidden panels and stuff. More, for all I know. Roly and I used to spend the holidays popping out of the priest-holes and scaring the tourists.'

'What's a priest-hole?'

'Gosh, you *are* wet behind the ears.'

'Don't suppose you'd know what to do with a funnel web, sweetheart. Educate me.'

'Hidden rooms. When the persecution of Catholics was going on.'

'Which was when?'

'On and off for the best part of a hundred years. People would build them into their houses and hide priests in them.'

'Sort of like a panic room?'

'Not dissimilar. Enormous derring-do involved, of course. Punishable by death.'

'Religion has a lot to answer for.'

We step through. From this side, the door just looks like a door. He pulls it to behind us. I pluck at his sleeve.

'How do you mean, *for all you know*?'

'It's a big house,' Rufus tosses out nonchalantly, 'and not all of it has ever been lived in at any one time. They'd just build new wings and move into them whenever they made a bit of money.' He scratches the back of his neck. 'For such an old family,' he says, 'they were very *nouveau*. Anyway, what it kind of meant was that they sort of lost track of what went where. They kept sticking stuff over things without keeping records. I'm pretty sure that there are rooms that no-one has been into for entire generations. Probably with all the furniture *in situ*.'

'Seriously?'

'Well, there was a terrible smell in the Tudor wing for about twenty years at one point – from before I was born right through to when I was a teenager – and no one could track down the source, so in the end they just moved out. We've never really moved back in. They were always doing stuff like that. And I remember spending an entire afternoon when I was seventeen counting the windows outside and trying to match them up to the rooms inside, and I could never manage it. It's a bit like one of those rings of standing stones.'

'It's all a bit Bram Stoker, isn't it?'

'The gothic novels were based on families like mine.' He leads me down the corridor as dead Wattestones glare at my jeans. 'Rumour has it that *The Mysteries of Udolpho* was written after my great-great-great-grandfather forgot he had a house party and half of the guests were eaten by the servants.'

We reach another set of stairs. These are made of marble, with cast-iron railings, like in a museum. Rufus sets off up them.

'Blimey,' I say, 'I should have brought my hiking boots.'

He laughs.

'So, have you just stopped wanting to know about these missing rooms?'

'Darl, we've got thirty-two already. And that's not counting the attics or the basement. Or the cellars. Or the bathrooms and dressing rooms. Or the public rooms. And we've only got two cleaning ladies. I think we're probably better off without them.'

'I'm getting a bit of a sinking feeling here.'

'Don't worry. There's been a bit of subsidence in the east wing, but you get that in old houses.'

'Don't tease me, Rufus. I didn't envisage my life as being one long round and with the mop and bucket.'

'Feather duster as well, sweetie. We've got several with twelve-foot handles because of the high ceilings.'

I stop dead in my tracks, remain silent.

He stops as well, two steps down, and looks up at me. 'Mel, you're going to have to be a bit of a chatelaine at some point, but it won't go further than that. We do actually employ people, especially in the tourist season. And besides, Granny's still alive, let alone Mummy. I should think you'll have a good couple of decades to get used to the idea . . .'

'I said don't tease me.'

'I'm not . . .'

'I didn't sign up for this . . .'

'No life is all fairy dresses and cocktail parties. Even Saint Princess Diana had to occasionally cut her toenails.'

'Never mind,' I say. 'Maybe we should do this one step at a time, eh?'

I don't think he gets exactly what I mean. 'That's the spirit,' he says, brightening up.

'Where the hell is this room, anyway?'

'Just round the corner.'

We reach the top of the stairs. It's taken a full five minutes to get here. 'Right,' he says, 'it's just along here, now.'

'Jesus. I don't even know which way we're facing.'

'If you were standing on the front drive, facing the house, our window would be on the left, on the first floor, hanging out over the moat.'

'I thought you said it was the second floor?'

'The first floor in England, sweetie, is the second floor everywhere else in the world.'

'I get it. Another trap for the unwary.'

'We like it that way.'

'I've noticed.'

Rufus turns a handle and presses a shoulder to a door. 'Hinges are a bit wobbly,' he explains. And leads me into our marital bedroom.

Chapter Sixteen

The Painted Hussy

'You go ahead,' I tell him. 'I'll catch you up.'

He looks doubtful. 'Are you sure . . .?'

'How hard can it be?'

'This is Bourton Allhallows,' he says. 'You'd be surprised.'

'So just tell me, OK? If it's that complicated you can write it down.'

'It's not *that* bad. You turn right out of this door.'

'OK.' I'm digging in my backpack, only half-attending.

'Then – Mel, listen. It might save your life.'

'Bit of an exaggeration.'

'Not necessarily. OK. Right, right, then right again. Then second left, then two more rights.'

I stop rummaging and look at him. 'So that'll take me back to here, then?'

He rolls his eyes. 'There *are* stairs. I was trying to keep it simple.'

'Ah.'

'Quite a few. Some you don't want to take. You'll have to take exactly the route I told you, or you'll end up in the dungeons.'

I bellow with laughter.

'Not a joke.'

'OK. Sorry. Not laughing.'

'Repeat.'

'Right. Right, right, right, second left, right, right.'

'No. Mel, I said listen. You've put one too many rights at the front.'

'Doh, stupid, the first right was a "Right", not a *right*.'

He folds his arms.

'Right, as in OK? As in "I'm complying, oh lord and master"?'

'Oh. Right.'

'Stop it.'

'They've got a one-way latch on the door. And a hidden spring. Once you're in, you don't get out until someone comes and finds you.'

'Nice.'

'It's damp down there.'

'You don't say.'

'With a slug population that's been there so long they've turned albino. And rats the size of squirrels.'

'Well, I guess I'll be able to spot them, then.'

'Not in the dark.'

'I love it here already.'

'I knew you would.'

Then he gives me a kiss and I start to feel better about Bourton Allhallows.

'’Zat what they call *droit de seigneur*?'

'Nope. That's me. Kissing you.'

'You're allowed.'

'You are the love of my life. Don't forget it.'

'Accept no substitutes, R.W.'

'See you later.' He leaves me to it.

Once I'm alone, I take a moment to look around my new habitat.

It's a nice room. And not as monastic as I've been afraid it might be. The walls are lined with what looks like fabric, printed with a pattern of bamboo and strange, Phoenix-like birds that peer down indignantly from leafy perches. There's a huge, faded rug, oriental design, in greens that go with the wallpaper, and heavy green velvet drapes at the huge bay window, which hang the full four metres from an ornate plasterwork ceiling to pool on the floor. There's a huge, squashy old couch that sags in the middle, a couple of polished tables with ginger-jar lamps and bits and bobs of ceramic and wood and silver lying casually just so on their surfaces.

And there's a four poster. Not the sort of cast-iron-and-mosquito-net construction I'm used to from Pacific resorts, but the real McCoy: the sort of bed people get born in and die in, and probably spend their lives playing card games and drinking toddies in as well. My marital bed: the huge screen of carved oak, and giant posts made to look like tree trunks, complete with vines and flowers and assorted wildlife. I approach for a closer look, duck in behind heavy curtains and spot a snake, a couple of birds and what looks surprisingly like a possum.

I'm not sure what I've got in my bag that's even remotely appropriate for this situation. All my formal gear – my wedding dress and two crumple-silk shifts designed for no-iron travelling joy – are unsuitable for the temperature both here and downstairs, and my less formal gear isn't a lot better. I resort to tipping my backpack out on the carpet to see what I've got, settle, in the end, on a pair of black cotton drawstring trousers from Thailand, a strappy black vest top and a dusty blue Mao jacket. At least I won't look like a feral, and if they think I'm a commie, then tough titty. I replait my hair, slap on a bit of mascara and eyeliner and lippy, and then I feel better.

Out in the corridor, you'd never tell there were a hundred people bellowing downstairs. The silence is unique: even my footfalls, the rustle of my jacket, are muffled, as if soaked up by the ancient air. Dust motes spiral in the shard of light falling from a window at the end of the corridor. Somewhere, a clock ticks self-importantly.

I turn right. Come almost immediately to a narrow passageway that leads to a flight of stairs. Follow it down – there are only half a dozen of them – and hook another right into a stepped corridor lined with hunting prints. Here, a set of small bedrooms leads off to either side. I can't quite work out how they can fit beneath what must be our bedroom, but somehow they do. Five doors along, the corridor is bisected by a wider, grander one, all rosewood and Benares Ware pots. I cross over it, take the next left, pause at the top of some stairs, because I can hear voices below me, just round the next bend.

Two women, in the process of greeting each other. The sort of accents you can only get through spending your formative years talking more to animals than to human beings.

'Well!' says one.

'Well indeed!'

'Did you bring a present?'

'No. You?'

'Always think there needs to be a *wedding* to give a present. I'll tell you what I *will* give them, though.'

'What?'

'About six months.'

A peal of laughter rings up the stairs.

They always say eavesdroppers never hear good of themselves. Being your old-fashioned masochist, I lean on the banister to listen.

'Have you met her yet?'

'Didn't get a chance. I haven't even seen her.'

'Quite a sight, darling. Not what you'd expect it all. Especially given his normal taste. Quite a scarecrow, really.'

'No! Rufus? I don't believe it. He's always had such . . . elegant taste.'

'I know. I could barely believe my eyes. Six foot tall and, well – swarthy is the only way of putting it. Hair like a bird's nest and dressed in the sort of clothes you wouldn't let your groom out in. Mary's devastated, of course.'

'Poor thing. What a shock.'

'I know. There he was with a lovely girl like Madeleine Christie all lined up and ready to go, and he gets his head turned by some Australasian masseuse.'

'No!'

'So I hear.'

'You're not serious. He wasn't . . .?'

'No, nothing quite as sordid as that. Picked him up on a beach, apparently. But all the same. I should think she's picked up a trick or two.'

I feel myself go red in the face. I mean, yes, I have picked up a trick or two, but so have most women my age.

'No!'

'Divorcee, I gather.'

'Well!'

'Mmm,' says the voice significantly. 'Hence the hole-in-the-wall nature of the wedding.'

My God, what is this? The 1930s?

The voice drops confidentially, continues at a murmur. '. . . Duchess of Windsor . . .' it says. ' . . . Cleopatra Grip . . .'

Once more the voice expresses scandalised denial.

'Well, you know what men are like . . .'

'I must say, though, I'm surprised. I wouldn't have said that Master Wattestone gave the impression that he might . . . need . . .'

'Oh, Patsy, they're all so spoiled these days. And obsessed with sex. Any kind of exotica's a thrill, whether they need it or not. And besides, she's been working her way round South East Asia with her . . . skills, apparently.'

'Gosh. And when you think about what those Thai girls have to offer . . .'

A significant 'Exactly.' I can just see the pursing of the lips that goes with it. 'It makes your toes curl. I wouldn't have thought he was the type.'

'Oh, come on, Lavinia, they're all the type. Men are frightful beasts. It won't last, of course. Sex never does. And they've nothing in common. It's an age-old story.'

I've worked out in a flash that 'nothing in common' is a euphemism.

'I dare say she'll do the same. I don't suppose she thought what marrying into somewhere like Bourton Allhallows was going to involve. Probably thought she'd scored herself a life of unstinting luxury.'

'Can she even ride?'

'Not that I know of.'

A sigh. 'Well,' says Lavinia. 'All Mary can do is hope he comes to his senses reasonably quickly.'

'She'll be trying to get herself *enceinte*, of course,' says Patsy. 'Girls like that always do. Better settlement that way.'

'Heavens! Can you imagine? I do hope Mary's given him a good talking-to about that sort of thing.'

111

'I know. Too awful. The thought of dear old Bourton being broken up for the sake of . . . well . . .'

'I know. Got away with it by the skin of their teeth with Edmund, and now the son's following the old man's example.'

'Appalling. Why on earth couldn't he just keep her as a mistress or something?'

This is too much. I barrel down the stairs to confront them, a hundred stinging put-downs ringing in my ears.

There's no-one there. The half-landing – white plaster walls and waist-high dado – is silent as a cloister. A floor down, I stop, perplexed, and hang over the banister in search of my slanderers. Not a sign: not below, not above. Just me and my burning cheeks. There's no door, not an opening, until the stone-flagged ground floor two storeys down.

Perplexed, I retreat back to where I first heard them. They're there, all right; have been joined by a man and have changed the subject.

'Didn't see you out last week,' Lavinia is saying.

'No,' he replies. 'Had to go to London. Ghastly. Went out on Thursday instead.'

I retreat a couple more steps. The voices disappear. Return, and there they are, clear as foghorns. Descend a couple of steps, and they vanish again.

I feel sick. This is one of those otic illusions you come across in cathedrals and suchlike, but whatever, the voices themselves were real. I've got to go downstairs now, face all those people, and I'll never know which of them it is that's just been talking about me in this way.

If it matters. After all, they were probably simply voicing what the rest of them think.

I wish I hadn't told Rufus to go on ahead of me. I take a couple of steps; realise that I am, actually, shaking. Feel my way down the rest of the stairs like an old person whose sight is failing. And when I get there, I realise that my distress has made me forget which way to turn.

It can't be too far. I must, by now, be at least on a level with the great hall. But I can't hear anything. Not a dicky bird. Eventually I just head for the nearest door, which leads into a room that looks like a scullery. Every surface is piled with more of the glassy-eyed game birds that accompanied us on our trip here from Moreton-in-Marsh. They've obviously been lying here for some time, because the place smells rank, like old sweatsocks and fear.

I back out, go in the opposite direction. The next room contains shelf after shelf of assorted silverware; the stuff at waist height – knives, forks, spoons, a set of claret jugs and a couple of dozen chargers – white and shiny and buffed to gleaming, the rest showing various degrees of tarnish and decrepitude. I work my way along the corridor. Small room after small room containing, in one, stacked plates, in many patterns and coats of dust, in another, wine glasses, in another, water glasses. Who needs separate cupboards for different types of glass? It's madness. Crazy. And here's another one that contains nothing but soup bowls.

I reach the end of the corridor, push open the door and find myself in another. And now, at last, I can hear the *obbleobbleobble*. Feel relief, tempered by the dread of all those googling eyes following me in judgement. *She's learned a trick or two . . . Cleopatra Grip . . . Girls like that always do*. My God, what have I got myself in to?

The sound gets louder. The party is obviously on the other side of the wall to my left. I can hear them in there, baying like a lynch mob, waiting for my return so they can set on me with their horsewhips.

Cleopatra Grip. What in God's name is the Cleopatra Grip?

I try a door. Vases. On shelves. Try the next. Spare armour, as if they don't have enough. Suppose they might need some extra siege equipment come the revolution, and they're keeping it to hand.

Girls like that always do.

Trays. Several dozen of them. I wonder if there is a cupboard somewhere that contains a selection of everything, all in one place. Somehow doubt it.

Things for opening wine with.

Coasters.

Hunting horns.

Guns.

There are no doors leading out the other side.

Cracked and desiccated leather boots.

Two dozen waxed raincoats.

I reach the end of the passage. The roar of chit-chat is as deafening as if I were actually in the room, but all I see is blank, peeling white wall. I put my hand on it. It vibrates with the noise. Press an ear against it.

They're all like that when it comes down to it.

Is Rufus? Is Rufus like that? Has he married me because he's mesmerised by my siren skills and can't think straight? Gozo is the island where Calypso trapped Odysseus for seven years, after all, and wouldn't let him go. Is that how they see me? Some long-haired sea nymph who's keeping him trapped while he weeps for home?

I tap on the wall, then thump with closed fist. I can't see how to get through. A couple of voices raise in bellows of laughter and I'm tempted to start shouting.

A toilet flushes behind me. Turning, I see a man in a tweed jacket emerge from one of the doors on the right, doing up his flies as he goes. He stops, gives me an amiable grin.

'Lost?'

I nod. 'I don't get it. I can't find a door that—'

'Ne'mind,' he says. 'First time, is it?'

I recognise his voice as belonging to the man who fell into conversation with Patsy and Lavinia. They must have been down in this corridor when I heard them, and have returned to the party from it. I guess it'll be years before I identify them now.

'Yeah. Yeah.'

'Always catches people out. Funny acoustics. Come on. Chin up. It's through here.'

To my surprise, he backs up the corridor and puts a hand on the handle of a door to the right.

'But—' I begin.

'Told you,' he says, 'funny acoustics. Catches everybody out.'

The door opens and the roar is suddenly all around me. My saviour, grinning the grin of the Cheshire cat, ushers me through with a grandiose sweep of the arm.

We've come through a door in the panelling to the left of the fireplace. No-one seems to have noticed our entrance. They're intent on their wine and their backslapping, complexions rosier than when I left, decibel level up another notch. I step through, look around. Rufus is over by the front door, deep in what looks like intense conversation with the pregnant lady. He's frowning, has a hand on her shoulder. She leans in to him intimately, almost resting on him. This had better be his sister, or I'm going to want to know what's going on.

Mary stands with Hilary, watching me. She catches me catching sight of her, smiles a sparkly smile and raises her glass in my direction. Hilary just looks inscrutable: a little dimple at the side of his mouth, hair so shiny it has to be synthetic.

I force a cheery smile and a wave in their direction, and plough my way through the crowd to Rufus's side.

'Darling.'

He puts his spare arm round my neck and hugs me. 'I was just about to send out a search party. Have you met Tilly yet?'

The pregnant lady takes my hand and squeezes it firmly.

'Heavens,' she says. 'You look like you've seen a ghost.'

Chapter Seventeen

Bedtime

I'm feeling pretty sick by the time we get to bed. It's turned out that those birds I came across in the cupboard, the ones I thought were rotting because they'd been forgotten, were actually what they call well-hung around here. The phrase means something else entirely in Australia. Whatever, it seems they eat them like that. Leave them lying around for a week, ten days, with their innards swelling up and fermenting inside, then they rip the feathers off and sling them in an oven and serve them with jam. The smell of decaying flesh was almost as stifling as the conversation, which mostly consisted of a blow-by-blow of a day out with the local foxhounds.

I am exhausted. Exhausted, but as wakeful as a soldier in the trenches. It's nearly midnight by the time Rufus and I break away from a debate about puppy walking, which is, apparently, a big deal in local society, and make for our own quarters and to the deep, damp warmth of the four-poster bed with its six layers of blankets and quilts and heavyweight covers. Every one of which is essential. Now darkness has fallen, the castle is shrouded in the sort of cold that makes your bones brittle. Rufus doesn't seem to notice. I've got undressed under the covers and pulled on two T-shirts to keep me warm.

'Wow,' I say, 'is it always that scintillating?'

Rufus laughs. 'I think they were a bit overtired tonight.'

'You think? I hope so.'

'Don't be a bitch, Melody. They're simple country folk. That's what they talk about. What do you talk about in Brisbane, then? International current affairs?'

I think about the nights I've spent listening to detailed

dissections of the day's play at Catch-me-fuck-me and decide not to pursue it. 'Fair dos,' I say. Then: 'Stop it, you sod.'

'Well, cheer up, then,' he says, and stops tickling me.

'Give it a rest. Who said I wasn't cheerful?'

'Oh, I don't know. I suppose I'm psychic.'

I don't say anything.

'That,' he says, 'and the fact that you've had a face like a slapped arse since half-past six.'

'You're turning into a right little ocker,' I tell him. 'Who's that guy Hilary, anyway?'

'Hilary? Mummy's walker.'

'What's that?'

'Her walker. Takes her to art galleries and things. Meets her in London for lunch during the hunting season when Daddy's too busy. Everyone's got one.'

'Is he gay, then?'

'We prefer to call it 'safe in taxis',' he informs me. 'Hilary's got the flat in Chelsea. The basement. Keeps an eye on the house when there's no-one there.'

'You have a house in Chelsea?'

'*We* do. Not a very big one.'

'Mmm. Got any others?'

'Not that I can think of.'

'Apart from a few dozen derelict ones up in the village.'

'Well, *you're* observant.'

'What's with that, anyway?'

He rolls away from me, throws a hand behind his head on the pillow and says: 'Can we not talk about that stuff tonight?'

'Why?'

'Because I've had a skinful of it already. I've had my ear bent by everybody today.'

'So, what? Don't want to worry the little woman?'

'Can it, Mel. You'll find out all about all of it. I just *really* don't want to spend the night going over the estate accounts.'

'OK.' I decide to change the subject. 'So, like, this Hilary geezer. It's some kind of work creation thing for

117

otherwise useless benders, yeah? A sort of upper-class charitable scheme?'

'Hilary works.'

'What at?'

'He has – his work.'

I raise an eyebrow.

'OK. He's writing a book.'

I raise the other one.

Rufus starts sniggering. 'On great British art collectors.'

'Uh-huh.'

'In Florence between the wars.'

'And how long's he been writing it?'

'Um . . . d'you know, I think it's been all his life? Well, since he left university.'

'Which was?'

'Umm . . . nineteen sixty-seven, I think.'

I start to laugh too.

'He has to go on a lot of research trips,' he says.

'I'll bet he does.'

'And he advises rich ladies on their art collections.'

'Uh-huh.'

'And sources antiques for them.'

'That go with their complexions.'

'Don't talk about it to Mummy like that.'

'Wouldn't dream of it. Does he help her with her shopping?'

'Takes her to smart hotel bars and buys her cocktails.'

'Tells her she's divine.'

'Well, she is, darling.'

'Of course she is.'

'Hilary's Mummy's best friend.'

'Oh, good. We'll be best friends too, then.'

His body language has improved. He turns in to face me, slips an arm over my torso.

'Who were all those people, anyways?'

'Just friends.'

'You've got that many friends?'

'Oh, those are just the *close* ones.' After about ten seconds, he says: 'Joke.'

'Oh, right.'

'Anyway,' he says, 'Hilary is my godfather. He's also one of Granny's godchildren's children. Like me. Only a generation older.'

'Your dad's his own mother's godchild?'

'D'oh. No. Mummy.'

'Strewth. You guys don't half like your incestuous relationships.'

'It's an effective weapon in the build-up and maintenance of wealth.'

'Yada yada yada,' I say. 'Your grandmother seems like an entertaining old stick.'

'Well, she's still got *some* of her marbles,' he says.

'Those diamonds she was wearing tonight: were they for real?' Against her wrinkled *décolletage* they looked like dewdrops on a basket of walnuts, but they were impressive none the less.

'Yes,' he says. 'Family ones. Her family.'

'Must be worth a few bob.'

'That's right. Bring it back to the venal. Don't you believe in sentimental value?'

'Oh, yeah, sentimental value. I'll believe in that when insurance companies start doing policies on the kiddies' drawings on the people's fridges. I've always noticed that the sentimental value of jewellery always seems to go up in direct correlation to its fiscal value. Wears a lot of plastic beads, ever, does she?'

'We don't usually let her out in the diamonds, truth be told,' Refus says. 'Everyone's always a bit nervous when she wears them. She's got a bit of a track record for losing things. I've grown up on the family legend of the Callington Emerald.'

'The Callington Emerald?'

'Gigantic thing, came down through the distaff side. Size of a pigeon's egg, set in gold with a string of diamonds.'

'Tasteful. Bet *that's* got some sentimental value.'

'*Had*. Plenty, I think, if she hadn't let it fall off the last time she wore it. Nicked from some Rajah in the eighteenth century.

Massively underinsured, of course. Could've got a couple of Lear jets and change out of it. People have been looking for it ever since but she doesn't even remember which part of the house she was in at the time. Just says she doesn't remember. And she was only sixty-odd at the time.'

'She *lost* an emerald the size of a pigeon's egg?'

Rufus shrugs. 'It's a big house.' Then suddenly, in a clunky change of subject, he blurts: 'Tilly's husband's done a bunk.'

I sit up. Think better of it. Lie back down again. 'No!'

'Seems like it. Gone off somewhere with his secretary.'

'But she's pregnant!'

'Is she? I hadn't noticed. That puts a whole new complexion on the matter.'

'Well, I'll be stuffed.'

'Bastard. And do you know what? It happened eight weeks ago and Mummy didn't say a thing.'

'That's weird.'

'Yuh.'

'What do you think she's playing at?'

'I don't know. I haven't had a chance to talk to her yet. I guess perhaps she's clinging on to some fantasy that he'll reappear and no-one will be any the wiser.'

'Pfff,' I say.

'That's sort of what I said. Especially when it turns out that not only has he cleared out the bank accounts, but he remortgaged the house and ran off with that as well. He transferred the documents into Tilly's name a few months ago, so she's liable for the lot. The house is on the market and she's going to be lucky if she gets out of it all with nothing.'

'But that's illegal, surely?'

Rufus shrugs. 'Don't think so. She signed the papers. She's quite unworldly, I suppose. I don't know. No. He was her husband and he said it was something to do with tax breaks, and she didn't have any reason not to believe him.'

'She can chase him for it.'

'I'm sure she would, if anybody knew where he'd gone. Last

120

heard of catching a plane to Addis Ababa, with a gal pal in a powder-blue power suit. No sign of him since.'

'Jesus.'

'Mmm.'

'Poor cow.'

'Mmm.'

'What are we going to do?'

'I like that "we",' he says, and smiles. 'Thanks for that. We'll work something out.'

'Christ. It makes what Andrew did to me look like chickenfeed. At least I didn't get bankrupted.'

'And you met me.'

'Yip. That's true. Rufus?'

'Yes, my love and helpmeet?'

'I overheard some people.'

'Ah. I'd been wondering.'

'They seem to think I'm some sort of hard-as-nails fortune-hunting divorcee.'

'Better get you a manicure and a big bottle of fake tan, then.'

'Not something to joke about.'

'Joking is the only possible way to react.'

'They think you're obsessed. Sexually, you know? That I've trapped you with my womanly wiles?'

He laughs. 'Well, they could have a point.'

He puts a hand on my breast.

'Do they really think that sort of thing?'

'Of course they do, darling. The older generation are completely obsessed with sex.'

'Not like us,' I say.

'No,' he says, 'not like us at all.'

'I love you, you know,' I say.

'Good. I love you. A lot. Almost as much as I love my dogs.'

'Glad you've got your priorities sorted.'

And then we're not talking for a bit.

I say: 'Rufus?'

He says: 'Mmm?'

'What's the Cleopatra Grip?'

'Where on earth did you hear *that* from?'

'Something to do with the Duchess of Windsor.'

'Ah,' he says.

'Well?'

He tells me.

'Oh, right,' I say. 'Sort of like this, you mean . . .?'

Rufus heaves a gratifying sigh.

'If I'd known you could do that,' he says, 'I'd have married you *days* earlier.'

Chapter Eighteen
The Earth Moves

I dream that we're on a rollercoaster and we've reached the top of a very high ascent, are looking down into the maw of hell, when the structure shudders underneath us. Lurches, first to one side, then the other. The car we're in lurches in response, throws me first one way, then the other. The metal holding bar clicks, flies open, and I find myself clinging on for life as the car tips once more, leans out over the edge.

I thrash back to consciousness, barely hold back a shout of terror. The bedroom is shaking around us. Creak of beams, crack of floorboards, a low drum-roll of shaking; even the air outside our high-piled blankets seems to be trembling. I think for a moment that I've brought the dream with me, that what I'm experiencing is a vestigial hallucination, but I hear something small rattle and fall from the bedside table to my left, and realise that it's the room that has brought the dream about.

Rufus is still asleep. How can he be? I'm clutching the nearest four-poster upright as though I'm going to fall out of bed altogether if I let go. The roof's about to cave in, and he's snoring as though nothing is happening at all.

Gradually, the movement subsides. With a couple of groans, the house goes quiet. Rufus grunts, smacks his lips on some tasty morsel, pulls the covers back up around his neck.

'What the hell was that?' I ask. He doesn't reply. I shake him.
'Nuuh?'
'Rufus, what the hell was that?'
'What?'
'Didn't you feel it? The whole bloody house was shaking!'
'Go'sleep,' he says.

'Rufus!'

'*Whaaa*'?'

'For Pete's sake! Didn't you notice *anything*?'

'Does that sometimes,' he mumbles. ''S a' old house.'

He's obviously still half asleep. I push gently at his shoulder. 'Rufus, that felt like an earthquake.'

He comes slightly closer to the surface. 'No. Don't worry about it. Old houses. They move. Settle on their foundations. ''Snothing.'

'How can you call that *nothing*? I thought the whole bloody lot was going to come down on top of us.'

Rufus heaves a sleepy sigh. 'Said. Happens. Been happening all my life. You'll get used to it. Stop worrying.'

'You have got to be *kidding* me! You call that nothing? That was the sort of thing you get just before a tower block collapses.'

Rufus sits up. 'Tower blocks,' he says, 'are poorly constructed things built in concrete in the past century. This house has been standing for many hundreds of years. Stop fussing, woman. It does that from time to time. It's like it's turning over in its sleep. Stop it getting bedsores.'

I shake my head. It's bloody freezing in here. I pull the bedclothes up around me.

'Seriously,' he says. 'You're just not used to it. Go back to sleep. It's nothing.'

Reluctantly, I slide back down into the warmth of the bed. 'Seriously?'

'Seriously.'

'I'm not sure I believe you.'

He snuggles in, puts his arms round me, kisses me on the temple. 'Mel, Bourton Allhallows has been around for a thousand years. I don't think it'll fall down just like that.'

Chapter Nineteen
Meet the Family

From behind the door, the clink of cutlery on china, female voices murmuring, and a single one, my mother-in-law's, raised in proclamation.

'. . . don't really know how she'll fit in,' she is saying. 'I mean, it was fairly obvious how out of it she was last night.'

Rufus opens the door. 'Now, Mummy, don't be beastly,' he says. I wonder if I'll ever get over the way they talk, like an Enid Blyton book.

Mary gets to her feet, showing no sign of discombobulation, smiles that warm, treacherous smile. 'I wasn't being beastly,' she says smoothly. 'I was worrying. We so want you to feel at home.' She approaches me and lands a cool cheek against mine. 'Good morning, Melody, darling. I do hope you managed to get a decent night's sleep. It's still rather bachelor-pad in there, I'm afraid.'

Instantly, and against my will, I feel the blood creep to my cheeks. Because, of course, we didn't spend a lot of time sleeping last night, and I don't suppose for a moment that she assumes we did. Or maybe she does. Yet again, I feel like the scarlet-taloned predator. That, or the fifteen-year-old who got caught going at it in Danny Rogers's pool house.

'Fine, thanks, Mary,' I tell her, in an effort to cover my discomfort. 'I found his old Subbuteo set in a cupboard, and we had a fine old time.'

'Of course, being foreign, she insisted on being Manchester United,' says Rufus. 'Which at least meant that I got to be Liverpool.'

'Still gave him a good old thrashing,' I declare, and my blush races up to the roots of my hair.

Tilly, wielding a huge silver teapot, says: 'Excuse me not getting up, Melody. I'm afraid it takes me about half an hour. Would you like a cup of tea? Come and sit down.'

Relieved, I obey. She fills an oversized china cup with something the colour of cat piss, adds milk without asking me and pushes it towards me.

'Earl Grey,' she says. 'I hope that's OK.'

Even their *beverages* have titles.

'Great,' I tell her. 'How are you feeling today?'

Tilly pats her distended abdomen with one hand, puts the other in front of her mouth and stifles a tiny burp. 'I'm ready to explode, to tell the truth. I feel like it's about to claw its way through my stomach like that monster in *Alien*.'

'When are you due?'

'Another two months, amazingly. I'm thinking of hiring a trampoline just to hurry it up.'

'Do you know what it is yet?'

'I am very much hoping,' she replies, 'that it'll be a baby. Sugar?'

Rufus takes a seat opposite me. 'What's for breakfast?' he asks.

'Sausages,' says Mary.

'Wow.' He seems disproportionately thrilled by this piece of news.

'And scrambled eggs,' says Tilly.

'What day is it? I thought it was Tuesday?'

Mary says to me: 'Melody, you'll find that my son orients much of his diary around his stomach. A habit he picked up from his father.'

'No, but –' says Rufus – 'we always have sausages on a Saturday.'

'. . . If you see what I mean,' says Mary. Then, to Rufus: 'We're having a proper breakfast in honour of Melody's first day. We also –' she addresses this to me – 'don't usually eat this formally in the daytime. We have a proper family dinner in the dining room, of course.'

'Mrs Roberts cooks that,' says Tilly, and helps herself to a piece of toast. 'Oh, Ruf, there's marmalade!'

'Marmalade?' cries Rufus. '*Wow!*'

'Every night?' I ask, heart sinking. I'd sort of hoped that last night's horror had been something of a special occasion.

'Every,' she says firmly, 'night. It's a family tradition. It's right to gather the whole family in one place. You'll soon get used to it.'

'No sense in fighting tradition,' says Tilly, and I detect a tiny note of irony. I attempt to throw frantic glances in Rufus's direction, but he seems to be engrossed in the construction of a marmalade and sausage sanger, and doesn't notice. So much for the king of chivalry.

Rufus's grandmother, despite the early hour, is already wearing a hat. It's a cloche constructed of feathers that have been dyed to match the baby blue of her coat-dress. She has been looking at me in silence since I came in, a dimpled smile of consummate sweetness clamped to her face. I have a feeling that she's already forgotten me from yesterday.

'Good morning, Mrs Wattestone,' I say. I figure you don't call someone of her antiquity by their first name until you're invited.

She bats her eyelashes. Beatrice has tiny little circular eyes set in creamy white skin, like raisins dropped carelessly in a snowdrift. The face has obviously been heart-shaped in the past: that soft, round look with the calcified points at the chin and jaw which was the feminine ideal in the 1920s and which modern medics associate with bulimia. Dame gravity has, over the years, pulled the skin downward so it hangs, like a washrag, half a centimetre from the bones.

'Is she my new nurse?' she asks.

Then she parts orange-painted lips and smiles at me with teeth of purest plastic.

'No, Granny,' says Tilly. 'She's Rufus's new wife. Your nurse will be in at ten, like normal.'

'But she's Australian,' says Beatrice. 'She must be a nurse.'

'Shall I get you some eggs?' asks Mary. 'You like eggs, don't you?'

Beatrice waves an imperious hand in acceptance.

'Morning, Granny.' Rufus puts down his sandwich in mid-bite and kisses the old trout above her shaven eyebrows. 'How are you?'

127

The head wobbles coquettishly, and the lashes bat once more. 'I'm *vurr*-uh well, thank you,' she lilts. 'Isn't it a beautiful day?'

Showering crumbs, he replies: 'Not really, Granny. Bucketing down.'

'But *so* good for the daffodils,' she says. Now, even I know that daffs don't usually appear in November.

'I'd better get up to the roof once I'm finished here,' he says.

'Oh, *thank* you, darling,' says Mary. 'Daddy will be *so* glad you're back.'

'Where is he, anyway?'

'Doing some lopping.'

'God, I wish he wouldn't do that,' says Rufus. 'Surely Martin Slatter could be doing that?'

'Martin's gone to the dentist,' says Mary, 'in Cheltenham.'

'Poor sod,' says Rufus.

'We're obviously paying him too much if he can afford Cheltenham prices,' says Mary disapprovingly.

'Absolutely,' says Rufus. 'Estate workers need estate worker teeth. I'll cut his wages immediately.'

I'm quite impressed by the way Rufus just ignores it when his family say something outrageous. I'll have to learn to follow suit.

'Sausages?' asks Tilly. I snag one on the end of a fork.

'Have more than that,' she says. I shake my head. Normally, with a breakfast like this, I'd be bogging in like nobody's business, but I seem to have lost my appetite.

Beatrice turns her attention back to me. 'Have you come far?' she asks.

'Yes, Granny,' says Rufus. 'We came from Gozo yesterday.'

A small frown, and a pout that doesn't go too well with bleeding lipstick. 'Gozo? I could have sworn she was A*w*st*ra*lian. Do they *have* nurses on Gozo?'

'She's not a nurse, Beatrice,' says Mary. 'She's a chiropodist. She can probably do something about those bunions of yours.'

'Oh, *no*,' says Beatrice, 'that won't do *at all*. Why would I want

128

a chiropodist as a nurse? And where did Nessa go? She didn't say goodbye . . .'

'Nessa's not gone anywhere, Granny,' says Tilly. 'She'll be here at ten.'

'So I have *two* nurses now . . .?' she muses.

'She's not a nurse, Granny,' says Rufus. 'She's my wife.'

'Nonsense,' says Beatrice.

'Not nonsense. We got married a couple of weeks ago.'

A flirtatious wag of the index finger. 'Ah, now I *know* you're teasing me,' she says. 'We didn't have a wedding two weeks ago. Our last wedding was Tilly's.'

'I'm not a chiropodist . . .' I say lamely.

'Chiropodist . . . oh, *sorry*, darling, *pedicurist*,' says Mary.

'Oh, fantastic,' says Tilly. 'I'd kill for a trim and a coat of nail-varnish. I haven't seen my feet in months.'

'Where *is* Hugo, anyway, darling?' asks Beatrice, suddenly.

'Um . . . Burundi, as far as I know,' says Tilly. Evidently Granny's being kept in the dark like the rest of the county.

'What's he doing in Burundi?'

'Business,' she says.

'I'd have thought he'd be here with his wife,' says Beatrice, 'waiting for their first baby.'

'Yes, well, he's not,' says Tilly bluntly.

'A woman's place is by her husband's side,' proclaims Beatrice in the manner of one repeating poetry learned by rote.

'Yes, well,' says Tilly, 'I'm afraid the global marketplace doesn't really allow for those sorts of pieties any more. I'm going to go and have a bath.'

She lumbers to her feet and stands there rubbing the small of her back. 'It's lovely to have you here, Melody.'

'Likewise,' I say.

'I was thinking,' says Mary, when Tilly has left. Wonders will never cease. 'I think I should give Melody a bit of a debrief on what she's taken on this morning. Would you like that?'

Oh, Gawd. 'Yes,' I say, 'thanks. That would be really helpful.'

'Great idea,' says Rufus. 'Thanks, Ma. That's really kind of you.'

My eyes are rolling so hard at him that I think they'll fall out of my head. Jesus, what *is* it with men?

'Tell you what,' he says, 'I think I should probably get up to that roof as soon as possible. Ma, did that plastic sheeting we ordered come, at all?'

'Yes, it's in the stables,' says Mary.

'Ah, great,' he says, pushing his plate away and standing up. 'Right. That's it. I'm off.'

As he passes my chair, he puts a hand round the back of my neck and kisses me on the forehead in that irritating brotherly fashion that men all seem to reserve for showing affection to their wives in front of the rellies. With a jolt, I realise that this is the first time he's ever done this. Even in front of the Marijas, with their monobrows and the metaphorical *mantillas* strapped about their heads, he was relaxed with his hand-holding and waist-squeezing, dropping casual kisses without thought on to my lips as he passed. Now, it seems, I've undergone a magical transformation into a twelve-year-old with no tits, clompy shoes and a pair of rubber-band-held pigtails sprouting horizontally out of the sides of my head.

'I'll see you later, my love,' he says. 'Don't let her wear you out, now, will you?'

I reach up and pat the hand. 'I'm looking forward to it,' I lie.

The three Mrs Wattestones hold their poses as he leaves the room, all of us smiling like waxworks, no-one willing to let the façade slip until the door closes. I'm not sure what's in store next.

I find out, double-quick. Mary gets to her feet, picks up some abandoned plates. 'I'm going to make a couple of phone calls,' she says, 'and do a bit of admin.'

The cordial tone has slipped right away now that there's no-one but senile old Beatrice to hear. 'If you would sit with Beatrice until the nurse arrives . . . I'm sure you can manage *that* without too many mishaps. There are a couple of the brochures we keep for the tourists on the windowsill over there. If you read that, I'm sure you'll know more than you need to.'

'Thanks,' I say.

'I dare say you won't be here long enough for a deeper grounding,' she tosses over her shoulder as she leaves the room.

Beatrice's bright button eyes study me as I click my jaw back into place. Steady, I think: keep the appearances going. I turn and smile at her.

'I think there's something you should know,' she says.

'What's that, Mrs Wattestone,' I ask.

'The doctor says I'm not allowed any more gin,' she says confidingly. 'But my normal nurse usually pops a little in my milk at elevenses.'

Chapter Twenty

Welcome to Bourton Allhallows

Welcome to Bourton Allhallows, home of the Callington-Warbeck-Wattestone family since 932. I do a double take here, before I understand that the printers haven't missed a digit off the date. The leaflet is printed on the sort of hard, shiny paper you find in cheap motel bathrooms. In fact, it's the sort of paper you find in the bathrooms at Bourton Allhallows. Whatever else goes on today, I'm going to be visiting the shops for essential supplies at some point.

We hope you enjoy your visit to our house, says the brochure. *Please remember that this is still our family home, and treat it accordingly.*

History: Bourton Allhallows and the Wattestone family are first recorded in the parish records of Wednesford and Sidbury, when Edmund Wattestone donated land and materials for the construction of a church in the Sidbury valley. The Allhallows estate was at the time little more than a large, lightly fortified farmhouse built on early Saxon foundations in an estate of some thirty virgates. The castle wall, or bailey, that can be seen today was certainly in situ at this time. The moat was added (by diverting the course of the Bourton river) in 1273-8 and the estate is recorded again in the Domesday book. The main source of income in the area at the time was wool, and it seems that the family were farmers on a large scale.

Sheep farmers. I've married a sheep farmer. Might as well have stayed at home.

The estate was enlarged when Rufus Wattestone married Anne Callington, sole heiress of a neighbouring landowner, in 1515; her estates were joined to the Wattestone land in exchange for the adjuncture of her surname. The family's landholdings further increased when they converted from Catholicism in 1538, benefiting, coincidentally, from the dissolution

132

of the Sidbury Priory. Many of the main public rooms of the house date
from this period. The family reconverted in the reign of Mary I, then settled
into Protestant life under Elizabeth I, successfully maintaining good
relations with both sides throughout the Civil War and Interregnum.

The direct Callington-Wattestone line of descent died out in 1727,
when, in the absence of a male heir, the estates were left to a cousin, Giles
Warbeck, of Plympton, on condition that the family names be preserved.

I pour myself another cup of half-cold tea. Wonder if it would
be rude to leave the table to settle a bit closer to the fire. Beatrice
is pretending to read a copy of a magazine called the *Lady*. She
sings as she flips through the pages: a Noel Coward song, 'I've
Been to a Marvellous Party'.

In the seventeenth century, the family's fortunes were boosted by the
discovery of a seam of gold in the Sidbury valley. The initial find proved
to be of disappointing quality, and operations became increasingly
intensive for decreasing rewards. They were enough, however, to finance
the additions to the house in the Jacobean, Queen Anne and Georgian
eras, and it is assumed that, though mining only officially continued for
some 175 years in the area, unofficial excavations were continuing to
provide revenues for the family for some time after they were producing
them for the exchequer.

I skip a bit. I can't help it. It doesn't make gripping narrative.

The current owner, Edmund, was born in 1930, and married Lady
Mary Fulford-Ffawkes. Their heir, Rufus, was born in 1976.

Not a mention of Tilly. Nice. I let the leaflet rest on the table
for a minute while I think and drink my tea. So this is my new
family. Over a thousand years, they've sat here in this valley, been
born, got married, bought a bit more land, reproduced, died, got
married, bought a bit more land again, reproduced. And that's . . .
well, that's it, as far as I can see. A thousand undistinguished years
of achieving doodly. No wonder they're so proud of themselves.
A real figjam of a family. The more I learn, the less I get how Rufus
has come out so normal.

'I danced with a man who danced with a gel who danced with
thuh Pri-*hince* of Way-*hales*,' warbles Beatrice.

I read on.

Great Hall: Part of the original structure of the house; hanging plaster ceiling by Nikolas Dowlet and scrolled oak panelling, 1567. Marble fireplace by Robert Adam, installed 1830s after the demolition of Tewkesbury March. Antlers over fireplace from a hart brought down by Edmund Callington-Wattestone during a hunt organised for Henry VIII. Pictures: Lettice Callington: school of Holbein; Caroline Callington-Warbeck-Wattestone: John Singer Sargent; The Hunting Party: after Stubbs; The Martyrdom of St Sebastian, Caravaggio.

It's a real one. Blow me down.

Selected furniture: George IV plum pudding mahogany and rosewood crossbanded sofa table; green painted parcel-gilt sedan chair, early 19th century; a pietra dura table; pair of oak and pollard oak antler chairs circa 1850; set of dining chairs, Chippendale; carved mahogany . . .

She's trying to bore me to death. This list is making my jaw crack. And there are another three pages to go. I think I've lost the circulation in my feet.

'Would you like to sit closer to the fire, Mrs Wattestone?' I ask Beatrice.

'Heavens,' she replies, 'it's like a sauna in here already. Have you come far?'

'From Australia, originally.'

'And are you staying nearby?'

'I'm married to Rufus, Mrs Wattestone,' I tell her again.

Beatrice shakes her head. 'Rufus isn't married.'

This is going to get a bit tedious.

'You don't mind if I . . .' I gesture towards the fire.

She inclines her head graciously. 'Please.'

There's a pile of magazines by the couch, which has a greasy stain at head-height on its high back. I take the opportunity to drop the leaflet casually on to a little metal trivet thing that sits uselessly by the fireplace, look through the dusty magazines. More copies of the *Lady* ('Jane Asher: Cake Decoration and Me'), something called *Country Life* ('Antiques Special') and something called *Horse and Hound* ('Adventures with the Pytchley'). I give *Horse and Hound* a burl.

'Do you enjoy country sports?' enquires Beatrice.

I lower the magazine into my lap. 'I'm not really sure,' I tell her. 'We're more sea where I come from.'

'Ah,' she says, 'so you'll enjoy fishing.'

I shrug. I haven't actually been out with a rod and line since the guy next to me pulled up a blue-ringed octopus and had to smash it apart with a boat hook while everyone else fled screaming across the rocks. 'I guess,' I reply noncommittally.

'My late husband was a great fisherman,' she informs me, fixing me with those shiny little button eyes. 'We used to stock the moat with a thousand trout every season. A great sportsman.'

Doesn't sound that much like sport to me, I think. More like the stately equivalent of shooting fish in a barrel. 'That's nice,' I tell her. 'They don't do that any more, then?'

'Not since the cracks started appearing,' she informs me. 'Too expensive, considering how many we lose to herons.'

I wait for a moment to see if she's going to say anything more, then return to *Horse and Hound*. Turn to the small ads at the back. They read like the lonely hearts in *Fruitcakes Monthly*: 'Schoolmaster, 11, sadly unable to compete due to tendon strain, but fit for hacking and schooling . . .'; 'Handsome black stallion, 15.2, huge potential but not a novice ride. Would suit strong, experienced boy . . .'; 'Rangy heavyweight, big jump, three seasons out. Only selling due to relocation . . .'

'Oh, yes,' burbles Beatrice, 'a great sportsman. There wasn't a day when he wasn't out with the Heythrop or off with his gun. The servants used to have it written into their contracts that they didn't have to eat pheasant more than three times a week.'

'Wow.' I try to sound impressed. 'You must have been very proud of him.'

'Oh, yes. The Duke of Beaufort used to say he was the best shot in the country.'

'Golly.'

'So do you hunt, in Australia?'

'We don't really have the right sort of foxes. Did you hunt?'

The beaming smile. 'Oh, yes. Three times a week. From when I was six years old. My grandmother was one of the first woman

135

MFHs. With the Dumfriesshire. I remember,' she leans towards me, cups her mouth conspiratorially, 'the day she died, we were all sent out, my brothers and I, to get us out of the house. It was a marvellous day: found immediately, and ran practically without a break. And we'd be galloping along on our ponies, and somebody would overtake us, and shout, "How's your grandmother?" And we'd shout: "She's dead!" Looking back, I suppose the modern psychiatrist would have a thing or two to say about that, but it was killingly funny at the time.'

And to show herself unaffected by the experience, she allows a peal of tinkling laughter to escape her, the sort of laugh that I thought that only Mary was able to accomplish.

I laugh too, to show that I'm not offended. Actually, I think it *is* pretty funny: the sort of story that my dad would appreciate, full on.

The laughter is cut off, just like that. Once again she tilts her head, hands crossed in her lap. 'Of course, I dare say you don't get too much hunting on a *nurse's* salary.' She pops me back into my box.

I don't have the energy. 'Can I get you a cup of tea or something, there, Mrs Wattestone?'

A little recoil as she corrects her deportment. 'A lady doesn't drink between breakfast and luncheon,' she informs me.

I try a little tease. 'Not even a drop of gin at elevenses?'

She gives me a look that leaves me in no doubt about the future of my medical support contract if I don't watch my lip.

The fireplace door opens and a woman in a green T-shirt and maroon leggings enters, pauses for a moment, then, to my astonishment, actually bobs a curtsy and says: 'Do you mind if I clear the table, now?'

I guess this is either the fabled Mrs Roberts, or Martin's wife, Sharon, who I gather helps out in the house as well. Probably the former. Whatever, I'm relieved to see her. But Beatrice, like the old Edwardian she is, pretends she isn't there at all.

I lay down my magazine, get to my feet. 'Sure. I'll give you a hand.'

She practically jumps out of her skin. I am just about to offer her a hand to shake, but think better of it when I see the way her eyes stand out on stalks. I make to walk towards the table, but she scurries into my path, blocks the route with a firmly turned shoulder.

'That's what I'm here for,' she tells me. None the less, I pick up the teapot and a couple of serving dishes as she stacks the plates, and follow her out of the room.

'I'm Melody,' I tell her as I pursue her down the passageway to the stairs. 'I'm Rufus's wife.'

She glances over her shoulder at me. 'I know,' she says.

'You're Mrs Roberts, right?'

She grunts in affirmation. 'Nice to meet you,' I say, and receive a noncommittal grunt in response.

We reach the kitchen, lay down our burdens on the table, and Mrs Roberts picks up a tea towel and wipes her hands. Looks at me in that way that I'm beginning to get used to, as though I've just sprouted a second head.

'I've got to say, Mrs Roberts, I could really do with your help.'

'Well, that's what I'm here for,' she says doubtfully, 'but I'm only kitchen staff, really, and a bit of cleaning here and there . . .'

'I'm sure you can be a lot of help. I mean, it's a bit daunting, this: I don't know who anybody is, where anything goes, or what I'm meant to do half the time. I could really do with a helping hand.'

'I'm sure you'll be fine, Mrs Wattestone,' she says.

'Yes, but you know how it is. A friendly face is always a big help. You can fill me in on the stuff I don't know about. I feel, you know – as though I'm in a wood full of bear traps. Like everyone's waiting for me to put a foot wrong. You know these people . . .'

She puts down the tea towel – she has gone quite red in the face – turns towards the sink and makes a big show of clattering about with the cutlery. 'I'm sorry, Mrs Wattestone, but I don't think that that's appropriate. I work here. I'm not a member of the family.'

'I'm not asking you to be . . .' I say. 'I was just hoping that—'

'Sorry,' says Mrs Roberts, 'but there it is. We have our ways, and I think everybody would be grateful if you'd respect that.'

'But,' I protest, 'how am I supposed to know what these ways *are* if no one will—'

'I suggest you ask your husband,' she says. 'I'm sorry. It just doesn't do, you know. You're family, I'm staff. That's how it is. It doesn't do to get too . . .'

'Too what?'

There's an edge of frustration to her voice. I'm obviously doing it again, blundering through etiquette hell without a handbook.

'Mrs Wattestone,' she says, 'we all have to know our place. I know you do it differently in Australia, but you're not in Australia now. Now, if you'll excuse me, I've got to get on.' She starts feeding dishes into the sink, turning up the tap so that any further attempts at conversation will be drowned out.

I don't know what to do, I really don't. I stand behind her for a minute, trying to think of something to say, but I understand that it's useless. I'm not just going to be rejected by the family, it seems: I'm going to be snubbed by the locals as well. I've walked into a minefield and I'm going to set off explosions wherever I put my feet. The back that's turned to me is rigid, resolute.

Eventually I say, in a cowed little voice: 'Well, I'm sorry I bothered you.'

She pretends not to hear.

Chapter Twenty-One
Up on the Roof

So here I am complaining about lies and untruths and people keeping things from other people, and the first thing I do is calm myself down as I make my way upstairs so that my husband won't know how rattled I am. Because I figure, you know, that if Mary's going to play the devoted mother whenever he's in the room, it's up to me to make sure as hell he's glad to be around his devoted wife. If the only ally I'm going to have around here is Rufus, I'd better make damn sure he's in the room to see the cause before he gets to see one of my sense of humour failures in action.

It's not too hard to calm down, as it goes, because I have plenty of time to do it in. It takes twenty minutes just to find my way up to the attics, and fortunately, the whole experience – the gargoyles carved into wood panels, the stuffed animal heads (my mum would love this place), the Brueghel grisaille hanging casually in a dark corridor – is weird and fascinating enough to restore some of my humour.

I reach my goal, and it's great. About as Narnian as you could get. A great jumble of history, like one of those huge antiques warehouses: room after room – thankfully all interlinked in a straightforward way; I suppose most of this floor was built all in one go – filled to the joists with the sort of furniture that has Beverly Hills decorators salivating. These people have never sold *anything*.

I walk on through, come to the room with the hole in the roof. It smells of damp, of rot, of the bumper crop of mushrooms piling out of the floorboards. There's a beautiful round pedestal table been rolled over to lean against the wall, but not before the rain has ruined it: once-ornate marquetry peels from a dull and spongy surface. It makes me want to weep, just looking at it. There must

139

be a few thousand dollars' worth there, just ruined for the sake of shifting it. Where it obviously used to stand is a collection of old tin baths, more or less full of rainwater. A hosepipe snakes from one, out through the hole, siphoning down to ground level. I wouldn't like to have been the poor sod who had to suck the other end and get it started. I'm probably sleeping with him, of course.

The tree has, at least, been cut down. It lies on the floorboards, its lower trunk wider around than my upper arm, branches, as long as I am tall, roughly lopped off and lain on the floor beside it. The stump has been painted with some chemical in a foul shade of Queen Mother turquoise. They'll probably keep it for another five hundred years as a souvenir.

I can hear Rufus moving about above my head; weave my way, treading carefully because I don't know how far the damage has gone with the floor, between the bathtubs, and look out of the hole.

I can't see him; he must be right up on top of the gable. A parapet runs the length of the roof, with a gutter-cum-walkway, lined with lead sheeting, behind. It looks safe enough. I haul myself up over the tiles and climb out.

He's astride the point of the roof, knees hitched up like he's on a horse, strong thighs in faded black jeans holding him steady. He's thrown his sweater down to the gutter, rolled up his shirtsleeves to reveal hard-muscled arms, golden from the Gozo sun. His arms were one of the first things I noticed about him: arms that have been shaped by use, not gym arms; arms that can carry a human body for ages without flagging. And I should know. He's totally absorbed in what he's doing: a sheaf of nails in his mouth, hammer and plastic sheeting in his hands.

I stand, hands on hips, and admire him for a few seconds, then say: 'Well, at least the builders come in nice packages around these parts.'

Rufus looks down, palms the nails and grins. 'Hello, trouble. How was the history lesson?'

'Got bored. Thought I'd come up and monkey about with the workers for a bit.'

'Good. They could do with a hand. Come on up.'

140

The roof is covered in tiles of a sort I've not seen before: stone of the same goldy-grey colour as the facings on the local houses, though crusted with orange lichen and patches of dark green moss. They must weigh half a ton each. I crawl up the roof, feeling them shift beneath me, grab his outstretched and do the last lot in a rush. Sit down with him, knees touching.

There's a fresh wind. Invigorating. And it's dizzyingly high. From here, I have a 360-degree view of the grounds, interrupted only by clutches of crooked chimney stacks.

'Wow,' I say.

'Thought you'd like it,' he says.

Up the hill, I see Edmund leaping from branch to branch of a tall tree like an aged monkey. The tree stands in the middle of a sweep of deer-mown grass that rolls down towards the house from a gigantic sky. I can see, now, that all the trees about the place have been planted artfully, scattered about asymmetrically to look as though they have grown there by nature, but each with a grand swathe of space over which to spread its noble boughs. Below us, a topiary garden shows signs of having once represented a half-played chess-game, in black yew and some tight-leaved red shrub. I can see Mary down among the rose bushes with a trug, making with the secateurs. Beyond the moat, in what were once obviously flat watermeadows, three horses graze good-temperedly in New Zealand rugs.

'Yeah,' I say, turning back to him. 'It's beaut. But it won't be much good to you when you catch your death, nothing on and all sweaty.'

'Sturdy stock,' he says. 'We've been getting cold and wet for hundreds of years. For pleasure.'

'So what's the deal?'

'Well,' he says, 'I need to get this sheeting over the gable and then run it down so it covers the hole. Only the roof-beam's a bit spongy and my nails just slip out the minute I bang them in.'

'Spongy?'

'Spongy.'

'Rufus,' I'm suddenly feeling just a little bit insecure up here in

141

the wind, 'if the roof-beam's spongy, isn't it time you just got the whole roof replaced?'

'Batman,' says Rufus, 'if I didn't have your brainpower to back me up, I wouldn't know what to do with myself.'

'Smartarse.'

'Back atcha,' he says. 'Have you seen the size of this roof?'

I look about me. From the ground, I haven't been able to take in just how much roof the house has, but now I see that the central mansard on which we're sitting has another mansarded wing sticking out at each point of the compass. That's a lot of square footage, what with the doubling up. 'Well, OK. But it's not like it's a cosmetic operation. How long has this hole been here?'

'Um,' says Rufus.

'Go on.'

'Well, since I was in the sixth form. It wasn't always this big, of course.'

'Sixth form. That's, like, ten–twelve years ago, yes?'

'Don't look at me like that. That's not all that long in the life of the house.'

'Well . . . have you ever heard of the stitch-in-time thing?'

'That presumes that you have a needle and thread.'

'Well, I don't want to do the I-told-you-so routine, but do you know how much that ruined table down there's probably worth?'

'Mel,' he picks up a loose tile, brandishes it at me, 'do you know how much one of these is worth?'

'Nuh-uh.'

'Around about two thousand pounds a ton.'

'Means nothing.'

'We need around six hundred tons to replace the whole roof. Obviously, some of them can be recycled, but most of them are on their way out. Plus, of course, because the ancestors have been making-do just like us, most of the rafters need replacing. Which means that the whole roof will have to come off at some point.'

I love the way he talks about The Ancestors. There's something very Japanese about it.

'Surely you could get cheaper tiles than that?'

'Listed building. We can't *move* without inspectors swarming all over us.'

'But if the house is falling down?'

'Doesn't matter,' he says. 'Doesn't work like that. They'd rather you let the whole place rot into the ground than let you use a material that's not in keeping with the vernacular. The whole place is a hodgepodge of jerry-built fashion, but it's got to be preserved in amber from now on.'

'How much are we talking, then?'

'Mmm? Hold on to your hat. We're not talking change from two million. Probably more.'

I suck air in through my teeth. 'Right-ho,' I say, thinking: you could probably sell half a dozen of those houses in the village, even in the state they're in, and raise the money, and still have another forty or so left over to rent to tourists. 'I guess I'll have to change your name to Roofless.'

'Ha ha.'

'It's a shame your nan had to go and lose that emerald, really, isn't it?'

Rufus sighs. 'Don't,' he says. 'You have no idea how many times over the last decade or so I've thought that. Mind you, I'd've had to prise it from her cold, dead fingers.'

I toy with the idea of offering him some help in that department, think, no, killing off old ladies is probably not a subject for flippancy. 'Think it'll ever be found?'

'Probably not in any of our lifetimes. There are an awful lot of sofas for it to have gone down the back of.'

'Oh, well. Guess we'll have to go for plan B, then.'

'Guess so,' he says distractedly.

I give the hole another look-see. Moss. Lichen. The slow drip-drip-drip of the roof-beams. 'Course,' I tell him, 'back where I come from, we'd get the whole thing sorted with a couple of sheets of corrugated iron and a staple gun.'

'Plastic sheeting is so much more sophisticated. And so much prettier.'

'And so handy in case of a dirty bomb,' I tell him. 'So if I shimmy backwards, do you think that beam'll hold me?'

'Wouldn't rely on it.'

'OK. I'll go round the long way.'

Down at parapet level, I have an idea. A bit of a blinder, though I say it myself. I love it when you realise you can use the stuff you've got to hand. It's the Aussie Battler in me. I call up to Rufus: 'Hey, mate, have you got some rope up here?'

His voice drifts down. 'Yuh.'

'Well, get down here, then. And bring the hammer with you.'

I hear him slide down the tiles, and his head appears at the hole in the roof. 'What?'

I've already dragged one end of the tree trunk across the floor. 'Take this. Let's get it out.'

'Oo–K. You're the boss.'

He takes the end and we feed it, between us, out over the parapet and back down until it lies lengthways along the gutter.

'Well?'

'What we do,' I explain, 'is nail one end of the sheeting on to this, and the other end to the underside of the roof overhang, if it'll hold. Then we can just sling the tree over the other side for weight.'

'Why didn't I think of that?'

'You married me for my sturdy artisan blood, didn't you?'

One of those little moments passes between us. Rufus smiles.

'Down, boy,' I say, but I can't stop myself smiling back.

It's only a bodge job, but the nails slip in sweet as a nut through the double layer of sheeting we've wrapped around the tree trunk. While he's doing that, I crawl around him, monkey-like, and hammer the other end of the sheeting into the lead lining under the tiles. I use an old jack I've found in a corner behind a mangle. I show him how to make a cradle out of the rope to hold the two ends and we clamber up opposite sides of the hole to the top.

'They don't teach you *that* at public school,' I tease.

The log reaches the apex of the roof. Rufus starts to unwrap his end of the rope.

'Don't do that, dingbat! We've got to lower it down, unless you

144

want it to hit bottom and rip the nails straight through the other end.'

'Ah. How do you know these things?'

'You can't make a habit of slapping your man down without something to base it on.'

'And you do it so well.'

'Ph.D. in it. Lower away, stupid.'

'You've got good muscles, for a girl.'

'Well, you've got a pretty good brain, for a man.'

'Not sure about the dress sense, though.'

I glance down over my chunky sweater with the grass stain on the front. His sweater.

'We're going to have to go shopping, I grant you.'

'We'll go soon. I'll take you on a spree.'

Spree. With tea and cakes and hard-boiled eggs thrown in?

'Like, when might "soon" be?'

'I don't know. There's a lot of catching-up to do. Soon, I promise.'

'I was rather thinking in terms of today . . .?'

'No can do, darling. We'll have to go to London.'

'You're yanking my chain. Surely there must be somewhere . . .'

'Well, yes, for jumpers and things like that. We could go really local and kit you out with half a dozen shirtwaisters and some corduroy pants.'

'Tell me you're joking.'

'Well, there are a few yummy mummy shops about the place, I suppose. Fleecy things that wash like rags, darling.'

'Sometimes you can be too camp for your own good.'

'Thank you. Can't you get the rest of your stuff sent from home?'

'That would make a lot of sense. 'Cause, like, even if I hadn't sold everything I had when I took off, it was all designed for wearing in sub-zero temperatures, naturally.'

'You sold *everything*?'

'Apart from what I could fit in the backpack.'

'Weird. Just getting rid of your past like that.'

145

'Bit of a family habit, I guess. Your family hangs on to history like it's a magic charm. Mine's had more fresh starts than a fish market.'

'I can't imagine it. Not knowing where you come from. Just – forgetting about all the stuff that went before.'

'Yeah, well,' I say, practising my British understatement 'I don't think my family's got quite as much to be proud of as yours. I guess if I had a thousand illustrious years of sheep farming in my background, I might feel differently.'

He sits back and takes a breather. 'It's quite sexy, in a way. Sometimes I look around all the . . . *stuff* here, and wonder what the point of it all is. What would it be like not to have all this baggage hanging round one's neck? Just to be free to do what I wanted.'

'Darl, you take your baggage with you, believe me.'

'Yes, but. I don't know. What if I just let it all go hang, and went off and lived on an island somewhere with nothing but a couple of coconut shells for company?'

'So, babe, if you *had* had a choice about it, what would you have done?'

He pauses, reflects. 'I think I'd've liked to have been an architect,' he says.

'Crikey. That's a bit coals-to-Newcastle, isn't it?'

'No,' he says. 'The opposite. I spend my life fantasising about lean white flat-roofed Araby buildings. All smooth and sleek and full of glass. No buttresses, no wings, no period clashes. Somewhere warm. Tiled roof terraces, that's what I want. Covered in pots of citrus.'

I shiver suddenly in the November wind. 'Nothing to stop us,' I say.

'Just a thousand years of history.'

'History can be overrated. Most of it wasn't particularly glorious.'

'Don't let anyone hear you say that around here. History's pretty much all they live for.'

'But not you?'

He thinks for a minute. 'It has to be taken into account,' he says eventually. 'And you've got to give it some respect, especially as it matters so much to the old, but on the whole, no, not really. History's an albatross slung round the necks of the aristocracy. It gives the worthless ones a sense of worth that saves them having to justify their own existence, and it manacles the talented. Traps them at the homestead.'

'And you?'

He glances up at me. 'Me, I don't know. I'm nothing special, but at least I know it. I'm sort of hoping you'll help me find out.'

'Bit of a tall order, darling.'

'You know what? I think you've got the steel to see it through.'

The sheeting reaches full stretch. I let go of my end of the rope, rub my aching hands together.

'There you go, matey,' I say. 'All snug and watertight for the winter. I don't know if I'm going to sort your head out for you, but at least I can keep it dry.'

'Excellent,' says Rufus. 'Now all you need to do is sort out the flooding in the cellar.'

Chapter Twenty-Two
Papering over the Cracks

'Hi, it's me,' I say.

'O!' roars my dad. ''ow you doin'?'

'Great!' I tell him, endeavouring to sound like a happy honey-mooner. 'All settled in!'

'Great! Good! We've been waiting to hear from you. What's it like, then?'

'Amazing,' I tell him. I always find that, if you're going to tell a lie, you're best to keep it as close to the truth as you can. 'It's really . . . old,' I say, 'and huge. Huge and rambling and full of history.'

'Just like your yaya, then,' he says, and chokes on his own laughter.

'Even older than her.'

'Wow. Thass pretty old. Bet it doesn't smell of piss, though.'

My father's attitude to my grandmother is fairly outrageous, all told. He extracts the Michael whenever he gets the opportunity. Something to do with having reached the age of fifty-seven while still expecting to be socked over the back of the neck with a wooden spoon at any moment.

'Parts of it. They have quite a few dogs. And a Granny who's even older than Yaya.'

'She living at home?'

'Yeah. She has a nurse.'

He makes approving noises. 'So what they like, then? Your new family?'

'Interesting.'

'Interesting.' He interprets this, correctly, with the Australian meaning of the word.

'Yeah.'

148

'What do they do?'

'Um . . . nothing, really.'

'Nothing? How can they do nothing?'

'Well, they have this property, and—'

'OK. So, what? If they do nothing, I guess they must be worth a few dollars. This husband of yours – he don't do nothing either?'

'Yeah – yeah, he does. He sort of runs things. His dad's largely retired.'

'Ah. So they're farmers.'

'No. Not really. It's really historic, like I said. It's open to the public in the summer.'

'Like a hotel?'

'No. Not really. More like a theme park, only no rides.'

'They got food?'

'Sort of. Scones. Those sort of bready buns with the raisins in. Oh, and fruit cake. Things called Melton Mowbray pork pies. Tell you something. British food is every bit as good as they say it is.' Says the girl from the land of the lamington.

'What, they don't do any hot food?'

'You know what, Dad? It's out of season. I don't really know.'

I hear him take time to digest this. To my father, a place of entertainment that doesn't also sell meaty treats is an opportunity wasted. My new family has just plummeted in his estimation to somewhere roughly on the level of The Vegetarian Society of Australia.

'So how,' he asks, 'are you getting on with the family? What are they like?'

I'm cautious. 'I've not been here long enough to get to know them. They're OK.'

I can tell he's not convinced.

'Well, OK. I think the mother-in-law's got a bit of a problem.'

A sigh, and a chomp on the cigar. 'Don't they all?'

'I guess,' I say doubtfully.

'If you think it's bad now, just wait till you have children.'

'Thanks, Dad. That's a great help.'

He does one of his cough-laughs. 'I know my girl. She ain't going to put up with no shit from nobody.'

'Glad I've got your confidence, old man.'

'Give 'em hell, Melody.'

'I'll do my best. Hey, where's Mum?'

'Where you think?'

'Oh. OK.'

'She took your yaya down to Sydney for a couple of nights. I think she needs some more black sacks and armour-plated control pants.'

'Hell. So you mean you've got the place to yourself?'

'I know. I'm surprised she trusts me after the last time.'

'You're not going to do it again, are you?'

'No. No. She confiscated the air gun, anyway.'

'Well, you're not going to let the opportunity pass completely though, are you?'

''Course not. What do you take me for? I know I've been married to your mother for years, but my balls aren't completely gone. So when we going to come and see this famous property, then?'

I've been sort of ready for this. It's not that I don't want to see them – God, I want to see them – but I've got to get a few things sorted out before they come. 'Anytime. Just give me the word. But I'd wait until the spring, or even the summer. It's really cold right now. And there's this rain – I don't even know how to describe it. It's not like proper rain. Doesn't come down and then go away. It's more like being stood in front of a windscreen mister. All the time.'

'Sounds awful.'

'It's been like that every day since I got here. Trust me. You don't want to come while it's like this.'

He catches something in my voice. 'Melody? You OK?'

'Yes,' I say quickly. 'Yes, I'm fine. Really.'

'You don't sound OK.'

'I'm fine, Dad.'

He gets that don't-lie-to-me tone. 'Melody?'

150

'Just leave it, Dad. I'm fine. Just a little bit homesick. But I'm fine.'

'We'll come, right now.'

'Don't. Just give me a little while to get settled in. And then I'll be fine.'

'No, but—'

'Dad. No. You've got to let me do this by myself.'

'I don't like to think about you, all by yourself . . .'

'I'm not. I'm not all by myself. I've got Rufus, remember? That's why I'm here.'

'You know what? I don't know this man. He could be doing anything, and I wouldn't know.'

'Dad? I'm hanging up now.'

'Don't do that, Princess. You can't blame me for worrying. After what happened the last time . . .'

'I'll talk to you soon. Don't worry about me. I'm absolutely fine.'

'Mel, I—'

'Bye, Dad. I love you. I'll call you soon.'

That went pretty well, I'd say.

Chapter Twenty-Three
Eavesdropping

It's a Sunday night in The Land That Time Forgot, and I'm on my way down to the dining room when I hear voices at the bottom of the stairs. They're so intent on each other that they haven't heard the schlick of my stilettos on the marble. It's Mary and Tilly, and they're having one of those 'the vicar's here, keep your voice down' rows. Well, Mary's having a row: it sounds like Tilly's crying.

'Please,' she says, 'Mary, I feel *awful*. I can't face it.'

It's odd how Tilly always calls Mary by her Christian name when she's 'Mummy' to Rufus. It's such a Modern Parent way of going on for such an old-fashioned lady. I feel it says more about the obvious distance between them than pretty much anything else. You'd have to have grown up a long way from human habitation not to notice who the blue-eyed boy was in *this* family. It's a testament to the strength of his character that he's not grown up with Little Emperor Syndrome, really.

'There's nothing wrong with you,' hisses Mary.

'I'm eight months pregnant.'

'It's not an *illness*. When I was pregnant with Rufus, I was—'

A rebellious interruption: 'Yes, yes, I *know*. You were opening fêtes and stalking deer right up until you went into labour. Well, I bow my head to you.'

'Oh, don't be sarky with me. Just pull yourself together and come in.' Mary's tone is sharp, bullying: like a bodkin prodding the small of a back.

Tilly again sounds tearful. 'Mary, my ankles have swollen up like balloons, my back's killing me and I've got a frightful headache coming on, and you *know* I'm not allowed to take anything for it. Please can't I just go and lie down . . .?'

'The table's already laid. I will *not* have your grandmother upset . . .'

'Granny won't mind. She'll understand.'

'If she thinks for a moment that there's anything wrong . . . if she finds out, I shall personally throttle you. I'm not having it.'

'Mary, she's *going* to find out! She can't possibly *not*. When the baby's born and—'

'*No!* Do you hear me, Mathilda? If your grandmother finds out what you've done, it will kill her! Do you want her blood on your hands on top of—'

Tilly sounds like her blood's just boiled over. '*What* have I done? What *exactly* have I done?'

'You know. Oh, my giddy *aunt*, you know. We do *not* have divorce in this family. You can do what you want after your grandmother is dead, but I will *not* have her heart broken.'

I hear a faint, catching sob. 'You bitch,' says Tilly. 'You bloody bitch. It's not *my* divorce. It's his. Do you think I *wanted* my husband to run off with some . . .'

Oy oy. I decide to eavesdrop a bit more.

'Well,' says Mary, 'in my day, women made damn well sure their husbands *didn't*. We looked after ourselves. We paid *attention*. No wonder he ran off with the first woman to look at him. *You* may be too spoiled to take your responsibilities seriously, but if you're going to come here and sponge off your father, you will have to respect the values of this house.'

A single, strangled sob.

'Now, come to dinner like an adult and behave. It's bad enough that we've got that . . .'

I know I'm about to come up.

'. . . hoyden at the table, without temper tantrums from you.'

I finish the stairs off in a split second, round the corner in a clack of heels, brightest smile at the ready. 'Hi,' I say, wringing every bit of mileage out of the vowel, 'I'm not late, am I?'

'No,' says Mary, and it's plain that it pains her that I'm not. Then: 'That's a . . . um . . . interesting dress. Are you sure you won't get cold?'

Despite Rufus's promises, we've not got any nearer the bright lights than a trip to the woollen-wear shop in Stow the weeks I've been here, so I'm wearing my wedding dress. Somehow I didn't feel like a painted whore in it in Valletta. Though, of course, I didn't have goosebumps all over my blue-stippled flesh in Valletta. 'I'd be cold whatever I wore, Mary,' I say pleasantly, 'so I might as well wear something nice. This is the dress I wore to get married in. Do you like it?'

'Very . . .' says Mary, and it sounds like the reminder of the solemn occasion makes her sick to her stomach. Then she frowns and picks up a corner of the shawl I've wrapped around my shoulders in a vain attempt to postpone the onset of hypothermia. 'Where did you get this?'

'The Chinese room. Over the back of a chair?'

I get one of those caught-the-sneak-thief vibes. So much for the old all-my-worldly-goods malarkey. 'It's very old,' she says. 'Valuable.'

'Oh, right,' I reply. 'I'll try not to get any fag burns in it, then.'

Write out five hundred times: do not attempt to bond with your mother-in-law by making jokes.

Another acid pause. 'Well, never mind,' says Mary. 'It's too late to change. Tilly's feeling under the weather. So we're *all* late now.'

I catch Tilly looking at me under her eyelashes. Her eyes are reddened and her nose looks like it would probably do as a traffic beacon. 'Poor old you,' I say kindly. 'We'll see you right.'

Tilly looks startled, like a guppy. I think she's afraid I might touch her or something. She attempts to shoot off. Does more of a lumber, what with the stomach and the floor-length maternity smock that ties her ankles together.

Mary stands to one side, face like stone. I stop; sweep my hand through the air, towards the dining-room door, like a ballerina; say: 'After you, Lady Mary.'

She says nothing, simply wheels on her heel and precedes me into the room.

Chapter Twenty-Four
Drinkies

So poor old Tilly's getting about as much support from her olds as she would have got if she'd been cuckolded by a Royal. I'd managed to work this out already but I hadn't realised the reason they were all keeping it under their hats. I'm shocked, though, at what seems to be Mary's idea of loving motherly behaviour. I'd have had her kiddies taken away years ago if I was Social Services.

They've got the vicar to dinner. The vicar and Mrs Vicar, and that guy Hilary, who's wearing a spotted cravat, no less, and two sets of people of indeterminate age – it's so hard to tell when the complexion's been eroded by driving rain – who talk like they've got raw eggs lodged between their back teeth and don't want to break them. They're called Patrick and Daisy Trice-Rickard and Jimmy and Patsy Something-Hyphen. I'm not sure if Patsy's the same one I heard on the stairs, but decide to give her as wide a berth as possible. Oh, and Roly Cruikshank. He looks like he's brushed his hair down with a nail brush and water. Looks like someone who deals in antiquarian maps.

She's done it again, of course. Ignored me right up to the door – she doesn't seem too bothered about Tilly knowing how the land really lies – and then slipped her arm through mine the moment it opened and paraded me around the drawing room with my bicep brachius pressed disturbingly against her right breast as though I was her new best friend.

I'm regretting the decision to wear the dress. I'm not sure what else I could have worn under the circumstances, but I feel virtually naked when I see that the A-line velvet is out in force tonight, combined with stark white blouses titivated by frilly jabots. Among the eight women present, four are wearing just that: one black

155

skirt, two bottle green, one claret. Tilly's smocky thing is made of velvet, slightly jaded by a liberal coating of long white hair that I suspect must come from Perkins. Beatrice wears something floaty in layers of peach and orange chiffon, which admirably hides the effects of ten decades of gravity by making her look like a caper blossom. Of course, they all know better than me. I'd naively thought that, with guests in the house, they might have indulged in some form of heating in the entertaining rooms, but aside from a two-log fire in the ten-log grate, the place is still cold as the grave. My nipples feel like walnuts.

'Well, how do you do?' asks Mr Hyphen, staring at them as he shakes my hand. 'And congratulations.'

Why do people keep congratulating me? Surely they're meant to be telling me how lucky Rufus is?

'We were sorry we didn't get to meet you the other day,' says Patsy Hyphen. She has a bananawood complexion and the Klingon head ridges of one who discovered Botox early. 'You seemed to vanish. One minute you were there, and the next – poof!'

I make a joke of it. 'You can always rely on me to be the party pooper. I sort of got lost for a bit.'

'Oh, my dear,' says Daisy Trice-Rickard, 'that's happened to me here so many times I can't tell you. I always make sure I have a piddle before I come, just so I can avoid having to go to the lav.'

'Tell you what, I almost gave up and went to the pub.'

'Well, bully for you,' says Mr Hyphen. 'Quite possible you'd have ended up there by accident anyway. There were always rumours that Edmund's father had a secret tunnel made leading straight to the Wattestone Arms.'

'You know, I'd never come across a family that was named after a pub before I met Rufus,' I tell him.

He bellows with laughter. 'Just wait till you meet the Duke of York,' he replies.

'Dear girl,' interjects Mary. 'Did you know, she's been clambering about on the roof like a little monkey?'

156

'Haveya?' cries Mr Hyphen. 'Haveya? Good for you! Didn't know you had it inyer! Thought you looked a bit *delicate* in that dress.'

He claps me about the shoulder, making me very glad I've got the shawl on. Even through the cloth, it stings like rubbing alcohol on a carpet burn, but I'm pleased to bear the pain. It's a noble scar of amity, after all.

'Have you met Paddy Trice-Rickard? He was always out on the tiles at Cirencester.'

Jimmy unclamps my mother-in-law's grip and leads me over to where Patrick Trice-Rickard is hogging the fireplace.

'Blushing bride,' he says, pumping my hand, 'how d'ja do? Very fetching frock, I must say.'

'Thank you. It was my wedding dress.'

'Jolly good. Must've looked splendid. Bit thin for church, though,' he says meaningfully. 'Must have given the vicar a bit of a thrill.'

'Registry,' I tell him, trying to draw the shawl a bit further across my décolletage without being too obvious about it. 'And it's still pretty warm in Malta in October. But I don't think it's going to do for the rest of the winter. I'm going up to London tomorrow. Do some shopping.'

'Poor old Rufus.'

'Naah. He's staying here.'

'That's the spirit. Just land the old man with the bill afterwards.'

'I was thinking of using my credit card.'

'A feminist!'

'Yeah,' I say. 'Burned my bra only the other day.'

'So I see,' he says. And the look on his face suggests he's glad of it.

From the corner of my eye, I notice that Beatrice is pulling some sort of face at me. I guess maybe she thinks I shouldn't be fraternising. What with being a servant and all. A week of sitting next to her at interminable family dinners, and she still thinks I'm her nurse. I mean, I don't *mind* cutting up her food for her, but when someone consistently dismisses you by saying, 'Thank you, you can go now', it can get a bit irksome.

157

Rufus arrives at my side, hands me a gin and tonic that's so strong I choke.

Tilly waddles over. 'I hear you're off to London?' she asks.

'Yeah. Just for the night. I've got to get some clothes in. Going to go to – where was it you said, Rufus?'

'Harvey Nicks.'

Tilly gets a dreamy sort of look. 'Ohhhh, Haaaahvey Nicks,' she says. 'I remember when I could get into clothes from Hahvey Nicks. Dreadful shoes, though. You must go to Bond Street. It's only a bus ride. The 137. Goes all the way. Oh, lucky you.'

'I'll pick you something up if you like.'

Tilly shakes her head, mournfully. 'No point. Once I've spawned it'll be corduroy the colour of babysick all the way.'

She's still looking horribly pale. There are lines of strain round her eyes and mouth.

'You look like you could do with a sit-down,' I tell her. Not that I fancy one myself, of course.

She glances surreptitiously at Mary over her shoulder. Beatrice and the vicar are the only people in the room who aren't standing up.

'I'll come and sit with you.'

'I . . . yuh, OK. That would be nice. Perhaps we can talk to Granny.'

I wait for Tilly to hoist her stomach over a Louis XV gilt armchair, follow her over to where Beatrice perches on the very edge of the sofa, nursing her gin and talking to the vicar.

'Good evening,' says Beatrice, with a gracious inclination of the head. 'So glad you could join us.'

'How are you this evening, Granny?' asks Tilly, parking herself on the far side of the vicar. I pull up a Victorian nursing chair and make a fourth.

'*Very* well, thank you,' replies Beatrice. Then again, she's the sort that would say that if her left leg were hanging off. 'And how are *you*?'

'Your grandmother was telling me,' says the vicar, 'about the war.'

Of course she was.

'Oh, yes?' says Tilly. 'Were you telling him about the refugees?'

'Cockneys,' says Beatrice. 'Ghastly. Used to scream when they saw a cow.'

'I don't suppose many of them had seen one before,' I interject. 'They'd come as a bit of a shock to most people if they didn't know what they were.'

Beatrice waits two beats and says, pointedly, to the vicar: 'I don't suppose you've been introduced to my new nurse, Miss Kalamata.' She lowers her voice, says in a stage whisper: '*Austrralian*, you know.'

The vicar clasps me into a clerical handshake: all trained warmth and practised distance. 'I'm so sorry. I thought you were—'

'I am.'

'Ah. And how are you finding our little slice of England? Quite a contrast with what you're used to, I should think.'

'It's . . . beautiful. Really beautiful.'

'I don't suppose,' he's got that fruity, pastoral voice, the sort that pauses for little lip-twitches every time he uses an adjective, as though they make him Oscar bloody Wilde or something. Useful for joshing with spinsters, I guess, 'I should be saying this as a man of the cloth, but it's as close to heaven on earth as one could come.' He pauses for effect. 'In my view.'

'Simply heaven,' says Tilly, and they all nod and murmur in agreement.

What is it with these people? Prenatal lobotomies?

Beatrice turns to me. 'And will you be staying with us long?'

I give it another go. 'I don't know. I was hoping for the rest of my life. Depends how long Rufus will have me.'

'I daren't really think that . . .' she begins. Then she stops, colours slightly, says: 'Oh' in a voice redolent with significance.

Then she hoists the chin and turns away, presenting a haughty profile like the queen on a stamp. 'I wonder,' she says vaguely to the room, 'how long dinner will be.'

'I think it's all ready, Granny,' says Tilly, 'on the hotplates. We can go in when . . .'

Goody. More congealed stew, dried-out potatoes and limp

vegetables that have been there since half-past five, when Mrs Roberts left. The food here makes hospital food look luxurious. Mary would rather put up with anything than have to turn her hand to domestics. I'd been hoping there might have been some sort of regime change for company, but it seems not.

Beatrice raises her voice. 'Mary? Mary!'

Mary breaks away from Mrs Vicar, smiles her perfect smile. 'Yes, Beatrice?'

'I think it's time we went through.'

'I thought we'd have another drink, first. It's only eight o'clock.'

'No,' says Beatrice firmly. 'I want to go through *now*.'

Something's up, obviously. I've put my clodhoppers in it again, but I'm not sure how.

Mary, surprisingly meekly, obeys her mother-in-law's command. Calls the party to order and starts to usher them towards the dining-room door.

Still keeping her face turned away from me, Beatrice fishes about for her cane, which is propped up against the sofa arm. I try and make up for whatever it is I've done, leap to my feet.

'Let me give you a hand, Beatrice,' I offer.

Cane in hand, she stops, looks at me with gimlet eyes, the way a magistrate would look at a burglar. 'I think not,' she says.

And those are the last words she addresses to me all night.

Chapter Twenty-Five
Packing

'What's eating your nan?'

'Oh, nothing. She's just bonkers.'

'Yeah. Even Blind Freddie could see that. What do you think I ought to take?'

'As little as possible, if I were you. You know what the trains are like, and it's not like you're going to end up short of clothes, after all.'

'True. What are you going to do without me all this time, you sad little man? A whole night?'

'I don't know. Drink a solitary bachelor whisky and cry into my pillow, I should think. Tell you what, though, I might bring Fifi in with me for a bit of company. Be good to have a beautiful face to wake up to for a change.'

I lob a shoe at him.

'No,' he says, 'I thought I'd go and hang around with Roly, actually.'

'Ah, charity work?'

'Don't be nasty about Roly, darling.'

'Well, come on, babe. He's a bit of a sad, isn't he?'

'Yyeess. But there's reasons for that.'

'I'm sure there are.'

'No, look. Seriously. He's my oldest friend, and I know he can be a bit of a buffoon, but most things that could have gone wrong have gone wrong for him. Pretty much from the start. The poor chap's frightfully lonely and doesn't know any other way of dealing with it than bluffing it out. You know what people are like around here. Hardly anybody bothers with him.'

'And none of that's his fault, of course?'

'Yes . . . I know. But the bullshitting . . . he can't really help it, you know. He had a horrid time of it as a kid. Parents were bullshitters too, and they couldn't be bothered with him. If he hadn't had us to come and stay with, he'd have probably ended up under a bridge somewhere. He lives in a shitty little ex-council bungalow over at Kingham, and he's done damn well to manage to scrape together enough for that, and every business he's tried to set up has gone belly-up, and all the little madams around here laugh at him, and underneath it all he's got this big, gentle, bruised heart and I'm not going to let him down like everyone else has.'

'OK. OK. You're a kind guy. I'll back off.'

'Yuh, I'd rather you did.'

He changes the subject. 'Now. Got the key to the house?'

'Mmmhmm.'

'Remember the address?'

'Yeah, yeah. Twelve Anderson Street, SW3. Off the Kings Road. Hilary knows I'm coming. Do I have to talk to him?'

'Yes,' he says firmly.

'Oh, Rufus, *pleeease*.'

He lobs the shoe back.

'Can't I just borrow one of the cars and drive up and back inside the day? They must have parking in London? Surely you can spare a car for a day?'

'Oh, darling, I'm sorry, but I haven't got round to changing the insurance yet.'

'Oh.'

'I know. I'm sorry.'

'So there are three cars out there and I can't drive any of them?'

He shakes his head. 'I'm really, really sorry. I've been snowed under since we got home, you know that. No-one's done a thing since I left. It's like they think the accounts fairy does everything.'

'Well, you'd better do it quick–smart, mate. I haven't been able to leave this place without asking someone to drive me. I'll go insane.'

'I know. It's wrong of me.'

'Tell you what, I'll hire one.'

162

'There's no need.'

I'm annoyed; dig in my documents pocket, looking for my passport and driver's licence, while I talk. 'Well, there is, actually. I don't mind playing the little woman now and again, but I'm not going to sit twiddling my thumbs in an unheated room while I wait for you to be finished with your important work. And come to that, how come you can't give me some of it, if it's such a bloody burden? I *did* run my own business back home, you know.'

'That's kind,' he says, 'and I'll take you up on it once I've caught up on the backlog. But it would probably take longer to explain to you than it would to do it myself.'

'Sorting a few receipts out would hardly be beyond me.'

'It's hardly a one-woman reflexology practice.'

'Don't be a patronising twat.'

'It's pronounced "twot",' he replies mildly.

'There you go again. Where the hell are they?'

'What?'

'My passport and driver's licence. They're not in here.'

'Are you sure you didn't take them out and put them somewhere?'

'No I bloody didn't.'

'Even when you dumped everything out on the floor the other night?'

'Yes.'

'Well, I don't know, then.'

'This is serious, Rufus. If I've lost my ID, I'm cactus.'

'I'm sure it'll turn up.'

'Yes, but you know what? I want to go and get on the net and book myself a car right now.'

'The net?'

'Yes. You know. Global interweb? Worldwide watsername? Electronic interface with all the world's businesses?'

'We're not on the web here.'

'You're not on the . . . what is this? Amish hour?'

'The lines are so old they won't support it, and we're so isolated we'd have to pay to have them upgraded. And anyway, Mummy thinks it will flood the house with unsolicited pornography.'

163

'God Almighty. You really are all obsessed with sex. Where the hell have they gone?'

'You *do* lose things, Mel. I'm sure they'll turn up.'

'Do I? Like what?'

'Your address book, the other day. And when you just left your wedding ring in the fruit bowl . . .'

'I didn't. Seriously. You've got a poltergeist. I *know* I left it by the side of the basin in the downstairs washroom.'

'Mmm,' he says doubtfully.

'You think I'd just forget about something like that?'

Rufus shrugs.

'I'm not that forgetful, Rufus. And you saw yourself. I was looking for the address book in the knicker drawer. You saw me. And the next day – bingo, there it was again.'

'There's a thing called negative hallucination,' he says.

'There's a thing called patronising the tits off people, too. Andrew used to do that. He was always on my back about being clumsy, and losing things, and in the end I got so tense it ended up being ten times worse.'

'Don't,' he says, 'compare me to Andrew. That's not fair. I thought we agreed.'

'Well, don't behave like him, then.'

'I'm not. I was just . . .'

I feel – got at. Slightly . . . I don't know. I hate losing things, and I hate the way men always seem to turn you losing things into an excuse for giving you lectures in life-skills rather than just giving you a hand. And because it's Rufus, not just any old guy, it suddenly makes me almost tearful.

'Well, don't! OK?' I snap. 'My vital documents have disappeared, and aside from the serious inconvenience, it's really weird!'

'Calm down, Mel. I'm sure they'll turn up.'

'And if they don't?'

'We'll get them replaced.'

'And in the meantime, I can't hire a car, and you couldn't put me on the insurance for the three bloody cars that are rotting away in the driveway even if you *could* be bothered to prioritise.'

I can feel myself getting worked up.

'I'll make sure,' he says, 'that someone will always take you about if that's what you want.'

'That's not the point! It's not the point!'

'No. No, I can see that. Look, can I suggest something?'

'Fire ahead.'

'Why don't you . . . just try and have a nice day tomorrow, and we'll worry about it later?'

'What, send the little lady shopping and it'll all be all right?'

'Mel . . . get a grip. I'm on your side.'

I'm about to explode. And then I remember who I'm talking to.

'Yeah, you're right. I was about to toss the dummy, wasn't I?'

'About to?'

'Point taken.'

'You're a proper little firebrand, aren't you?'

'He said, twiddling his moustaches.'

'Come here.'

'Come and get me.'

'That's a very nice vest you're wearing, Mrs W.'

'Thank you. I stole it from my husband. It's a bit big, of course.'

'Could probably fit the both of us in it if we tried.'

'You think?'

'Want to try?'

'We could give it a go. Just stick your head up here.'

'Golly. I can see your bosoms.'

'That's where I keep 'em.'

'Haven't lost those, yet, then.'

'Ha ha.'

The door opens. 'Darling,' says Mary, 'I was just – oh.'

I slap Rufus about the head. He struggles back out from under my underwear, pink-faced and giggly. 'Oh, hi, Ma. Mel just lost her . . . I was just looking . . .'

'I'm sorry to interrupt. I was just going to offer you a hot-water bottle.'

'Um . . . thanks. I don't think we need one, do we, darling?'

I can't hold back a giggle. 'No. No, you're all right, Mary. Thanks for the offer.'

She looks like she's swallowed a plum stone. 'Sorry for . . . disturbing you.'

'That's quite all right,' I say nicely. 'I'm sure it was more of a shock for you than it was for us.'

Mary retreats, quick-smart. Pulls the door to without a sound.

Once we're sure she's out of earshot, we look at each other and start to laugh.

'You must've had a hell of an adolescence,' I say.

'Boarding school,' he says. 'You never get any privacy. So I suppose you don't even think about it at home.'

'God, I can just see all the furtive fumbling you guys got up to.'

Rufus shakes his head, starts to peel the vest off. It's bloody freezing, despite the morose efforts of the two-bar electric fire. I shimmy round the side of him, dive into bed.

'You've really got to get a lock for that door,' I tell him.

Chapter Twenty-Six
Clompy Shoes

So it's not long into the day – half-past breakfast to be exact – that I get my reminder of just how much of a prisoner I am at Bourton. Because just as I'm about to get into the car for my lift to the station, the phone goes and it's the Customs and Excise, and Rufus has to go and take the call because he's the only person in the entire household who knows anything about it, everyone else just wanting to live off the proceeds without having to dirty their hands with commerce. So I'm left hanging about, watching the precious time tick away. I decide to go and hang about in the front courtyard and wait for him.

The rain's stopped, anyway. I suppose one should be grateful for small mercies, especially in a climate like this. I pause on the threshold, listen to the drip-drip-drip of the drainpipes, sniff the sweet damp air. You can almost smell the cleanness. God, it could be heaven, this place: it's just amazing how people can make a hell. Folding my arms, I crunch my way across the gravel. I've got no idea where I'm going, but I'm not hanging around here for anybody's money.

Halfway across the yard, I begin to pick up a distinct whiff of nicotine. I can't see where it's coming from. But it's a smell that's seriously attractive. There's a low murmur of voices somewhere: two female voices. A giggle, a returning laugh, and someone says: 'I think the worst thing, on top of all the other humiliations, is having to wear these clompy bloody shoes. I never knew how much I loved my kitten heels till I started falling off the things. I mean, how can anybody feel sexy in rubber-soled moccasins?'

'You're right there,' replies the other voice, which, to my interest, is Australian. 'But at least you're not condemned to them for bloody life like I am. Anyway: I don't know if you've noticed, but you've got a basketball stuck up your skirt.'

'Thanks for the reminder,' says the first voice wryly. 'And there was me having managed to forget about it.'

They laugh again. It's the sort of relaxed, easy exchange that I've so far failed to register in my brief time at Bourton Allhallows. Mildly curious, I head towards the gate, because I assume that the voices must be coming from the other side of the wall. And just as I get there, the Aussie voice, raised for my benefit, suddenly says, from the depths of one of those foul variegated evergreen bushes with the shiny leaves that look as though they have been extruded in a plastics factory: 'And talk of the devil. How's it going down at the Fight Club, then?'

I take a couple of steps closer, peer in among the foliage. The bush, massively overgrown because it has the space to be so, has created, in straining towards the distant sunlight from its north-facing position, a perfect little outdoor room between itself and the wall, maybe two metres across. And standing inside it, in the process of passing a cigarette from one pair of extended fingers to another, are my sister-in-law, Tilly, and a woman, around my age, whose practical mouse-coloured bob is lifted by streaky golden highlights, and who sports the navy-blue polyester-and-wool uniform of a private nurse above brown boat shoes. She grins: a toothy, open faced grin that goes all the way up to the eyes.

'G'day,' she says. 'Just topping up our dopamines.'

'For God's sake, don't lurk,' says Tilly. 'If Mary catches us, there'll be hell to pay.'

I push my way through the thinner leaf cover by the wall, land up in their damp, composty hideout. The ground is littered with butts. They obviously come here on a regular basis.

'Hi,' I say.

'Hi,' says Tilly. 'Please don't tell anyone. I don't do it very often. I was just a bit wound up this morning, and—'

'Not my place to judge,' I tell her. 'There are quite enough people turning pregnant women's bodies into guilt factories without me putting my oar in.'

She looks relieved. 'I don't suppose you've met Nessa yet, have you?'

The nurse and I shake hands. I've caught the odd glimpse of her wheeling Beatrice about the place, but to be honest, I've tended to wheel myself off in the opposite direction when I have. 'Glad to meet you,' she says. 'Nessa O'Neill. Welcome to the house of fun.'

Tilly bursts into a peal of half-tearful laughter. 'God, Nessa,' she says, 'I don't know how I'd get through the day if it wasn't for you.'

'Steady on,' says Nessa cheerfully. 'There's always methadone.'

'Don't suppose I could have one of those, could I?' I gesture at Nessa's packet of Superkings. 'I'm not having the best day myself, so far.'

She presses them into my hand. 'You'll get used to it. Might even start to find it funny, one day.'

There's an odd, choked little laugh from Tilly. 'Well, I suppose if car crash vids are your idea of fun. . .'

'Come on,' says Nessa kindly. 'I keep telling you, darly: treat it like you fetched up in the middle of a drag show.'

Tilly snatches my cigarette from between my fingers, pokes it between her lips. Takes a tiny, teenager's mouthful of smoke and puffs it out immediately. The baby's going to get far more oxygen from the hyperventilation than it ever is nicotine, the way she's smoking.

'I thought you were going up to London today?'

'I was. Still am if Rufus can ever tear himself away from the accounts for five minutes.'

'God, and you must have been looking forward to it so much.'

'You're not wrong there. I'm starting to get cabin fever down here.'

'Castle fever,' says Nessa.

'Going to get dry rot of the brain soon,' I say.

'I'm sorry,' says Tilly, 'if I'm not . . . you know. . . I know it must be difficult for you, and really, I can't tell you how happy I am that Rufus. . . And you seem really. . . anyway.'

I wonder, not for the first time, if it's the hormones that have made her lose the ability to finish her sentences. 'No worries, Tilly.' I take the cig back. 'I'm made of sterner stuff than you think.'

'Ooh,' she says, 'I don't think you are.'

I'm about to get a bit narky when she stutters, continues: 'I mean – I mean . . . sorry. My mouth doesn't seem to work any more these days. What I mean is, I thought you were made of stern stuff the minute I clapped eyes on you . . . no, that's not what I meant, either. But, you know, I'm not under . . . underestimating . . . that's what I mean. Oh God, I wish my back didn't hurt.'

'As your medical adviser,' says Nessa, 'I think you should go and put your feet up on a large sofa somewhere. Read a book. There must be something you can read in that library.'

'I can't,' she says. 'Someone'll come along and tell me I shouldn't be wasting time lying around reading on a lovely day like this.'

'It's not a lovely day,' Nessa points out. 'It's a typical shitty British early winter day. If you don't go and clock up some rest, I'll set your grandmother on you.'

'Oh God. Anything but that,' says Tilly. 'Can I . . .? Thanks.'

I hand her the cig.

'*Anyway*,' says Nessa, 'you'll be best off in the library. I don't think any member of your family has ever gone in there in the time I've been working here.'

Tilly hands me back the cig, does that pregnant-lady thing of prodding at the small of her back with opened fingers. 'Daddy sometimes goes in to look up Latin for the *Telegraph* crossword. I'm not sure what there is to read, though.'

'Books?' ventures Nessa.

'I suppose there might be some Dickens in there. And a full complement of gothics.'

'That's the spirit. Try *Hard Times*. That'll cheer you up.'

'Knowing my luck,' says Tilly, 'all I'll find is the complete *Clarissa*, and strain my wrist trying to hold it up.'

'Is your back really bad?' I ask.

Her hands fly immediately to the small of her spine. 'Awful. Feels like red-hot needles. It's 'cause the cartilage is softening.'

'And stress,' adds Nessa.

'We don't suffer from stress in this family.'

'No,' says Nessa drily. 'Well, I can think of certain individuals who have managed to avoid it most of their lives.'

'If you like,' I offer, 'I could come and give it a bit of a rubdown when I get back from London. Your back, I mean. You look like you could do with it.'

Tilly brightens visibly. '*Would* you? All this waddling . . . I don't know . . . Bit tense, I suppose . . .'

'Sure.'

'Awfully cold in there, of course . . .'

Tilly is wearing a maternity sack in weighty corduroy, woollen tights, a thick wool jumper with a roll neck and, on top of that lot, a heavy woollen cardigan. You can't tell how fat, or thin, she really is. 'No need. I can do it under your jumper. I can't really give you the full works in your, um delicate condition, anyway. But I can certainly help your back.'

'God,' says Tilly, 'that would be . . . yuh. Thank you.'

'That's a date, then. Hopefully I'll've got myself fully kitted out in Harvey Nicks' best designer thermals by then.'

'God . . . poor you . . . gosh. Are you dying?'

'Not dying, exactly. But my fingers turned blue the other day.'

'Happens to me every time,' says Nessa. 'Though I'm not sure if it's entirely related to the heating. Go *on*, Tilly, for heaven's sake. You look like your bladder could do with emptying, as well.'

'Well . . . you know . . .' says Tilly, clomping from foot to foot, 'coffee in, coffee out.' She starts to push her way through the leaves, turns and says: 'I don't know why people keep insisting on calling it a delicate condition. I feel like an elephant.'

'Look like one too,' shoots Nessa, leans back against the wall, taps another cigarette out into her hand and says: 'I don't go on duty for another five minutes.'

Tilly shooshes her way away. Nessa sparks up, raises an eyebrow over the flame and says: 'So how about you, girl? How you doing?'

'OK,' I say.

'No, really?'

171

'I'll survive.'

'That bad, eh?'

'They're quite a family.'

'Sure are. You've got your work cut out for you there. When I heard Rufus had married an Aussie, I thought, I'll bet she doesn't have a clue. Probably thinks they *all* talk like they've got lockjaw.'

'You were right there,' I say.

'Always am,' says Nessa. 'I mean, how could you imagine a spunk like Rufus could be related to a gaggle of inbreeds like this lot? Tell you what, he's a credit to himself, that boy. And Tilly, too. Amazing how some people can get hopeless parenting from the word go and *still* come out on top, isn't it?'

'Yeah,' I say. It is pretty amazing, really. But I know quite well that kids don't always come out like the people who raised them. 'You know what?' I continue. 'I wouldn't mind, but it's the way they're under the impression that *they've* got the raw end of the bargain.'

She laughs. 'I'm afraid that's pretty much all the English, all the time. I've never met such a race for thinking they were giving benediction to the rest of the world. Not quite all of them, mind. A fair number have moved on, especially in the cities, but you get the impression that a lot of them have never got over losing the empire. Still congratulating themselves on bringing bureaucracy to India.'

'How long have you been here, then?'

'Eight years, going on. Married a pom.'

'And you get used to it?'

'Fairly much?'

'Where did you come from.'

We're slipping into the Aussie inflection: one minute talking, and all our statements end with question marks. Except, of course, the questions.

'Melbourne? You.'

'Brizzie?'

'You don't sound like you're from Brizzie?'

'No,' I tell her. 'We were in Sydney at first? Then Canberra? We didn't fetch up there till I was eleven?'

'Oh, right. I know how that is. We started off in Perth? Didn't go to Melbourne till I was eight? Your mum and dad OK with you taking off like this, then.'

'They have to be?'

'They coming over for a visit.'

'Sure. I don't know when, though? Thought it might be an idea to wait for spring?'

'Wise,' she says. 'It's a lot better here once the days get a bit longer. If you can put them off till June, all the better. They might have some chance of two days on the trot without rain, then. So how you getting on with Mary?'

'Pass.'

Nessa laughs. 'Never underestimate the attachment of the *grande dame* to her firstborn.'

I don't even really notice it at the time. Dismiss it as a slip of the tongue. Firstborn son is what she means, of course.

'She's one scary lady,' continues Nessa.

'Oh, thank God,' I say. 'I was beginning to think it was just me.'

'Huh-uh. Scares the hell out of me, and I don't scare for *nobody*.'

'What do you reckon's my best tack?'

Nessa considers this. Takes another drag on her ciggy. 'Keep your head down for forty years and hope for the best?'

'Thanks. That's a big help.'

'I'd move to the other side of the world and change your name. Maybe have surgery?'

The Great Hall door opens and footsteps crunch across the yard.

'Talk of the devil,' says Nessa.

'Oi!' shouts Rufus. 'Nessa! Have you got my wife in there with you?'

'What's it to you?' she shouts back.

'I've come to take her to London.'

'About bloody time,' I say.

Nessa slouches against the wall again. 'Just finish this off. Have a good time.'

'Thanks. Good to meet you.'

'Good to meet you,' she says.
I start to push my way out through the foliage.
'Oh, and Mel?'
I turn to look at her.
'You know where I am, eh?'

Chapter Twenty-Seven
Brief Encounter

Well, I'm not going to pretend otherwise: I like to shop. I like it a lot. Not to the degree my mum likes it, where it's near obsessive-compulsive, but after my weeks of freezing rural dowdiness the sight of Knightsbridge is enough to set off a feeding frenzy. Within four hours of touching down at Paddington, I am staggering under the weight of the ankle-length dresses, knee-boots, velvet trousers, high-grade woollens, gloves, vests, hats and coats that will make life bearable in my new world. And with Christmas racing up towards me at an alarming pace, I've taken the opportunity to load up with what I hope might be appropriate gifts. It isn't so easy, buying stuff for people who make it so clear that they don't value anything that hasn't been inherited. I have been so enthusiastic that I have amassed a collection of sixteen separate carrier bags, and realise at about three o'clock that I am no longer capable of manhandling them without the help of wheels.

So I hail a taxi on Sloane Street and tell it to take me round the corner to the house where Hilary lives in solitary splendour.

I'm in a good mood. Successful shopping does that to you; it satisfies some sort of base hunter-gatherer instinct and leaves you feeling as though you are competent to survive in a fertile world. I guess that's why those bad shopping trips – the ones where every spot of cellulite stands out under the changing-booth lighting like the gone-cold skimmings off a stockpot, where clothes dig in under your stomach and make your breasts look like bags of slugs, where your toes poke out of dainty open-toed mules like chipolata sausages – are doubly depressing. It's not just the grim realisation that the flesh is not only weak, but stretches as well: it's the sense of failure. The feeling that someone, somewhere has got some quarry with your name on it. Usually someone whose arse doesn't resemble a sack of marbles.

The house is medium-sized, white, elegant, understated. Not unlike my husband, really. I pay off the cabbie, finish listening to his Ph.D. thesis on the evils of immigration and mount worn stone steps, dropping bags all around me as he separates out his tip from his fare, elbow leaning on the doorframe.

Behind a discreet navy-blue door, all shiny brass handles and knockers, I find myself in a narrow, high-ceilinged hallway – polished wooden floor, and a couple of wishy-washy oil paintings depicting dusty vistas that I guess are probably somewhere in Tuscany. A walnut console table displays a Staffordshire bowl brimming with short-stemmed white roses. A couple of Arts and Crafts wooden chairs stand on either side. Now, this is more like it.

I drop my bags by the table and call out: 'Hello?'

Over the swoosh of London's perpetual traffic, a sudden change to the nature of the silence. As though someone, sitting quietly somewhere, has stopped what they were doing and is listening. 'Hello? Anybody at home?'

I feel slightly bashful, despite the fact that I know that I have every right to be here.

A door under the stairs opens, and Hilary's head pops out. 'Ah,' he says. Not what one would call an effusive welcome.

I flash him a smile. 'Hi.'

'I wasn't expecting you until later,' he says.

'Yeah, well, I sort of ran out of arms.'

Hilary glances down at the pile of bags at my feet. 'So I see.'

'I'm gasping for a cup of tea,' I inform him. 'And a wash up. Is there anywhere I can . . .'

He flicks his eyes stairwards. 'The kitchen and the drawing room are on the first floor. Master bedroom at the top.' No offer to give me a hand or show me about.

'Oh, OK. Thanks,' I say with an irony that goes unacknowledged.

I walk past him and mount the stairs, feeling conspicuous. The kitchen is on the half-landing: tiny and twee, with floor-to-ceiling cupboards and not a stitch out of place. The exact opposite of the one at Bourton. I rifle through the cupboard nearest the sink and find a box of Earl Grey teabags, go to fill up the kettle.

He speaks from close behind me, over my right shoulder. He's followed me up the stairs so silently that I have been unaware of his presence.

'So,' he says, 'we're alone.'

I jump out of my skin. If I were a cat, I'd be hanging from the ceiling wallpaper.

'Jesus!' I say. 'You made me jump!'

He's standing far too close. Smiles a crooked little smile at me, purses his lips. 'Why?' he asks. 'Guilty conscience?'

I flip round to look at him. 'Sorry?'

'Why?' he asks. 'What have you done?'

'No, I mean – I'm not sure I heard you correctly . . .'

'Oh, I wouldn't think that if I were you,' he says. Smirks.

OK. So we're playing silly buggers.

'Would you like a cup of tea?' I ask.

He hasn't moved back. Still stands so close I can practically feel his breath.

'You're very quick to play the hostess,' he says.

I don't rise to it. 'No? OK,' I say. Try to sidestep round him to get to the fridge. I feel deeply uncomfortable. Not surprising, really. That's what I guess he's trying to make me feel.

He doesn't shift out of the way. To get to the milk, I'll have to put my head at crotch-level to his knife-pressed twill trousers. 'Excuse me,' I say.

Hilary puts a hand on the countertop. 'Why? What have you done?'

I stand back up. 'Never mind.'

'Mind what?'

I look him up and down. He's quite a fascinating specimen, in a way. Gay men don't come like that in my generation. Maybe that's just because we're not old enough yet. After all, it takes several decades of plucking and cold cream to achieve that shiny, plasticky, testosterone-free texture to the skin. Hilary looks like he's gone at

177

his masculinity with an ice-cream scoop. I suspect that the way men like him made themselves socially acceptable among a generation who were still, many of them, saying things like, 'I just can't bear to think about the things they *do*' was to make it look like they would never, ever, dirty themselves up with something like sex, to turn themselves into effective eunuchs. He must spend hours every day shaving and ironing and arranging things *just so*. His trousers are waisted and loose-cut around the groin to make it look like there's nothing inside them. His hair looks like it's been extruded rather than grown. The backs of his hands are pumice-smooth, the nails filed and buffed, the knuckles waxed hairless. In his top pocket he sports a spotted silk handkerchief which I doubt has ever seen the contents of a nose.

I could take him in a fight, any day.

I don't want to, though. Not just yet, anyway.

I smile pleasantly. 'I'm sorry if it's a pain, me turning up like this,' I say. 'Please don't feel you have to hang about with me out of politeness. I can look after myself.'

'I'm sure you can,' he says. And then he reaches out and, with one of those sexless hands, cups my right breast, firmly and contemplatively, and gives it a squeeze, as though he were testing a melon.

Chapter Twenty-Eight
A Conversation

'Bourton Allhallows.'

The pips go. I push in my fifty pee. They go away. I add 'cellphone' to my mental shopping list.

'Hello?'

'This is Bourton Allhallows.'

'Mary?'

'Yes?'

'Hi, it's Melody. I'm on a payphone.'

'Oh, yes?' She says this in the sort of voice you use when someone calls back from the electricity company to tell you how come your bill has suddenly doubled overnight. Maybe she's distracted or something.

'Mary, is Rufus about?'

'No.'

A pause. I wait for her to qualify the statement and watch the pennies ticking down on the crystal display.

'No, he's not about, or no he's not near the phone?'

'I—'

'Because if he's not near the phone, could you let him know and I'll call back in five minutes?'

'He's not about.'

'Oh. OK. I'll try him on the cellphone.'

'All right.'

She hangs up. No bothering with pleasantries or suchlike.

I have to pop into a shop to get some change. The nearest one is a health food shop. I have a hell of a time identifying anything at all that will actually produce any change from my five-pound note, eventually buy a bag of liquorice root. It costs £2.95 for five sticks. Unbelievable. Chew as I dig in my bag for the number.

'Hello?'

'Oh. He's left it behind, then?'

'I'm sorry?'

'He's left it . . . it's Melody again, Mary.'

'Oh.'

Well, who the hell did you think it was? The Queen Mother?

'I guess he's left it behind.'

'Yes. It was on the table.'

'Right. Is he due back at any point?'

'Yes.'

'Well, could you give him a message for me?'

'Yes.'

'Thank you.'

Another silence.

'Could you tell him,' I ask, 'that I've decided not to stay up in London? You wouldn't believe it, but I've got everything done already.'

'Oh yes?'

I don't mention Hilary. I've decided not to till I can see him face-to-face and there's no point telling *her*. It's too extraordinary a story to waste on a phone call.

'Yeah.' I attempt once more to engage her interest. 'It's great shopping up there. I've had a great time. I've bought some fabulous things.'

Now, any normal woman would, at this point, want to know what. Mary, instead, says: 'Oh yes?'

'So anyways, I thought I'd jump on the four forty-eight. Can you ask him to come pick me up?'

'If I see him.'

'Well, where is he? Is he somewhere I can call him?'

'I think he went out,' she says, 'to see Roly Cruikshank.'

Oh, yes, he did, didn't he?

'Oh, right. Have you got the number there?'

'No.'

180

'Mary, I'm running out of money. Can you call him, please, at Roly's, and let him know? I'm sorry to be a nuisance.'

She sounds like she's staring out of the window. 'Of course,' she replies vaguely.

'The train gets in to Moreton just after six.'

'Yes.'

'If you could let him know. Please?'

'Have a nice trip,' she says.

'Thanks. I'll see you later.'

'Thank you for calling,' she says. 'Goodbye.'

Chapter Twenty-Nine

Stranded

He's a nice guy, my cab driver. A man called Matthew Baker. There's a Gloucestershire type that's got a casual dignity about them that really warms your cockles. Mind, I think I'd probably have fallen in love with a one-armed jelly-wrestler after ninety minutes on Moreton station. It's not come as a hundred per cent surprise to me, after the tone of my exchange with Mary, but there's been no sign of Rufus, and every phone I have tried – house, office, and, with sinking heart, the abandoned cellphone – rings out with an unfriendly finality. By the time I've tracked down the business cards taped to the inside of the firmly locked ticket office door, located an eye-pencil at the bottom of my bag and scribbled the numbers on the back of my hand, called three men with garages who said they only picked up personal friends of their wives at three weeks' notice, finally found Matthew and waited, huddled on a bench that's only half-sheltered by the roof overhang of the padlocked waiting room, until he got finished with his pickup over at Kiftsgate, I'm dripping, and so are my new clothes, and I'm as glad to see him as I would have been if he'd been Keanu Reeves come sauntering out of the sea in a skin-tight rubber T-shirt.

'You're soaking,' he says, observantly.

'That'll be because it's raining,' I tell him.

'It does that,' he informs me. 'Don't suppose you're used to a lot of rain where you come from.'

'Oh, no, we get rain. Just not twenty-four/seven. It stops, sometimes, back home.'

'Sometimes,' he says gravely, 'it stops here too. You can go . . . ooh . . . two, three days with nothing but sunshine come June, July.'

He leads me to an old but lovingly maintained Ford Escort. The seats are protected by a sturdy layer of shrink-wrap plastic, and the interior smells strongly of pine air freshener. There is one of those cardboard things in the shape of a Christmas tree dangling from the rear-view mirror. Combined with the smell of my wet shoes, wet hair and sodden clothes, it produces a fug so powerful that I have surreptitiously to wind the window down and lean my face into the damp breeze in order to stop myself from chundering.

'Bourton Allhallows, was it?'

'Got it in one, Matt. You've just about saved my life, I reckon.'

'Someone forget to come and pick you up, did they?'

'Something like that, yeah. And now no one's answering the phone. The lines must be down or something.'

'That,' he says, looking to left and right as he waits to pull out on to the main road, 'sounds like the beginning of one of them old black-and-white horror movies.'

I shiver, but from cold and dampness rather than anything else. 'Oh, don't. Don't get me started.'

'So what you doing down there? Staying with the family?'

'No. Worse than that. I've married one of them.'

I see him glance at me, interestedly, in the mirror.

'Ah, so you're the one we've been hearing about.'

'All good, I assume,' I half-joke.

A fractional pause. Then his natural politeness kicks in. 'Of course . . . nothing you need to worry yourself about. Mostly speculation.'

'I'm sort of getting used to that,' I say.

'Give it twenty, twenty-five years and they'll be treating you like a local.'

I tuck my hands between my knees in an effort to warm them up. 'I can't wait.'

'So what do you make of your new home, then?'

'It's . . . interesting,' I say.

Matthew laughs. 'I see you've got your diplomatic skills sorted out.'

We're passing through a darkened Moreton-in-Marsh. When it

looked like I wasn't going to have any luck getting a cab I had thought of walking up into town for warmth and company, but it's all too grimly evident that, out of tourist season, no one keeps their business open longer than they have to. The main street is eerily empty: not even the usual gaggle of teens gathered on a bench somewhere. The tea shops have given up on the crumpet trade for the day. Only the Bell and the Black Bear are open, in a desultory fashion.

'I'll tell you something for free,' says Matthew, 'I don't envy you.'

'Really?'

'What? Go and live in that mouldy old pile? Not for all the tea in China.'

I sit forward. 'You know what, Matthew?'

'What's that?'

'If you didn't have them on the steering wheel, I'd be shaking you by the hand right now.'

'Why's that, then?'

'Do you know, you're the first person who's said anything like that to me since I got here.'

'Sorry if I've said anything out of place,' he says.

'No. The opposite. I was beginning to think I must be mad, or something, the way they all talk. Every time somebody opens their mouth and talks about that place, it's the way people talk about bits of the True Cross or something?'

'Well, you do get some odd people . . .'

'Yes, but it's almost like a religion. You know the word I hear most often in relation to Bourton Allhallows? Heaven. Do you get it? I don't.'

'Hell, in my book.'

'I mean, seriously.'

'Creepy sort of place as well. I should think there's people been done away with up there and nobody any the wiser.'

'And some.'

We come over the crest, and Bourton is laid out below us in moonlight that filters through a break in the cloud cover. In this

184

light, in the distance, it looks spookier than I've ever seen it. Great clods of it lie in utter darkness, shadowed by the wings. The moat is black and oily, and laps against the lower walls as though it wants to swallow them whole. Blank windows stare, empty like the eyes of a psychopath, at us as we approach.

'There aren't any lights on,' says Matthew.

'Probably just looks like it. You know what those windows are like.'

'Are you sure there's someone at home?'

'Yeah. No-one said anything about going out.'

He shrugs. 'Great big cave of a house. I don't suppose you bump into each other all that often.'

'You'd be surprised. The family generally live in four rooms, apart from their bedrooms. You trip over them all the time.'

He shakes his head in amazement. 'Doesn't make sense. All that space, and you're more overcrowded than in a council house.'

'Beats me too. But there you go.'

We get closer. The house really does look dark. I scan the frontage for a chink of light, but nothing shows. I know Rufus is out – or I guess he is. But the family must be scattered about the place somewhere. If we were approaching from the back, the windows would probably be lit up like the fleet, but from this angle the house looks almost derelict.

Matthew pulls into the yard, switches off the engine and looks up at the lowering edifice. 'Are you sure?'

'Yeah, yeah. No worries,' I tell him.

'Do you want me to wait till you're in, at least?'

I'm halfway out of the car, bent double to hook the bags off the back seat. 'That's really kind, Matthew, but you don't need to.'

'You got a key?'

'Left it inside.'

'Oh, well, then. I'll definitely wait.'

I shake my head. 'There'll be my grandmother-in-law and her nurse, if there's no-one else. You go on. You must want to get home. You've saved my life already. What do I owe you?'

Once more, he glances up at the house. 'That's eight pounds, my love.'

I give him my last tenner. I forgot to go to the ATM, I was in such a rush to get the train.

'That's very kind of you,' he says.

'Don't mention it.'

'Are you sure? About me not waiting? You're a long way from anywhere. I wouldn't like to leave you stranded.'

'Stop it,' I say firmly. 'You're starting to sound like one of those movies again. I don't want you giving me the heebie-jeebies.'

'Well, if you're—'

'I am. Thank you.'

He shrugs again. Sparks up the engine. 'All right then. You have a nice night.'

'You too,' I call. Stand in the headlights and wave as he backs up and turns around.

Then once he's beeped the horn and taken off up the drive, I pick up my bags and walk towards the front door.

Chapter Thirty

The Fortress

When the sound of Matthew's engine dies as he crests the hill and enters the woods, the remoteness of Bourton Allhallows becomes crashingly evident. There's the drip of a plaintive gutter, the crackle and fssh of wind in conifers, the sludgy, sulky movement of water in the moat. But there are no comforting background noises, no sounds that help me know that I haven't just dropped off the edge of the world.

My footsteps sound out like an intrusion as I cross the gravel. Now I'm alone I feel vulnerable, as though hidden enemies watch and wait for their moment. I can feel their eyes on me: veiled figures hidden by foliage, crouched among shadows, regarding me with old, old eyes. I am not wanted here, a creature of the new world, disruptor, cranky-voiced invader: with my bright colours, my lanky gait, my unwitting flouting of a million unwritten rules. Mist rises off the surface of the moat, drifts across the water-meadow. I step up my pace, hear my footsteps change as they move on to flagstones, put my hand on the great iron handle, try to turn it.

It holds, solid as though carved from the door itself. I lay down the bags, try again with the full force of both hands, but without success. The door is locked.

A sigh behind me. I jerk to look over my shoulder. The courtyard is empty.

Get a grip.

A bell sits to the right of the door, set in the stonework: one of those old-fashioned ceramic handles attached to a wire that runs all the way to the heart of the house, where a deep-toned brass elephant bell, a souvenir of the Raj, hangs on a pivot. I grasp the handle, haul back against it with all my weight, hear the eerie dong–dong–dong echo through corridors and walls, up desolate staircases, and die away, soaked up by drapes and panels. Then I turn my back to the door, lean against it, for I would rather know what's coming towards me silently across the gravel, and wait.

Nothing stirs within. The house, accustomed for centuries to repelling invaders, sits, broods, awaits my next move.

It's cold. It feels as though the air in this courtyard has been imported direct from the Arctic. I wait for five minutes, hands tucked inside my sleeves like a Mandarin, but there is no welcome sound of approaching footsteps.

Just silence.

Then I try again, though I know that if no-one has responded the first time, they are unlikely to do so to a second. Again: dong–dong–dong, then nothing.

I consider my choices. I don't really have any.

Damn you, Rufus. Why did you bring me to this place?

I don't understand it. It isn't possible that every member of the family has gone out. In the weeks I've been here, nothing of the sort has ever happened. There have been comings and goings, of course, but Beatrice, at the very least, is too old and too gaga to go anywhere much beyond the front step. I leave my shopping bags by the front door and take myself nervously off towards the alleyway that runs between the house and the offices towards the topiary garden.

The house breathes beside me. I pause at the doorway, peer into the gloom. Light barely reaches here, and the path turns the corner of the house before it lets out again. Going in will be like plunging into a cellar. The temptation is to bolt down it, get the ordeal over as quickly as possible, but the paving is a mass of moss and lichen, and my leather-soled town shoes have no grip. I'll have to walk it, feel my way slowly, make certain of each step before I put my weight on it.

Into the dark. Three steps in, and it wraps around me: sodden and grasping, the temperature that of a place that never sees the sun. Before: blackness. Behind: the promise that some figure might block out the light. I edge my way along the house wall, back against it, hand over hand, prickling hairs on the back of my neck, hearing only the sound of my own breaths.

Maybe I should go back. Maybe I should sit on the doorstep and wait.

And no-one will come.

My foot sinks into something deep and slippery, ripping the ground out from beneath me. Going down, I grab and clutch at the wall, scrape skin, fail to save myself. Flounder and bang my head. Damn it, damn it, damn it. The ground is soaking wet, my jeans drenched. I crouch, a hand on each wall, see stars, swear under my breath.

Hear another sigh.

Oh God.

'Who's there?'

No-one answers. Of course they don't.

Sick, sick fear now. Not something you can control. Not a sensation that comes from reason. Somehow I pull myself to my feet and find myself frozen against the wall. Go forward?

I can't see. I can't see what's there.

Back, then . . .

There could be anything.

Breathe. Just breathe.

My mouth is open. I pull my lips together and swallow. Concentrate on breathing in, out, through my nose.

Eventually get my heartbeat under control. My blood still races, but the flutter dies back. *Get a grip, Mel.*

I unstick my feet, move forward. Pass the office window, the tongue-and-groove door. My hand touches a drainpipe. Greasy, wet, icy cold. But manageable. I slide round it. Halfway, now. Something drips on to my shoulder. I shake myself like a dog to get it off, slide forward.

White painted door of the gents' toilet. Something rustles inside.

Rats. It's rats, or some other wildlife in out of the rain. It won't be anything bigger. Just go past.

Another door: the ladies. Almost there now.

A sudden flurry of wings at the far end. Something – one of the doves, perhaps, that roost on the front elevation of the house – taking off and resetting somewhere else.

Yes, but something disturbed it.

I cover the last ten metres at a stumbling, sliding run. Burst out into the moonlit garden with a combined rush of relief and terror. My flight mechanism is well and truly primed now. Stork-like legs carry me across the garden at a speed I hadn't known myself capable of, dodging round the topiaries without allowing myself to register what might be hiding behind them. I lob myself against the garden door, crash through into the backyard and bolt towards the kitchen door.

Not a light on this side of the house, either. I know before I even try it that the door will be locked.

Where are they? Where the hell are they?

The big pines sough above my head.

Where are they?

There is no bell on this side of the house. Tradespeople are supposed to use their hands and wait, I guess: not disturb the residents. I hammer on the door with both fists, shout at the top of my voice: 'Hello? Is there anybody there? Somebody! Let me in!'

The house laughs at me. I can hear it. I can feel it, mocking me: the scorn of bricks and mortar.

'Where the hell are you! Somebody! For God's sake, let me in!'

Nobody comes. These hateful people: they've left me here, out here in the dark. They want me to know.

This is a lonely, threatening place. The drive leads, silver in moonlight, through an avenue of ancient yews, winter foliage dripping, mysterious ticks and clicks as wood and leaf catch the breeze. I don't want to be alone here. Too many spirits, too much history.

In the dark, a figure steps out on to the road in front of me, turns and walks away. It wears a long, black hooded cloak, like a monk or a highwayman, or someone dressed up for Hallowe'en, and moves with a smooth, thoughtful tread. I don't know who it is. Frankly, I don't care.

'Hello!' I call.

He doesn't respond. Just carries on walking, slowly, deliberately, towards the stable block.

I try again. 'Hello? Can you help me? I seem to have got locked out.'

The head is bowed, arms folded across the body. The cloak brushes the ground so that I can't see the feet. He stops. Stands stock still, as though listening.

I've got goosebumps.

'Hello?' I say again, less confidently.

Slowly, the figure turns to look at me.

It has no face.

Chapter Thirty-One

In The Deep Woods

Halfway up the drive, I burst into tears. I'm zonked, and frustrated with myself for being so jelly-kneed that I've actually started hallucinating, and it's as dark as it could be and as cold as a witch's tit, and my husband hasn't even noticed I'm missing, and to cap it all, it's coming back on to rain – a sort of misty, sleety sideways rain that turns my lips blue and cakes my eyelashes – and I'm suddenly fully aware of why the snotty-arsed inhabitants of this shonky bloody country wear anoraks. And yes, I'll admit it: I am scared. I am jangling with it.

I don't believe in ghosts. Any more than I believe in angels or demons or mischievous pixies. But I saw *something* and the brief glimpse of the blank nothingness under that hood before it whisked away into the shrubbery was enough to leave me jittery.

So now I've got bush oysters coming out of my nose, double-wet all over my face and my feet are killing me as I haul butt up the hill in shoes made for swanning about city pavements in. And for some reason, in my head I'm singing a little song to the tune of 'Camptown Races', only it goes 'Who-the-fuck-do-you-think-you-are? Do-dah, do-dah . . .' I'm going to kill Rufus, if I survive long enough to get hold of him.

The anger, at least, is a source of warmth. I could swear the drive has doubled in length since I came down it. By the time I reach the top, sweating inside sopping clothes, it's nine o'clock. The woods, which just seemed raggedy and unloved when we were going down, have taken on an altogether more menacing flavour now that I can't see more than a couple of metres.

Over the soft-shoe shush of my feet on the pitted road, I hear vague rustlings to my left: furtive, creeping, chasing-and-fleeing sounds. Snuffles and lolloping. The crackle of breaking under-growth.

I'm a hundred metres in, and I don't know what to do.

It gets darker with every step. I have to take it slowly, though my instinct is to bail at speed. But I'm mindful of the fact that every time we've come down this way, the Land Rover has bounced through potholes like a fairground ride. The last thing I need on top of my current miseries is a sprained ankle.

Something shrieks over in the forest to my left, and I have a momentary out-of-body experience. When spirit finally reunites with flesh, I am shaking, my heart scrabbling to escape my ribcage, and I seem to have got a good fifty metres further down the road. In fact, I seem to be running, though I have no memory of having started to do so. The edge of my foot hits a hole, and I stumble, stagger, regain – just – my footing and force myself to slow down. It's an effort of pure will. And once again, I'm cursing myself for a sook, because it's not like we don't have owls in Australia.

I walk on, try to keep my thoughts under control, but my pulse still tells me that I'm being stalked by something three metres high with teeth made of old tin cans. I can feel its eyes on my back in the dark. I can feel its breath on my neck. I wish I'd never come here. I'm going to die thousands of miles from home and no-one will ever know. It'll drag me into its lair and make merry with my intestines, and all they'll think is that I took off at the first sign of pressure, probably open a surreptitious bottle of champagne to toast my defeat.

A crash of undergrowth to the right. This time, I know I'm not imagining it. Something burls through the woods at a rate of knots, and it's large enough to break everything it brushes up against. It makes terrible, golloping, slurruping noises as it goes.

I'm not hanging around to see what it is. Belt up the road like greased lightning, don't care if I hit a bump or a hole, because I've got so much adrenalin in my system I could break a leg and not notice till I'd worn the bloody stump all the way to the hip. My vision, suddenly acute despite the gloom, makes out flashes of white keeping pace with me between tree trunks and behind bushes. My tongue is dry and clouds of fog burst from my lips. And the whatever-it-is in the woods is going gloffle–gloffle–ploff–ploff–ploff as it lollops along, demolishing saplings and spraying toadstools in its wake. It seems like a million years till I reach the broken–down gate, bolt through it and scream round the corner into the village.

But there's no salvation here. Bourton Allhallows is a ghost town. The empty-looking houses we passed on the way down are still empty. My pace slows involuntarily as I take in the fact that I'm in a village with no villagers. My pursuer seems to have dropped back when I left the estate, but I'm not out of the woods yet.

I've never been somewhere so quiet. What the hell is going on here?

My ankle hurts where I twisted it on the pothole, and I limp gingerly along the road towards the green. On either side: sightless windows, sagging thatch, stones tumbled from walls left lying at their bases, little plots of front garden strangled by ivy and weeds. I feel like I've been written in to *The Day of the Triffids*.

Another shriek from the woods – a different tone, this time: more panicky, more desperate – cuts off suddenly, encouraging me to step my pace up once again.

There's a light on in the pub. I feel the breath slip from me in a great gush of relief. It's not much of a light, just a single-bulbed lamp in the window of the downstairs bar, but in this lonely gloom, it's as welcome to me as Liberty Island must have been to a zillion refugees.

And then my heavy-breathing woodland pursuer is coming up fast behind, the sound of beastly claws on tarmac, clittering towards me at high speed.

I don't wait to look round. Just take off across the green towards safety. Whatever it is, it's close, now: ghastly, rasping, drool-laden breaths, great slobbering grunts, heavy footfalls on the grass. I don't even stop to think when I get to the creek, just launch myself out over the water, slip as I land and fall in the mud. Push myself up and scarper, soaking and filthy, up the far bank. Gain a couple of seconds as I hear my stalker pause on the other side. Then there's the heaving groan of muscular exertion, and I catch the splash as he – it – lands in my footsteps.

Ten paces away, now. It's gaining on me. I find reserves, deep down, where the bad things are, and put on a final surge. Burst through the door, arms outstretched as it bangs back and bounces off the wall, and tumble into the dark haven of the bar.

Chapter Thirty-Two
No Dogs

Three men sit on high stools under a string of horse brasses, almost brushing the dust from the low beams above their heads. They stop talking as I appear, turn and look at me. And the barman, slowly polishing a pint glass with a piece of grey cloth, says, in a kindly enough tone of voice, 'Sorry, love. We don't allow dogs in the bar, I'm afraid.'

It takes me a moment, through my panic, to make out what he's saying, partly because I don't know what he's talking about, but mostly because I've never heard anyone speak in such a songlike, fifteenth-century way before. This is my first real rural accent. Matthew was Prince Charles in comparison. It's a combination of glottal stops and vowels that manage to be both long and clipped all in one go. It's sort of 'Surryluv. We dow'mer leaw dugs inder baaarrr, Oimer frayed.'

A voice speaks up from a darkened corner, under a display of dust-covered plastic carnations. 'Zpashly no' thapwom,' it says. It belongs to a wizened little goblin with a silver skull dangling from his ear. He cradles a pewter tankard, and has a damp-looking durrey dangling from his lower lip. He gives me a friendly nod.

'Zpashly no' thapwom,' echoes the barman. 'Keeps bringing vermin in. And that don't go down too well with the 'Elf'm'Safety.'

The three bar drinkers are still transfixed, staring at me. One takes a long draught of dark brown beer from a mug, and leaps to his feet.

'G'waaaarn!' he shouts, jerking a hand in the air in my direction. 'Geddewt, y'bugger! And take that with you!'

I start backward. 'Jesus, I'm sorry,' I say.

He bursts out laughing. 'No, not you, darling,' he tell me. 'That bloody dog.'

I look over my shoulder, and find that Fifi is squatting on the stone floor behind me, front paws straddling the bloodied corpse of a rabbit. 'Gloof,' he says, and opens his mouth in a big slobbery grin. I'm so relieved to see that this is my ogre, that I burst out laughing in turn.

'Oh, shit,' I say, 'I'm sorry. He must have followed me.'

'Yeah, he does that,' says the barman. 'He's a friendly old sod, but he dudden half scare the lights out of the tourists.'

'Scared the lights out of me, actually,' I tell him. 'Thought I was being tracked by a werewolf. Fell in that creek out there, trying to get in here before he got me.'

'You're Australian,' says the man in the corner. No shit, Sherlock.

'You're covered in mud,' says one of the men at the bar. I guess stating the obvious is another of those English things I'm going to have to get used to.

I grab Fifi by the collar and drag him, bodily, towards the door. He doesn't resist, but he doesn't co-operate either. You'd never credit how much a full-sized bulldog can weigh until you try to pick one up. There's a metal draught-excluding strip let into the concrete door-sill, and I have to lift him, grunting, over it, limb by limb. As I turn back to collect the rabbit, I hear the clitter of claws, and look round to find that he's back inside the room. Sits, back feet out in front of him, with a big doggy grin on his face like a Chinese Buddha.

'Throw the rabbit,' says the barman. 'He'll go arter it.'

The rabbit, eyes wide open, lies in a small pool of blood, mud and saliva at my feet. 'You've got to be kidding,' I say.

'She's squeamish,' says a voice from behind me. 'Don't they have rabbits in Australia?'

'One or two,' I say slowly, eyeing the smudgy fur for a spot where I might get a handhold, 'but we haven't made throwing them into a competitive discipline yet. We tend to stick to dwarves.'

'Just pick 'im up. 'E's dead, inn'e? 'E ent gonna bite you.'

Fifi watches me speculatively. Goes back further on his haunches as I bend closer to the object of our discussion.

''F'you don't want to touch him,' suggests another voice, 'just get 'im by his hind leg and flip 'im.'

'Thad'll do it,' agrees someone.

I try the charm that seemed to work on Edmund. 'Can't one of you guys do it?' I ask, and bat my eyelashes till I think they're going to take off.

''Snot my rabbit.'

'Well, technically speaking, it's not mine either.'

'You brought it in with you. Just chuck 'im out and get that door closed.'

I swear I'm going to tear Rufus's arm off and beat him to death with it.

I do as I'm told, grab the limp body by one sad little rear paw and hoick it out into the night. Fifi grunts his pleasure, lumbers to his feet and trots off in pursuit. I get the door shut as fast as I can.

I turn back to see three smirks buried behind the rims of beer glasses. All the men at the bar look remarkably alike. Each sports sideburns you could sweep a floor with, and each has hair that curls just below the collar of his leather car coat and a single gold earring, the ring type.

'Sorry about that,' I say.

''Sorlroight,' says the barman. 'What can I get you?'

'Ah,' I say, 'I was rather hoping you might let me use your telephone.'

'Sure,' he says. 'You can use my phone once you've bought a drink.'

'Yeah, look, I'm in a bit of trouble, here.'

All five members of my audience sit forward, eagerly. This is probably the most exciting thing that's happened here all year.

'Thing is,' I continue, 'I've got split up from my husband, and I've got no English money on me.'

'Got split up from your husband?' asks the barman.

'It's a long story. I've got a hundred–dollar bill, if that's any good . . .' I always keep it, folded inside the lining of my bag, against emergencies.

'This is a pub,' says the old bloke in the corner, 'not a bank. You want a bank, go up Moreton.'

'Only it'll be closed by now,' says the man in the footie shirt. 'They ent open all night.'

'I understand that. You see, if I could just borrow the phone and call my husband, he could come and get me, and he could pay you back.'

'How,' asks the man in the stripes, 'do we know you've really got an 'usband?'

I'm not quite sure how to answer this.

'Why have you got American money if you're Australian?' he continues.

'It's easier to change.'

He bellows with laughter. 'Not here it isn't,' he says. 'Looks like you've not been as bright as you think.'

I put my bag down.

'Thing is,' says the barman, 'I've got a business to run here. And I'm not going to be paying the rent if everyone who comes in just uses the phone.'

'I know,' I tell him. 'I'm sorry. But I don't know what else to do.'

Unfriendly bastards. They all just carry on looking at me. 'At this juncture,' I say, 'I'll happily give you all the money I've got if you'll just let me make a call and sit in a corner.'

'Thing is,' says the barman, 'how do I know they'd be real dollars? They could be fakes, for all I know.'

'Yank money,' says Lacoste man wisely. 'Easy to counterfeit.'

I'm gobsmacked.

'See, you can't be too trusting these days,' says striped shirt. 'Asylum seekers and that. For all he knows, you've got some international campaign of terror up your sleeve and he's going to end up chained up blindfold in a Cuban prison camp. Aiding and abetting.'

'That hundred-dollar bill,' says OUFC, 'could be impregnated with deadly spores.'

'Yes,' says Lacoste. 'You could be trying to bring Bourton Allhallows to its knees.'

'I'm not a terrorist. I'm an Australian, for fuck's sake.'

'Ah.' Lacoste wags a knowing finger at me. 'You *say* you're Australian, but for all we know you're fresh from the Osama bin Laden accent school in Afghanistan.'

'Probly,' says OUFC, 'got one of them bourqas on under your jeans.'

'Probly ought to call the police right now,' says the barman. 'Get it over with.'

'Now, hold on,' I begin to protest. Then I notice that all three drinkers have once again buried their faces in their glasses. I relax. Put my bag down. 'Oh, I get it. You're shitting me, right?'

'I thought,' says Lacoste, 'you Australians were meant to have a sense of humour.'

'And I thought,' I put my hands on my hips, 'you poms were meant to have manners.'

'Don't know what gave you that impression.' Soccer man puts down his glass, digs in his pocket and produces a crumpled five-pound note. 'Landlord, a draught of your finest nut-brown ale for the young lady.'

They all snigger. A running gag, evidently.

'Very nice of you, Gary,' says the landlord. He must be in his mid-forties, wears a yellow V-necked pullover. 'What'll it be, young lady?'

'Jeez,' I ham up peering into the gloom around the room. 'I didn't realise you were talking to me.'

They like this. Shift on their bar stools and chortle.

'Thanks, Gary,' I say, 'I'll have a fourex, if you don't mind.'

A hiss of insucked breath. As a man, they point to a plaque screwed on to a vertical beam alongside a list of bar snacks. They do something called Scotch eggs. Sounds tasty. The plaque has the word 'camera' on it, spelled wrong. Which obviously means something.

'Only real ale here,' the landlord informs me. 'None of your fizzy pop.'

'Famous for it,' pipes up the man in the corner. 'Get coach parties coming in the summer. Forty, fifty people, and every single one with a beard like bindweed.'

'OK,' I say, having no idea what the difference between 'real' and – what? virtual? – ale is. 'What have you got?'

He reels off a list. 'Hooky, Dirty, Manky, IPA, Partlington's Old Cock Crow, Badger's Snatch, Wooky, Old Cheeseparer, Chadlington Red, Speckled Beauty, Burpitt and Lurker's Murk. Only that's a porter, which is good on a winter night like this one, only I don't s'pose you'd like it, given that you're used to . . .' He raises an eyebrow at me and enunciates the next word as though throwing down some sort of challenge. '. . . *lager*.'

'Gets in folk singers and all,' continues the man in the corner. 'Hey nonny haystack and that. Cheesecloth. Can't tell Eve from Steve, as they've all got beards. *And* Morris dancers. Out on the green. Kickin' their heels up and making arses of theirselves.'

'Don't confuse the girl, Ian,' says Gary. 'Give her a Hooky and let her get on.'

'Hooky's a bit lively tonight,' says Ian. 'Phone's over there. Why don't you go and call your hubby, and I should have it poured by the time you're done.'

'She'll need 10p,' says Gary.

'So you will.'

He tings open the till and gives me a coin. I duck beneath a collection of dusty thistles and have a go at dialling Rufus. On the third go, after I've taken off some fours and added in some zeros, I get through to his voicemail. Suddenly, instead of sounding mondain and sexy, like it sounded to me in Gozo, his voice sounds dismissive, exclusive, superior. I bite back a rush of misgiving, speak after the tone.

'Yeh, hi, it's me,' I say. 'While you're enjoying yourself, I'm in the pub with a load of blokes in leather jackets. If you want to know why, maybe you'd better ask your mother. I've got no fucking money, and I'm pretty pissed at you, and if you don't come and get me soon I'm giving the landlord my engagement ring in exchange for a lift to the station. OK? Just thought I'd let you know.'

And then I add in a quick loving note at the end for good measure. 'Arsehole,' I say, and hang up.

I feel a bit better after that. Random name-calling is good for morale.

Back at the bar, a glass of something semi-opaque and brown awaits. It's got a few globs of desultory froth on the top.

'Get your mouth round that,' says Ian, flicking at it with his tea-towel. 'You'll never drink your fizzy pop again.'

I take a sip. It's delicious: nutty, bitter and sweet all in one mouthful, twice the density of the beer I'm used to, like drinking a chestnut tree.

'Wow,' I tell him. 'That's really something.'

'Be poetry readings next,' says the fella in the corner. 'Sun-blushed *tomatoes*.'

'You get hold of him?' asks Ian.

'I left a message. Just hope he gets it.'

'It's hours till closing time,' says OUFC. 'We don't mind. You got a name, or shall we just call you Sheila?'

'Melody Katsouris,' I tell him.

He nods. 'Paul.'

'Hi, Paul.'

'And this,' he gestures to the man in the striped shirt, 'is Derek. Only we call him Del-boy.'

'Like on the telly,' says Del-boy.

'He's a little bit bish, he's a little bit bosh, he's a little bit woooah,' says Gary, and they all laugh. I guess barflies speak in secret code the world over.

'And over there, that's Samson.'

'Hi, Samson,' I raise a hand.

Gary lowers his voice to a stage whisper. 'His mum had twelve kids,' he tells me. 'I think she ran out of inspiration.'

'Why is he sitting over there?'

'I'm playing dominoes,' says Samson.

'So what are you doing up this neck of the woods, Melody?' asks Ian.

'My old man's a pom.'

'Local?'

'Just down the road.'

'You're covered in mud, you know,' repeats Paul.

'Soaking wet too.' I'm surprised by how cheerfully I say this. I swallow another mouthful of beer. Beats the hell out of Edmund's wine.

Del-boy offers me a cigarette. I take it, spark up. Accept another half of Hooky and look around me. I guess this must be a traditional British pub. Stone floor just inside the door, red-and-black-and-sludge patterned carpet everywhere else. Nicotine-coloured walls – whether by choice or habit is hard to tell without actually licking my finger and running it over a surface – and hard black beams from which hang several dozen dust-covered objects: a corn dolly; a bit of an old ploughshare; postcards from Benidorm, Tenerife, Kenya, Egypt; a giant cobweb in which a red-and-black butterfly lies mummified; a pair of copper warming pans. Behind the bar, handwritten signs read: 'Please do not ask for credit, as a smack in the mouth often offends', and 'You don't have to be mad to work here, but it helps'. On the bar, a little collection of cruets, paper-napkin-lined plastic baskets full of cutlery, squeezy bottles in red and yellow and brown, and a huge jar of what look like pickled eggs.

'So your old man live around here, then? Or are you just passing through?'

'No. Just down the road.'

He raises his eyebrows, gives the pint glass in his hand a loving rub with a tea-towel. 'Zat so? Where's that, then?'

'Oh for Christ's sake, Ian,' says a familiar female voice, 'do you really want people to think you're as stupid as you look? This is the poor sap who's married Rufus Wattestone.'

Chapter Thirty-Three

The Maven

It's a relief to see her. She must have been in the ladies while I was making my dignified arrival. Nessa advances. 'You're looking glamorous tonight.'

'I've been exploring the local amenities.'

'I didn't know we had a swimming pool.'

'I don't think it's usually open in the winter. They opened it up just for me.'

Nessa laughs. 'And they say you don't need contacts to get the things you want. Paul! Do you not listen to a word I say? Didn't I say we'd got an Aussie living down at the big house?'

'She said her name was Katsouris,' says Paul. 'Not my fault if she's a bra-burner.'

'Melody, meet my first husband, Paul. Paul, this is Melody Katsouris, a.k.a. Mrs Charles Rufus Edmund Callington-Warbeck-Wattestone.'

'Mel.' I shake his hand.

'Come and take a pew,' says Nessa.

'Don't mind if I do.'

We settle at the table in the far corner of the bar, elbows on the surface and knees almost touching.

'So how's your evening shaping up, Mrs W? And what are you doing back already?'

'I'd say I was just about ropeable,' I tell her. And it's such a relief to say it.

'You don't say,' says Nessa. 'What brings you to this genteel hostelry of a winter's night?'

I fill her in on what's happened to me so far. Leave out the ghosties and the ghoulies. I don't want to be carted off on the strength of a figment of my imagination.

'I just don't get it,' I finish. 'None of it makes sense.'

'Mmm,' she agrees.

'It's just – weird.'

'Well, it's unlike them to all go out, certainly.'

'And Mary didn't say anything when I spoke to her. You'd have thought she'd have said something if she was . . .'

'Well, it must have slipped her mind,' says Nessa. 'I mean. You've got a choice of interpretations, here. Either it slipped her mind or they were hiding in the cellar and pretending not to be in. I mean, which would you say was the more likely?'

'Yes. I know.'

'I mean. They'd have to be pretty much clinically insane . . .'

'I know.'

'So,' she says.

I think for a minute. 'They're pretty odd people, though.'

Nessa laughs. 'They are that. But I've got to say, there's a difference between pretty odd and psychotic. I mean.' Then, with typical Aussie overstatement, she says: 'I get the impression you're having a bit of trouble settling in.'

It's as though someone's opened the sluices on a dam. I've been holding it back so assiduously that the pressure is at bursting point.

'How do you deal with it?' I ask, all in a rush. 'This country . . . these people are so . . . I don't know. How do you *talk* to them?'

'Oh, they're not so bad. They've got kind hearts, most of them.'

'The ones I've met before tonight?'

'Mmm. You've got a point, I guess. Trouble with that lot, they're so terrified of losing status they can't loosen up for a minute.'

'I get that.' I wonder if I can trust her, and think: I have to talk to *someone*. Lower my voice, so the others can't hear. 'I'm beginning to wonder if I haven't made some terrible mistake.'

As I say it, I feel a lurch of sadness. It all seemed so easy. So perfect. I was sure we would make it, certain I'd found my soulmate, and here I am less than a month later, telling a virtual stranger that I'm not sure any more.

She blinks a couple of times. 'No,' she says eventually. 'No, you've not done that. But you've got your work cut out.'

'Yeah, I'd guessed that much.'

We both pause as Ian arrives with another round of drinks.

'So what,' I continue once he's safely back at the bar, 'do you think my main problems are?'

'Ah Lord, there's the million-dollar question.'

'Well?'

'Well, there are two main ones.'

'Which are?'

'First up, you've married into one of the world's most mysterious cults. They make the Sufis look transparent.'

'Go on.'

'They're odd, the upper classes,' she tells me. You don't say, I think. 'They're not like us. It's almost like an obsession. They're trained up from birth to believe that property is the most important thing. I mean, they go on about manners and history and duty and that, but what really matters, deep down, is owning every scrap of land you might be able to see from your house. Even if it's bankrupting you. Villages like Bourton, they were all built to service the big house and the estate, back in the days when everything had to be done by hand. It made sense, then. But of course, the estates themselves were actually producing money, so they could afford to keep all these servants in tied cottages. There's no money in agriculture. Hasn't been in – ooh – a hundred-odd years. But they're stubborn. They just carry on like nothing's changed and get angry because everything's falling apart. Simple fact: your husband can't afford to keep up these houses.'

'That much I'd worked out.'

'Yeah, but holding on to them is like holding on to their identity. Selling things, to people like that, is the equivalent of murdering your granny or something. They'd rather sit on it and let it fall apart than face reality and enter the modern world.'

Golly. Politics.

'But I know Rufus. He's not like that.'

'No, I don't think he is. If it was up to him he'd take a more realistic attitude. He's the one who opened the place up to tourists, and believe me, the rows it took to get them to agree to that were monumental. They may say they've handed over the reins, but they never actually do.'

'Well, that's true enough. So what's my second problem, then?'

'Oh God,' says Nessa. 'This is the real humdinger. You're up against the aristocratic matriarch.'

'Oh.'

'It's the womenfolk you have to watch out for,' she says. 'They're the ones who keep the whole thing going. You'll find that they're the ones who are unfriendliest, the ones that suck in their breath when you're not quite quite, the ones that adhere to all the unwritten rules, and write a few more in when you're not looking. Comes from getting all their status from the men in their families. That's why they're so possessive of their sons. Their sons are their only hope of having any status once their old men are dead. Mary ain't going to let go of Rufus without a fight. And especially not to a chick like you. And don't fool yourself that she's your only problem. Beatrice is just as bad, if not worse, and she rules that family with a rod of iron. It may be wrapped up in pink chiffon, but there's iron in there. Just look at the way they're all treating Tilly, just so Beatrice doesn't get to find out about it.'

'What's the big deal, anyway? Surely the fact that she's family counts for more than—'

'Divorce. She's fanatical about it. All those Edwardians are. You've got to remember, the Royals wouldn't have a divorcee in their presence until so many of them did it themselves it got embarrassing, and the rest of the country spend half their time copycatting them. What the Royals do, they do. I think she thinks it's a bigger shame than having a murderer in the family. Seriously, I wouldn't be a bit surprised if she didn't think it was *better* to have a murderer in the family. And besides, it's bad financial sense, isn't it? You get divorced, you break up the money. Wattestones didn't get to be Wattestones by letting go of a single red cent. If she thought Tilly was bringing disgrace on their spotless record, she'd have her out in the snow before you could say Jack Sprat.'

'That's really . . .' I try to think of a suitable epithet, give up the struggle and just say, 'shitty.'

'Yeah, it is, isn't it? Still. You've got the best part of the family there. That Rufus, he's a goer. He's – oh, talk of the devil . . .'

And the door opens, and a familiar voice says: 'Hello, Ian. I'm looking for an angry wife. Don't suppose you've seen one, have you?'

Chapter Thirty-Four
Jesus Bloody Christ on a Bike

There's a silence you could throw a brick at.

'Oh,' I say. 'There you are.'

Rufus doesn't seem to want to look at me. Looks, instead, at the drinkers by the bar. Fifi has come in with him and is sitting by his ankles, and no-one has a word to say about it.

'Thanks so much for looking after her,' he says. 'Bit of a mix-up at home, I'm afraid. Crossed wires everywhere.'

'Well, it's lucky she found us,' says Ian.

I toy with the idea of telling him that it's been a relief, that I've had a more relaxed time in his pub than I've had in the whole of the past few weeks down the hill, but I get the feeling that Rufus won't want to hear it. 'I've had a good time,' I assure him, 'seriously. You guys have been great.'

Another pause. I don't seem to have improved matters any.

'Well,' says Rufus, still not looking at me, in that we-are-going-to-have-such-a-row-when-I-get-you-out-of-here voice, 'are you ready to go now, darling?'

I get up from the table, discover, to my consternation, that I am not entirely sober. 'Nessa's been looking after me,' I say.

'So I see,' says Rufus grimly. I don't know what he's got to be grim about. I don't suppose *he's* spent the evening dodging bunyips. I start to look about for my stuff. I don't know how it happened, but I seem to have spread belongings over the entire room. My coat hangs over a bar stool, a small puddle on the floor beneath. My scarf is draped over one corner of a hunting print called *Gone Away* and my bag seems to have fetched up over on the bar, by the telephone. How long have I been here again? The clock says it's going on eleven. Who'd'a thunk it?

I seem to have lost my shoes.

'I seem to have lost my shoes,' I inform the room.

'They're over there on the heater,' says Del-boy. Well, blow me down. I don't remember how they got there.

'I'd better go get them, then,' I say.

Rufus starts feeling about inside his jacket. 'Thank you so much, Ian,' he says. 'How much do I owe you?'

'Doesn't matter,' says Ian. 'On the house.'

'Come on,' says Rufus, 'she's been here for ages.'

'Too bloody right I have,' I say from over by the heater. My shoes seem to have shrunk as they have dried out, and I'm having to stand on one foot and strain with an index finger to get the left one on at all. Have to catch on to the back of a settle before I plummet floorwards. God, I've let my yoga slip.

'No, really,' says Ian, 'it's fine.'

'Well, if you're sure . . .' Rufus sounds doubtful, but I can see from the way he's glancing at me that he'd rather get me out of here than get into an argument about it. 'I'll be taking her home, then. Come on, darling, if you're ready. . .'

I give up on the shoe. Hobble over to take his hand. Rufus puts an arm around my shoulders, but I can feel that it's more of a proprietorial gesture for good public form than it is one of affection.

I raise a hand in farewell. 'Listen, you guys. It's been real.'

Six pairs of eyes study me.

Eventually, Derek speaks. 'It's been nice meeting you, Mrs Wattestone.'

The place stays unsettlingly quiet as we make our way out into the car park, Fifi grumbling along in our wake like a disgruntled vacuum cleaner. Then as we pass a window on our way to the car, I catch the sound of a great gust of laughter. It sounds as though the people inside have been holding their breaths until we have gone.

Neither of us says anything until we're both settled in our seats, and the car doors are firmly shut.

Then Rufus says: 'Jesus bloody Christ on a bike.'

And I say: 'What do you bloody *mean*, Jesus bloody Christ on a bike? It should be bloody me that's bloody saying that.'

Call me quick on the uptake, but I have a feeling that our first marital row is about to kick off. I knew the harmony would be too good to last.

'Why did you have to go to the pub, of all places?' he asks.

'Where did you want me to go? Did you want me to walk to bloody *London* before I got out of the rain?'

'No,' he says, in that infuriatingly patronising tone that men reserve for speaking to women in, 'but you didn't have to . . .'

'Didn't have to *what*?'

'Well . . .'

'Don't you bloody 'well' me, mate. I'm not the one who didn't bloody notice I was missing for *five bloody hours*. I could have frozen to *death* out there.'

'I don't think so,' says Rufus. 'Why didn't you just go to the house, for God's sake? And what the bloody hell was that message all about? You've got some mouth on you, do you know that?'

'You know what? I was pissed off.'

'*You* were pissed off? How do you think *I* felt, coming home to a stream of abuse?'

'Well, how do you think I felt? You left me sitting on Moreton station for *two bloody hours*!'

Our voices are rising as the exchange progresses. 'Well, how was *I* meant to know you were there? Osmosis? I mean. It's all very well changing your plans, but you can't just expect . . . why the hell didn't you call?'

'I did!'

'Oh yeah?'

'Yeah! Your mother, she didn't—'

He cuts across me, stops me in my tracks. Just for a second it's like being slapped in the face. 'No you didn't! There's not a single message on my phone before your bloody stream of dirtymouth.'

'You weren't bloody *answering*, idiot.'

'Well, I wasn't expecting you to suddenly come home twenty-four hours early, was I?'

'I didn't have a lot of choice. Welcome I got from Hilary would have turned you grey overnight.'

'What do you mean?'

'Well, first he was rude to me, and then he suddenly started coming on to me. I wouldn't have felt safe sleeping in the same house.'

'*Hilary?*'

'Yeah. Hilary.'

'But Hilary's as bent as a nine-bob note!'

'Well, for a gay man he certainly did a good impression of someone with his hand on my tit.'

'You are *kidding* me. You don't seriously—'

'Who are you going to believe? Me, or him?'

'It's just that . . . come on, Mel. It's not exactly something you'd have on your likely list, is it? Are you *sure* you weren't . . . misinterpreting . . .'

'No! Fuck! Thanks for the show of support.'

'Well, we'll have to see about that. I don't know what to make of it. But honestly, even if it *did* happen . . .'

'It did.'

'OK. Whatever. But why on earth didn't you call someone and let them know you were coming back?'

I fold my arms and let out a noise that's somewhere in the region of a 'huurngh!' 'I did!' I continue. 'Your bloody mother said she'd pass the bloody message on!'

'Don't swear about my mother.'

'I've got every right to swear about your mother. She's the one who dumped me on some bloody station in the middle of bloody nowhere.'

'What on earth,' he asks, 'do you think you're going to achieve by lying about it?'

'I'm not bloody lying!'

'Well, it may not be lying where *you* come from . . .'

'What's *that* supposed to mean?'

He just pulls a face.

'Love it,' I say. 'Love the 'tude.'

He turns the key in the ignition, slams the car into first. 'Let's just go home,' he says, 'I'm not in the mood . . .'

'Oh, I'm so sorry,' I say sarcastically, '*you're* not in the mood.'

We take off, showering gravel behind us.

We swish through the gates and, heading down the drive, he speaks again. 'And another thing,' he says.

'Oh, right. Here we go.'

He ignores me. 'What I don't understand. If you could make it to the village, why on earth couldn't you come down to the house?'

'Rufus, *listen*. I called your mother and told her I was coming back. And then no-one came and picked me up, so I had to find a taxi. But when I got down to the house, it was all locked up. No-one came to the door, and all the lights were off.'

I catch a glimpse of his face in moonlight. It's slack with astonishment, disbelief. 'Oh, come *on*.'

'*Listen!*'

'Melody, you're talking *bollocks*.'

It's my turn to be flooded with disbelief. 'Why would I do *that*?'

'I don't know,' he snaps. 'I don't have the foggiest fucking idea.'

I'm devastated. 'So I'm a liar, is that it?'

'You're – n'well . . .'

'You *bastard*!'

'Well, I don't know, Melody. What am I supposed to think?'

'You're supposed to believe me! Why don't you believe me?'

'Because it doesn't make any sense!'

'Of *course* it bloody doesn't! I *know* it bloody doesn't!'

'Do you have to bloody swear so much?'

'Yes I bloody well do!'

We subside into resentful silence. The house comes into view: lights on all over; on the ground floor and the second. The back yard is lit up like a football pitch by the security lights fixed to the upper walls.

'Mummy says they've been in all evening,' he says.

'Well, *Mummy* –' I emphasise the word with all the contempt in my body – 'is lying.'

Again he shakes his head. It's obvious he doesn't believe a word I'm saying.

'I could have broken my leg out there,' I tell him. 'Don't you give a damn?'

'I don't know what you're talking about.'

'Look, arsehole! I had to walk all the way up here in the dark!'

'Don't *use* that word.'

'Arsehole.' I repeat. Then, overcome by my inner child, I say, 'Arsehole, arsehole, arsehole,' for good measure.

'Jesus,' he says, 'do you have to be such a pain?'

So I pinch him. Not very hard, and on the upper arm, but enough to make him gasp and slam on the brakes.

'What the *fuck* did you do that for?'

He rubs his arm and looks at me with a heart-wrenching combination of surprise and reproach. 'Ow.'

Having been on the edge off giving him the gobful to end all gobfuls, I find myself, instead, covered in mortification. I never thought anyone would push me to that point again. I swore I was done with that sort of behaviour after Andy. I thought I'd learned my lesson. What'm I doing here? Leading by example?

'I'm sorry,' I tell him. 'I'm really, really sorry.'

He rubs the assaulted arm again, though this time in more of a point-making fashion than anything else. I didn't pinch him *that* hard. 'So you bloody well should be. What do you want to do next? Black my eye?'

'I'm sorry. I am really sorry, darling. But you weren't listening to me, and—'

'So you bash people for not listening to you?'

'Not as a rule, as it goes.'

'By the way,' he says accusingly, reaching across me. 'I found your passport and your driving licence. They were in the glove pocket.'

'What were they doing there?'

His voice has gone quiet. I don't like it. 'I don't know, Melody. Maybe *Hilary* put them there.'

'WHAT?'

He reins himself in. 'Sorry. That was uncalled for. But you must have put them there and forgotten about it or something.'

'Of *course* I didn't.'

'Well, you seem to have forgotten to call and let anyone know your travel plans.'

'Oh, Jesus. This is *impossible.*'

'Yes,' he replies. 'It is.'

'Look, I—'

'No, look!' He's snarling at me, now. 'It's not all *about* you, Melody! Not everything in the world is *about you!*'

'Oh, forget it!' I snarl back.

'Right!'

'Yeah! Right!'

He slams the car back into gear, and drives on. The silence is overwhelming, the gulf between us so huge it gives me vertigo. I want to cry, want to howl at the moon. This isn't the way it's meant to be. We're meant to be adults. We're meant to talk things out, not shriek and snap like feral dogs.

After a hundred metres, I say: 'Rufus, can we start this again?'

He heaves a sigh. 'Yes. Of course. I'm just – really confused.'

'So am I.'

'They've been in all evening. Mummy says she didn't hear a thing.'

'Well she's—' I just stop myself from renewing my accusation. 'Maybe she needs to get her ears tested.'

'Maybe,' he says. Then, as an olive branch: 'It must have been horrid for you.'

'Yeah, it was. It's really – creepy here by yourself.'

'Yuh. Yuh, I should think it is. I'm sorry. I wouldn't have left you if I'd known.'

'I know you wouldn't,' I tell him.

He puts a hand on my knee. I pat his arm.

'But please don't pinch me again.'

'I won't. I promise.'

'OK.'

I give it a two-beat pause, then: 'I'll smack your arse for you if you like.'

He laughs, and the atmosphere in the car lightens.

'They do call it the English vice.'

'Don't push it, Mrs.'

'Push it? That's a new one on me.'

'I was really worried about you, you know. I didn't know what had happened.'

'You don't need to worry about me. I've been looking after myself for a bit now.'

'Yes, but ... seriously, it would have been a bit bloody embarrassing . . .'

'I can see that. Yeah, I can see that it might be a bit embarrassing, telling people you'd lost your *wife* . . .'

'Nothing like,' he says, 'as embarrassing as finding her in the pub.'

'What's the problem with the pub, anyway?'

'They gossip.'

'Oh dear. *Gossip*. That'll be the end of the world, then.'

'From some points of view.'

'Oh, Jesus, Rufus. So people fill their time in with a bit of talk. Seriously. What does it matter?'

'I don't know. People can get their lives ruined by gossip.'

'I know that. But I just went to a pub and had a couple of beers.'

'Mmm. People like us . . . we don't . . . women don't . . . you know.'

'People *like us*?'

'Yes. That's what you are now. If you want to fit in.'

'Hmm. Rufus, do I detect a smidge of snobbery?'

'Not at—'

'I dunno. If you guys won't admit you've got a caste system, how on earth am I going to avoid the tripwires?'

Typical Englishman. He clams up.

'Seriously, Rufus. I'm going to need help.'

'Yes, and then you'll accuse me of being a snob if I give you any advice.'

Touché.

The stableyard comes up on our left. I have to think fast. If I pursue my current line, we'll have nothing sorted out by the time

216

we get back and we'll be going into the thick of it still at odds with each other. And maybe . . . I don't know. Now I'm even starting to doubt myself. No. I can't have made that sort of mistake. But if that's so, the only obvious reason would be that someone is trying to create discord between Rufus and me. And if these women are as possessive and rigid as Nessa says, the last thing I need is for seeds of doubt to be sown in his mind.

It's going to be a case of winkling him out. And you know how it is with winkles. Grab on and pull, and they'll hang on to their bit of rockface like they're welded. The only way to get a winkle off a rock is to slide your blade in there, slowly, slowly, so they don't notice you're doing it. And once you're firmly in there, embedded beneath the suckers, all it takes is a twist and a wrist-flick to get them free.

I'll put it another way: softly softly catchee monkey.

Or another: if you've got a great white circling you, you'd be well advised not to splash about too much.

It's better, I think, if I make my peace now and live to fight another day. 'Well, babe,' I say, 'I don't understand what happened, but I'm sorry I swore at you and I'm sorry I shouted at you.'

Rufus sighs. 'And I'm sorry you had such a gruesome experience. I have no idea what can have happened. I really don't. But it's OK now. I've found you.'

'Perhaps,' I offer, 'there was something wrong with the bell?'

I know that this is rubbish: the sonorous ding-ding-ding of the early evening is engraved on my memory. But you've got to offer olive branches.

'I wouldn't be surprised,' he says. 'Everything else is falling apart, after all. I'll look at it tomorrow.'

Chapter Thirty-Five
Brekkie

I have to get a grip on this listening at doors thing. But it's not easy. I'm paranoid by nature as it is, and the setup at Bourton Allhallows is calculated to feed my weakness. It's all very well *thinking* that people are talking about you behind your back; when you *know* they are, the urge to snoop is well-nigh irresistible.

Mary's got her reasonable voice on again. That let's-have-a-houseparty tone that sets my teeth on edge.

'Well, *darling*,' she is saying, 'it's possible that Melody is making it up, of course.'

I'm relieved to hear that Rufus isn't having any of it. 'Melody doesn't make things up,' he says. 'I'm certain of that. She's the most truthful person I know.'

I've been so low on compliments lately that this show of support sends a warm glow all through me.

'Well, you don't really *know* that, do you, darling?' asks Mary. 'It can take *years* to find out what people are *really* like.'

'No, Ma,' says Rufus. 'If she says it happened, it happened. I'm more than prepared to accept that there's been some sort of unholy cock-up, but I'm not going to go any further than that.'

'But, *darling*,' she says, 'it simply never . . . you'd have thought I'd have remembered if I'd spoken to her on the phone, wouldn't you?'

'Yes, you would have,' he says, with an edge to his voice.

Tilly speaks. 'It *is* a bit weird,' she says doubtfully. 'Of course, I was dead to the world from seven onwards. Didn't even hear the dinner bell. But I'd have thought I'd've heard something.'

No-one responds.

'Of course,' she says falteringly after a few seconds, 'I've been so tired lately. I could have slept through an earthquake. Thanks for letting me miss dinner, by the way. I'm grateful for the sleep.'

'Well, I don't know,' says Mary, ignoring her, 'if you're not prepared to listen to other people's points of view . . .'

'Go on, then,' Rufus says. 'Give me your point of view.'

'I just think,' she says, pauses as if considering her words, 'that perhaps . . . well, perhaps she's feeling rather neglected.'

I feel myself redden, feel the intestinal lurch that has become such a familiar sensation over the past few weeks. Is she really suggesting that this is a hysterical attention-seeking put-on? She can't be.

You've got to hand it to her: she's skilled in the art of the veiled put-down.

'I mean,' she says sympathetically, 'we *are* rather dull, here. And I should think that after the glamour of such a protracted honeymoon . . . especially if you're used to a . . . *lively* social life . . .' She leaves this hanging in the air.

'What are you saying, Mother?'

'Well, darling. She's not used to our sort of structures, is she? I know it was an odd way of going about it, but perhaps, with you being so busy and so few young people around . . . one can hardly blame her if she feels the need to go to the pub and find herself a *p'tit ami* . . .'

I don't know a lot of French, but I know when I'm being insulted. I open the door and enter the breakfast room, in the full knowledge that my expression is murderous.

They all look up. Well, all except Beatrice. I spot her seeing that it's me and turning her head away with *grande dame* deliberateness. Edmund clutches a copy of the *Telegraph*, peers at me over his specs with a small smile and immediately reburies his face. This is roughly how he has coped with morning small-talk since I got here. Tilly moves her chair round to make room for me. Mary beams at me like the treacherous witch she is.

'Good *morning*, Melody,' she says. 'I hope you're feeling better today.'

I slip into my chair and say, 'I wasn't aware that I was ill, Mary.'

I hear a sigh from Rufus.

'Not ill, darling. Though I did hear you'd drunk a certain amount of beer last night.'

'Well, I don't know what else I was supposed to do. I was in that pub for the best part of three hours.'

The smile spreads. 'So I hear,' she says archly.

Ooh, you *bitch*. I am *this* close to giving her a slapping.

Mrs Roberts enters the room. Lays a plate of kippers lovingly down in front of Rufus, bangs one down in front of me, wheels on a heel and leaves.

'I don't know why you couldn't have just called the house,' says Mary, the smile never wavering. 'Someone would have come and picked you up.'

I just give her a look.

'Mummy says they were at home all night,' Rufus tells me.

I struggle with my manners, lose. 'Well, *Mummy*'s lying.'

The *Telegraph* rustles. 'Melody!' mutters Edmund reprovingly.

That's all I need: upbringing from someone who almost certainly has a shot of whisky in the bottom of his teacup.

'Well, if they were at home all night, how come the lights were off all over the house?'

Tinkle tinkle, goes Mary. 'But darling, why on *earth* would we want to have the lights off?'

A big '*graaargh*' rises in my gorge. I ram it back down, dig my nails into the palms of my hands under the table.

'I'll think you'll find,' I say, once I've got myself under control, 'that that was *my* point.'

She knits her eyebrows, tilts her chin and gives me the sort of look you give to stupid children. And people you want to insult.

'But, darling, it's just *silly*. What did you think? That we were creeping about in the dark playing hide-and-seek?'

'She shouldn't be living in the house anyway,' announces Beatrice. 'There are plenty of houses in the village for that sort of thing. I don't know why you put up with it, Mary.'

'Morning, Beatrice,' I say. Her mouth collapses in on itself. She goggles at me for a single second, turns away.

'Well, I'm sorry,' says Mary, 'if you think we all turned the lights off and hid from you.' She leaves the sentence hanging in the air.

'Oh, *please*,' I say.

'Rufus!' says Beatrice. 'I will *not* have her talking to the family like that!'

'What, I'm not allowed to express my opinion?'

'Mel,' says Rufus. And I think: yeah, well, perhaps I *should* go a bit easy on the old girl. She is nearly a hundred, after all. A hundred years old and crouched over this family like a corpulent old spider in a web.

'Excuse me,' says Tilly, scraping her chair back and standing up, 'Toast. Must walk it off.'

'How's your back?' I ask.

Her hands fly instinctively to the top of her hips. Then, remembering the house rules, she plasters a smile on and Doesn't Make A Fuss. 'It's fine. Thank you for asking.'

'Would you like a bit of a rub-down later?'

Her eyes dart about. In the world of Bourton Allhallows, massage still only means one thing: anonymous doorways with red lights. I don't know if you've ever heard someone pursing their lips, but I know for a fact that Mary is doing it right now. Then suddenly, Tilly shows a bit of intestinal fortitude. 'Thank you, Melody,' she says. 'That would be very nice.'

'I'll come find you.'

She smiles, and the tight, white little face is transformed for a moment. I can see the skinny, freckly teenager Tilly once was, and I like what I see. Now, *there's* Rufus's sister, at last. Here's something I can build on.

I attack my kippers with new enthusiasm. They are dried out like shoe leather. Pinpricks from tiny bones assail my throat.

'Stuff and nonsense,' says Beatrice, apropos nothing. 'In my day we just got on with it. Didn't make all this fuss.'

No-one responds. Mary sips her Earl Grey. Rufus snatches a handful of sliced bread and slathers Tesco Value butter over it.

I'm stupid and rise to the bait. 'There's a fair body of evidence,' I tell her, 'that massage can help a lot in terms of pain. And getting ready for childbirth. I wouldn't go just knocking it for the sake of scoring a point.'

She throws me a look that would freeze mud. Turns her face away and addresses the fireplace. 'I suppose that this is all one can expect if one brings staff to the table,' she says.

I give up. Give her my most charming smile. 'Would you like a cup of tea, Beatrice?' I ask.

She pretends – actually pretends – she hasn't heard me. It's like sharing a table with a six-year-old.

I raise my eyebrows. Pour Rufus a cup of tea and one for myself.

'I should like a cup of tea, if it's not too much trouble for you, Rufus,' says Beatrice with more than a hint of reprimand.

Rufus pours her one.

'D'you want milk with that?' I ask.

No reply. I sling some in anyway. Slide it over.

Beatrice pretends, after a few seconds, to notice it with surprise, as though it's turned up by magic. Takes a sip. Pulls a face like she's just been given a cup of hemlock. I wish. She lays it down, pushes it away.

'Is that not right, Granny?'

'Never mind,' says Beatrice.

Rufus heaves a sigh. He seems to have been doing a lot of that, lately. Adjusting his napkin in his lap, he speaks. 'OK. Would someone mind letting me in on what's going on?'

Edmund heaves a sigh and turns a page. 'Bloody socialists,' he says. 'Destroying the country.'

I think Edmund is probably completely unaware that there's such a thing as an atmosphere.

Rufus waits for an answer. Breaks a piece of bread and wraps it round some kipper. 'Well, it's obvious *something's* going on. I mean, I know you're all capable of amazing rudeness, but this ignoring-Melody-altogether thing takes the biscuit, even for you.'

I've never heard him talk like this before. My nape prickles with the thrill of it. Maybe there's hope for us yet.

Mary sips her tea, glances at him. Says nothing.

'Granny?' asks Rufus.

222

She's silent for a bit. Eventually, she says: 'If you don't know, you should.'

Rufus slaps a hand down on the table-top. 'Well, if no-one will say, how am I *supposed* to know? I'm not a bloody mind-reader.'

'Rufus!' says Mary. 'Please! No swearing at breakfast.'

Beatrice pulls a face that makes me hope for a second that her teeth have come loose and are about to slip down her throat.

'I'm getting really sick of this,' says Rufus. 'Can't you *try* to be civilised?'

'Well,' says Mary, 'I didn't notice that *I* was swearing at the breakfast table.'

'If you don't talk to me, I'm going to swear a bloody lot more.'

Edmund lowers his paper. 'Rufus,' he says. Raises it back up again.

Rufus sighs. 'OK. Granny, you seem to be the one with the biggest snit on. What is your problem?'

Beatrice comes over all dowager duchess.

'I will *not* discuss family matters in front of your . . .'

'My what? Melody *is* family matters. I'm not having her shut out. If there's a problem, I—'

Beatrice responds sharply, spitefully. 'Don't you *dare* speak to me in that tone of voice! *You're* the one who has caused this problem. You and your . . . you bring your . . . doxies into the house and expect to get away with it?'

'What are you *talking* about?'

She flicks a hand at me. 'Your mistress. Did you think I wouldn't notice? I know I'm old, but I'm not *stupid*. I'm not *blind*.'

'Well, actually,' I say, 'you are.'

It doesn't help, of course. Rufus says: 'Christ, Melody! Don't you have an *ounce* of tact?' Mary says: 'Rufus! I *asked* you not to swear!' and Beatrice, voice shrill like a hand blender, shouts: 'I want her out of here! Out of my house! I don't care what you say! Pay her her notice and tell her to leave!'

'What the f—' I quickly correct myself – 'on earth are you talking about?'

Suddenly, she's glaring at me, meeting my eye for the first time this morning. There's nothing little-old-lady about her now. I'm looking into the emotionless eyes of a boa constrictor. 'And where did you get the impression you could call me by my Christian name? I don't expect to be talked to like that by my staff. And especially not by a . . . a *kept woman*.'

'Granny!' protests Rufus.

'Oh, get over yourself,' I snarl.

'Don't speak to me!' she snarls back. 'Don't speak to me at all!'

'Granny!' he shouts again.

'Get out! Get her out of here! Go on! Get out!'

I slap my napkin down. 'It's OK. I'm leaving.'

'Mel!'

'No, Rufus. I've had enough.' The strain of having kept a grip on my emotions over the past few weeks gets to be too much, forces tears into the back of my throat. '*Nothing's* going to make these people happy. I can try till I'm blue in the face and they'll just keep throwing up new things to beat me up with. It's just one bloody thing after a-bloody-nother. Well, fuck 'em. Fuck 'em all. I'll see you later.'

He's torn. Knows he's not going to get anything sorted out if he comes after me.

'Wait,' he says.

I shake my head. 'I'm sorry. I'm too angry.'

'I'll . . .' he says. 'Look. I've got to get this . . . I'll come and find you.'

'Whatever,' I snap, and stalk out of the room.

I pull the door to just as Rufus explodes.

Chapter Thirty-Six
A Bit of a Rub-Down

Tilly's sparko on her side in the library, on a chaise longue whose bottom is a mass of protruding horsehair. It's got the look of mice about it. No doubt they've never been culled because they were recorded as living there in the Domesday Book and they're traditional. She's covered herself up with a motheaten mohair, and hugs her bump like a teddy-bear. Django, tail thumping, grins at me from where's he's perched along the length of her body. I'm not sure who's relying on whom for body heat here, suspect it might be symbiotic.

Instincts fine-honed, she starts awake the moment I enter the room, tries to look alert – I don't know if you've ever seen a pregnant lady trying to look alert, but it doesn't work too good – and then, seeing that it's me, drops her head back down on a cushion and blinks instead.

'You gave me a fright,' she says. 'For a horrible moment I thought you might be Mary come to tell me I shouldn't be moping.'

'No worries,' I tell her. 'I thought you might like that rub-down.'

'A rub-down and no lectures.' Tilly's voice is uncharacter-istically blissful. 'I can't think of anything nicer. Get off, dog.' Django thumps his tail again, remains steadfast on his mistress's well-covered hipbone. His tongue lolls downward as his grin widens. Tilly pushes at him. 'Bloody hell,' she says, 'he's got me trapped like a kipper.'

'Please don't talk about kippers,' I beg her. 'I think those ones of Mrs Roberts's will be with me till next week.'

I grab Django by the scruff – Wattestone dogs don't have collars,

as the chances of them wandering off Wattestone land are slim –
and haul. Every muscle in his body goes limp. Suddenly, he weighs
roughly the same as a baby elephant. Even the dogs are passive-
aggressive.

'Christ, girl,' I tell her, 'I think you're trapped for life.'

Tilly groans. I insinuate my free arm between the dog and my
sister-in-law's swollen abdomen, and lift the unresponsive form on
to the floor, give her a hand, and with three heaves we get her
upright.

'Bit of a palaver, this pregnancy thing.'

'Really,' she says, 'don't do it. Ever.'

'Got to be done, I guess.'

'The sooner they can grow them in Kilner jars, the happier I'll
be,' she says. 'A stomach like a laundry bag, veins like road maps,
piles like chicken droppings. Men don't know how lucky they
are.'

'What was that you were reading there?'

She reaches down and picks her book off the floor where she's
dropped it. Flips it over to reveal *The Well of Loneliness*.

'Never read it. Any good?'

'Not really. I thought it was meant to be about lesbians, but it
just seems to be about wanting to wear trousers and breed horses.
I don't know, maybe it's a metaphor. Instant soporific, mind you.
I'll take it up with me tonight and guarantee myself some kip. So
how do we go about this, then?'

'Tell you what. You sit at the end with your feet on the floor
and I'll get behind you.'

'It's a bit like a *Carry On* film, isn't it? Do I need to take anything
off, Matron?'

'Not a lot. Maybe just the top three layers or so.'

'Lucky,' she says, obeying, 'it's not winter yet.'

Oh hell. And there was me thinking that Christmas *was* the deep
midwinter. There's only a few days to go, after all.

I kneel up behind her on the chaise, and start warming her back
up with an all-over rub. It's not easy. Corduroy tends to snag, if
you've not exfoliated your palms lately. I run through the choice

of hairdresser-style small talk in my head. Been anywhere nice lately? How's work? Lovely weather. Got any holidays lined up?

None of them seems particularly appropriate. So I say: 'Jesus, girl, you've got a back like a board. When was the last time anyone had a go at it?'

This is the equivalent of asking who was responsible for the state of your client's hair. It either makes them apologetic, and therefore putty in your hands, or confused, which has a similar effect.

'Never,' says Tilly. 'It's not the sort of thing we do much of around here.'

'Have you been cricking your neck at all?'

Tilly nods. 'Like an eight-gun salute, three times a day. I'm surprised you haven't heard it.'

'I guess I must have mistaken them for real gunshots.'

'Ha ha.'

I roll up my sleeves, lay my forearms either side of her spine and start rocking.

'Oh, lovely,' says Tilly. 'Ah, God, that feels nice.'

I realise, with a glum little twist, that this is probably the most kindly human contact she's had in ages. Poor girl. Tilly must have been crying her eyes out for months in the isolation of her room, then getting up and washing her face, because Wattestone women don't indulge in unnecessary displays of emotion. I'm not sure whether to broach the subject. Hopefully her tongue'll loosen with her muscles. Otherwise, I might give her a bit of cranial.

'So,' she asks, 'have you found out what the old people are in a tizz about yet?'

'Oh, yeah. You won't believe it. I don't believe it myself. Your gran's only decided that I'm Rufus's mistress. She wants me horsewhipped from the property.''

I feel her tense beneath my arms, then she starts to laugh. 'Stop! Stop! I have to sit up!'

I cease, and Tilly lets her head fall back against her shoulders. She is shaking with mirth. 'I d-d-d that's the funniest thing I've heard in ages!'

'Not so bloody funny for me.'

227

She laughs a bit more.

'I mean, I don't get it,' I say, resuming. 'How come people can't just tell her? It's got to sink in eventually.'

'Granny's mind is a weird amalgamation of sponge and granite,' says Tilly. 'She soaks up all the tiny nuances of everyday life, but the big picture just washes straight over her. It's partly because she's a bit gaga with her age, but it's just as much that if she simply denies the existence of something that doesn't suit her, she can usually make it not exist. And if you try to force things, she'll have a whoosh–dada to end all whoosh–dadas. You saw what she was like this morning?'

'Hard to miss.'

'Well, imagine that, multiplied by ten, and going on till the middle of next year. Believe me, you don't want to get on Granny's bad side. Nobody does. That's how come,' she clears her throat, then mentions the elephant in the corner, 'they can all convince themselves that she'll never find out about Hugo. Because it would be so much easier if she didn't.'

So there we go: it's out in the open. I make sure I don't break my rhythm.

'I was wondering about that. Do you want to tell me about it? I don't want to – you know . . .'

A huge sigh. 'Nothing to tell, really,' she says, and the strangled little Kristin Scott-Thomas voice is back. 'Just one of those things . . . I married a shit and he's running true to his personality.'

If I've learned one thing in life, it's that there's no point in pushing someone who doesn't want to be pushed. You're more likely to make them angry than to help them out.

'Well, I'm sorry,' I tell her. 'You know, if there's anything I can do . . .'

'You're doing it.' She pushes back against my elbow, and the lump does a crunch, dissolves. 'Hunnh,' she says. 'To be honest, this is the most anyone has done in months.'

I start on the lump's twin on the other side. We're quiet for a bit, reflecting. Then she says: 'Well, that's what you get for making a suitable marriage.'

'You weren't to know, Tilly. Nobody really knows.'

'I did,' she says. 'God, everybody in the world knew that Hugo was a bolter.'

'So why did you marry him, then?'

'Because I'm stupid. Because I'm wet. Because I was thirty-four, and nobody else had asked me, and I felt a failure, and I saw the way Granny and Mary despise all the local spinsters and I didn't want to have to cope with the fact that they were starting to look at me the same way. And Granny thought he was marvellous. He's the grandson of one of her oldest friends, you know.'

'Jesus. You lot might as well live in a trailer park, the way you intermarry.'

'Well, you know what they say about the upper classes and the working classes . . .'

'Yes, and *you* know that's just so much bull cooked up by the upper classes to avoid getting their heads cut off.'

She laughs again.

'So you married this guy to keep your nana happy?'

She doesn't answer. Then, in a small voice: 'Well, I've got my reward now, haven't I?'

'I don't think that's quite how I'd put it,' I say. 'I'm really, really sorry, Tilly. You must feel awful.'

I've got the heels of my hands either side of her nape, pressing in and out like a happy cat. There's no give at all. It's like kneading teak. 'So what are you going to call it,' I ask, 'when it's born?'

'I thought Henry if it's a boy. Lucy if it's a girl.'

'Lucy's good.'

'Thanks.'

'Henry's a bit . . . smoking jacket, isn't it?'

Tilly laughs again. 'You're a blast,' she says. 'It's another family name. My grandfather. And countless others before him.'

'Lucy's not, though?'

There's a slight pause. 'No. Not a Wattestone name, no. It's—'

The door bursts open and Rufus stands there. 'Oh, *there* you are. I've been looking everywhere for you.'

229

'Oh, right,' I say. 'Well, here I am.'

'You do look odd, you two. Like a pair of dogs humping on a lawn.'

'Nice image. What can we do you for?'

'Um, well, um . . .'

'Spit it out.'

'Granny wants to talk to you,' he says. 'I think she's finally got the message and wants to welcome you to the family or something.'

Chapter Thirty-Seven
Barbara Cartland

Beatrice is waiting for me in the brown study. Nessa is still getting her settled in, propping her into an ancient office chair behind the desk with the aid of half a dozen cushions and, I dare say, some hidden ropes. She's got the chair set at the highest notch, doubtless in an effort to be intimidating (there's a footstool placed pointedly on my side of the desk, bless it), and her feet dangle three inches from the floor. Nessa winks at me. I maintain a poker face, but look her straight in the eye for a full two seconds.

'There you go, Mrs Wattestone,' she says. 'Can I get you anything else?'

'No, that will be all,' says Beatrice imperiously.

'Okey-dokey,' says Nessa. 'Fair enough.'

Once she's gone, Beatrice raises her chins and says: 'Would you care to take a seat, Miss Kalamata?'

I don't bother correcting her. I mean, in a way she's got it right. Miss. Ms. It's a minefield of my own creation. I fetch a proper armchair from where they're lined up by the wall. 'So. I gather you've something to say to me.'

Beatrice is dressed to kill today. She wears a floaty chiffon dress-and-coat combo in mint, which loosely swaddles her old-lady undergarments. They must be made of pressed steel, because anything that can pummel a sack of marshmallows into human form must be pretty robust. Her face has been whitewashed, and her eyes drawn in with thick black pencil, false eyelashes like pipe cleaners glued to the pinky lids, a crinkly line of marmalade greasepaint slicked across what remains of her lips and bleeding up into the cracks like candlewax. It's the sort of look that has courtiers dropping to their knees, mumbling about vibrancy and vivaciousness. To me it looks like a couple of bats have lost their echo-sounding equipment and run slap into a factory wall.

She's topped it all off with a hat. In a darker shade of green than the dress, it's a confection of silk laurel leaves. Beatrice has an entire wheel-in closet full of hats, all lined up on polystyrene heads whose facial features have been coloured in crudely with crayon, next to her room in the neo-Gothic wing. I stumbled across it once and thought for a moment that I'd unlocked the door to Bluebeard's cupboard and found the heads of Rufus's previous wives.

'Indeed I have,' she says, and launches into one of those significant pauses.

I give her a good looking at while she's doing it. The trouble with Beatrice is, she reminds me, more than anything, of a character in one of those old British sitcoms you get playing late-night to fill airtime for tuppence. Mrs Slocombe in *Are You Being Served?*. Whenever she opens her mouth to let out a few more of those strangulated vowels, I half-expect her to start banging on about her pussy. It doesn't help, you know, when you're supposed to be treating someone with respect.

'So fire away,' I say.

Beatrice, of course, doesn't. Decades of bollocking housemaids has taught her not to just jump in until your opponent starts to look twitchy.

I give her a cheerful smile.

Beatrice drums her crabby old talons on the desktop. Eventually, she says: 'Miss Kalamari. I have called you here today to talk woman to woman.'

'Great,' I say. 'I've been thinking we ought to get to know each other.'

A slight widening of the eyes. 'I want you to leave my grandson alone,' she says.

I think about this for a bit. 'Sorry,' I reply eventually. 'No can do, I'm afraid.'

I guess she has been expecting some sort of response like this. Scarlet women, after all, aren't, on the whole, the sort who just go 'Oh, OK', and toddle off. 'I'm sorry, but I don't think I have made myself clear,' she says. 'Rufus is a very attractive young man. Of course he is. Any gel would fall in love with him. I *do* understand that. But this simply won't do. I'm sorry, but there it is.'

'Don't you think that's sort of up to Rufus?'

Beatrice starts to drawl, like someone in a costume drama. 'My *deah*,' she tells me, 'you don't understand, do you?'

'Oh, I think I do,' I reply. 'You don't think I'm good enough for your grandson and you're warning me off.'

'And you, poor child, are harbouring some naïve belief that he'll marry you, I suppose.'

'Er,' I say.

She barely takes breath. 'I've seen it all before, of course. Oh, I can't remember *how* many times. But please, dear, I don't want you to labour under any illusions. Boys like Rufus don't *marry* gels like you.' She waits for this information to sink in.

'I wouldn't be so sure about that, Beatrice,' I say.

A sharp expulsion of air through the nostrils. 'Permit me to remind you that I am a good deal older than you and have probably seen something more of the *real* world.'

Heavens. I'm in the middle of a Barbara Cartland novel. She'll be telling me he's a rake next. With a gambling problem and a cruel glint in his eye. Either that or she'll be calling for Mr Humphries.

'I know,' she continues, 'that you are probably cherishing hopes and dreams, making romantic plans for your future as the mistress of Bourton Allhallows, but I'm afraid, dear, that it simply isn't going to happen.'

Too right, I think: not if I can help it.

'You'll hardly be the first,' says Beatrice, 'and I'm sure you won't be the last. A man like Rufus, with his history and his charm and his wonderful house, is fatally attractive to young women. But he will never, *ever* marry you.'

My eyes wander as I listen to this lecture. There's a crack in the wall behind Beatrice's head. It must be an inch wide. I wonder if she's noticed it. Probably not. Blinded, I should think, by the sand she's buried her head in.

I realise she's waiting for me to say something. I think fast. Come up with: 'Is that what you think?'

'No, dear, it's what I *know*.'

'Oh.'

'I'm so sorry,' says Beatrice.

'Have you talked to him about it?'

'Of course I have.'

'And?'

A sigh. 'I won't pretend he's not attached to you,' she says. 'I'm sure he's fond of you, in his way. But Rufus is a sensible young man. He knows as well as anyone that marriage would be unthinkable. He has a strong sense of responsibility. I'm sure you've seen that. Responsibility and duty. These are our family watchwords. They are the words he has been brought up to value above all others.'

'I know,' I say. 'It's one of the things I love about him. The fact that you can trust him to keep his word.'

'Oh dear,' says Beatrice, 'I'm not making myself clear, am I?'

'Oh, I think you are. It's just that I'm not going to pay any attention.' I say this a bit more sharply than I mean to. Repeat to myself: I will not pick a fight with a hundred-year-old woman. I will not pick a fight with a hundred-year-old woman. 'Sorry,' I say as an attempt at amelioration.

'Very well,' she says. 'It is evident that I have misjudged you. I was under the impression, I must say, that you were rather nicer than the usual run of your sort, but it seems that I was mistaken.'

I'm beginning to understand something about the clunky dialogue in Barbara Cartland novels. This is actually how the aristocrats of that generation, brought up, at least in their formative years, by servants – generally by literate servants, but by servants none the less – spoke when they were being formal. A sort of language lifted from the sort of novels servants would get out of penny-lending libraries. So a manner of communicating that only existed in the fevered minds of popular scribes transferred itself back, over a generation, to an entire nanny-raised class. Who wrote it down in their own popular novels.

'It was foolish of me, I suppose,' Beatrice says, opening a drawer and fossicking about inside. 'I always *have* had a fatal tendency to try to see the best in people. I honestly believed, from talking to my grandson, that you were the victim in all of this. I really didn't want to believe you were an adventuress in search of profit. Still . . .'

'Beatrice . . .' I begin, but she isn't listening. I've a pretty good idea of what's coming. Half of me is horrified, half is full of glee. A giggle rises in my throat.

'. . . have it your way. How much would you like?' As I had suspected, she has produced a cheque book from the drawer, and is looking at me with an air of contemptuous expectation over the top of it. 'How about twenty thousand?'

'How's the weather in Lala Land?'

She doesn't get my drift. Thinks I'm holding out for more. 'Well. Perhaps you could name the sum *you* had in mind.'

I'm interested here. I'd like to know how much someone like Beatrice actually values Rufus's freedom at.

'How about a million?'

There she goes, tinkling like a bloody sleigh bell. 'Come *come*, Miss Kalamari. Even *you* cannot be so blinded by greed that you believe that I can write you a cheque for a million pounds. Still. At least we have opened the bargaining and I know I am not mistaken.'

My word.

'Well, I dunno . . .' I say doubtfully.

'Ah,' she says. 'Well, it's a pretty penny. A gel from your background could do far worse than a tax-free lump sum to get her started in life.'

'Twenty grand's hardly enough to buy a decent car these days.'

'All right,' she says. 'Shall we say thirty?'

I look at her.

'That and the family jewellery I see he's given you should certainly . . . you could buy a little . . .' a pause as she searches her database for the sort of pastimes that might get a gel like me's juices flowing '. . . *hat* shop . . .'

235

It's too much for me. I should have brought a tape recorder. My desire to laugh overcomes me. Looking at her sitting there in her big hat, all serious with her pen poised, is almost as funny as seeing someone slip on a banana skin. You know you shouldn't laugh, but the laughter comes anyway. I'm unable to stop myself, try to cover it up by putting my hands over my mouth, but realise, too late, that my shoulders are shaking and tears have sprung to my eyes, and that someone with the mindset of the woman in front of me will interpret it as . . .

The head tilts. Little beady eyes attempt to glisten with sympathy.

'There, there, dear. Never mind. I know it's come as a shock, but the money will be a great compensation, I'm sure.'

'No,' I stutter round my fingers, 'no, it's not that. It's that—'

'Money is a very important commodity,' she tells me, 'though I'm sure I don't need to remind you of that. I don't blame you for thinking you could get the blue ribbon, but I can assure you . . .'

Out of the corner of my eye, I notice movement through the window, out in the park. There seems to be a car approaching.

I pick up my bag and get out my own chequebook. 'No, you're right, Beatrice. Money *is* important. And I'll tell you what. How's about I write *you* a cheque for *fifty* grand to get off my case? Then maybe you could buy a bit of family jewellery of your own, eh? Make up for the stuff you've mislaid over the years? I know it's not enough for a Callington Emerald, but it'll certainly get you more than a *hat shop*.'

It's like watching someone pick up the strings on a marionette. All of Beatrice's limbs go at once, in all different directions, eyes bulging in her tapioca face. For a moment I'm afraid she's going to slide off her chair and break her hip or something, but she recovers, grips the arms and says: 'I *beg* your pardon?'

It's not a car. It's a limo. A big, white limo with blacked-out windows. It looks totally out of place in the park. I can't think which of the Wattestone social circle would be likely to turn up with such a flourish of ostentation. It's the vehicular equivalent of pink plastic flamingos. It's a pimpmobile.

'Looks like you've got visitors,' I say.

She's still gawping at me. '*What* did you say?'

'What? Oh. I said I'd give you fifty grand to shut the fuck up,' I say.

She winces at the swearword.

I can hear how my drawl sounds in her ears; ham it up for good measure. 'Thing is, Beatrice,' I tell her, 'it's not all about money. Or status. Or any of your not-in-front-of-the-servants gibberish. It's about love, actually. It's about the fact that I love your grandson to bits, and he loves me to bits back. And if anybody in your family could see past their own precious prejudices for one blind second, they'd probably have noticed that, far from being after your bloody money, I'm bringing money *with* me. I've tried to respect your age and allow for your brain not being what it should be and all, but talking to you today's convinced me your marbles are perfectly intact when you want them to be. As is your hearing. You've got selective deafness, Beatrice. But if you listened for one blind second, you'd understand that it's too bloody late. Rufus married me nearly two months ago and it's no good being in denial about it. Get used to it. I'm here and I'm not going away.'

Beatrice is stunned into silence. I don't give three toots what they say. It may be the preserve of the inarticulate, but swearing is a bloody powerful weapon.

I leave it three beats. Look out of the window and notice that the limo seems to have come to a halt halfway down the drive. It seems to have skewed slightly on its course, as though it's skidded. The front door has come open and the driver has got out, is looking at the ground just under the front wheel.

'So,' I say, 'would you like that cheque now?'

She doesn't answer. I look over and see that she is craning round in the direction in which I've been looking. The hat is bobbling like nobody's business. I've lost her. I've forgotten the old saying about never arguing with someone with an attention span of less than ten seconds, and I've lost her.

'What a ghastly car,' she comments. 'Who on earth would be coming here in a car like that?'

'Search me,' I say.

'Well, it can't be anyone *we* know,' she says. 'They would know better than that. It must be something to do with *you*.'

And when she says it, I have a sudden, blinding realisation as to who it is, and I'm up and off like a bride's nightie.

Chapter Thirty-Eight
The Mummydaddy

I don't even pause to find a coat: just belt down the stairs and through the Great Hall – Rufus, who's been waiting outside the study door, on my heels – fling open the front door and cannon over the gravel to the drive.

Emerging from behind the wall, I see that not only have they really hired an honest-to-God white limousine, but the chauffeur is standing by the bonnet, scratching the back of his head, with his hat in his hand. The back door has come open and a set of legs is emerging.

Oh God. Trust my family to hire a limousine. Any number of Mercedes and Audis and Jags and Beemers and even, God help us, Bentleys for hire to make a splash with, but oh no: they have to go the whole hog and plump for something designed for New Jersey prom parties. I don't know why it's stopped on the drive, but I've certainly got an excellent view of its eight metres of gleaming white paintwork and bulletproof tinted windows. I can just see the white-leather-and-varnished-woodwork-cocktail-bar interior. It's even got strips of pink neon lights running up the sides; they flash, gaudy and bold, in the gathering gloom, and the creeping colour on my cheeks is not just the byproduct of this unexpected burst of exercise. You can always rely on the Mummydaddy to do things by tens.

I set off up the hill. Have to slow to a jog to manage it. The limousine's occupants move into my sight-line around the sides of the car doors. My heart leaps. They're here: my dad, short and squat and cuddly in a baseball jacket; my mum, blonde hair and a white velour leisure suit. I wouldn't be surprised if she hadn't changed into it in the toilets at the airport once she'd verified what colour the car was. They look exactly the way they looked when I last saw them. I can feel emotion welling up inside me like a flash flood. It's funny how sometimes you only realise how much you've been missing someone when you catch sight of them again.

Several sets of eyes bore into my back from the study window.

My mother's voice drifts down the hill over the chilly air. Well, drifts isn't really the word for it. My mum is descended from a long line of Buchan fishwives. Brawny women who followed their menfolk, rolling pins at the ready, down to Cape Town and on across the Indian ocean. They didn't start breeding out until they'd been in Oz for a couple of generations. My mother's bloodline is near intact, and her vocal chords with it.

'What the bloody hell's going on, Don? My teeth damn near bounced clean out of my mouth.'

As I hear her, I feel my heart swell close to bursting. Great gouts of joy swoosh through my circulatory system, freeze up my throat, bring tears straight to my eyes. And, oddly, I find myself slowing down over the last couple of hundred metres, as though I'll get to savour the moment better that way.

My mum! My dad! Here in this silvery field, rooks exploding from the empty treetops. My people!

'I don't bloody know,' says my father, who is bending, hands on knees, beside the chauffeur, gazing down at the front wheel. 'Looks like there's a bloody great hole or summink.'

'Gone into it right up to the axle,' adds the chauffeur.

'Well, what the bloody hell did you drive into *that* for?' bawls Mum.

'Pretty hard to avoid it,' says Dad. 'It's right across the way and halfway across the field.'

'Christ, have you brought us the wrong way?' asks Mum.

'Well, *I* don't bloody know!' replies Dad. 'It's what's on the bloody map, isn't it?'

They are so intent on their argument that they don't notice Rufus and me approaching. That's my family all over. Squabbling their way across the hemispheres. I break back into a half-jog as I get closer.

A small figure, bundled up in black, emerges from behind my mother. Oh my God. Yaya! It's my yaya! She's not been beyond Sydney in twenty years! Swore that the only thing that would get her on an aeroplane again would be if they could scatter her ashes at Famagusta! My entire family, all here, large as life and twice as brassy!

I reach them. 'My word,' I say.

Mum looks up. 'What are you crying about? You're meant to be glad to see us.'

And then she enfolds me in a hug and rubs my back like she's trying to light a fire there. And I'm squashed into the middle of the three of them, Rufus and the chauffeur standing on the outside like spare pricks at a wedding, and I'm bawling my eyes out, rubbing mascara down my cheeks and touching their dear, dear faces like I'm trying to check that they're really real. I know I'm only here because I was running away in the first place, but there are no people you miss more than the ones you run away from.

'What are you doing here? What are you doing here? Why didn't you tell me? I've been trying to call you for days.'

'Well, it wouldn't have been a surprise if we'd told you, would it?' asks Mum matter-of-factly.

'No, I . . . oh my God! Yaya! How are you?'

Yaya does her usual trick of staring you out before she opens her mouth. Yaya has piercing blue eyes. I don't know how it works, because the rest of us are moo-cow brown. 'I tired,' she says eventually, in her customary reproachful tone, the one where she hams up her Cypriot diction, 'and I cold. Why you got a hole in your road?'

Rufus steps forward. 'I don't really know. We've been having a few problems with subsidence recently. . .'

The lot of them clam up, like the blokes in the pub yesterday. They look at him like he's an exhibit in a waxwork museum. Practically walk round the back to check out the joins.

'You must be this man,' says Yaya.

If he's at all taken aback by this novel address, he doesn't show it. 'Yes,' he says. 'Rufus Wattestone. How'd you do?'

241

'Good to meetcha, Rufus,' says Dad, and claps him on the shoulder with a hairy brown hand. Then they all line up to shake his paw.

'I thought,' Mum says to me, 'you said his name was something-something-something.'

'It is. But they call it Wattestone for short.'

'Pretty smart,' says Ma. 'You'd waste an entire year of your life saying it otherwise. So how's my girl? How are they treating you?'

'Great,' I lie. Then follow it up with a truth: 'All the better for seeing you.'

'That's the spirit. So where's the rest of this famous family, then? Couldn't be arsed to come out and meet us?'

I glance over my shoulder. I had sort of assumed that at least one or two of the family might have made the effort, but the drive behind us is empty, and the courtyard as well. The entire Wattestone clan has stayed indoors, observing the interlopers from the safety of the shadows.

'Probably killing the fatted calf as we speak,' I joke, embarrassed. 'They always keep one to hand for unexpected visitors.'

Dad has gone back to looking at the front wheel. 'Well, it looks like we're totally cactus here,' he says.

'We'll bring the tractor up in the morning and pull it out.' Rufus takes the lead at last. 'If that's OK,' he adds to the chauffeur.

The chauffeur turns out to speak fluent cockernee. He opens his mouth and it's like finding yourself flipped into the middle of an Ealing comedy. 'Naah skin off my nose, myte,' he says. 'Dey got me for a wee'. Makes no odds ter me where vey want ter dump da'motah.'

Apples and Pears. Cup of Rosie Lee. Charlie Chester. Gareth Hunt. It's a relief to hear someone speak like this at last. I'd been beginning to think Guy Ritchie was making it all up.

'I'll go down and get the Land Rover,' says Rufus. 'Then we can get your bags down to the house without too much grief.'

'Yaya's not so good on her legs,' says Dad.

'I'm not bloody dead yet, sonny,' says Yaya. 'Show some respect.'

'Well, perhaps you wouldn't mind coming with me and bringing up one of the other cars,' Rufus says to the driver.

'Whoo, *one of the other cars*,' says Mum. Don't start, Ma. Not yet. You've got plenty of time to put the buggers in their place.

'No' me, myte,' says the driver. 'Ahnly errlaird 'er drive ver wum car. More'm my job's wurf.' We really are in an Ealing comedy.

'I'll go,' offers Dad.

'Oh, don't worry about me,' says Yaya. 'I'll just walk. Someone fetch my cane for me, wouldya? If it's not too much trouble.'

'I told you I was going, Ma,' says Dad. 'Keep your hair on.'

'Making an old lady walk miles in the pouring rain,' says Yaya. 'No wonder I never go nowhere.'

She climbs back into the limo, behind the chauffeur, who has settled down in the driver's seat, arms folded, with his cap pulled firmly down over his eyes. Mum and I watch Rufus and Dad descend the hill. They look relaxed together, Dad walking with his hands in his pockets, Rufus's swinging loosely by his sides.

The moment they're out of earshot, Mum sticks an arm through mine and says: 'So how you doing, lovey? Really? It's not like you to burst into tears.'

'I'm fine, Ma. I'm fine. It was just the shock of seeing you, is all.'

'It was a relief to see you,' she says. 'We weren't so sure if we'd come to the right place at first. Tell you what. From a distance it looks like it's practically derelict.'

'Don't let them hear you say that. Round here, that place down there is what they call heaven.'

'But there's a bloody great hole in the roof!' she begins. 'That and the bloody great hole in the *road*. If you left a house in that state back home . . .'

'Different culture, Ma. You've got to give it five minutes. How was the trip?'

'Qantas,' says Yaya, as though this is an explanation in itself. 'Tell you what, I'm bloody glad we can fly Business. I went out the back to stretch my legs and they had them packed in there like sheep in a slaughterhouse.'

'Never again,' says Mum. 'Tell you what, I won't even fly Economy internally these days. They don't even give you enough legroom to read a magazine. Let your table down and you cut off the circulation to the bottom half of your body.'

Yaya's voice drifts through the door. 'These people. Do they know we here? Why they not come to meet us?'

I guess I know the answer, but something makes me protect them anyway. They're my husband's family, after all. It would slay me if my folks judged Rufus on the strength of his family's manners.

'I'm not sure,' I reply. 'It's a big house. Maybe they don't know you're here yet . . .'

'I seen t'ree people at that window there.' A gnarly hand emerges from the limo and points at the first-floor drawing room. Her eyesight hasn't deteriorated since I left home. 'They were watching us.'

'God, then they're probably running around getting tidied up. I don't know. They weren't exactly expecting visitors.'

'No need to go to trouble on our account.' Mum pats the back of her barnet and shakes her Rolex. 'I'm just wearing what I threw on out of a suitcase.'

Glancing in through the open limo door, I see that she's brought her entire range of Vuittons: the portmanteau, the suit carrier, the midsize suitcase, the wheel-on cabin baggage, the shoe store, the vanity case; even the hat box.

She's travelling light, then.

Chapter Thirty-Nine
Could Do with a Dusting

By the time we reach the front door, they've pulled themselves together enough to form a welcoming party. To my surprise, it includes Hilary. I shouldn't be surprised, really. We were supposed to be travelling down on the train together today so he could stay for Christmas, and he must have arrived while I was closeted with Beatrice. Doesn't have a family of his own, of course. Or not one with a bloody great mansion on offer, anyway. Mary has managed, while we have been manhandling Yaya down the hill, to change into a dark green woollen dress topped off with a string of pearls and a pair of matching stud earrings. She has treated her hair to a comb and half a bottle of lacquer and slicked on another layer of her shell-pink lipstick and an application of powder. And sports a pair of high black court shoes which she must have carried down and put on just inside the front door, as she would have broken an ankle trying to walk in them on the uneven surfaces inside the house. She looks, as always, elegant.

Beside her, my mum looks dumpy in her Nikes and leisure wear. It doesn't help that she has slung a bum bag around her hips that makes her look like she's just stepped off a Disney cruise liner. Edmund hasn't changed: is still in his customary uniform of twill trousies and a checked lawn shirt, but has definitely tidied his hair up, and Hilary looks, as usual, like a comedy cad.

They've turned the lights on in the hall. I glimpse Beatrice looking down from her bedroom window, Nessa silhouetted behind her.

The three of them stand in the doorway, Mary a step forward, one hand on the lintel, while her menfolk take up position, hands behind their backs, to her rear. I'm relieved to see that she is smiling.

'Welcome!' she cries, once we're out of the Land Rover. 'What a surprise! And what a treat!' She totters gingerly out on to the flags in front of the door, extends a hand to my mother.

Edmund steps out after her, does the same to my dad. 'Edmund Wattestone,' he says. 'How do you do?'

'Mary,' says Mary.

'Great to meetcha, Mary,' says my mum. 'Colleen. I guess we're related now, eh?'

Mary doesn't turn a hair. 'Lovely girl,' she says. 'And what a treat to be able to put faces to names at last.'

Mary has asked me precisely zero questions about my family in the past seven weeks.

'I've heard so much about you,' she says.

'Likewise,' lies my Mum right back at her. 'So this is the old homestead, eh?'

'For its sins,' says Mary. 'Come in. Please.'

There's a pointed cough from behind us.

Oh God, sorry.

'This is my grandmother,' I say, 'Penelope. Yaya, this is Mary, my mother-in-law, and Edmund, my father-in-law. And this is Hilary. An old family friend.'

'That's a chick's name, isn't it?' asks Dad.

Edmund steps forward gallantly, takes my Yaya's hand and bows over it. 'ἄσμενος σε ζενιζω ἐν τῃ μου οἰκιᾳ,' he tells her. 'τιμᾳς δη ἡμας φοιτησασα.'

'What'd he say?' asks Mum.

'Δεν ζερ'ω.Σαν Ελληνιφ'α μου ακο'υτ'αι η δι'αλεκτος ε'ιναι περ'ιεργη' says Yaya. 'Λαμβ'ανοντας υπ'οψ'οψην και την προφορ'α.'

'λυπουμαι γε· ἐνομισα γαρ σε Ἑλληνα ἐιναι,' says Edmund.

'Well, I am,' she says, getting what's going on, 'But I'm only seventy-five. Not four thousand.'

'Ah. You speak English.'

'I guess after thirty years in Australia I might have picked up a bit.'

Yaya turns to Dad and says: 'Καλ'α αυτο'ι τα 'εχουν χαμ'ενα.

246

Τι στην ευχ'η γυρ'ευουμε εδ'ω π'ερα? Το αγ'ορι φα'ινετ αι καλ'ο 'ομως. Επ'ισης, ε'ιναι και μοστιμο'υλης.'

'Σταμ'ατα γιαγι'α.' I tell her.

'Μπορε'ι να ,ιλ'αει αρχα'ια Ελληννικ'α, αλλ'αθαρρ'ω πως καταλαβα'ινει αυτ'α που λες.'

Yaya looks at me, then at Rufus, then back at me. 'Ωρα'ιος πισιν'ος. Τ'ωρα βλ'επω ποι'ο 'ηταν το θ'εαμα.'

Rufus flashes my yaya a flirtatious look. 'Thank you. It's all the riding.'

I find myself blushing. Yaya cackles.

'Well,' says Edmund, 'come in. You must be exhausted. I should think you could do with a drink.'

'You're not kidding,' says my mum. 'I'm as dry as a nun's nasty.'

There's a moment's silence in honour of this statement. 'Well,' says Mary faintly, 'we'll see what we can do . . .'

As we enter the hall, I hear Mum gasp. I know everyone else has heard it too. They, of course, will be thinking she's impressed. I know, and Dad will know, that she's thinking about the dirt. Mum has a bit of an allergy to housedust. It makes her angry.

'Well, this is . . . interesting,' says my mum.

'It's colder inside than out,' says Yaya.

'Hey!' says Dad, advancing into the room. 'That's some weapons you got there!'

'Do you like them?' asks Edmund. 'That one over the fireplace is the axe my great-great-great-great-great-great-great-great-great-grandfather used to behead witches with.'

'Radical,' says my dad.

'Very advanced, of course,' says Edmund. 'Most of them were still tying them on to bonfires at the time.'

'Hmm,' says Dad, 'nowadays we just send them to Queensland and call them politicians. You mind if I smoke?'

'Not at all,' says Edmund.

'Want one?'

Edmund glances at his wife and declines.

'Go on. I've got plenty. Havanas. I get them sent over by the case.'

'No, really,' says Edmund. 'Under orders, I'm afraid.'

'They're really good,' says Dad, and elbows Edmund in the ribs. 'Rolled on a maiden's *thigh*, you know what I mean?'

'Adonis!' barks Yaya. 'You watch your mouth! You want to show us up in front of your daughter's new family?'

Dad just lets out one of his emphysematous chortles and claps Edmund on the back.

Yaya turns to Tilly. 'What joy you have beneath your dress,' she says.

Tilly looks startled, glances down and remembers that she's pregnant. 'Yes, I – thank you.'

'It will be any day now, I think,' says Yaya.

'Another few weeks, I'm afraid,' says Tilly.

Yaya shakes her head firmly. 'No. Next few days. And it will be a boy.'

'Oh, I *do* hope so,' says Mary, who seems to have recovered her composure.

'I am always right,' says Yaya. 'In fifty years, I never been wrong.'

'Well!' says Mary. 'At least *that's* something to look forward to!'

'You got to be strong to have children,' says Yaya gloomily. Pats Tilly's belly absentmindedly as though she were a passing moo-cow. 'First they rip you apart when they come into the world, and then they rip your heart from your body when you are old. It's no life, being a woman. A vale of tears.'

Rufus brings in the last of Mum's bags. He's looking a bit pink about the face. 'I think that's the lot,' he says.

'Oh, thank you. Now come into the light and let me have a proper look at you.'

Rufus looks sheepish, ducks his head and steps in front of her. Looks down at her. Something passes between them and they both smile. Then Mum stretches up and pinches him on the cheek like a little boy. 'Not bad for a pommy.'

'I've seen worse ockerinas.'

'You're going to look after my little girl, aren't you?'

'I shall cherish her like finest porcelain.'

Mum bellows with laughter. 'Cheeky monkey.'

'You've brought plenty of luggage,' says Mary faintly.

'Oh, you don't need to worry about that,' says my dad. 'She takes a suitcase on wheels when she goes out to lunch in case she feels like a change of outfit.'

'Didn't really know what to pack,' adds Mum. 'It's kind of hard to believe that it's really going to be cold in December. So I packed a bit of everything. And besides, you need the odd special gear for Christmas, don't you? Plus, of course, the big trunk is gifts. You'll have to wait for the big day to see what they are, though.'

Hilary finally finds his voice. 'You've come for Christmas?'

'Yeah. Only period Don can get the time off. As it is, we've had to leave Melody's brother behind to look after the shop. But we couldn't leave our little girl to fend for herself in a strange country over the festive season, eh?' There's a little pause as this information sinks in, then Mum, suddenly remembering her manners, adds: 'If that's OK, of course. If we're not putting you out.'

'No, no,' says Mary.

'Cause I'm sure we could still check into a hotel,' says Ma unconvincingly.

'I told you we should have given them some notice,' says Yaya.

'But that would have spoiled the surprise,' says Edmund. 'We've plenty of bedrooms.'

'That's good. Was wondering when we came down the hill if it wasn't a lunatic asylum,' says Mum. Hastily adds, when she sees how well this is going down: 'I can give you a hand with the cooking.'

'How kind . . .' says Mary.

'Or I'll tell you what,' offers Dad, 'maybe there's a hotel or a restaurant around here that does Christmas dinner? Maybe I could take us all out, eh? My shout.'

'How kind . . .' says Mary again. I think she's gone on to automatic. I can see her gazing at my mum's trainers, at the spectacles held round her neck by a white plastic chain (she's got chains to go with all her outfits), at Dad's bomber jacket, at Yaya's old-Greek-lady black dress and furry boots. 'So!' she says brightly. 'Let's go up to the drawing room and get you a drink!'

'Thought you'd never ask,' says Mum drily.

'We've some champagne in the cellar,' says Mary.

'Christ, no,' says Mum, 'hate the stuff. Gives me terrible wind. Have you got anything else?'

Chapter Forty

Delilah

The cellphone I insisted on going to buy in Bicester yesterday arvo
while the olds napped off their jet lag wakes me, bimbling out the
chorus of 'Delilah' in the dark, pulling me slowly out of sleep like
a mosquito buzzing in my ear. Seems like I'm the only one to hear
it. Rufus and Buster slumber on oblivious, tandem snores filling
the room as I feel about the floor for my bag.

Eventually I track the phone down by the green light on top.
Notice that the time display reads 06:24 before I answer.

It's Mum.

'Hi,' I say.

'Sorry. You're going to have to come and get me.'

'Where are you?'

'I haven't the foggiest. I came out looking for the dunny an hour
ago and now I'm lost.'

'But it's only one door down from your room.'

'Someone must've moved the doors,' she says firmly.

My husband sighs in his sleep, mutters something about
pheasants and buries his face in the pillow.

I sigh myself. 'Tell me where you are.'

'Well, if I knew that,' she tells me with faultless logic, 'I'd be able
to find my way back, wouldn't I?'

I manage to hold back a second sigh. 'Look around you, and tell
me what you see.'

'Oh. OK. Well, I'm in a room . . .'

I wait.

'It's . . . I dunno. Looks pretty much like all the rooms I've been
in. Covered in dust, wallpaper hanging off, cobwebs in the corners,
little piles of plaster flakes, drapes haven't been cleaned in years . . .'

'Is there anything at all that's different from the other rooms? Have you got any idea which floor you're on?'

'None at all.'

'Well, look around you, Ma. There must be something you can give me a clue with.'

'I don't know. Oh, yeah, OK: there's a couple of statues.'

'What do they look like?'

'Naked chicks.'

Plenty of those about.

'What are they doing?'

'I dunno. Washing, I guess. That or stripping'

'Does one of them have eight arms?'

'That's the one.'

'OK. I'll come and get you.'

She's somehow found her way to the Indian gallery, two floors and a wing-and-a-half away from their quarters. I turn on the lamp to find some clothes – I'm not walking those dark and haunted corridors in just a nightie; I've seen *Friday the 13th* – and Rufus, disturbed, opens his eyes.

'Hi. What's up?'

I explain.

'What time is it?'

'Half six, quarter to seven.'

'Ugh. God, I hate these dark mornings. Suppose I might as well get up now I'm awake.'

'Naah. Stay in bed for a bit, doll. Place won't fall down without you.'

My husband rubs his face, sleepily. 'Wouldn't be so sure of that.'

'Mind if I take this sweater with me? She's probably halfway to hypothermia by now.'

He raises the counterpane, sends Buster tumbling over on to my side of the bed. The dog barely reacts, just rearranges himself, smacks his chops and resumes his snoring. 'Sure. Can I have my morning kiss, please?'

'I've not brushed my teeth yet.'

'Doesn't matter.'

This is the stuff about marriage: the stuff I find surprising, the stuff that delights me. This intimacy, this no-need-to-impress, these small rituals that keep you warm on chilly mornings. I go to him and hold him as he comes awake. Stroke his hair and feel the comfort of his arms round my waist, the flex of his shoulders under my forearms. Rufus smells of bonfires and toffee this morning. I will never let him go.

'Where did she say she was?'

'Sounded like the Indian gallery.'

'Oh, OK. Know the quickest way to get there?'

'Down to the hall and back up the Broad Oak Stair, eh?'

He shakes his head, grazes my neck with his night-beard. 'No, darling. You just turn left out of here and go down to the end of the corridor. It's the other side of the door there.'

'I thought that was a wall?'

'No. We don't use the door much, so it seemed like a sensible place to hang the tapestry when the water got into the Henry the Second room.'

I shake my head back at him. 'I'm never going to get it, am I?'

''S'all right, baby. Give it another twenty years or so.'

'Funny fellah.'

'Funny ha-ha.'

'Funny bloody weird as hell. I'd better go.'

'Mmm. I love you, you know.'

'I know. I do too. I love you.'

'Good.'

He lets me go, lies backs on the pillows and smiles.

I don't see her when I first enter the gallery, because she's sitting in an old howdah, shrouded by curtains. Eventually I track her down by the smell of cigarette smoke.

'Christ,' I say, 'it's not even seven. Couldn't you at least wait until after breakfast?'

'It's four thirty in the afternoon as far as I'm concerned,' she says reasonably. 'And I've been up since half three anyway. Had to do something to fill the time.'

'You took your cigs to the loo?'

'Didn't want to disturb your father.'

'And your phone?'

'Took my bag for luck. Bloody glad I did.'

'So did you manage to find one?'

She harrumphs. 'No.'

'You must be busting.'

She laughs. 'You can say that again. If you'd been five minutes longer you'd've found me squatted over one of those pots over there.'

'Come on.'

'Hold up. Let me finish my cig first.'

Mum takes three huge lungfuls off the end of her butt. 'Where can I stub this out?'

'Well, I dunno. You should have thought about that before you lit it.'

'Yep, that's what I came for,' she says dismissively, 'to be brought up by my own daughter. Ah, look. This'll do.' She lifts the lid of a pot set into one of the howdah's upright posts, daintily crushes out the cigarette inside.

'Mum!' I am scandalised. 'You can't do that!'

'Just did,' she points out. 'And besides, what is it if it ain't an incense holder? It's just another sort of ash.'

'But it's probably hundreds of years old!'

Mum does one of her sniffs. 'I dare say it hasn't been opened in all that time, neither. By the time it gets opened my butt will just be another historical artefact. Anyway, let's get to that bathroom, eh?'

I'm not so good on the geography of the Georgian wing. I decide to get her down to the ground floor so that at least she can orientate herself enough to navigate her way back to their bedroom, which is in the Edwardian section.

'So you haven't had a lot of sleep, then,' I say as I lead her out to the Tollbooth stair.

'No. Bloody jet lag. Tell you what, Melody. This house is weird.'

'You don't say?'

She misses the irony in my tone. 'I mean, I must've opened forty doors, and not a single one of them a khazi. What is it with these people? They think it's common to wash, or something?'

'I think some of them have their bladders taken out at birth.'

'Christ. I'd heard about the chinectomies, but I didn't know about that.'

'It's in case they meet the Queen. They're not allowed to go to the loo till she does, or something, so they have to get into practice.'

'I'll tell you, I almost got spooked wandering around in the dark. Half the light switches don't work and even when they do, mostly all you see is junk.'

'That's heirlooms, Mother.'

'Nonsense. Heirlooms is stuff you care about and treat with love. This is room after room of discarded second-hand furniture. Covered in dust. I gave my pillow a bit of a punch before I lay down last night and we couldn't see anything for half an hour.'

'I wish you wouldn't talk about Dad like that.'

'Oh, ha bloody ha.'

I get her to the door of a bathroom at last. Stand outside as I hear her settle on the throne, sigh with relief. Through the door, her voice carries, muffled.

'And another thing. It wasn't just the jet lag that woke me.'

'No?'

'No. I don't know. Maybe it was a nightmare. But I don't think it was, because it seemed to go on after I woke up. Are you sure this place is stable? Only I could swear the whole house was shaking.'

'Oh, yeah. It does that.' I can't believe I'm so blasé about it already.

'It does that?'

'Mmm hmm. Rufus says it's because it's so old.'

Mum shifts behind the door. 'Come on, love. There's more to it than that. God, it was like being in the middle of an earthquake.'

'I know. That's what I thought the first time. But you get used to it. It happens all the time. I don't even remember it waking me tonight.'

'Well, it did me. Didn't wake your father, of course.'

'He wouldn't hear it over his snoring, anyway.'

'Too true. By the way, who was that ancient old baggage I saw staring at me from an upstairs window when we came in? Looked like someone had stood her too close to a heater?'

'Oh, that's Beatrice,' I say. 'Edmund's mother. A treat in store.'

'Looked like it. Looked like she'd lost a quid and found a button.'

'Yeah, she does rather, doesn't she?'

The thunderous flush of hundred-year-old plumbing and she emerges, tugging her top down over her waistband.

'And who's the pregnant one?'

'That's Tilly. She's Rufus's sister.'

'Oh, right. Doesn't look much like him.'

'No, I suppose not. She looks a bit like Edmund, though.'

'I guess so. Suppose that's something. She seems nice enough. At least she hasn't got a stick up her backside like her old girl. Where's the babyfather?'

'Done a bunk. They don't talk about it, though. They say he's in Burundi.'

'Gone to Burundi. I like it. Nice euphemism. Like having the painters and decorators in.'

'Hugo Hunstanton.'

'Oh, well, there you go. Stands to reason he'd do a bunk with a name like that. How come's they're not going after him with the shotgun?'

I puff from inflated cheeks. 'God knows, Ma. I think Edmund might, if he ever noticed, but he's had the wobbly boot on for years and nothing much impinges on his consciousness. Mary just seems to want to blame Tilly and all of them want to keep it from Beatrice.'

'Poor kid,' she says.

'I know.'

She makes use of her talent for dropping subjects when she's done with them. 'What do you think the chances are of a bit of brekkie now I'm up?'

'Let's go and see what we can find.'

We pass through the hall and start down the kitchen stairs. 'How's Costa?' I ask.

'He's good. He sends his love. He'll try and come next year. Had to stay back and keep an eye on things, you know?'

'Yes. Is everything OK?'

'Oh, yeah,' she shrugs. ''course it is. You know how it is, though. Can't turn your back for a second or someone'll be in there trying to take over. Jesus, Melody, you're not telling me people actually make food down here, are you?'

Fifi and Django have got down from the couch to greet us. Fifi stands up on his hind legs and gazes longingly up at my mother. He looks – I've got to say it – adorable. What's happened to me? Since when did I think bulldogs looked adorable? I even found myself dropping a kiss on the head of Roly's dog Perkins the other day. But he looks so – big and cute and cuddly, and I find myself forced to bend down and catch him up in a big bear hug. He wriggles his backside and rolls his strangulated eyes. Makes for my mouth with a long schlumphy tongue. Mum makes a noise of combined disgust and contempt.

'You mean they leave the dogs in here all night?'

'Some of the time, but . . .' I suddenly think better of telling her about where they spend their nights if they're not in the kitchen. 'No. Not always. What would you like to eat?'

She pulls out one of the wooden chairs that sit round the table, checks it for stains and lowers herself on to the seat. 'I don't know. Everything. I feel like I haven't eaten in a decade.'

'Well, you didn't make much of a go of last night's dinner, that's for sure.'

'Yes. What was that?'

'Toad in the hole.'

'Oh my God. You're not telling me those snags were made of toad?'

I laugh. 'Just you wait. They have something called spotted dick.'

Mum lights a cigarette. 'I will personally,' she says, 'garrotte anyone who tries to feed me something called spotted dick.'

A voice from behind me: 'I'll thank you not to smoke in my kitchen.' We whirl round to find the happy smiling face of Mrs Roberts mooning at us from the back door. 'It's unhygienic,' she adds.

Fifi squirms his way towards her using only his front paws, dragging his backside along the floorboards. She bends down and rubs the top of his head, accepts a good licking and advances into the kitchen. Puts a plastic bag down on the table and folds her arms.

'Can I help you with something?'

'Hi, Mrs Roberts,' I say. 'How are you this morning? This is my mother. They arrived from Brisbane yesterday.'

'Nobody told *me*,' she says suspiciously.

Mum sticks out a hand for shaking. 'Pleased to meet you, Mrs Roberts. We sprung a bit of a surprise. Didn't tell anyone we were coming.'

'I hope there's enough to go around.' Mrs Roberts ignores my mother's hand.

'Actually, she's pretty much starving,' I tell her, 'after the journey and all. We were sort of hoping . . .'

'Breakfast is at nine,' she says firmly. Opens her plastic bag and starts digging within.

'Well, maybe we could make ourselves some coffee and some toast or something . . .' I can't believe how tentative I sound.

'Breakfast is at nine,' she repeats. I sort of feel sorry for Mrs Roberts, in a way. It must have been bad for her, missing her calling as a seaside landlady and all.

'But if we—'

'If you'll excuse me,' she says, 'I must get on.'

'Don't mind us,' says Mum. 'We'll be out of your hair in no time.'

Mrs Roberts doesn't respond. Pulls a bag of what looks like

bacon rashers out of her bag and slaps it down on the tabletop. Crosses the floor and gets herself a large knife from the block by the sink.

Mum gets to her feet and makes for the kettle.

Mrs Roberts stabs the knife into the table-top.

We freeze.

'Mrs Roberts—' I begin.

'Breakfast,' she says, 'is at nine.'

'But we—' I begin.

'Lady Mary likes her meal-times regular. Mrs Wattestone liked them regular before her. When Lady Mary says it's all right for all and sundry to come in here and help theirselves, and smoke all over the food, then they can do as they like. But in the meantime, I'd be grateful if you would let the running of the house go on as it always has,' she says.

'Christ,' says Mum, 'what do you *sound* like?'

'If you've got any complaints,' says Mrs Roberts, 'you should take them up with Lady Mary. She'll be down to breakfast at nine o'clock, like normal.'

This is going to deteriorate, fast. There's one of those unstoppable force/unmoveable object situations developing in front of my eyes, and I'm not sure the house's foundations are strong enough to take it.

'Now, look, my lady—' begins Mum.

I raise my voice. Pointedly. 'We'll be getting out of your way, then, Mrs Roberts,' I say.

'I want a cup of tea,' says Mum.

'You'll get one at nine o'clock,' I tell her. 'And I'll get you a kettle for your room this afternoon.'

'You can't let her talk to you like that,' says Mum. Her voice is starting on that familiar build. If I don't get her out of here within the next minute, the whole of Gloucestershire will know my olds have come to stay.

'We'll talk about it later,' I say. I take her by the arm and guide her back towards the hall stairs.

'What is going *on*?'

'Don't, Mum.'

'Who *is* that woman?'

'She's the housekeeper.'

'And you let her talk to you like that?'

She's right, of course. Time was I would never have stood for that kind of talk.

'For now,' I say.

'I wouldn't put up with it.'

'Sometimes it's better to wait for your moment.'

'Revenge is a dish best eaten cold?'

'Indeed.'

We pause in contemplation. 'So what time is it, anyway?' she asks.

I check my watch. 'Another hour till breakfast, I'm afraid.'

'I've got an idea. Why don't we just take a car and go to a greasy spoon?'

'Good thinking, Mother. I don't suppose the chauffeur would be up for taking us?'

'What, that jobsworth? No chance. Let's just take one of the cars.'

'Don't shout at me.'

'What?'

'I'm not insured.'

Mum gapes at me. 'How long have you been here, again?'

'Seven weeks. I know. I know. It's just, Rufus keeps forgetting and I don't think it's a very high priority with anyone else.'

'But you used to *love* your car.'

'I know.'

'Well, we'll see about *that*,' she says. 'Where's that husband of yours?'

'No, Ma. When I said not to shout, I meant at Rufus either.'

'Ah God,' she says, 'I'm too hungry to shout. I'm going to get him to drive us up to town.'

Relieved, I say: 'He'll be out in the grounds somewhere. He always checks that nothing's fallen down in the night first thing.'

'Great. I can get a chance to see the famous grounds, then. Hope

260

they live up to the promise of the house. I mean, I know it's hard, but you never know. Because if this is anything to go by, they'll be something really spectacular, then, eh?'

'Shaddap.'

'An Englishman's home is his pigsty. So what are we going to see? Triton fountains? Swimming pool? A collection of pink plastic flamingos? No, don't tell me: there'll be some hedges with big holes in and something dead somewhere.'

'You can be a real smartarse, Mother.'

'That'll be where *you* get it from.'

'It's a thousand years old. Or so they keep telling me. You can't expect it to look like new.'

We step out of the front door, and she says: 'Well, OK. I wasn't expecting it to look like new, but I was right about the something dead. Jesus. Who cut the dog in half?'

The courtyard is filled with the sulphurous smell of drains. Drains and dead vegetation, and something vaguely fishy, to boot.

'I take it all back,' says Mum. 'It's a paradise on earth.'

'Something's wrong,' I tell her. 'It doesn't usually smell like this.'

'Of course I believe you.'

I shout, 'Rufus? Rufus!'

'I'm over here,' calls his voice, and it sounds – drained, empty. Weary.

'Where?'

'Here.'

I see him over by the moat. He's sitting on the wet grass, knees pulled up to his chin, fingers linked at the back of his neck.

'Hey!' I say, and we start towards him. 'What's going on? What are you doing there and what in the hell is that smell?'

And then I stop, and stare. Because where there should be a limpid expanse of noble water there is, instead, a muddy ditch, brown trout gasping at the bottom.

Chapter Forty-One
Crack in the Earth

Even Mum has the tact to withdraw at this point. She mutters something about checking on Dad and goes back inside. Rufus doesn't move. He's breathing deeply; his shoulders are heaving with the effort. I'm not sure if he isn't actually crying.

I go to him, lower myself down to sit next to him, pressing up against his side.

'Oh, baby,' I say, 'I'm sorry. I'm so sorry.'

Rufus doesn't speak.

I can see what has happened now. The crack which the limo fell into last night has extended all the way across the park, and enters the moat just outside the courtyard walls. And I'm thinking: yes, but for a moat a couple of hundred metres long and four deep to drain completely overnight . . . the water had to go somewhere. I'm thinking: what the hell is down there? But I don't say anything to Rufus because he's not in the mood for idle chitchat.

Eventually, he stirs, says: 'I'm sorry. You didn't deserve this.'

'Oh, Rufus,' I say. It's funny how many words you can encapsulate into just two. Because I'm saying: *what on earth are you on about?* And: *don't be stupid*, and: *I love you so much that I don't even know how to begin to tell you*, and: *it'll be OK, darling, we'll find some way*, and: *I do understand that this is a major disaster, darling, you don't have to tell me*, and: *shit, shit, shit, shit, shit.*

'Don't worry,' I tell him. 'I married you for your body not your house. If you let *yourself* go to seed, it'll be another matter.'

'I'm so sorry. I should have told you the truth. I'm such a selfish, lying . . . and now you're trapped with all this and I wanted to give you something so much better.'

262

'Ne'mind. Look on the bright side. At least you won't have to give me any money when I divorce you.'

Rufus half laughs. 'Don't even joke about it. You've no idea.'

'I've got *some* idea.'

'We'll go bankrupt,' he says, and his tone is uncomfortably matter-of-fact and emotionless.

'No, Rufus. We won't do that.'

He twists round to look at me and says: 'You can't say that, Melody. You don't know. You don't know *any* of it. I've dragged you into it and now you're going to be dragged down by it along with the rest of us, and I'm really, really sorry.'

I try reasoning. Sometimes that works, I've found. 'Rufus, you're demoralised. Anybody would be.'

'No,' he says, with an edge of finality to the word. 'I mean, yes, I'm demoralised, but my state of mind doesn't alter the facts. We're stuffed. Insolvent. Out of business. Broke. Bust. Cleaned out. Ruined.'

'Insurance?'

A shake of the head. 'Not for subsidence. Not around here.'

'They can do that?'

'Of course they can do that. That's the point of insurance. They only insure you for things that aren't likely to happen, not for things that might. They double your premiums for being old, you know, as well. It's how they make profits.'

'Jesus.'

'This is going to cost – Mel, we're not going to be able to find that sort of money. And Health and Safety won't let us open for the season with the building unsafe, so there's no prospect of any income.'

'Can't you borrow?'

Rufus's laugh sounds out across the mud like a funeral knell. His meaning takes a moment to sink in.

'OK. So how much do we owe?'

He names a figure that makes me gasp.

'How? *How?* How does *anybody* borrow that sort of money?'

'By being at school with someone whose family own a bank. And, of course, it wasn't that much when he borrowed it.'

'He?'

'Daddy. Borrowed it in the nineteen seventies. Old mate's interest rate. That sort of thing still went on, back then. He wanted it for one of his get-rich-slow schemes. I think it was the ostrich farm. That or the Alaskan goldmine. Or maybe the offshore trust with the unbelievable rate of return based on the fact that the man who was running it was tucking it all into a trust of his own in the Caymans. That one shook him, I can tell you. Said he'd never do business with a Harrovian again. But then, you know, there was Big Bang, and the nineteen eighties, and all the big banks started noticing that the small private banks were run by old Etonians without a brain cell to rub together, and so did the con merchants, and before you know it, your bank's gone down with all hands and your debt belongs to some chap in Hong Kong who doesn't have the same reverence for the Old School as Daddy's friends had, and the silly old bugger hasn't bothered to have limited liability to Lloyd's when they go bust because everyone knows it's just a licence to print money, and you're running along only just managing to make the interest payments, and the roof's falling off, and everyone in the village thinks you're a laughing stock, and your forebears are spending money like it's going out of style and just scattering bits of priceless jewellery about the place like they've come from Claire's Accessories because they will not – *will not* – get their heads around the fact that there isn't any any more, and running up tabs at all the local shops if you try to impose some sort of allowance on them because it doesn't count as spending money, only it does, God knows it does, especially when they hide the accounts when they come in and you don't know anything about it till there's a bailiff on the doorstep, and I'm in *despair*, Mel. They just don't listen to a word I say. They think that the fact that we're an old family is enough, that Bourton has always been here so it always will be, and they don't understand that you can't just *have* money, you've got to *make* it. It took me five years just to get them to open up to the public. I don't know what to *do* . . .'

Oh God.

A trout flaps and struggles in a tiny pocket of sludgy water below us. Poor creature: slowly suffocating in the place that should have been its haven.

I try a tentative suggestion. 'Well, you know, you could always sell something . . .'

'Like what?'

'I don't know. There must be something. Isn't that a Brueghel on the corridor up to the Lady Chapel?'

'Oh, darling,' says Rufus, 'that would be so nice. You're so nice. Solutions. God.'

'Well. Why not?'

'It's a copy. Not even a very good one. That's why it's hung in that dark old corridor, so you can't see too clearly.'

'Oh.'

'The original went for death duties some time in the nineteenth century.'

'Oh. How about the Caravaggio?'

'Granny would eviscerate anyone who touched that.'

'Oh,' I say again.

I pick a stalk of grass, start shredding it between my thumbnails. 'Babe, we can find something. I know we can. It won't come to that.'

'It will, you know.'

He puts his head in his hands and to my shock I realise that he's doing it to hide the fact that he really is crying. My heart does a huge, dizzying lurch. Seeing someone you love cry is the worst thing. It's the time when the lies, the mutual fantasies that bind love together, are shown in all their tawdry worthlessness, like paste diamonds under strong light. When the belief we all cling to that we are one as two, that love confers invincibility, is shown for what it is: a hopeless expression of the search for heaven. Because I love him, I love him with all my life, but I can't reach him. Maybe that's what love is for: it's a confidence trick we play on ourselves to fool us into believing we're not alone.

I reach out and take him in my arms, press kisses on his temples, stroke away his tears with faltering fingertips. Whisper soft assurances like you would to a child. *Hush, my love, be still. I'll take care of you. I'll bind you safe and keep you warm.*

'I so want to walk away,' he says. 'My whole life I've wanted to walk away. Run away. When I was a child. Looking at the damp streaming down my bedroom wall and the rats scurrying off when you turned the light on in the cellar and the plaster coming off in chunks from the Great Hall ceiling and the elms crashing down in the park and the houses in the village emptying out one by one and the peacocks dying on the lawns and mould inside the wardrobes and silverfish pouring out from under the lino and beetles in the carpets and paint peeling from every single wall, and everyone told me, over and over again, how lucky I was, what an awesome responsibility and an incomprehensible privilege. Mummy and Granny, talking about sacrifices and determination, battles and wars, bravery and grit, all of it so that I could be the heir to Bourton Allhallows, and take on the noble duty of preserving it to pass on to my sons. And I knew even then that it wouldn't be possible, that there was dry rot in the timbers and woodworm and Dutch Elm and deathwatch beetle and something very, very wrong with the foundations, and that I was going to be the last one. That I wouldn't be able to keep it going any longer. It's beyond anything. There isn't a lottery win, or an upturn in the market, or a mystery benefactor or a surprise legacy that could sort this out. It's just a matter of time.'

It's all right, my love. I'm with you.

'And yet even though I've known it was inevitable,' he says, 'I feel like a traitor. If I have to walk away, I will be betraying everything. All the ones that came before me, and all the ones that will come after, will look on me as the coward, the one who wasn't up to the job, the one who sold his birthright. That's all that's kept them going, you know, over the last hundred years. Each son, terrified that he was going to be the one. Each one of us pretending he loved the place that smothered his ambitions. It's destroyed Daddy, and it turned Granpa into a raging drunk, and it'll get me in the end, whatever I do to stop it.'

I'm speechless. I'd not thought of it this way. I've thought of all these people as rendered helpless by privilege, and now Rufus is wanting me to believe that they've been sucked dry by a house.

Are people really like that? Is this what happens to great families, as the bloodline to the high-achieving villains that once headed them gets thinner and thinner? At what point in a family's history does the stuff they have accrued become more important than the family members, the offspring merely custodians of bricks and mortar, rather than individuals in their own right?

I suddenly understand, now, why Mary and Beatrice put so much store in status, why Tilly is apologetic as though her very presence in a room were an embarrassment. Surrounded all their lives by husbands and fathers and brothers whose only function was to caretake an architectural vampire, they have been raised to be nothing but addenda to the caretakers. Status is the only thing available to them, and Tilly, husbandless and undereducated, has no more status in the world than the girl behind the checkout at Tesco. I find myself quietly grateful for the Aussie Battlers who raised me. Far better to be the offspring of the working classes on the way up than the overlords on the way down. No wonder they don't like me. No wonder. Snobbery is so much more complicated than simply looking down on people. People aren't really offended by their social inferiors. They're threatened by what they represent.

'Rufus,' I say, 'I feel obliged to point out that you'd be doing our kids a favour if you broke the chain. Why not call it quits? There might still be a pop star, or an IT billionaire or something, who'd think it was worth the small change for the big-face cachet of a slice of history like this.'

He shakes his head. 'I can't. It would kill Granny. And probably Dad, too. It would break them, and I can't do that.'

'But if it's a choice between—'

'Anyway, it's not really my choice,' he says. He's sitting up now, and he's surreptitiously wiping his face as though he thinks I might not have noticed his tears. 'Apart from anything else, I can't do a thing without the trustees' say-so.'

'Well, surely the trustees will be able to see that there's nothing else to be done? Seriously. I don't have any brief for living in a castle myself. It's ruining my clothes and I'm getting chilblains.'

'Darling, think about it. Who would you think the most likely people to be trustees *are*?'

'Oh,' I say.

'You'd be much better off divorcing me now.' He puts an arm behind my back. 'Even without children you'd probably get a nice little settlement. We'll have bugger-all in a few years' time.'

I pinch his thigh, hard. 'That's not even funny.'

'We've got excellent accident insurance, as well. After Granpa got killed out hunting and we realised we could have completely refurbished the orangery with the settlement.'

'I'll bear it in mind. So what are we going to do while I wait to bump you off, then?'

'I don't know. Same old story, I suppose. Job by job and hope for the best. I'll have to get the surveyors in to look at this. It obviously wasn't a fluke last time. So we'll just have to keep our fingers crossed. Maybe I can fix it. Maybe there's a way.'

'Well, you know what we say in Australia?'

'What?'

'If it can't be fixed with pantyhose and fencing wire, it's not worth fixing.'

Chapter Forty-Two
Dad's Big Gesture

We're down in the cellar, wearing waders, alternately loading a couple of wheelbarrows with Edmund's wine and wheeling them to the door, where Tilly lumbers it, bottle by bottle, up the steps, when Edmund's voice echoes from up in the house. None of us has exchanged a word about the fact that the grownups, as Rufus and Tilly refer to the olds, have been conspicuously not in evidence all morning, none of them so much as sticking a head out of the front door to tell us about breakfast, which we missed.

'I say!' calls Edmund.

Rufus and I are in that weird state where you are both freezing cold and covered in sweat all at once. Tilly's hair sticks to her forehead and she already looks fit to drop. But she won't go and rest, and, though the work we're doing is probably less demanding than hers in a lot of ways, none of us is prepared to accept the potential consequences of making a pregnant lady wade in backed-up drain water.

It stinks down here. Where the rest of Bourton Allhallows smells faintly fungal, the cellar smells of rats and rotting things and old earth and, now, sewers. I have sent Mum off in the limo to pick up some medicated shower stuff – there's a craft fair on in Stow anyway, and I'm sure the ceramic-cottage shops will keep her entertained for most of the day – but we'll still probably go down with Weil's disease, maybe a spot of cholera. God knows what ancient spores are lurking in the bones of the house, just waiting for a bit of water and an unwary passerby to wake them up.

'I say?' calls Edmund again.

Tilly wipes her forehead with the back of a hand that clutches a bottle of 1974 Petrus. 'Down here!'

Footsteps, then a silhouette blocks out the feeble light. We've got a gas lantern lit at the far end, by the wine racks. The leccy has long since died. Probably sometime around 1953.

'Good show.'

'You're welcome,' says Rufus.

'You *are* being careful with the labels, aren't you?'

'Doing our best.'

'Only, it won't do if I can't tell what everything is.'

I draw breath to say something sarcastic, but feel Rufus's hand on my arm.

'I'm doing what I can, Dad. You might want to put in a bit of time with a magic marker after lunch.'

'Do I?' says Edmund. 'Well, yes, I suppose I might. Good thinking.'

I slop my way through thigh-deep slurry towards the stairs. If Edmund is going to create a hiatus, I intend to make the most of it. Tilly has already sat down on a step, and I've got the one where her feet are resting earmarked for myself.

'Was there something we could do for you, Edmund?' I ask.

'Was there?' he says vaguely. Edmund is quite infuriating, sometimes. 'Oh, yes. Your father wants us all in the breakfast room. Says he has a proposition.'

I reach Tilly and settle below her. She puts a sisterly hand on my shoulder. I glance up, gratefully, and give it a pat.

'Can't it wait till lunchtime?' asks Rufus. 'We're a bit busy . . .'

'No,' says Edmund, 'it can't. Honestly, you young. We don't ask a lot of you, Rufus. I think you could at least—'

'We're saving your wine cellar here, Edmund,' I say sharply.

'Well, it's *your* father,' he says, with ineffable reasoning.

'What time is it?' I ask Rufus quietly.

Tilly removes her hand to check her watch. 'Half twelve.'

Rufus sighs. He seems to be sighing a lot, lately. 'Well, I suppose we could do with a break.'

Then, for Edmund's benefit: 'We'll be up in a couple of minutes.'

'Right-oh,' says Edmund cheerfully, and goes away.

Once he's out of earshot, Rufus lets fly with string of expletives. 'Bloody bloody bloody bloody bloody *hell*. Bloody bollocking buggery.'

'You forgot bastards,' I remind him.

'Bastards,' he says. 'Right, well, better see what the old sods want *this* time.'

'Are you sure you don't want to swear a bit more first?' asks Tilly.

'No, I'm done. But thanks for asking.'

'Can I just say fuck it?' she asks.

'Well, normally it would be fine, but I'm not sure if you should be doing it in front of the baby.'

'Sorry,' she says. Then she bends her head and strokes her tummy and says: 'Sorry, baby.'

I affect a little squeaky, foetus voice, put my face near her navel and say: 'Piss off.'

For some reason, this strikes all of us as hysterically funny. A relief of tension, I suppose. I laugh till my belly aches, leaning on my sister-in-law's thigh for support. I can feel her shaking next to me, hard belly and soft breasts pressed against my side. And suddenly, out of the blue, in the middle of my laughter, I feel almost tearful.

'I do like you,' says Tilly.

'Yeah?' I tell her, and gulp back my emotions. 'Well, back atcha.'

'Come on, you old slags,' says Rufus, sloshing his way towards us with an armful of what looks like champagne, 'on your feet or they'll be sending Roberts in after us.'

Tilly takes two attempts to get up, uses my shoulder for leverage. 'Bloody *hell*,' she says, 'I can't wait till this is over. I feel like a water buffalo.'

'Look like one too,' says Rufus.

'Mmm. That was why I came home. For the loving support of my family.' She grabs four bottles of red and waddles up the stairs.

Dad's grinning like a shot fox. He's practically rubbing his hands together. Obviously he has something up his sleeve or he wouldn't have sent for us all in this drum-roll fashion. Both families are gathered in their entirety for his announcement, Beatrice and Yaya eyeing each other from opposite sides of the room like baleful walnuts. You couldn't get two more contrasting grannies. Each is a granny-stereotype in her own way – Beatrice the fluffy, scented granny with the heart of industrial diamond, Yaya the resentful, gloomy Mediterranean granny with the pockets full of contraband sweeties – but neither is recognisable to the other as an acceptable example of dignified old age. Mum is telling Hilary some involved story about a row she won with Harrods in Kuala Lumpur Airport and Hilary has one leg crossed over the other at the knee, and jigs his ankle. Why do Englishmen do that? Seriously. You'd think Hilary was pretty poofy even if you didn't know he was. If you see what I mean.

There are no seats left. I know it's the warmest room in the house, but I'd swap that for a chance to sit down for a bit. The three of us stand, vaguely dripping, on the rug.

'They think they're really something,' says Ma, one of her favourite phrases; 'way they go on in there, you'd think they *owned* the shop, not worked in it.'

'Mmm,' says Hilary, his tone suggesting that owning a shop wouldn't be a lot different from working in one.

'Darling, do mind the paintwork,' Mary tells Tilly, who is leaning against the wall. 'I do wish you children would be a bit more thoughtful.'

'Maybe someone should give a seat to the pregnant lady,' I say. 'I know it's not a bus, but similar rules apply, surely.'

I'm feeling a bit sweaty and peculiar myself, truth be told, but I reckon Tilly's need is probably greater than mine.

Edmund, always more vague than he is deliberately selfish, leaps to his feet. 'Here we are, darling,' he gestures to the tapestry couch by the fire.

'Darling, *no*! Look at her! She's *covered* in grime!'

Tilly shows an uncharacteristic burst of mettle. 'You know what? Sod the sofa covers.' She flings herself into the seat, bouncing Yaya up and down like a jack-in-the-box.

'That's right, lovey,' says Yaya, 'you get all the rest you can.'

She gives the tummy another pat like the one she gave it in the hall last night.

That poor baby: it must have an impression of the outside world like it's a cold, stinky place where people beat each other up. It'll be hanging on to her ribcage by its fingernails.

Once we're all in, my dad clears his throat and speaks. 'H'OK, everybody.'

Voices drop and people look round.

'Listen,' he says, 'I couldn't help but notice that things aren't going good around here.'

Oh God, I think. What's he going to say?

No-one moves. They're all thinking the same thing.

He cackles. 'It's OK,' he says. 'I just thought, you know . . . Colleen and me, we thought . . . well . . . with Christmas coming and all . . .'

'Spit it out,' I say. 'The suspense is killing me.'

'Well, when we went into Stow this morning, you know, we were thinking, you know, with the drains broken and everything, it's going to be pretty difficult, and here we are turning up out of the blue and all, it can only add to the trouble. So we were thinking . . . what do you say to the idea we all go and spend Christmas in a hotel, maybe? Nice and dry and warm, and room service and all to keep up the festive spirit?'

I can't say he's overwhelmed by the enthusiasm of the response.

'Stuff and nonsense,' says Beatrice. 'I've never heard anything so absurd.'

'Mummy,' says Edmund.

'I . . .' says Mary.

'Ooh, lovely,' begins Tilly, then glances around and subsides.

'Um,' says Rufus.

'A fool and his money are soon parted,' says Yaya. Dad waggles his head at her like a donkey.

'Well, don't all be too enthusiastic,' he says.

I speak up. 'It sounds like a lovely idea, Dad, but I should think everything's sorted for Crimbo already.'

I can't think of anything nicer, not in the whole world. Hot showers. Clean bedlinen without darns. No need to have dogs with you for warmth. Dirty martinis instead of dirty moatwater.

Dad does an expansive shrug. It doesn't matter, it says. Who cares? Forget about it. Adonis wants to spend some money. 'And you don't need to worry about the money, neither,' he says, as if reading my thoughts, 'because it's my shout.'

Oh, Dad. What a way to say it. Half of me is cringing, the other half rejoicing. Being able to walk barefoot without getting frostbite. Club sandwiches. Minibars. I feel my spirits surge at the thought.

'Mr – Don,' says Mary, 'it's not a question of money. We aren't paupers.'

'Didn't say you were,' starts Dad, but fortunately, she ploughs on before he can dig any deeper.

'We have arrangements.'

'Like what?' asks Mum.

'I've not spent a Christmas away from Bourton Allhallows in seventy-five years,' announces Beatrice.

'Do you good to have a change, eh?' says Yaya sharply.

'Well . . . we have people.'

'Who?'

'Hilary, obviously . . . and Roly. Roly Cruikshank.'

'Who's Roly Cruikshank?' asks Mum on the side to me.

'Local boy,' I tell her. 'Bit of a loser.'

'Oh right. Inbreed?'

'Wouldn't go that far, but I don't suppose he can cook for himself. If brains were elastic, his pants would fall down, that sort of thing.'

'Oh. Fair enough. Can't leave the charity cases.'

She speaks to the room. 'That's not a problem. Hilary, you're welcome, as our guest, and Roly can come to dinner too. God, he can check in with us if he can't find a tin-opener.'

'Yes, but all the food . . . and Mrs Roberts is expecting to cook.'

'She can take the day off, can't she?' asks Mum. 'Wouldn't that be normal? Spend it with her family?'

'Mrs Roberts always cooks on Christmas Day.'

'Good Lord. Doesn't she have anything better to do?'

There's a puzzled silence. I realise that no-one has ever thought about this before.

'But the food . . .'

'Stick it in the freezer. What were we going to have, anyway?'

'Beef.'

'Beef? You haven't got a turkey?'

'The traditional English Christmas dinner is beef,' says Beatrice. 'Turkey is a colonial affectation.'

'God, well, I'm sure we can get you some beef if that's what you want,' says Dad.

'I was thinking more a big plate of fat prawns,' says Mum.

Mmm, I'm thinking. A little spoonful of caviar. Eaten off my husband's stomach. I can feel the excitement growing. I don't care. I don't care if it's déclassé, I'm new money and I like my luxuries.

'I must say,' says Edmund, 'it *does* sound rather tempting.'

'I'm not spending Christmas in some flea-pit,' says Beatrice. 'We don't stay in hotels. We stay with *people*. A Wattestone has never had a bed bug.'

'Oh, for heaven's sake, Granny,' says Rufus, 'you used to go to Baden Baden all the time. You never stop going on about it.'

'Yes, but *everyone* went to Baden Baden. And they didn't have bed bugs.'

'Who said anything about bed bugs?' asks Mum.

'Αυτ'η η γρι'α μου φα'ινεται ε'ιαι για δ'εσιμο,' says Yaya.

'I heard that,' bellows Beatrice.

Yaya smiles at Tilly. 'So what if she did? What's she going to do? Come over and hit me with her stick?'

I give her a face like I'm going to come and hit her with a stick myself, and she purses her lips in that way she has, which you're aware is actually a smile if you know her well.

'What about the dogs?'

'We can put some food down and leave them in the stables,' says Rufus. He's come on side, thank God. I think he's thinking the same sort of things I'm thinking. Sex without having to wear a jumper, that sort of thing. 'Someone can come down and let them out. They won't know it's Christmas. I think it's a lovely idea. Thank you, Don. Thank you, Colleen.'

'You're welcome,' says Ma. 'Call it a honeymoon.'

Our eyes meet for a split second. I get a flashback to Gozo, to making love by moonlight in a boat off Ramla bay, and shiver. Bite my lip. My Rufus.

'And there's the meet,' says Mary.

'The what?'

'The meet. Boxing Day. They've had to move it from Chipping Norton because of the antis and we said they could have it here. The whole county will be turning out.'

'Well, we're not going to *Australia*,' says Dad. 'You can drive over in the morning. What's the biggie?'

'I . . .' Mary runs out of excuses. 'Well, I don't know.' Then she brightens. 'Of course, it's all academic. A lovely idea, but completely impossible.'

'Why's that?' asks Dad.

'Well, what hotel is going to take us at this sort of notice at Christmas? It may be possible in Australia, but it certainly won't be here.'

'Oh, you'd be amazed,' says Dad, waving his new money credentials about in the fusty old air of Bourton, 'what a couple of hundred in the manager's top pocket can do.'

I find myself bouncing up and down on the balls of my feet. 'You mean you've done it already? Dad? Have you?'

'Quieten down, Princess,' says Dad. 'You'll find my daughter's quite a little capitalist when you get to know her,' he tells Edmund. 'All that alternative therapy nonsense wears off pretty fast if you put her in front of a Jacuzzi and flat-screen telly.'

Soap in little packets. Shampoo in teeny tiny bottles. Pedicures. Remote-control movie channels. Chocolates on the pillows. Oh, wheee!

'Anyway, yeah, I sorted it already. We went past a place called the Bardmoor Manor while we were trying to find our way to Stow. Big old place, bit like this, only –' he catches himself, veers away just in time – 'a hotel, five star, all suites. So I went in and slapped down the old black plastic and it's all sorted.'

'Ah, Bardmoor,' says Beatrice. 'The Raynesforths. Do you remember, Edmund? Forced out in nineteen seventy-three. Ginny would be turning in her grave at the thought of it being a hotel.'

'Well, it looks pretty comfortable to me,' says Dad, blithely ignoring the niggle. 'So if it's all right by you, we all check in tomorrow night and come back sometime before New Year.'

I let out a whoop of joy, and Tilly, bless her, claps her hands together like a little kid.

'Oh, well,' says Mary, ever the gracious recipient, 'perhaps it might have been nice if you'd checked with us first.'

Chapter Forty-Three
Contains Sexual Content That Some Might Find Disturbing

We've got a suite. The olds, good as their word, have put us up in the honeymoon suite, where the drapes on the four-poster are purely for decoration rather than warmth. We've a suite with three huge French windows that overlook acres of manicured, loved and planted garden, and miles and miles of the Cotswolds, from our hilltop position.

White carpet. Clean white carpet. With a couple of hole-free rugs that don't crunch under your feet as you cross them. Heating that permits nudity. A couch that doesn't stab your buttocks when you sit down, a coffee table with a big basket of fruit. An electrical supply that still works when you turn the hairdryer up to hot. A help-yourself honesty bar. A sliding door. Big white fluffy towels and bathrobes. Gold brocade curtains. A fireplace with a huge arrangement of gaudy flowers flown in fresh from the third world. A power shower. A bed that's – oh, heaven, thank you, God – got four pillows that retain their shape when you put your head on them, rather than vanishing in a pile of dust-mite remains – and a lamp on either side so you don't have to get out in the middle of the night and run across the room to hit the switch by the door. I'm as blown away as a frog in a windsock.

Oh, but this is bliss. I'd almost forgotten. Nearly two months at Bourton, and this single day of freedom has made me feel like a kid released from the drudgery of term into the endless balmy days of summer. I'd thought that time had stood still on Gozo, but in comparison with the tedium of days at the Big House, our love-bubble was one long whirl of activity. It's wonderful, wonderful,

wonderful: a fairyland with endless hot water. And best of all, a lock on the door.

Despite my mother-in-law's image of the frantic, chandelier-swinging couplings with which she knows I trapped her son, we actually celebrate with a long, slow luxuriant session of love-making, the sort of fucking you never get in one-night stands or porn movies: the sort of one-touch-at-a-time, whisper-and-stretch body-worshipping that you imagine sex will be like when you're a little girl, and it so rarely is.

But that's it: that's why I married him. It's why I knew from the first time, that he was something other, something *real*. It's not the primal pursuit of pleasure. When we are alone together, when we're not worrying about roofs, and interruptions, and lies and deceits, we are perfect. We are everything. Rufus and me, we don't just caress with our handslipsbodies. We caress with our minds.

He goes into me as we lie on our sides, face to face, my legs wrapped around his waist and my hands thrown wantonly behind my head. And once he's buried, deep as deep, lovely big warm cock matching me pulse for pulse, he stays, stays still, and we wrap each other in an embrace, faces, bellies, breasts pressed as close as close as close, fingers tracing smalls of backs, the curve of upper arms, butterfly kisses on flushed and ardent cheeks. I feel as though, if we pushed a little harder, closed our eyes and held a little tighter, that barriers of skin and flesh would melt, that we would slip without resistance into each other's bodies and become one.

It's worn me down, Bourton Allhallows, so quietly and with such resolve that it's only now that I'm away from it that I see how much it has stolen. No warmth, no privacy, no time – a million demands and worries and tiny disasters going drip, drip, drip between us. It's no place for lovers, no quiet space to whisper *you, you, you*.

I can barely keep my eyes open. I am shivery and hot, breath deep in my body, his palms on my buttocks, hair meshed together like a Chinese puzzle. He moves, so slightly, and my back arches in an involuntary spasm of pleasure. A starburst: nerve ends tingling, fingers frozen, suddenly, in his hair, heat rolling through my groin, my stomach, my back, my head.

'I love you,' he says. 'You saved me.'

And I cry out, *no, it was you, it was you*.

He reaches down, hooks my knees around his elbows, and we roll together until I am beneath him, head between the pillows, his knees, bent, either side of me. And he stoops, bites softly at my throat, my ears, my shoulders, and I whimper, feel neck-hairs prickle, tell him to fuck me because I'm going to die.

He thrusts. We both gasp. I say, *my darling, you make me feel, you make me feel . . .* and the words are snatched from my throat and I cry out, instead, to the God I don't believe in. I can feel myself going, now, grip the bars of the bed head, voice rising, ripping out yelps, sobs, howls, mouth open, the undignified sounds that we can never imagine each-other making when we're dressed up ready for church.

I love you, I love you, oh GOD . . .

And when I open my eyes, close my mouth, feel my spirit return to my body, he is still there. He will always be there, all rough and sweaty, with his hair in his eyes and stroking the hair out of mine, grinning like a shot fox like he always does when he's made me come, that look-at-me-I-scored-a-goal look that makes me want to hold him for ever. And he stays with me. He stays. Rufus always stays. Wrapped in my legs and my arms, feeling our heartbeats slow together, skins cool, limbs slide into blissful butterscotch languor.

He murmurs: 'We were right. We were so right. I am never, ever going to let go of you.' And I say: 'I know, my darling. You're mine.' 'I always will be,' he says. 'And I yours,' I tell him. Kiss his eyelids, touch his wonderful mouth.

'We can be OK,' he says. 'We can make it be OK.'

'I know, my love,' I reassure him. 'We can be OK.'

Chapter Forty-Four
Happy Crimbo

I give Costa a bell before we go downstairs on Christmas day. He's on his cellphone; the house phone rings out. When he picks up it is to a background of raised voices. He goes: 'G'day?' then shouts 'Sis! How's my little sister? How's your Crimbo? Is it snowing up your way?'

'Some bloody chance,' I tell him. 'More like a faint drizzle mixed in with the odd hailstone. Sounds like you're having a good time, anyway.'

'You know what they say. Cat's away.'

'And there was me imagining you sitting all alone at the dinner table in a party hat blowing feebly on a squealer.'

Costa laughs.

'So all under control over there?'

'Yeah,' says Costa. 'You know. A couple of people getting a bit big for their boots so I had to play the heir apparent while the old man was out of the country. You're an alibi.'

'Oh great. And there was me thinking it was a social visit.'

'They won't be bothering us again,' he says.

'Poor guys.'

'Poor guys my clacker. They should've known better than to try it on in the first place. This ain't the playground. How are you anyway, Sis? You settling into married life?'

'Yeah,' I say, still feeling the glow of lurrve dying on my skin, 'You know?'

'He treating you good?'

'Of course.'

'Tell him he'll have me to answer to if he steps out of line, yeah?'

'Sure.'

'No, I mean it. Tell him I'll have his guts for garters if I hear anything . . . literally . . .'

'Yeah, yeah, yeah. Costa, don't start with that 'bidness is bidness' stuff, OK?'

'No, really, Sis. You know I don't make idle threats.'

And I'm all grown up. I don't need my family paving the way for me any more. 'Especially when you've been on the sauce,' I say.

The sound of my brother putting a bottle to his mouth. A schlup and a popping noise as he unsticks the neck from his face. 'Naah, just the odd stubby or twelve. What about you? You not started yet?'

'It's only just gone noon, stupid. We're just about to go downstairs and have dinner.'

'Oh, right. Figgy pudding and the works, is it?'

'I don't think so. The old man's booked us into a hotel for the duration. Which is something of a relief, as pretty much everything's fallen apart back at the house.'

'I thought these people were meant to be rich?'

'Rich is a bit different over here,' I say. 'Seems like it means not having any money.'

'Oh, right? So what does being poor mean?'

'Oh, that's not having any money, too. Only with a different accent.'

'Uh-huh?'

'And the middle classes are all poor too, because they're spending all their money on sending their kids to schools where they'll learn not to talk like the poor people.'

'Makes sense,' says Costa.

'And it rains all the time.'

'Sounds like heaven,' he says. 'So are the old people behaving themselves?'

'Not too bad.'

'Dad splashing his money about much?'

'God, yes,' I say. 'He keeps ordering up those carts with the Napoleon brandy on. And we haven't even got to presents yet.'

'You're going to love yours.'

'Am I? Oh God. What is it?'

'Godda go, Sis,' he says. 'People to do, places to see.'

'No, come on, Costa. Don't leave me like this . . .'

'Wait and see, greedyguts.'

'You bastard. What did he get you?'

'Nothing remotely like yours, Princess. Oh Jeez I've really got to go now. There's a pair of hotpants with my name on them and they're getting into Danny Rogers's car as I speak. Love you.'

'Love you,' I say, but he's gone already.

'My brother –' I tell Rufus as we go downstairs – red patterned carpet, dark varnished oak banisters, sacrilege on this wood, but what can you do? – 'says you'd better be nice to me or you'll have him to answer to.'

'To be honest,' says Rufus, 'it's answering to you that really fills me with fear.'

Chapter Forty-Five
Beware of Greeks Bearing Gifts

The hotel dining room has been done out overnight. The staff must be having a great festive season. The room is festooned floor to ceiling in tinsel, the carpet covered in *faux* polar bear rugs, the normal chandeliers replaced with new ones from which huge opalescent icicles dangle. Each time someone comes through the double-doors from the kitchen, the draught catches them and produces, instead of the tinkling you'd expect, the dull rush and clitter of clashing plastic. The windows, largely covered by a drawn curtain, are further obscured by a covering of spray-on snowflakes. And amid all this theme-park fakery, the tables themselves have been done up like props for the medieval banquet in *Westworld*.

It's gorgeous. I find myself laughing with pleasure like a kid.

The guests, even more overawed than usual by the opulence of their surroundings – you don't get a lot of English talking in loud voices in public at the best of times – have dropped from customary mutter to wide-eyed whispers and minimal movement. The waiting staff, mostly matronly fiftysomething women, have been made to dress up like Santa's elves. Bells attached to the toes of their curled slippers, they jingle as they walk and avoid meeting anyone's eye. For many of them, this is probably the most dignified moment of their lives, and they all seem determined to make the most of it.

Beatrice, never one to be intimidated, sits halfway up our table – Dad, of course, has managed it so that we are, effectively, sitting at the high table, an eleven-person affair on a raised dais under the main window, dripping with giant iron candelabra and holly wreaths – with a face like a slapped arse and a pair of gaudy green earrings on her that look like they might have been part of a matching set with the famous lost emerald. And all along the tabletop, beneath her raised nose, pile upon pile of gifts. Wrapped in gold, silver, tinsel, ribbons. Mum must've been beavering away up there in their room every minute she wasn't laughing at the house. Beatrice is ignoring Mum and Dad, who are, oblivious, talking to Tilly, who has put on a pair of festive plum pudding earrings for the occasion. They bobble about at her cheeks in a determinedly cheerful manner, though she herself looks pretty grim.

I go and sit next to her. There's a slight film of sweat on her forehead.

'Hell,' I say, 'you're not going to do a yuletide parturition on us, are you?'

Tilly shakes her head. 'It's just indigestion or something,' she says.

'Well, go and lie down, woman.'

'No.' She's firm. 'I'm not going to make a fuss.'

'It's not a fuss. You should take care of yourself.'

'Fuss,' she says. 'Please don't make one yourself.'

I shrug. 'OK. But if you look any worse I'm going to.'

Tilly sips at her water.

'Merry Christmas, Mrs Wattestone,' I say to Beatrice.

'Yes,' she replies. 'And there's my boy! Happy Christmas, darling! Come and give your granny a kiss!'

Rufus presses his cheek fondly to the old bag's powdered dewlaps. 'Happy Christmas, Granny, darling. Happy Christmas, everyone.'

Everyone responds. A few seconds later, Mary and Edmund arrive, and the greetings start up again. Then Yaya, then Roly, my parents and, last of all, Hilary in a gold brocade waistcoat. The word is dapper. And I don't mean it as a compliment.

'Happy Christmas,' they say.

'Merry Christmas.'

'Merry Christmas.'

'Merry Christmas.'

It's a Wonderful Life without the feel-good factor.

We sit. An elf jingles over and places a champagne glass in front of me. Fills it up.

'Ah, champagne,' says Edmund.

'Cristal,' says Mum.

'The best,' says Dad. 'We had it sent down by carrier. From Harrods.'

I take a sip. Belch quietly.

'Good shop,' says Mum.

'We always used to call it "Horrids",' says Beatrice.

'Very good,' says Mary.

'Isn't it run by Jews?' asks Beatrice.

'No,' says Rufus. 'An Egyptian.'

'All the same,' says Beatrice. 'Actually, it was Marks and Spencer, wasn't it? They were Jews.'

'Anyway,' says Mum with surprisingly tactful haste, 'cheers, everybody.'

'Bottoms up,' says Dad.

'Your health,' I say.

Everyone else sort of murmurs and raises their glasses half-heartedly as we clink ours together.

'My son married a Jewess,' continues Beatrice, unperturbed. 'Dreadful. Awful mistake. Tried to warn him, of course, but the young . . . what can you do?'

There's a moment's uncomfortable silence. I don't have the faintest idea what she's on about, but even our kind know that this isn't the sort of conversation you have over the dinner table. Tilly picks up a cracker, says in a loud voice, 'Did these come from Harrods as well, Don?'

'Yes,' he says. 'The good ones.'

'Of course, a society needs the Jews,' continues Beatrice. It's weird how her gaganess shows in some ways and not in others. My cheeks are burning out of sympathy for Rufus. 'To keep the wheels of trade turning.'

'I'm going for some air,' says Tilly.

'No, don't go yet!' cries Mum. 'We've presents to do yet!' She leaps to her feet, almost toppling her glass in her haste to change the subject.

Under the kerfuffle, Rufus leans over and says: 'Granny, that's enough about the Jews. Nobody wants to hear it.'

'I was only saying—' she begins, and he raises a finger to his lips. Then he turns and goes, 'Look! How embarrassing! I'm so sorry, darlings, I'm afraid we've come completely unprepared. We don't usually do Christmas presents, as a rule.'

'No,' says Beatrice. 'Usually we go to church.'

It hangs in the air. No Jews in church, it goes. Goes away.

They've bought presents for everyone.

'I say,' says Roly, eyeing a gold-plated cigarette lighter. 'Wow. Spiffing.'

'Thought you might like it,' says Ma. 'Just the thing for impressing the ladies.'

'I shall take up smoking forthwith,' he says.

'Not at the table, though, darling, please,' says Mary.

'Of course not, dear lady.' Roly sits back and polishes the lighter with his cuff. There's a little glow of pleasure on his cheek. He's genuinely chuffed.

Which is a good thing, really, because Hilary looks at his diamond-inlaid golfing tie-pin, manages to mutter something about thanks and lays it straight down on the table. Mum, fortunately, is so excited about the whole process that she doesn't take it in at all. For Mum, the shopping is the best bit of Christmas. And Easter. And Australia Day. And birthdays. And Saturdays. And the rest.

'What'd your husband give you, Princess?' she asks.

I show her. It's around my neck. I found it on the pillow this morning, when I woke up. Tell you what: he got a lovely present in return.

'Nice,' says Mum. She's sprouted another ring herself, I notice. She could do some serious damage if she got into a fight, these days.

'That's a family necklace,' says Beatrice.

'That's right, Granny,' says Rufus. 'Good spot. Suits her, doesn't it?'

'And I promise,' I assure her, 'not to just go and *lose* it.'

Bea clamps like a bearded mussel. The Callington Emerald, it seems, is a valuable device for the silencing of matriarchs.

Edmund seems pleased with his hunting flask. Gold plated it may be, but it's practical. And apposite, if you get my drift. Yaya's got her usual crucifix and rosary beads. She's had the same every year since I remember. That and a life of luxury and all the halwa she can stuff in her gob. Beatrice has a new hat. I don't know where Mum heard about the hats – I guess I must have mentioned them in a call home – but she's done the old girl proud. It's made of peacock feathers. A huge, attitudinal saucer of feathers, straw and net. She gazes on it with the awe of a child seeing its first carthorse, and she's shut up about the Jews. She holds it up to the light, gawps with open mouth. A hit, then.

A stunned silence emanates from Mary's corner. Mum, I can see, is more excited about Mary's gift than any of the others. Keeps peeping out of the corner of her eye to see when she's opened it. My mother-in-law, meanwhile, is struggling for a reaction. I don't know if you remember that bit at the end of *Terminator 2* where the bad terminator is getting melted up in the furnace and its face keeps popping back up out of the molten steel in, one by one, all the different incarnations it's had throughout the movie, but that's what Mary's face looks like right now. I see: horror; offended taste; pride; the giggles; depression; manners; disapproval; *noblesse oblige* all flicker across her visage in a matter of a second. Mum's picked a corker.

'You shouldn't have,' she stutters out eventually. 'It's so . . . generous . . .'

'Do you like 'em?' asks Mum confidently.

Mary draws out a plate that's obviously part of a set. I can only see the back, but recognise the mark of Australia's premium producer of heirloom porcelain. They advertise regularly in *Women's Home Journal* and the TV listings rags.

'They're . . .'

Mary loses the ability to speak for a moment.

'. . . extraordinary,' she finishes.

'They're a set,' says Mum.

'So I see,' says Mary. Lays the plate down on the table and reaches into the box for another. I see that the picture transferred on to the surface of the plate seems to be of a sheep-shearer, complete with a panicked-looking ewe gripped between his thighs.

'*Trades and Crafts of Old Australia,*' says Mum.

'Well I never,' says Mary. 'I've never seen anything like them.'

'That one's a sheep shearer, see,' says Mum. 'And you've got your opal miner, your swagman, your fencer, your rabbit-catcher, your aboriginal tracker . . .'

'Well I never,' says Edmund. 'The things they think of.'

'The carpetbagger, the fencer, the jackaroo . . .' continues Mum.

I hear Hilary murmur: 'What? No convicts?'

'They've got hanging wires,' says Mum, ignoring him, 'so you can put them on the wall, out of harm's way.'

'Modern heirlooms, those,' says Dad. 'They'll be worth a few quid eventually.'

'Got a certificate of authenticity,' says Mum. 'Limited edition. Not just any old tat.'

'Why . . . thank you,' Mary manages. 'It's too kind. I'm . . . embarrassed.'

'Don't be embarrassed,' says Mum kindly. 'You weren't to know we were going to be turning up on your doorstep.'

'You'll have to think of a really *special* place to put them, won't you, Mary?' says Hilary nastily.

I raise a glass to him. 'Cheers, Hilary. And Happy Christmas to you. Like the bow tie, by the way. Very . . .' I give it a couple of beats, '. . . *Christmassy.*'

Hilary pretends not to hear me.

Tilly is gazing, aghast, at what's come out of her wrapping paper. It looks to me like a giant teddy bear. Then I see that she has an envelope in her hand, and her eyes are full of tears. 'I can't take this,' she says. 'I can't. It's too much.'

I glance over. It's a voucher for baby stuff. Harrods, of course. The amount makes even me draw my breath in sharply. Tell you what, they may be parvenus, but you can't fault my olds for generosity.

'Enjoy it, lovey,' says Mum. 'You've got to welcome a kiddie into the family.'

'Yes, but . . .' says Tilly.

'No buts. Just take it. We'd heard you'd had some bad luck lately.'

'Oh had you?' says Mary. There's an ominous tone to her voice. 'Well, I'm glad people are seeing fit to wash our dirty linen in public.'

'It's not public, Ma,' says Rufus. 'They're Melody's family.'

Christmas is shaping up well, then.

The staff emerge from the kitchen with the first courses. A plateful of smoked salmon with a little dish of caviar on the side is placed in front of me by a grey-haired woman dressed entirely in red felt. The Katsouris half of the table choruses thank-yous. The Wattestone contingent behave as though the food has arrived by magic, pretend they don't see the wait staff at all. I've sort of got used to this over the period of my stay – as long as you understand that being used to something is not the same as accepting it as right – but my family exchange glances. I know what they're thinking. How rude. Trying to act like they're royal or something. I thought it myself when I first noticed it. Where we come from, you only behave like that if you've got tickets on yourself. Or you're from Melbourne, which is the same thing.

'Anyway,' says Rufus once the servants have gone, 'while we're on the subject of Tilly, darling, I've got a present for you as well.'

He digs in his pocket and places a bunch of keys on the table in front of his sister. She looks at them like they're some sort of alien artefact whose use she doesn't understand.

'What are these?'

Rufus gives her one of those faux-patronising pats on the shoulder. 'Keys, darling.'

'I know they're keys,' she says slowly, 'but what are they for?'

'Limehouse Cottage.'

Her eyes widen. As, I notice, do Edmund's, Mary's and Beatrice's.

'What do you mean, Limehouse Cottage?'

'Yuh, I'm sorry,' he says. 'It was the one of the untenanted ones that had least to do to it to get it liveable. And I wanted you to . . . you know . . . before the baby was born.'

God, I love him. He's so wonderfully inarticulate when he's doing something emotional.

'Seriously?'

'Please don't blub,' says Rufus. 'I know it's not the nicest place in the village, but you can always sell it and—'

'Excuse me?' says Mary.

'Yuh?' says Rufus.

'Sell it?'

'If she wants to. If that's what she wants. It's up to her.'

'But it's part of the estate,' says Edmund.

'I know. But it's going into Tilly's name.'

'You can't just . . . *chuck* bits of the estate around,' says Beatrice.

'Please let's not make a scene,' he says. 'I'm trying to do something nice? For my sister? And my nephew or niece? Who haven't anywhere to live when we've got nearly sixty houses to choose from?'

'Stuff and nonsense,' says Beatrice. 'No-one's breaking up the estate in *my* lifetime.'

Tilly isn't saying a word. All our eyes bounce from speaker to speaker like we're on the centre court at Wimbledon.

'It's not breaking up the estate. It's giving Tilly a house. Tilly.' He turns to Edmund. 'Your daughter?'

'She doesn't need one,' says Beatrice.

'Well, I think she does.'

There's still not a peep from Tilly's corner. Why does she take this sort of treatment? I want to reach out and shake her, only I'd probably make the baby fall out right here at the dinner table.

'She has a perfectly good room at the house.'

'She's an adult. With a child. It's absolutely unacceptable to expect her to live off charity in some sort of scullery-maid accommodation.'

291

'It's all right, Rufus,' says Tilly, 'you don't need to—'

'No, shut up,' he says. 'Sorry, but just shut up and take it. I'm sick to death of you being walked all over so I'm going to bully you myself. Here's your bloody house, and if there's one more word about it . . .'

He pushes the keys further in her direction and looks seriously pissed off. I guess having your ball-tearer of a surprise present treated like a disaster can do that to a guy.

'Well, you can't do it, anyway,' says Beatrice, triumphantly.

'I said *not another word*,' he snarls, picking up his champagne glass. 'I'm not having a row about it. Not here, not now, not in front of our visitors. Not in front of all these people. Just shut up, Granny, and be nice.'

She ploughs on regardless. 'You can't just hand out bits of the estate without our say-so. You know the rules. The trust has to agree. Not you.'

The glass slams down on the table. There's a crack, and the stem breaks off in his hand. 'Well, here's the way it is! OK? I said I didn't want a scene, but if you want one you've got one. I'm sick to death of you all being so bloody selfish. I'm sick of you treating me like an unpaid estate manager. I'm sick of you behaving like my sister is some sort of leprous charity case who only survives on the milk of your kindness and I'm sick of you behaving like my wife – my *wife*, get it through your head, Granny – is some interloper you're all keen to see the back of. So here you go. Here's your ultimatum. If I get one whine – *one objection* – out of the trustees about this, you can stick the whole lot. I'll wash my hands of it all and walk away. Right now. OK? Do you understand?'

'Rufus!' cries Mary.

'Yuh, Mummy. That means you too.'

I catch the look on her face and it's tragic. Mary is the mistress of self-control, but just for a second, she looks so lost, so ripped apart that I almost feel sorry for her. Because whatever else I feel about her, I know that she loves her son. Truly, wildly. He's the whole focus of her existence. Always has been: raising him, teaching him manners, getting him ready to take on the mantle of the Wattestones. He's more than a child: he's a whole career. And on top of that, when I see the way she looks at him sometimes, I know, also, that, in the end, what he is is her baby boy.

She catches herself. Catches me catching her. 'Well, we'll talk about it later,' she says. 'Though I just want to say what a thoughtful, generous brother you are.'

No-one quite knows where to look. Apart from Yaya, who's having the time of her life. Other people's family discord is like manna to her. Her eyes are glittering, she's enjoying herself so much. Everyone else looks down at their plate. I take a bit of caviar on the tip of the tiny spoon that comes with it. Pop it on to my tongue, close my eyes to feel the eggs pop-pop-pop against the roof of my mouth. Salty seawater heaven. It makes you shiver, caviar.

Dad clears his throat. 'Well, I don't know if I can beat that,' he says. 'But tell you what, Mel, there's something in here for my girl.'

He throws me a small gift-wrapped box from his end of the table. Oh God: the present Costa was going on about. I'm not sure if I want to open it.

I do. Inside, nestled on a bed of shredded tissue paper, is a key. A car key.

I look up at him. He's chewing furiously on his cigar, looking like he's just swallowed a turkey whole.

'Is this what I think it is?'

'No, it's a pumpkin.'

'Dad . . . I . . .'

'Well, don't get excited or anything.'

'Oh my God. Oh my *God*!'

'That's better,' he says. 'And it's all insured and ready for you to drive,' he adds, pointedly.

I'm out of my seat. 'Where is it? Where *is* it?'

With a flourish, two of Santa's little helpers pull back the curtain that has been hiding the window behind our table.

Parked on the drive, gleaming and gorgeous in a giant silver ribbon, stands a Mercedes coupé. No: not a Mercedes coupé: an

SL 600. A convertible SL 600 in black with alloy wheels and – I can see it from here – *cherry-red leather interior*.

'Oh my God,' I say. There's a hundred grand's worth of sports car standing on the drive, and it's *mine*.

'She likes it,' says Mum. 'I told you she'd like it.'

'Like it?' I say. 'I friggin' love it. I've got a fucken hard-on for that car.'

And then I remember the company I'm in and shut up. Walk round the table and give my dad the biggest hug of his life. 'I love yer, you old sod,' I tell him. 'You're a little belter!'

'Steady,' says the old man.

'I could sit on your knee and call you big boy! I couldn't be more chuffed!'

'Oh, I think you could be,' says Mum.

'I couldn't. I'm as stoked as it's possible to be!'

'Oh, get on with it, Don,' says Yaya. 'You're confusing the girl.'

'OK,' says Dad, and gets to his feet. Oh God: he's going to make a speech. Right here in front of the whole dining room. Attracting attention. I can see the whites of Mary's eyes.

Dad takes his cigar out of his mouth and taps on his glass with his knife. That does it. Anyone who wasn't rapt at our little display before is surely aware of us now. The muttering in the dining room dies to silence as he stands there and digs in his pocket. Clears his throat.

'H'OK,' he says. 'Well, here we are.'

I'm not used to my Dad making speeches. Nor is he, of course. He's always been of the low-profile persuasion that way.

He shows us why by not saying anything at all for a full minute because he's come over all gulpy. Grabs a napkin and dabs furiously at his eyes. There's not a sound in the room: not a tinkle of crockery, not a whisper, not a footfall. I find myself blushing on his behalf.

He speaks. 'Melody's my daughter,' he says, 'my princess. We call her Princess back home, you know. We call her that because that's what she is. A princess. Our – little – I would do anything for her. *Anything*.'

Dad is overcome by sentimentality. He stumbles to a halt, going all watery about the eyes, and blows his nose, loudly and at length, on the white damask clutched in his hand. It's funny, isn't it, how these men, the ones who are capable of extreme ruthlessness in their outside life, are also capable of such extremes of sentimentality when it comes to family? I've seen it all my life among Dad's business associates. Stabbing people in the back with one hand while they hold handkerchiefs to their eyes with the other.

On the edge of my field of vision, Mary sits stock still, one palm on the table.

He recovers, continues: 'Anyway. Since she was a nipper, there's been one day I've looked forward to with all my heart, and that was the day I gave her away. And – well – I guess I've been robbed – no, not robbed – it just wasn't to be . . .'

He drinks half a glass of champagne in a single gulp. Champagne is a dangerous drink. It loosens tongues. Rufus looks uncomfortable. Mum looks down at the tablecloth. '. . . but at least we're all together now, eh? The families. And maybe we can give them a toast now, like we didn't get to make on the day.'

Dad is, bless him, oblivious to many things he doesn't want to see. He beams waterily around the table and recharges his glass. 'So if everyone,' he says, 'would like to raise their glasses, here's to the bride and groom.'

It's one of those moments. Rufus takes my hand and squeezes it while Mum, Dad, Yaya, Edmund, Tilly and Roly bellow 'The bride and groooooom!' with an enthusiasm that almost drowns out the half-hearted mumbles that come from Hilary and Mary's end of the table and the 'stuff and nonsense' that comes from Beatrice. The toasters slug enthusiastically from their glasses. Mary and Hilary sip the tiniest drops from theirs, lips pursed, like hamsters at a water bottle. Beatrice just glares.

He puts his glass down. Starts digging in his breast pocket.

'Anyways. I've been thinking about what to get you, and it wasn't easy. I'd wanted to maybe sort you out with a house or something, but when I got over here, I realised that you're not really short of houses.'

You can feel the tension. Well, I can. Dad, evidently, can't. 'So, well, I thought maybe what you *really* need is a bit of help with the houses you've got. I couldn't help but notice,' he says to Edmund, who has stopped grinning and started looking for the exits, 'that you've got a bit of a hole in the roof, there.'

Ever a one for understatement.

'So I thought –' he finally locates the piece of paper he's been looking for, brandishes it triumphantly. It's a cheque. I can see the ANZ logo from the KebabCab cheque book. Crikey. He must have been putting some serious wedge through that account – 'maybe the best thing would be just to give you a little . . . help.'

Chapter Forty-Six

Dad of the Year

So this year's Embarrassing Dad award goes to Adonis Katsouris of Brisbane. And, like all Embarrassing Dads, he hasn't even realised.

That state of affairs doesn't last long, though.

Edmund, hand trembling, takes the cheque and looks at it like he's never seen one before. To do him credit, I think the tremor is more to do with alcohol – he's a nice old stick, Edmund, even if he can't get through an hour without a top-up – but when I catch sight of the sum the cheque's made out for, I wonder if emotion isn't also a factor. But he's not the sort who would get in a strop or anything, whatever you did to him.

Not the case with his mother.

'Good *God*,' she says in a voice that's calculated to bring anyone in the room who might have lost interest right back on to the radar. 'Do you think you can *buy* us?'

Rufus isn't saying anything. I think he's in shock, especially as the digits on the cheque have swung into his sight at the moment they swung into mine. The amounts of money that have swapped hands in the past half-hour would even shut Elton John up for a few seconds.

'Ay?' says Dad. This is not the sort of reaction he'd been expecting, I'd wager.

Beatrice pushes her glass away from her like it's poisoned. 'We can *not* be bought,' she says.

'Now hold on a minute,' says Mum. 'Who said anything about buying anybody?'

Bea's off and running. 'Your sort of people,' she says, 'think money is the answer to everything.'

'Well, it's the answer to quite a lot,' says Mum wryly. 'I don't think it's exactly bypassed your own life.'

'I suppose,' says Beatrice, ignoring her, 'that in exchange you'll be wanting introductions. And invitations.' She addresses the room. 'I've seen it all before, of course. *Arrivistes* thinking they can buy their way into—'

Rufus finally moves. 'Shut *up*, Granny,' he hisses.

'Christ,' says Dad, 'it was just an offer.'

'Wattestones don't parade their problems like dirty laundry,' says Beatrice, 'and we don't like other people doing it for us.'

'Well, *that* wasn't the idea,' he says.

'I suppose you thought we'd be impressed by —' she waves a hand over the table, at the caviar and the champagne and the gold-rimmed chargers — 'all this. Rented finery. Gewgaws. And cheques.'

'We're no show ponies,' says Ma. 'Got it all for real back home.'

I will her to shut up. *Shut up, Mum. It's not helping.*

Edmund tries to cut in. 'Mummy – enough.' He turns to Dad and says: 'Don, I appreciate this gesture. It's immensely generous. But I can't take it.'

'Nonsense,' says Dad. 'You've already got it. And it's family, ain't it? I've been putting it aside against Melody's wedding anyway, so it's no skin off my nose.'

'It used to be the Americans, of course,' says Beatrice. 'Coming over here and thinking they could *buy* a bit of class. I suppose it was only a matter of time before the Australians—'

Rufus glares at her. 'Be *quiet*, Granny.'

'What's the problem here?' asks Mum. 'Our money not good enough for you?'

'No,' says Beatrice.

'Shut up, *both* of you!' I say. 'Not another *word*!'

The people in this dining room must be having their most entertaining Christmas ever. I can imagine the pleasure they must be getting from having the traditional family row without having to participate themselves.

'Please,' says Edmund, 'take it back.'

298

'No,' says Dad. I think he's under the impression that this is some British politeness ritual. That if he refuses a couple more times, they will accept it and all will be well. No-one says no to my dad. He's not used to it.

'No, really,' says Edmund.

'Aah, take it,' says Dad.

'No. Thank you, but no,' says Edmund.

I dread to think what Rufus must be thinking. Because though Dad's got the subtlety of a discarded condom in an alleyway, this sum of money is the answer to his prayers. It's enough to put the roof back on. Seriously. Not to mend the foundations, but at least to stop the rot from above. And here's his father turning it down and his grandmother hurling invective at the givers.

'Ah, come on,' says Dad. 'Let's face it. It's not like it's not obvious you could do with it.'

I actually hear a groan escape my lips.

'What I want to know,' says Beatrice, 'is where this money came from in the first place.'

'Granny, how *dare* you?' says Tilly.

'Oh, right then,' says Mum. 'If *that*'s the way you're going to play it, then we might as well forget about it.'

Great wafts of despair drift over from Rufus.

'Look,' I say, 'maybe we can talk about it later? Dad, I think you're amazing. I can't even begin . . . but why don't we leave all this till later?'

'*What* a good idea, Melody,' says Mary, voice oozing sincerity. 'What a *good* girl you are.'

Mum glances at me speculatively as she hears the tone, but I just smile. No way. No way am I getting into this now.

I turn to my mother-in-law as plates of turkey with all the trimmings land in front of us. 'So what's the deal with Boxing Day, Mary?' I ask. 'Are you all going out with the hunt?'

'Every able-bodied person in the entire county will be out,' she assures me, with the absolute certainty of the totally sheltered.

'What, all two million of them?' asks Mum. I attempt to kick her under the table, but my leg doesn't reach.

'Ah-ha-ha-ha-ha!' tinkles Mary. 'Ah-hah-haaa!'

Conversation sort of dries at that point. Everyone concentrates on the plate in front of them. I cut into a Brussels sprout. It gives off the sulphurous scent of the overcooked brassica and takes several chews to get it down.

Beatrice still looks murderous. Peers round the table like a malevolent little gargoyle. Never been one to let things lie, that woman.

'It's her fault,' she announces. 'That woman. Twisting his mind. Turning him against us. It was all fine before *she* came along.'

I stretch my eyes. Rufus takes his serviette off his lap and slaps it down on the table. Stalks out of the room.

'Oh *God*, Granny,' hisses Tilly.

Yaya lifts her glass. Says, loudly and ironically: 'Well! Happy Christmas, everybody!'

Chapter Forty-Seven
Mum's Opinion

I storm off after Rufus. He's not in our room, not in the lounge, not out in the grounds in any obvious sort of way. My family doesn't last a lot longer at the table: Mum, letting loose a couple of choice adjectives, storms off after me, Dad storms off to have a smoko and Yaya, suddenly deprived of people she can make asides to in Greek, just storms off, in a hobbling sort of a way. Tilly, who knows perfectly well that once we've all gone she's going to be in for it despite the fact that she's not actually done anything, waddles off to her room holding her stomach. When I pass the dining room five minutes after I first left it, there's nothing left but a pile of wrapping paper, a couple of dozen delighted fellow-guests and the Wattestone party, all eating their roast turkey with their elbows tucked in and gazing, blankly, into the middle distance.

Serve them bloody well right.

I can't seem to find Rufus anywhere. He must be really distressed if he doesn't even want *me* to find him. I decide to give our room another go. Maybe he's curled up in a cupboard somewhere, doing the old rocking routine. As I mount the stairs, I find Mum coming in the opposite direction.

'There you are!' she says. 'I've been looking for you everywhere!'

'I've got to find Rufus,' I say.

I get a hand on the arm. 'Not yet, you don't, young lady. Not until you've had a serious word with me.'

'I don't have time, Mum. Give me a break, huh?'

'No, I won't. I want to know what's going on and I want to know now.'

'It's nothing I can't handle.'

301

'Well that's not the way it looks from here. What *is* going on here, Melody? Have you gone out of your mind? What are you doing, letting people talk to you that way?'

'Please, Mum. Just leave it, OK?'

'Leave it? I didn't bring you up to let yourself get walked all over by snobs like that. I'm not bloody putting up with it. I'll tell you something: we're not staying around here to get talked to like that. We're out of here and if it was up to me we'd be taking you with us. You've got to stand up for yourself, girl. Haven't I told you a million times? I can't be here to do it for you all the time.'

I've managed to get a couple of steps above her by now. Stop and turn to face her. 'I'm not asking you to.'

'Well, you don't seem to be doing a very good job of it for yourself.'

I take a deep breath, try to find the right words.

She ploughs on. 'It's pathetic, Melody.'

And this is the problem. My parents are so afraid of anyone getting one over on me that they've never let me sort things out for myself. I love them. I love them to bits, but I've had to cross several oceans to get to make my own mistakes. It's about themselves, of course. But it's not really about me. If they see someone dominate me, insult me, overlook me, ignore me, they feel it as a reflection on themselves. And they can't bear that.

I lean against the wall, arms folded like a sulky adolescent. 'Mum, it's my problem, OK? I'll handle it my way.'

'Your way isn't *working*. I'd say *that* was pretty obvious. Don't be such a bloody *doormat*.'

The trouble is, she has something of a point. I *am* being wet, I know that. But I'm like someone trying to put in central heating without a monkey wrench. And if there's one thing I *do* know, it's that if you ain't got the tools, you're bound to make a few cock-ups along the way. I tried doing it the Katsouris way, with Andy, and all it did was drive him off. There has to be another route, and I haven't worked out what it is yet. But one thing I do know is that nagging isn't going to help.

She goes on, 'And another thing. How come Rufus lets people

302

talk to you like that? What sort of a guy lets his wife—'

'No,' I say, 'leave Rufus out of this. You've only been here five minutes. You don't have the first idea—'

She does a sort of *hah*-type laugh. 'I've got a good enough one. You're living in an armpit of a house with a load of people who think they're too good for you, right down to the —' she pauses to emphasise the word — '*employees*, and your husband — well. Presumably he thinks *he's* too good for you and all. I'll tell you, Melody, if you don't do something about it, then I will.'

I unfold my arms and take a step forward. 'If you do anything of the sort,' I say, 'you can go back on the next plane. I've got enough on my plate without you putting your oar in. I'm an adult, Mum, and I'll deal with my own problems, OK?'

'But you won't,' says Mum. 'You never do!'

'You never give me the chance!'

'Well, what do you expect? We're your parents! We've always looked after you! How can you expect this to be any different? I can't just stand back and let this disaster fall in on your head, Melody! I've stepped in before and I will again!'

And I step back as she says this, look her in the eye and say: '*Please*. If I don't get a chance to make my own way in the world I'll never survive it. Please. This time. Let it be me, even if I do screw it up.'

She looks at me. 'But these people . . . You can't be serious. You can't want to be like them.'

I take two steps up the stairs. Look her straight back in the eye. 'No, I don't. And I don't want to be like us, either.'

Chapter Forty-Eight
Daddy's Girl

I love them. Love them to pieces. They're my people and they're where I come from, but they're not good people. They're my people, and they started from the bottom of the heap and made it close to the top, and I'm the indulged, spoiled little Daddy's girl who doesn't know how to get away. Because my folks are rich, yes: far, far richer than the Wattestones give them credit for. Far, for that matter, richer than the Wattestones themselves, probably. And you know what they say: behind every great fortune there's a great crime. Dad's no honest son of the soil. He didn't toil his way to riches by scrimping and saving till he got the deposit for his first car. He got there because that genial exterior is the packaging for one nasty bastard. He got there by being the sort of man who can watch someone beg and remain unmoved. You don't get rich by owning a cab company and fast food service. Not *rich* rich. People like my dad own companies like that because a business that deals almost entirely in cash is the most effective way of laundering the spoils of their other businesses.

Yes, I'm a little rich girl, and yes, just like Mary thinks, I've got no class. But I'm rich because my people would beat you up and throw you in a ship canal as soon as look at you.

Some things I remember. I don't remember all that much. And besides, they wanted me, at least, to have the chances they'd never had, to grow up with all the advantages of Daddy's money and none of his criminality. Costa was a different story, of course. He's the legitimiser, the investor in the straight and narrow, but he's Daddy's son and heir. When I was eight we moved out of Sydney into our neoclassical spread with the six-pillared, broken pedimented porch and the swimming pool with the retractable roof and the mega-gas-fired barbecue pit and the collection of shotguns under the beds because Dad's firm was expanding up north and they needed someone to head it up. And at that point I largely got separated off from how Daddy made his money: I got the self-congratulatory suburban upbringing my mum had always yearned for, and apart from the wads of cash in the shoeboxes and the occasional cortege of Mercedes rolling up the drive and the odd door closing suddenly as I passed it, my life was pretty much normal. Only with more money.

Though they had their own sweet way of sorting out my problems. You'll see.

I don't know if I remember very little because I'm suppressing the memories, like a dodgy shrink would probably say, or if it's that they just didn't let us see much of what was going on in Dad's working life, but I suspect it's the latter. But here are the things I do remember.

King's Cross, 1978. It's my fifth birthday. My daddy takes me out with him, all dressed up in my party dress, while Mum organises a surprise shindig. My daddy's got his business suit on, and he looks *sharp*: giant collars, one on top of the other, and a tie covered in pictures of ladies in bikinis with their hands linked behind their heads. My daddy's got one of those haircuts where the front is bouffant and the back hangs down below the collar in lank locks. He has magnificent sideburns, bushy and black, that run all the way from his ears to the point of his jaw.

We go down one of those streets you find in most cities that's full of a mixture of ethnic shops and bordellos – a street of a thousand yayas, where every third woman is an old one in black and a lot of the rest are wearing clothes constructed of nylon and spangles. Dad says he has to do some business, that he's got to just drop in and see a few people, and in each shop, the people behind the counter stop what they're doing the moment we come in, greet me with an enthusiasm that I now realise was probably not as wholehearted as it felt at the time.

I'm hoisted up on to counters, congratulated for being such a pretty girl, and in every shop I go into, an assistant is left to pick me out a birthday present while Dad disappears into the back with the owner. And people are going: 'I didn't know your dad *had* any children. How old are you? And look how pretty you are. Look at your *hair*! If I had hair like that, I'd be a model!'

I get some chocolate in the coffee shop. A gateau is wrapped to go in the baker's. In the newsagents, the assistant, a lovely-looking girl with black eyes, a green mohican and six earrings dangling from a single ear, digs me out a colouring book and a multi-pack of felt-tip pens. I emerge from one Italian restaurant with a box of little tiny macaroons wrapped in tissue paper, and from the one next door with yet another cake, this time in a tin. The chemist showers brightly coloured hair bobbles on me, and the hippie shop gives me a small plaster cat.

It's a great birthday. This street, barely touched by the backpacker's paradise around it, is a seedy, glamorous, cosy mix of sex and family, and no-one can do too much for the pretty little daughter of their local loan shark and protectionist.

And then Daddy ducks down some steps into a basement, and I find myself in a witch's cave. It's dark down here, red and black on the walls, a series of black curtains, and it smells sort of damp, sort of salty, with a faint whiff of cheese.

'O!' shouts my dad.

A head appears from behind a curtain: a man who seems, in this light, to be red and sweating, a grimace that I don't understand written across his face. 'Uh,' he says, and his head disappears.

At the end of a corridor, another curtain moves back and a man with a moustache appears. Looks us up and down and says: 'You're a day early. You're not due till tomorrow.'

'It's my little girl's birthday,' says my daddy. 'Getting her out of the house.'

The man stares at me. Says: 'Happy Birthday, sweetheart. You shouldn't have brought her here,' he says to Dad. 'It's not a place for a kiddy.'

'Well,' says my dad, 'hurry up, then, and we can get out of here.'

'Like I said,' he replies, 'you're early. You can't just—'

My dad takes a step forward. I can't see his face, but the man can. A muscle moves on his jaw. Raising his voice, he bellows: 'Lindy! Get out here!'

'Customer!' a voice bellows back.

'Now.'

'Oh for fuck sake . . .'

'Language!' shouts my dad. 'There's kiddies here!'

A curtain moves and an irritated-looking woman pokes her head into the gloom. Sees us standing there and says: '*Oh.*' Vanishes again for a moment and re-emerges, wrapping a slightly greasy satin robe around her.

'Need you to look after the little girl,' says the man.

She approaches. Doesn't look at my dad. Crouches down in front of me. She's wearing stockings, red garters. She smells salty, like the premises, and has smeared red lipstick on. Reaches out a hand that looks a lot younger than her tired, lined face and traces my cheek with a chipped nail. 'Hello, darling,' she says. 'My name's Lindy. What's yours?'

'Melody,' I tell her.

My dad walks away.

'That's a pretty name,' she says. 'I've got a little girl about your age.'

'I'm five.'

'That's nice. My little girl's six. She lives with her nan.'

'It's my birthday,' I tell her.

She raises eyebrows that have been drawn roughly with black crayon on to shaven skin. She looks about a million years old to me at my age, but looking back, I think she was probably not a lot more than thirty. The red mouth forms an 'O' of feigned astonishment. 'Your *birthday*! Happy birthday, darling. Have you had your presents yet?'

'At home,' I say. 'Though some people gave me some things.'

'I'll bet they did,' says Lindy. 'What did you get?'

I tell her, counting the list off on my fingers.

'That's lovely, darling!' says Lindy.

The sound of raised voices drifting down the corridor. Lindy glances briefly over her shoulder, turns back to me and raises her voice. 'So your daddy brought you out for the day?'

I nod.

To my surprise, Lindy shakes her head. 'Well, that's just wrong,' she says, more to herself than to me.

From the cubicle emerges a man so fat he can barely squeeze through the entrance. Hairy hands, rolls of fat on the back of his neck, one, two, three, a waistband that has vanished beneath a rippling waterfall of a stomach. He totters on legs that look like strings of faggots. He's tying his tie and carrying his jacket over his forearm so I can see the great patches of sweat under his arms, which leach down all the way to the first fold of his hips. He waddles down the corridor towards us, and I see that he is, of all things, pouting.

'I'll be with you in a minute, love,' Lindy says.

'Don't bother,' he replies.

'Sorry,' she says, not reacting. He gets level with us, and I reel at the smell of unwashed underpants that comes off him.

'You're too old for it, anyway,' he says.

'Yeah,' says Lindy, 'well, it's been a pleasure for me too.'

We have to squeeze to one side to let him pass. Her face is a mask of non-reaction. Once he's gone, she turns back to me.

'If everyone else is giving you presents,' she says, smiling, though even in this light I can see that there are tears in her eyes, 'I'd better give you something too.'

Something in me, even though I'm only five, makes me say: 'No. No, really.'

'Oh, bless her,' she says. 'It's not your fault. It's not.'

My dad's still shouting. He never shouts at home. I shuffle, strain to look round Lindy and catch a glimpse of him. Behind another curtain, someone moans repeatedly. It sounds like they're in pain, or dying.

'Don't worry, darling,' Lindy puts a hand on my face and guides me back to looking at her. 'You're so pretty. Daddy'll be back in a second. He won't be long.'

But I'm only five. I start to blub.

'No, look . . .' Lindy reaches behind her neck and unhooks the necklace she's wearing: a cheap filigree crucifix, hanging from a slender chain. Later, on Gozo, I'll realise that it's a Maltese cross. 'Look. See this? Isn't it pretty? You want to wear it?'

I sniff. Look as the metal catches the light from the red bulb above our heads. It glitters wondrously, makes me open my mouth in awe.

Lindy stretches her hands round the back of my neck, clips it on. 'There,' she says. 'There. You look ever so pretty, darling. Beautiful. Now, you wear that for ever, and it'll keep you safe, I swear. And every time you touch it, you can think of your friend Lindy.'

'Thank you,' I say.

Another touch to the face. 'Take care of it, darling.'

Dad reappears, marches up the corridor. Sees the tears drying on my face and snaps: 'What have you done?'

'Nothing,' says Lindy, looking up. 'She got nervous, waiting. You shouldn't have—'

'You look a mess,' he says. 'Clean your face up. Shit.'

And he grabs me by the hand and pulls me towards the exit. As we get out into the sunlight, I look at the hand holding mine and notice that there's a graze on his knuckles.

Jump forward seven years. I'm twelve and we've been up north a while and things have started to go bad at school. It's not that – you know, I'm not such a pariah that I've got no friends, but I'm gawky and goofy-toothed, and what with the foreign dad and the gaudy mum, I'm not high on people's invitation list. And then Reggie Harper steps in and things get a whole lot worse. Because Reggie doesn't like me and, though I do my best to persuade myself that she's only turned out like she has because Regina is no name to be carrying through the Australian state school system, it doesn't make it any less painful when she hits me.

She does it daily. Just for the hell of it, really. Reggie and her friends Babs, Dinah and Linda Ho have a little click: lumpen, high-coloured girls with habitually challenging expressions, they swagger round the playground looking for people to pick on. And those people are mostly me.

It starts off small: a bit of pushing, some tripping up. But then I make the mistake of trying to fight back one day, and things escalate, because Daddy's brought me up to be his princess, not a brawling Greek like he is, and I have no more idea what to do with my fists than I would what to do with a Black and Decker Workmate. The four of them, a year or so older and several inches taller, simply hold me by my hair as I flail at their faces, then throw me to the ground like a piece of flotsam. And now they've had their reaction off me, it just keeps on coming. Every day, every dinnertime, same thing: hello *Millerdy*. Doof. Oops. *Sor*-ree. Aww. Is she *cry*-ing? Aaah. There there.

It goes on for months. Every day, same thing: doof and down I go: great wedges of skin off my thighs and knees, school blouse hiding atlases of bruises on arms and shoulders, never the face because then the staff might have had to notice. Anyone who's been bullied will tell you the same thing: the teachers never want to know, never want to shift themselves to champion the awkward ones, the fat ones, the ugly ones, the lispers, the odd-ones-out who always come in for the worst of it. And the teachers' idleness depends on that great rule of schoolyards the world over: you don't dob your mates in. You don't dob anyone in, not even your enemies, because then your mates will cut you out, too.

And then one day Dinah's foot slips, or I curl up too early into the foetal position I've got used to adopting and, instead of kicking me in the ribs like she'd intended, she catches me one full in the face. Draws blood from my nose, imprints a livid toecap mark on my cheekbone. And I go home and refuse, resolutely, to dob through the interrogation that ensues, do the old walked-into-a-lamppost routine, but none the less, three days later, when I come back to school, I find that it's all over. My persecutors have left the school. Not sacked, or suspended. They've simply left, all four of them, and they aren't coming back. Dinah's father's taken a job up in Darwin. Babs has gone to family over in Canberra. Linda's been

310

taken to another school, twenty Ks away in central Brissie, and Reggie – well, the Harper family are just *gone*. The neighbours saw them packing up a rental truck in the middle of the night and reckon they must've left some bad debts behind.

Whatever; they're gone.

Except that somehow the other kids seem to be treating me with a little less familiarity. They've not turned rude or anything: just jump back like a woman in danger of touching a Buddhist monk when I go down the corridors, pull back their hands so as not to overhit when they tag me in playground games. I never have trouble of any sort at school after that. I don't have many mates, either, mind.

Jump back four years. Our unit in Manly. We've already moved up in the world, got a sea view, hot tub on the deck. I'm seven, and I've woken up with a powerful thirst. There's a murmur of voices from downstairs.

We live on the third and fourth floors of a sixties block that's filled from floors to ceilings with the sort of luxury goods normal people still only really see on television. We are a white-leather-sofa, giant-screen-TV, cut-glass-cocktail-bar, marble-bathroom sort of family. We've got fluffy rugs and chandeliers and a twelve-setting dinner service rimmed in fourteen-carat gold. My mother wears chunky chains and earrings to do the weekly food shop, my dad has a watch that would sink the *Titanic*. I've got toys, toys, toys, and a wardrobe of tiny replicas of my mother's designer gear. Costa has a Chopper bike, a TV and video recorder of his very own. It doesn't occur to me that it's unusual, because everyone my parents know lives the same way.

I lie in bed for a minute or two, listening to the action downstairs. What sounded like conversation now sounds like it's been replaced by the sounds of the television. *The Sweeney*, maybe, or *The Professionals*. They like their English TV. Certainly, it's something that involves an amount of hardman discourse and the occasional pause for violence. My mouth is as dry as a pommy's towel. I'm not going to be able to get back to sleep unless I have a drink. And needing a drink gives me all the excuse I need to get a look at Bodie and Doyle, like all small girls want to.

I get up. I'm in Barbie pyjamas. I pick up my monkey for company. I slip my feet into my rabbit slippers and make my way down the stairs, past the collection of resort goods my mum insists on collecting on our thrice-annual trips to the islands. It's dark on the stairs and in the hall; all I can see by is the sliver of light that peeps out from under the lounge door. Whatever's on the TV is dead realistic. I hear someone hit someone else, a sort of wet thud, and a soggy groan in response. I push the door open, walk inside.

I'm in the middle of one of those nineteenth-century drama paintings: *When Did You Last See Your Father?*, something like that, only bloodier. And the clothes are a lot less stylish. Someone's spread plastic sheeting on the white carpet and the white suite, and in the middle of the floor sits a man on one of our kitchen chairs. Only, he's not just sitting there: he's handcuffed, and my dad is standing over him with a band of steel wrapped around his knuckles. Uncle Phil and Uncle Ern – my dad's business associates – sit on the settee, wearing bomber jackets emblazoned with the logos of American sports teams from cities they probably wouldn't be able to point out on a map. My mum's in the kitchen, on the other side of the lounge; I can hear her, rattling pots. Uncle Ern's wearing dark glasses. The man in the chair is covered in blood: his head has swollen up like a football.

But the thing that's most striking is the fact that they have all frozen as I entered, which is how I get the image of them as figures in an oil painting. I stand, one hand on the door handle, and stick a thumb in my mouth.

It's the man on the chair who speaks first. Tipping his head back, he spits out a tooth and gives me a wide, gory grin that reveals that he's lost at least two more.

'Why, hello, darlin',' he says, and his accent is the broadest Strine. 'What're you doing up at this time of night?'

'Good evening, Melody,' says Uncle Ern. 'Did we wake you up?'

312

'I need a glass of water,' I say, staring all the while at the gash on the captive's left cheek. It looks like it's turned inside-out. Red stuff and clear stuff runs down his face as he grins again and winks a black and swollen eye. 'Sure you do,' he says. 'That's a lovely monkey you've got there. Has he got a name?'

'Ringo,' I say.

'Now, that's a good name for a monkey,' he says. 'Isn't it a good name?' He appeals to the uncles for affirmation.

'An excellent name,' says Uncle Phil.

'Where'd you get that name from, sweetheart?' asks Uncle Ern.

Wide-eyed, I suck harder on my thumb.

'I'll get you your water,' says my dad. 'Stay there, darling. Don't come any further in. We don't want you messing up your lovely slippers.'

Uncle Ern leans forward as he leaves the room, looks at my slippers over his glasses. 'What're they?' he asks. 'Gonks?'

'Rabbits.'

'Well, b— I never,' says the bleeding man, like a man correcting himself at a vicarage tea-party. 'The things they think of. Ginger rabbits. Where'd you get those, darling?'

'Market.'

'Well, I must get our Siobhan a pair of those,' he says. 'She'd love a pair of those.' Then he shuts up, manages a watery smile. The uncles shift on the sofa.

'How you getting on at school, Melody?' asks Uncle Ern.

'OK.'

'You're in what . . . year two?'

'Three.'

'Three already? Aren't you the clever one?'

The man in the chair does an enormous cough, sprays blood over his front. 'Best days of your life,' he tells me. 'You listen to your teachers and work hard, and you'll not regret it.'

Phil nods, sagely. 'Nothing more valuable than your education,' he concurs. 'Get your exams under your belt, you can be anything you want.'

Dad comes back, followed by Mum. 'I thought you said you'd

locked that door,' she says. 'Here you are, sweetheart. Drink that down and we'll get you back to bed.'

'No harm done,' says the man in the chair. Gives me another flash of his toothlessness.

I drink my water.

'Right,' says my mum, 'let's get you off.'

'Say good night,' says Dad.

'Good night,' I say.

'C'm 'ere and give your Uncle Ern a kiss,' says Uncle Ern.

I tiptoe over the plastic sheeting, stretch up and buss the cheek he offers me. He rubs my hair. 'Sleep tight, little one,' he says. 'You take care of yourself, now, you hear me?'

'Night night, Uncle Ern.'

Mum takes me by the hand and leads me towards the door.

'Night night, little one,' calls the man tied to the chair. 'You make sure you do your homework.'

Mum closes the door behind us and leads me up the stairs.

Chapter Forty-Nine
The Meet

So I go home, because it's where my husband is, and my family stay on at the hotel because they're still riding high on their dudgeon, and Rufus's family have already decamped, with the exception of my sister-in-law, who's got more sense than the lot of them put together, to spend Christmas night with the rats and the rain and the possibility of the roof falling in on their heads – would that it did. And my mum's not talking to me, and nor, by extension, is my dad, and nor is my yaya. I feel like I've just survived the Battle of the Somme.

I've got to get it all sorted before they fly back to Brisbane, but I don't know where to start. All I know is I've got the sort of car that makes you melt with joy, though my guilt and confusion take the shine off the experience somehow and I still don't know how seriously yesterday's shenanigans have damaged things between Rufus and me. But Tilly seems to enjoy herself anyway, riding all the way back with the top down and her red hair streaming out behind her like a Chinese flag and a big grin on her face at the thought of the move ahead of her. There was never any question about it: Rufus is getting his way and Tilly and the baby are getting their new home.

We crawl down the drive because it's lined with horseboxes – everything from single-pony trailers attached to clapped-out Fords to the sort of pantechnicons that contain everything including three Filipinas and a bouncy castle.

I'm surprised, to be honest. I'd sort of expected everything around hunting to be more related to the latter. My impression of foxhunting is wall-to-wall Maseratis and the sort of women who would horsewhip you as soon as look at you, but the route to the house has as many hairy-looking blokes in beanie hats riding ATVs and kids in ratcatchers on ponies so short-legged they're running to catch up with themselves as boot-faced blondes or those sort of men who fill their shirts up as much with hot air as flesh.

The house looks as grim as ever. Someone's covered the hole in the drive with floorboards from somewhere, so at least the park isn't strewn with the twisted metal of a multiple traffic pile-up, but the crack itself is still starkly visible, snaking across the grass. The drain – sorry, moat – has emptied itself completely now, is nothing more than a deep, mud-lined ditch. But outside the fortifications, on the grass, is a magnificent sight. I don't have a lot of qualms about hunting *per se*. As far as I gather we only evolved the way we did because we are bloodthirsty, organised carnivores, and trying to turn us all into open-toed bean eaters would seem like a pointless exercise, even aside from the global warming from the extra methane. But, well – wow.

Huge, shiny patchwork hounds – I don't know why, but I'd always thought of foxhounds as being something around the size of beagles, but they're big, lolloping creatures with paws like soup plates – press mournful faces into unwary crotches, scratch and wag and do doggy stuff, occasionally letting rip with a sonorous chorus when one of the hunt servants decides to change his position. It's a beautiful sound. Tuneful, optimistic, tragic, fierce all at once, and musical, like a chord played on handbells. I've never heard anything like it. It bursts across the valley and catches me somewhere around my heart.

'Good God,' I say to Tilly.

'I know,' she says. 'People think of it in this abstract sense, like it's some gathering like Nuremberg, but if you see it . . .'

I've slowed to a trickle, now. Around the outside faces glare at me: those beaky arrogant female faces that make people hate the country, wrapped tightly in headscarves and full of venom for my townie attire.

'Ah well. Don't suppose we could have got through Boxing Day without some bloody antis,' shouts one to another as we pass.

'Don't be stchoopid,' yells her companion. 'That's Edmund

Wattestone's daughter. Mathilda. The one whose husband's ran orf.'

'Would have thought she'd know better than to turn up in a car like that. Who on earth's the trollop she's got in tow?'

I lean over my door. I've got sunglasses on, *Thelma and Louise* style, and drop them down my nose to give her a beatific smile. 'I don't know if you realise,' I say, 'but one of the things about having the top down on a car is that it means that you're, like, open to the outside world? We've not got a force field around us.'

She looks at me like I've just spoken in Martian. A cross face. Full of resentment at the thought that other people might enjoy life differently from her. Full of contempt for them and fear that they might not respect her. The sort of face I'll always associate with the countryside, wherever it is.

'That must be the Awstralian daughter-in-law,' she bellows. 'Poor Mary.'

I toss my hands in the air, force a laugh and drive on. 'You'd've thought they'd have *some* sense of shame,' I tell Tilly.

'I think she was talking in an undertone,' she says. 'They spend so much time shouting at the dogs over the top of the Channel Four racing that their vocal chords forget that they're adjustable.'

'Sorry about the car. I didn't mean to attract attention.'

'It's a lovely car. Just needs half a ton of dog hair and some mud on the seats.'

'Of course. Silly me.'

We park up in the courtyard and I make to go back out, expecting her to follow me, but Tilly, after taking three goes to lever herself out from my roadholding suspension, leans instead against the side and waves a hand. 'I think I'll give it a miss. I'm just going to go inside and get on with the packing. If that's OK. I might have a quick lie-down.'

I come back towards her. 'Of course it's OK! Are you? Can I give you a hand?'

A shake of the head. 'No. No, don't be silly. Bit of leftover indigestion and a backache, but nothing much to worry about. Go and have a look. I'll see you upstairs.'

'OK. I won't be long.'

'Take all the time you want,' she says.

I find myself in the middle of a big crowd of horses, the atmosphere an electric mix of anticipation, tension, excitement, good humour. I thought these people didn't *get* excited about things. I'd expected the same sort of stolid, emotionless, lowered-eyelid attitude I've come across at parties, but it's as though someone's attached electrodes to them. It's as though they have suddenly come alive. They wear an interesting mixture of British racing green, of long black jackets with starched white stocks, of tweed and of britches, and the occasional pink coat. I don't know how the coding works – though you can betcha that there's some unreadable class element involved – but I'll tell you this: put an English person on horseback and you'll see a creature transformed. My neighbours, with their stuffiness, their lack of enthusiasm, their suspicion and superiority, have vanished overnight, have been replaced by creatures of grace and elegance. They have turned into centaurs.

I spot the family party, over by the park fence. Mary's riding side-saddle, looks chic and calm in her long skirt with her hair caught up in a net beneath a shortened topper. She wears very little makeup – all the women do, I notice – just mascara and a little slick of neutral lipstick, and it suits her. Edmund is distinguished in green; long and lean and wiry. But they all look good. Roly, on a cob the size of a small tractor, moves with the animal as though they were glued together. He's riding one-handed, the other being taken up with a glass of port. Even the stumpy little vicar looks almost attractive on his grey gelding.

There's an old army type sitting glumly next to me on a mountainous bay. He has a large white moustache and slurps his stirrup cup through it gloomily, looking about him with watery eyes. I try a small smile, get a look of pure pathos in return. Well, I suppose that's an improvement. Three little kids on skewbalds conduct a squabble over a Gameboy. Glad to see the country doesn't deprive them of *everything*.

''Scuse me, coming through,' calls a voice, and I jump aside as a woman in a tweed coat manoeuvres her horse through the crowd towards the army type. I swipe a sherry from a passing tray – carried by Mrs Roberts, I notice – and settle in to listen. The good thing about the English upper class conversational tone is you can never be accused of snooping.

'Colonel!'

The colonel turns slowly and manages a mournful smile. Touches the brim of his hat with the handle of his whip.

'Glad to see you out! Weren't expecting to! I hear you buried your wife on Tuesday.'

'Yerrss,' says the colonel. Thinks for a moment. Adds: 'Had to. Dead, you know . . .'

'Hi, Mrs W,' says a familiar voice behind me.

I turn, heart rising. If he kisses me now, in front of all these people, it will be all right.

'Ms Katsouris, if you don't mind.'

Rufus leans down from the back of the Brigadier and plants a kiss on my lips. 'Thanks for coming, darling,' he murmurs. 'I do love you. I'm sorry Christmas was such a washout.'

'Me too,' I say.

He sits back up. 'So what do you think?'

'It's . . . incredible.'

'Just wait till you see them running. Makes your hair stand on end.'

'I can't wait.'

'Did you bring Tilly with you?'

'Yes. She's upstairs packing.'

'Oh, good. So she's going, then?'

'She's beside herself. That was a good thing you did, Rufus.'

'Nonsense.'

'You could have let me know about it, though, you dope.'

Brig performs a nifty little two-step and Rufus is forced to pay attention to him for a moment. I don't know enough about horses to know whether he's set it off on purpose to give himself thinking time. 'Sorry. I wanted it to be a surprise.'

If ever there was a moment when you just wanted to ruffle a

guy's hair, this would have to be it. I can't reach, though, and there's a hard hat between me and the barnet.

'Yeah, you see, the idea of surprises isn't necessarily that *everyone* has to be surprised. Just Tilly would probably have done it.'

I hear him say 'pshaw'. So *that's* what pshaw sounds like. 'What do you think the chances would have been of her not getting to hear about it if they'd been going off on one at the breakfast table?'

'Fair point. So when do you move off?'

'Fairly soon, I expect. Are you going to follow for a bit?'

'How, exactly?'

'Well, you got a car now, haven't you?'

'What, and scratch my shiny new paintwork? Anyway, I'm going to help your sister get moved. Think of the shopping lists.'

'Bloody hell. I really *have* married a townie.'

'I'll do it once my dad's left the country.'

'Don't tell me you're scared of your father?'

'You don't know my family very well, do you?'

'I was aware of that, yes,' says Rufus meaningfully. He's not going to let the cheque incident lie. I change the subject as quickly as I can.

'You look very dashing today, Mr W. You scrub up well. If you didn't have a horse underneath you I'd be throwing you over a haybale.'

Rufus shows the hooded eyes of a Victorian philanderer. 'Why, thank you, my dear. I'll keep it on for later, shall I?'

'And how long will that be?'

'Only as long as it takes, m'dear.'

'Promises. You're all promises.'

'Ah,' says Roly, coming up behind me, 'sexual banter. Jolly entertaining Christmas, Melody, I must say. Haven't enjoyed myself so much since my stepfather shot himself in the foot.'

'Thanks, mate.' I give the cob a good slap on the neck. 'Glad to be of service.'

'Tell you what,' he says. 'Don't suppose you could do me a favour and take Perkins off my hands, could you? Sort of forgot to lock him in the Land Rover and he'll be trying to go off with the pack if I don't get him under control.'

'Sure,' I say.

'Here,' he digs in his pocket, produces a wodge of binder-twine. 'Put this through his collar. He's a good old dog, but he does get a bit excited.'

I bend over Perkins, whose eyes goggle with the thrill of it all. He wags his whole back end as I slip the string through, shakes his tongue at me. I tell him he's a good boy, like you do.

'By the way,' says Roly, 'have you met Camilla Warrington-Campbell?'

Roly's accompanied by a hefty red-faced woman who seems to be handling her horse without use of reins. A bit of a swamp donkey, if you ask me. She eyes me with all the grace of Fifi eyeing a shin of beef. And when I shake her hand, it feels like it's actually going to come off. 'Not coming out yourself, then?' she asks.

'Don't know one end of a horse from the other,' I say gaily. Her mount presses a warm velvet nose into my palm, snuffles about in it. 'This is the end that bites, right?'

The lights go out. 'Think we're in for a good run today?' she asks Rufus.

'Shouldn't be too bad,' he replies. 'There's a dog fox up in the woods that's been causing bother at the home farm. They've lost thirty chickens to him already this season, so he should have some go in him. How are you? I thought I'd heard you'd broken your arm?'

Camilla pulls a dismissive face. 'Lot of fuss. Only a break, for God's sake. Tried telling me I had to keep the plaster on for six weeks. Ended up cutting it off myself. Only ruin your muscles as well as spoil the season.'

'Good Lord,' I say. 'Are you mad?'

'Can't let a few bumps get in the way, especially when it might be the last time.'

'What? Because you'll be dead?'

'No. Bloody Labour.'

'Ah,' I say wisely.

'What's happened to the park?' she asks.

'Wish I knew,' says Rufus. 'We've got the surveyors coming in.'

'Spoils the look, I must say. Still, never really been the same since the elms went, anyway.'

'I'm wondering,' he says, 'if the two aren't related, actually. If there's some sort of geological fault, I suppose the roots might have been the only thing holding it together.'

'Mmm,' says Camilla. Pulls a face like Fifi eating a cowpat, does a twist in the saddle. A loud clunk emanates from somewhere on her body. 'Bloody pins,' she says. 'Wish they'd just take 'em out, but they say they're what's holding the back together.'

'How did you do that?'

'Horse rolled on a bank in Ireland.'

'God, poor you.'

'Awful,' she concedes. 'Had to shoot the horse.'

They all fall silent in contemplation of her loss.

'He was a good chap,' she says. 'Big heart.'

She turns back to Roly. 'Any idea which way we'll be running today?'

'I heard someone say something about the Barringtons.'

'Oh, God, I hope not. Those pylons make the plate in my head sing.'

I decide to cut loose. Give the Brigadier a clap on the shoulder and wander away among the crowd. Give a wide berth to what even I can see are London riders down for the day on rental horses – the brand-new clothes and the fact that they don't seem to be able to make them stand still gives it away – and go over to stand among the foot spectators.

They're an odd lot. They divide down the middle between hatchet-faced women of a certain age and jolly men in flat caps and cords. The women catch sight of me, and the reaction is spontaneous. If they had skirts, they would be picking them up and swishing them as they turned their backs. I mean, OK, so palazzo pants and a purple velvet Shanghai Tang jacket probably isn't the most practical attire for wading in mud, but there's no need to look like I just vomited in their strawberry patch. Oh, well. I start talking to the man nearest to me.

'Good day for it,' I say.

He pulls his cap slightly forward on his face. 'Ar.' He has a broad Oxfordshire accent, I hear to my relief. 'Bin a bet of a dew, though. Scent won't be so good.'

'Uh-huh,' I say, trying to look knowledgeable. Venture an opinion. 'Still. At least the wind's dropped.'

It works. 'You're right there. Didn't hardly get a whiff of a fox over at Great Tew on Friday. Load of antis down from London wi' a video camera and we couldn't give 'em no sport at all. And they was hopin' to throw theirselves in front of the foxes and get ripped apart for *Channel 4 News*. Went home wi' faces like pitchforks.'

'There don't seem to be many here today.'

'No. Well, there wouldn't be. Too many Heythrop Blondes out on a Boxing Day.' He jerks a tidy thumb in the direction of our companions. 'They'd never stand a chance in a fair fight. Never mind the foxhounds: that lot'd rip 'em to shreds in seconds. So where are you from, then?'

'Australia.'

'Australia! Ever ridden a camel?'

'Couple of times. Plays merry hell with the back, though.'

'I rode one once in Dubai,' he says. 'Tell you what. Saved myself the cost of a vasectomy.'

There's some movement over among the hounds. A couple of the guys in green are collecting their horses and ushering them into order. Forty tails go up in the air, eighty ears flap in the breeze and the singing rises, chorally, into descant. It's lovely, lovely, lovely. I'm nowhere near a horse, but even I can feel the adrenalin.

'Oop, looks like they're off,' he says. 'You following?'

I shake my head. 'Got stuff to do in the house.'

A nod. 'Oh, right. Staying with the Wattestones, are you?'

'Sort of.'

'Well, wrap up warm.'

'I've learned that already.'

The foot followers stream towards cars and ATVs. And the horses, picking up the vibe, turn as if at the flick of a switch from docile domestic to wild outdoors: muscles bulging in necks and rumps, wide eyes bright with excitement. I run for it as a young 'un with a green ribbon in its tail executes a balletic solo, carving great divots from the four-hundred-year old sod, his rider seeming to sit the whole thing out without moving a muscle. They gather, wheel and light out up the park drive at a smart trot.

I drag Perkins inside, leave him on the sofa in the Great Hall and go in search of Tilly. The drain smell has permeated the hall, and a nasty-looking crack, a good couple of inches wide, has appeared in the central wall, running all the way from the ceiling into the fireplace. But otherwise, Bourton is unchanged since we left it; broods on with the air of one who will resist change until blood is spent.

I cross the hall, go through the drawing room, notice a faint sludgy give in the floorboards that I'm sure wasn't there before. I'm not going to think about it. If Rufus doesn't want to go, he doesn't want to go. I've got to make the best of a bad lot.

In the Long Gallery, up on the second floor, I pause at the window, catch sight of one of the most beautiful things I've ever seen. On the brow of the hill, a lone figure jumps up and down, takes off its cap and waves it. And suddenly a green-jacketed horseman bursts from cover and gallops towards him, hounds racing ahead. And then they come, like a waterfall: bay and chestnut, grey and black and roan and dapple, dun and skewbald, palomino, pie and fleabitten: two hundred noble thundering horses, ears pricked, hoofs flying, tails streaming out behind them, racing across the park, coming to the crack in the earth and taking off over it as though lifted by wings, under a huge sky in which cloud piles, tower on tower, like meringue. I can't help it: my heart leaps into my throat. Horses. You barely see the riders: just soaring, stretching, hauling, fighting beasts running for the sheer joy of it.

I stay and watch in awe. I've never seen anything like it. You can sneer all you want, but then you see what it's all *for* and it takes your breath away. They cross the ground in less than a minute, stream away over into the next valley and I continue to stand for a while longer, thinking about what I've seen, hoping foolishly that they might come back.

Tilly is up another floor, in her old bedroom. I wander through empty halls and think of what to tell her. Hear the tick-tick-tick of the deathwatch beetle, see motes of dust catch in shafts of light and dance their way floorward. *I think I understand, now, I want to say: I think I see that there's more to it all than an obdurate adherence to how things used to be done. I think I get why Rufus can't go away, why you came back into this hell when you had nowhere else to turn.*

But I don't say anything in the end. Because Tilly is lying on her side on the bed, white as snow, hair plastered down with sweat, clutching with desperate hands at her stomach.

Chapter Fifty
The Immortal Stain

So much for worrying about the paintwork.

'I'm so sorry,' says Tilly though her tears. 'I'm so sorry. Your poor lovely new car . . .' And then she gets another spasm of pain and practically takes my hand off.

I'm in so way out of my depth. I don't know anything about what I'm supposed to do, because it never occurred to me that Birthing Partner might be one of my life's titles. I sort of know about – I don't know – hot water, and telling people to breathe, and something about ice chips. But I haven't even had time to go and look up exactly what it was on the internet, because the stupid, stupid English bint has left it so late by Not Making A Fuss (so much for whingeing Poms), that she was eight centimetres dilated by the time I'd manhandled her over to Chipping Norton hospital.

Jesus. At least she's read a *book*. All I've ever done is wonder how actresses manage to get so red in the face pretending to give birth in the movies. And now I hear something about something-or-other dilated and seeing the baby's head and I don't know whether to laugh, cry or throw up.

It passes. The white light that's been blocking out my vision gradually fades to dancing grey and I say: 'Don't worry about it. Stop it. It doesn't matter.'

But a bit of me's thinking: thank God the old man chose Berry Red for the upholstery, because I don't suppose you can ever really get the sort of mess we're talking about out of nappa leather.

'It's only a car,' I say. 'For God's sake, we've got bigger things to worry about.'

She's obsessing. I guess maybe you do when you're trying not to think about the fact that you're about to wave horoo to your twinkle.

'But it was such a beautiful car,' she sobs, 'and now it's all . . . it's all . . .'

'It's still a beautiful car. Come on. It's just, now it's always going to have that something extra special about it . . .'

I'm crying inside myself. Less than twenty-four hours I had it: my lovely gleaming status symbol. I hadn't even managed to soil the ashtrays.

'I'm *sorry*,' says Tilly. 'I'm *so so sorry*. Everything I do I fuck up. I can't even . . . can't even . . . *ngaaaaagh* . . .'

I'm starting to recognise the look on her face so I can brace myself before the pain hits. I think I'll need the name of that Camilla's bone doctor by the time this is over.

'That's it, babe,' I say ineffectually. 'Keep breathing.' Knead her back the best I know how, kicking myself for not having taken the childbirth massage leg of the course when I was training. Though I'm not sure how my sister-in-law would take it if I went down to the business end and started having a go at her perineum. Some intimacies are probably best left to strangers, even if you *don't* come from a family that wears its inhibitions as a badge of honour.

'. . . *ggghhaaaaghghhhh* . . .' She reaches the end of the contraction, slumps, panting like a winded hippo, on the bed–table–whatever.

'Shit,' she says.

I dab at her forehead with the sponge, like a Victorian nurse.

'I thought it was Braxton-Hicks,' she says. 'I've been having them for days. How was I supposed to tell the difference?'

'I don't suppose you were,' I fib kindly, through gritted teeth.

There's a lot of bustle down by her ankles: the midwife and the doctor, who looks about ten and has a pustule on his neck that I just long to pop, jostling for prime position with, as far as I can see, their elbows. 'That's great,' says the doctor, 'you're doing fine. Try not to push, if you can. You don't want to rush it if you can help it at this point. Baby's doing a fine job.'

The word 'episiotomy' dances in front of my eyes in lurid green

80-point. I realise that I have, involuntarily, crossed my knees and wound my ankles around each other.

'It's not like they got any worse . . . much worse . . . oh hell . . . until. Why can't I just die right now?'

'That's the spirit,' I say.

'Fuck off,' she replies.

'You too,' I say back. 'Betcha want to throttle Hugo right now.'

'Shit,' she says, 'with cheese wire . . . Oh God, what's going on down there? *Nnnnaaaaggghh . . .*'

Oh, good grief.

The midwife looks up from between her thighs, says something about doing well and crowning, but I can't really take it in for the pain. Good God: how on earth is Tilly supposed to, if I can't?

'I *really* want to push,' she says.

'Nearly there,' says the midwife. 'You can bear down again when the next contraction comes.'

She gives me one of those reassuring healthcare smiles. 'Do you want to have a look?'

Ah, Jeez. I'm not that grounded in delivery-room etiquette. I mean, what do you do, here? I can't say I particularly want to be going down for a gander. I've seen about as much as I'd like to on the Discovery Channel. The gynaecology of strangers is somehow a lot easier to take. I'm not sure, though, if refusing might not cause some sort of offence.

'It's OK,' she encourages, 'it's really very beautiful.'

I glance down at Tilly, see that a look of horror is pasted on over the pain. She doesn't want me down there any more than I want to be there.

'Naah,' I say, 'you're all right.'

Tilly's clutch crushes down again, but I am so relieved that I bear the pain without a flinch. 'Gaaa–FAAA!' she yells.

'That's it. Yes! We have a head!' says the doctor.

I can glimpse something round and slimy on the other side of her thigh, rubber-clad hands fiddling about its squashed little alien features. Well, blow me down. It's actually very, very exciting, this. My God: it'll be squawking in a few minutes.

'You're doing great, girl.'

'I wish my mum was here,' she says.

I feel guilty. I don't know why. It's not like Mary was exactly offering to take the day off from hunting in case. 'I know,' I say. 'I'm sorry.'

She doesn't say anything. She looks like she's just done a couple of rounds in a cement mixer. A bead of sweat hangs on the end of her nose. I dab it off, offer her a chunk of ice to suck; she shakes her head, no.

Someone mutters something about the cord being out. Tilly jerks forward, showers me, snaps: 'Yeah, can you talk to *me*, please? Brain up this end?'

God, it ain't like it is in the movies. Shouldn't she be crying weak tears of joy right now, passively gathering strength for that final push-and-sob moment of delivery?

'Sorry,' says the midwife. 'It's all fine. Everything's lovely. The cord's free and baby's just turning.'

'Is it a boy?' she asks me suddenly.

'Er . . .' I brace myself, have a peer. It's covered in gunk and blood. I can barely tell that it's a baby, to be honest.

'Ah, fuck,' she says. 'I'll know myself in a—'

And then there's one of those slithery moments that just goes on and on, and then Tilly's crying full-belt and I am pretty choked up myself, because it's amazing – it *is* amazing. All this gore and blood everywhere and suddenly, held in the midwife's hands as the doc checks her over and hoovers her out, there's a real life here. This greasy lump has hands and feet and a tiny little face that's screwing itself up to let out the first bellow of life, and I've got a lump in my throat the size of a marble as I squeeze Tilly by the shoulder and say something like, 'oh bloody hell. Bloody *hell*, girl!'

'What? What is it?'

'It's a girl,' says the midwife, lifts the bloody little bundle up and places it, all limp and snuffly and red-faced, on her deflated stomach. Tilly's hands fly up to hold her, and her weary face is suddenly lit up like the sun's got through the curtains.

329

'It's a girl,' I tell her, and burst into tears myself. 'Well done, darling. You've got a little girl!'

And Tilly's pouring tears, and kissing Lucy's fragile head and touching her cheek with the flat of her knuckle like she's made of glass, and it's wonderful, wonderful, wonderful. And she goes: 'I want my mum. I want my mother *so* much.'

'Hey, kid.' I'm staring in rapture at the baby. You know what they say, how you don't get what it's all about till you see one that's attached to someone you love? Well, this baby looks so like Rufus it's like recognising a stranger. Family resemblance, I know, but . . . she's got his expression: she's got that frown he gets when he's trying to work something out. She's all slimy and bloody, and she really is a little miracle. And I'm thinking: this is what ours would look like. If we made one, it would come out looking like this. And, I swear, I feel a great lurch somewhere between my heart and my womb, a lurch that makes me feel weak and feverish for a second.

'They can't be long, now,' I say absently, and run my own knuckle down Lucy's cheek. 'Nessa was going straight out to look for them. Your mum'll be here the minute she can, darling.'

'What are you talking about?' asks Tilly. Looks up at me, all sweaty and tear-stained, but more than that, suddenly angry. I've said the wrong thing somewhere, cast back in my memory to try to work out what it was.

'Your mum,' I say. 'She'll be here in a minute. Don't worry.'

'Not *her*,' says Tilly. 'I don't want *that* bitch.'

Then she stares at me, and the same working-it-out frown I've just seen pass across little Lucy's baby face passes across hers.

'Good grief,' she says. 'You didn't think Mary was my mother, did you?'

Chapter Fifty-One
The First Mrs Wattestone

I don't need to wonder if Nessa's in the yard. The minute I step out of the door, her voice says, from behind the bushes: 'Holy Cow. There's a right old ding-dong going on in Castle Wattestone this morning.'

I duck in to join her.

'Walls have ears. How do you know all this stuff?'

Nessa winks, and produces a blue-and-white placcy baby alarm from behind her back.

'Oh, you cheeky minx,' I say.

'Necessary tools of the job,' says Nessa. 'Even nurses have to take a break from time to time.'

'So you just spend your life listening in on the family?'

'Got to have some entertainment,' she says, stamping out her half-smoked cigarette butt, 'and besides, I need to know when I'm going to be needed. So what's all this I hear about Christmas? Sounds like a laugh.'

'Don't get me started, Nessa. I hope I never have to live through another . . .'

'Folks still at Bardmoor?'

'Far as I know. I'll have to go and look for them later. Mum's switched off her cell so I can't get hold of them.'

'That's mature.'

'Sure is.' I gesture at the baby alarm. 'Let's have a listen, then.'

'Cheeky minx yourself.'

Obligingly, she turns up the volume control on the side of the machine.

Beatrice is talking to someone. '. . . shared a governess with

Ruth, Lady Fermoy,' she is saying. 'Of course, she was part of the old school. Took her duty seriously. None of this chasing orf after fulfilment the young seem to think so important.'

Mary sounds like she's not listening. She's talking to Edmund. 'Poor old Tilly,' she says, 'going through that and it's only a girl. And I don't suppose she'll get another chance now, will she?'

'Nothing wrong with girls,' says Edmund. 'Keep themselves clean, at least.'

'I suppose you'll be wanting to visit her,' says Mary. Rufus went up yesterday evening, but none of the older generation could be prised from their traditional hunting baths for long enough to go over to Chippy.

'Well, it's customary,' says Edmund. 'She *is* my daughter, after all. And my first grandchild, come to that.'

Mary says something like 'humph'.

'Of course, I call them,' says Beatrice, 'the *me* generation. Because all you hear from them is me, me, me, me, me. We used to know what had to be done and accept our responsibility.'

Nessa turns the volume down again. 'Hilarious. Going round and round in circles. Don't suppose Edmund's going to make it up to the hospital for a good few hours yet. I'll offer to give him a lift when I come off shift. I suppose you'll be wanting to sponge a ciggie off the hired help, then?'

I shake my head. 'Thanks anyway.'

'So I hear you did the honours in the birthing suite.'

I pull a face. 'Don't know if it hasn't put me off for life. They don't exactly tell you about the blood, do they?'

'Of course not. Do you think women would let men near them if they knew the whole of it?'

'I know a few who wouldn't, anyway. So how did you hear?'

'Village. Living in an English village is like working on a tabloid newspaper. They're all obsessed with uncovering the doings of the upper classes. It's like a local sport. And self-feeding, of course. Because the more they find out the more paranoid people like your family here get and the more they try to cover up. And everybody pretends to everybody else that they're not doing it. Clam up like

332

cats' backsides when they think the family might get to know about it. Spill like beer kegs when they don't.'

'Which, I suppose,' I say gloomily, 'is how come I never knew about Tilly's mother.'

'Wow,' she says. 'Seriously? Rufus never told you that?'

'No.'

'Wow,' she says again. 'Strikes me you and your hubby have a bit of a communication problem.'

'No we don't.'

A raised eyebrow.

'We don't. He just . . . doesn't tell me stuff, is all . . .'

'That's what we call a communication problem where I come from.'

'I thought you said you came from Melbourne.'

'Ha bloody ha.'

'OK. You're right. Even I can't deny that someone not telling me something like this might be a bit weird. Why didn't he do it? I keep asking myself, and I can't come up with a rational explanation.'

'I've got a theory on that as well,' she says.

'Well, I'd guessed as much.'

'I think they believe that if you pretend something doesn't exist, then eventually, it won't have. And besides, I don't think it's such an important thing in Rufus's mind as it is in other people's. Lady Mary is his mother, after all, and whatever Tilly thinks of *her*, she's always doted on *him*. You have to remember that. He's the darling baby boy. It probably just slipped his mind.'

'Slipped his mind?'

A shrug. 'You'd be amazed. And besides. It doesn't change *your* relationship to her. She's still your mother-in law.'

'My luck.'

We mooch about in contemplation of this for a minute.

'So, what does the village have to say on this one?' I ask.

'How so?'

'Come on. The amazing vanishing wife. There must be some goss.'

'Oh yeah. Of course. They reckon Edmund did away with her to avoid alimony.'

I look at Nessa. Nessa looks at me. I can't tell if she's joking or not.

'By all accounts, she wasn't a very satisfactory wife. Or not by Wattestone lines, anyway.'

A bit like me, then. I stay silent, waiting.

'Right, well,' she begins.

Arms crossed, I look at her.

'OK. Well, the story as it goes out there among the proles is something like this. I guess you must have noticed that Edmund is quite a lot older than Mary?'

I nod. 'I sort of gathered that it was a bit of a habit in this family.'

'Well, yes and no. It's true, for sure, that Beatrice got herself married off to a guy who could barely get out of his bath chair, but actually Edmund was quite a normal age the first time he tied the knot. I mean, surely you must have wondered a bit? Mary would have had to have been, like, fourteen when she got up the duff if she was Tilly's mother, and that's going it some, even for people of their class.'

'I guess I wasn't thinking. I guess I thought she was older than she is. Put it down to the famous English complexion.'

Nessa sparks up a new ciggy.

'Nope. She's as young as she looks. Wasn't much more than eighteen when Lucy disappeared. That was her name, by the way.'

'I know. Tilly's calling the baby after her.'

'Good for her,' says Nessa.

'So?'

'Oh, yeah. Right. Mary's a goddaughter of Beatrice's, you know. Daughter of a playmate of Edmund's.'

'Oh, God, not again. That's a bit yuk, isn't it?'

'A bit, I guess. I'd say the likelihood was that Beatrice had had Mary lined up all along and Lucy was not only an aberration but a serious inconvenience. And the not-having-sons thing would have been close on a final straw.'

'You *are* joking, aren't you?'

''Fraid not. She'll have been lined up in some sort of nod-and-wink agreement from practically the day she was born. No use to anyone for anything else, after all, being a girl: the only thing she's good for is keeping the bloodlines intact.'

'It's medieval.'

'I don't know. A lot of religions deal in arranged marriages and no-one thinks it's odd, after all. People like Beatrice believe that they've been given their position by God and it's their religious duty to maintain the *status quo*. You know how superior God-botherers always seem to feel? It's the same thing. Of course, if Lucy had been a breeder I dare say people would have gradually got used to it, but as it was, they were looking at the end of the bloodline, even if he'd got divorced. If he'd remarried someone his own age, the chances of dropping an heir would have been pretty slim. As it is, women like Mary are largely brought up to get themselves wed off and pop out a couple of boy-spawn, and part of that includes doing it before they're thirty.'

'You make her sound like a brood mare.'

'Not far off. It's all done on breeding. And given Edmund made his own choice the first time round, I dare say he didn't have much option but to follow orders the second.' Nessa pauses for breath, takes in another gust of nicotine with it. 'Aaaah,' she says, breathing out, 'norepinephrine. Can't beat it.'

'So come on. Shoot.'

'Oh, right. What do you want to know?'

'Um . . . everything?'

'Well, I'll tell you what I know. Which is probably more than you'll get out of anybody here. Tilly wasn't but a little thing, and I don't suppose Rufus has ever been particularly curious. She was OK, so far as I hear. Beatrice didn't like her much. Middle class. Jewish too. I heard there was some sort of stink from her side when she married Edmund – religious separatism, again, ordained by God and that. Possibly one of the things they had in common. Anyway, all accounts, they held a funeral service for her the day she got married and never made any contact after.'

'Sheez.'

'It was the nineteen fifties.'

'I though anti-Semitism was the problem . . .'

'Oh, believe me, babe, it can cut both ways. Especially back then. Not that I'm saying that this lot would have welcomed her with open arms. Believe me, they weren't exactly dancing for joy at the prospect of Jewish offspring.'

'Oh right. You *do* surprise me. I'd never have thought it of 'em.'

Nessa laughs one of those would-ya-believe-it laughs. 'Riddled with The Protocols of the Elders of Zion, the upper-class olds. You know that's what they mean, don't you, when they lower their voices and tell you someone's 'clever' in that tone of voice?'

'Oh. Oh right. I see. I didn't realise.'

'Yes. And it's one of the reasons they're nervous of clever people. They're not particularly threatened by clever *per se*. Most of them don't have the brains to be threatened. No. They're afraid they might be Jewish.'

'So this chick was clever, then?'

'A degree in Latin or somesuch. Nothing useful. But that's the way people talk about her. They've picked it up in the village, though I think most of them would be pretty appalled if they knew what they were really saying. 'She was clever,' they say. And usually they wink. I think they think it means she was neurotic, or something.'

'OK.'

It's always interesting how people will interpret simple words in different ways. My parents, for instance: if they said someone was clever, they'd probably mean that they big-noted themselves. Either that, or that they were some type of illywhacker.

'So what's the real story?'

'Well, I think some of it's probably spot on. She wasn't a hundred per cent right in the head. I don't know. It can't have been easy for her, poor thing, locked up in this bloody great pile with only Beatrice and a few of Beatrice's servants for company, and Edmund arsing about the place thinking his one act of rebellion was enough, more than likely. Probably just expected her to fit right in without any help. Them being so perfect and all.'

This is disturbing. I am finding this disturbing. The similarities between father and son are suddenly a lot clearer to me. For all I know, I could be Rufus's final kick over the traces before he capitulates to a life of gin and hunting. And where does that leave me?

'OK. And?'

'Well, she went a bit gaga. She was fine at first: got involved in the village, started teaching down at the school. That was back when they still had a school. But people started noticing things, after a bit. Funny stuff. Just odd things. Losing stuff, at first. She'd open up her bag to hand out the homework and find she'd brought the stable accounts with her instead. Or she'd get to the shop and find she'd left her wallet down at the house. Stuff like that.'

'Well, that's not all that odd.'

'No. But it got odder, over time. Her clothes. All the people who were kids then remember her walking down the high street in Stow one day with, like, a great big tear down the back of her dress. All her foundation garments hanging out for everyone to see. Or she'd have, like, stains, or odd shoes or something. And after Tilly was born, she got increasingly weird. Paranoid. Stopped talking to half the people about the place. Accused a couple of folk of spreading rumours and stuff. And she got this thing about the house. Started telling people it had it in for her. Turned up at a couple of county-type parties in some sort of mumbling state like a zombie. They'd just invented post-natal depression about that time, so people thought it was that. Beatrice actually turned quite nice about it at that point, funnily enough. Used to sweep in and settle bills and explain things away. I don't suppose it was from any particular urge to look after Lucy, mind. More the usual don't-let-the-common-folk-know-too-much-about-our-business stuff. And maybe some protection of Edmund, I suppose. Anyway. Poor cow. The depression never seemed to let up. It got worse with time, if anything, even though the doctor had her on a pretty ferocious drug regime by that point. Barbiturates and Valium and the like. There was talk of ECT at one point. Beatrice asked Marjorie Slatter — that's Sharon's mother-in-law. She died ten years or so ago – about it, because she'd had it when she got bad with her nerves, whatever that means. Asked her in confidence, of course, so it was all round the village in no time. But I don't know if they went through with it. It certainly didn't do any good if they did. She started going AWOL. Was found wandering a couple of times in her nightclothes, once over by the Rollright Stones, once all the way to Cirencester. Never seemed to know what she was doing there.'

'Poor bitch,' I say.

'Too right. And Tilly. Neglected's not the word for it. Spent most of her time being brought up by Roberts, if she was lucky. Otherwise it was dump 'er on whoever came in handy – mostly the grooms and the ground staff.'

'Mmm.' Well, it certainly explains the constant need to apologise for her presence. 'So what happened?'

'It's hard to say. It went on for a while like this. Obviously. As I said, Tilly was four by the time she went. But the AWOLS got bigger, and longer, and by this time the rows between her and Edmund could be heard all the way to the village. I mean, obviously, half of them would happen in the village. She'd come storming out of the place and he'd come after her, and she'd be going 'You hate me! You want me dead! All of you! You'd rather I was just gone, wouldn't you!' and he'd be going, 'Darling, you've not taken your medication' and, 'Come on. Come back. You're making a fool of yourself' and stuff like that. You can't expect thirties man to know what to do in circs like that, but Edmund was particularly inept. And then one day she took an AWOL and just never came back. Poof. Vanished into thin air.'

'How do you mean, vanished?'

'I don't really know. No-one knows exactly how she went. Chucked a spaz in the middle of a dinner party and by the time the men were done with the port, she was gone. Took a suitcase, not much else, and one of the cars was found at Moreton station a couple of days later.'

'Good God.'

'Yuh. Of course they all kept it quiet down at the house.

338

Hoping she might turn up somewhere, I suppose. But there came a time when people started noticing that she wasn't there any more, and eventually Mrs R let slip that she'd done a bunk, and that was that. That's what I heard.'

'Hold on. That was that? Are you serious?'

A roll of the eyes. She pauses to take another drag of her cig. 'Well, no, of course that wasn't that. But I wasn't there at the time, so I don't know the details overmuch.'

'Surely there must have been some sort of kerfuffle? You're not saying she disappeared and no-one did anything?'

'Of course not. They had her on the missing persons'. Put up posters all over. Dragged the moat and everything, but they never found a sign of her. But to be honest, I don't think they made all that much effort. She'd become, you might say, a bit of a burden. Truth be told, they must have been pretty relieved to be shot of her. So, no: he didn't go chasing off trying to track her down. He just waited seven years and divorced her for desertion. Probably a pretty good solution as far as he was concerned. If there's one thing Edmund can't be doing with, it's high-maintenance women. If anybody's going to get any maintaining around here, it's him.'

'And her family?'

She spreads her hands. 'I told you. She was dead already as far as they were concerned. I don't suppose they even let them know.'

'Shit,' I say, bringing all my articulacy to bear. 'Bugger me dead.'

'Yeah. I don't think it was exactly the top time for anyone. That was when Edmund took to the gin, of course. And Mary came to stay soon afterwards – she'd been here at dinner the night Lucy went, so there wasn't a lot of dissimulating to be done about it where she was concerned – and sort of picked up the reins and got rewarded with the wedding ring.'

'But good God! She was only eighteen! How could she possibly have taken a place like this over at eighteen?'

Nessa pauses to inhale another lungful. 'Well, obviously it wasn't just her. It was a nice cosy cabal of her and Beatrice together, with the dedicated backup of Mrs Roberts and Mrs

Roberts's mother. I don't think she found it too difficult, especially as I dare say everyone was going out of their way to remind her that she was the Chosen One.'

'Oh my God. Poor Tilly. And poor Edmund.'

'Yeah. Sort of explains a bit, doesn't it?'

'I don't understand,' I say, 'how Rufus could possibly not remember to tell me something as . . . well . . . significant as this.'

'You would wonder, wouldn't you? You know what? I think it's all a matter of perspective. I mean, obviously it's a big thing as far as pretty much everybody else would be concerned, but as far as Rufus is concerned, it's something that happened a long time before he was born. After all, they'd hardly be the first family to gloss over history for the sake of convenience, would they? And Mary is Rufus's real mum, after all, and she'd been in place for so long before he was born that it's like the waters had long since closed over Lucy's head.'

'God, families. I have to say I never thought Edmund would've had it in him.'

'Well, I guess that's where Rufus got it from, eh? And I think he learned his lesson pretty good. He's not stepped out of line since. The only thing is, looking at you, and Rufus, and the way those women are going on, I can't help but worry that history might be repeating itself.'

'Oh, don't. I'm not blind to the similarity. Still. Maybe I'm made of sterner stuff.'

'I hope so. For Rufus's sake as well as yours. I'll tell you what: you're amazingly patient. Haven't you ever been tempted to lose your temper? Just really let rip?'

'Er, yeah. I have that.'

'Well, why didn't you? I know I would have by now.'

'That's not my way of doing things. I don't like losing my temper. It always causes more harm than good in the long run.'

She looks at me, speculatively. 'Funny. I'd have got you figured for a chick with a bit of a mouth on you. Especially – don't take offence – now I've had a look at your family.'

'Yeah, well,' I say, 'you've got me figured wrong.'

And then I shut up, because the truth is that I haven't lost my temper in over two years, because I know, when you do it, that bad things happen.

Chapter Fifty-Two

Souvenirs of the Apocalypse

We think we've evolved so much as a society, but really, we've just moved the goalposts. We've developed a new set of pieties over the past fifty years that are just as abusable as the last lot, and we're too damn arrogant to see it. So that, now that women have finally persuaded men – and each-other – to take rape seriously, we've also spawned a type of ruthless harpy who'll scatter accusations about, for revenge, or for profit, regardless of the cost. And now women have hard-won the right to work, we use it as a justification for shirking our responsibility to the vulnerable, a cudgel as hefty as any of the old moralities.

And there's the piety that has shaped my own life, has affected me the most: the piety that says that a man, any man, who hits a woman, any woman, is by definition a bad 'un. Straight up. Black and white. No ifs or buts or maybes or provocation. No second chances. You're better off without him, girl. Your dad's no angel, but he never hit your mother.

'Cause I'm no angel, either. Andy and me, it was bad towards the end: really bad. But I'm talking six to the half-dozen. It was a bad relationship, I understand that now. A spoiled princess and a princeling with commitment problems. A man who never, ever introduced me to his family, and a woman whose family were never out of the picture, not even for a day. A guy who reacted to pressure with brutal off-pushing and a woman who reacted to rejection with bursts of uncontrollable rage.

I'm a hypocrite: I'm such a hypocrite. I complain and complain about secrets, and most of my life has been about staying shtum one way or another. I guess I got so much early training in not letting people know how the land really lay, that I never really learned to do anything much else. I didn't talk about the way things were deteriorating with Andy until they'd gone a long way down the road, and by the time people found out the truth, it was far too late. And they still don't really know the half of it. To this day, the family think of me as the victim, as their hard-treated little Princess. And me? I'm scared. Scared to death. Scared of getting trapped in another situation I can't get out of. Scared of people finding out about me, that I'm not as nice as they think. Scared I'll drive Rufus off, make him leave me the way Andy did. And most of all, I'm terrified of my temper. I've not learned the happy medium. Where before I would have reacted like a wildcat, I now just roll over and play dead. I disgust myself, sometimes, with the way I just let myself be stomped on. But you see, I learned the hard way that if I don't shut my mouth and take what's doled out to me, that disaster will inevitably follow.

Love has a lot to answer for.

Some Souvenirs of the Apocalypse

Saturday, 11.30 p.m., Brisbane. Driving home from the Mummydaddy's. I'm driving because Andy always seems to need a drink to handle time with my family. Or so he says. I think it's more of an any-excuse thing. Andrew has spent an hour in the den with my dad and Costa while Mum and Yaya and I cleaned up after dinner, so it can't have been that much of an ordeal.

Except that, while we're sitting at the lights on an empty junction, he announces, apropos nothing, that this has been his last visit to my family home.

He doesn't say it quite so elegantly, of course. The phrasing comes out more like: 'Well, that's the last bloody time I bloody go there. You can stick your bloody family up your bloody clacker.'

Andrew's speech has always been peppered with the Great Australian Adjective.

I count to ten, and reply: 'Excuse me?'

343

Having had his little outburst, he adopts the accusatory-silence mode of expression, and glares through the windscreen.

I count some more, then say: 'And would you mind telling me where this has come from?'

'I can't stick them,' he says, 'And I'm not putting up with it any longer.'

'Since when?'

This has genuinely come as a surprise. Andrew has been coming with me on the weekly home visit without a complaint for years. Matter of fact, I had always been under the impression that he enjoyed them: clapping people on the shoulder and calling my father an old bastard. He showed all the signs of an Australian male in his element.

'Since for bloody ever. Anyway, I'm not going back there. Wild horses wouldn't drag me.'

'What's eating you?'

'Nothing. I've just had enough, is all.'

The lights change. I move off, hang a right through dark suburban streets.

Neither of us says anything for a bit, then he starts up again: 'They think a whole lot of themselves, your family. You'd have thought they were royalty, the way they go on.'

My father was wearing a string vest this evening. And my mother was wearing a towelling playsuit in frosted pink. Not a tiara between them.

'Bullshit.'

'And that's another thing. Where do you get off being so bloody foul-mouthed?'

'You can bloody talk.'

'It's not bloody ladylike. Just shows the sort of family you come from.'

'Well, make your bloody mind up, Andrew. They can't be the scum of the earth *and* royalty at the same time.'

This is not, by the way, a political viewpoint I particularly subscribe to, but the point itself is reasonable.

'Well,' he says, 'you can let them run your life if you like, but

344

they're not bloody running mine.'

'What's got into you?'

Andrew suddenly starts gesticulating. The alcohol he's consumed during the evening exaggerates his gestures, so that I find myself ducking around his hands as I try to keep an eye on the road.

'No, I guess you probably wouldn't see any of it, would you? That's the trouble. You don't see anything wrong with it.'

I find myself thumping the steering wheel. 'Of course I bloody don't! What do you want me to see?'

'That's it,' he says. 'Bring out the threats. Typical. Daddy's little girl. Bloody princess bloody Melody, can't get her own way so she goes berko. Can't take criticism, can't take the truth. Things get a bit hot so she goes running to Daddy.'

'I never—' I begin.

'Stuff it,' he interrupts.

'Has something happened I don't know about?'

'I very much doubt it,' he says meaningfully.

'Don't talk riddles,' I say.

'I'm just telling you,' he says, 'that I'm sick of the way your family interferes. They're bloody stickybeaks. Can't keep their bloody noses out of anything.'

'Well, at least you've *met* my family. Yours might as well be dead as far as I've seen of them.'

'Well, are you surprised? If they met you, they'd have to meet your family, and—'

'*Now* who thinks they're bloody royalty?'

'Well, we've gone a bit higher up the social scale than kebab shops,' he says crushingly.

I realise I'm grinding my teeth. 'I never realised you were a snob, Andrew. Anyway, I don't know what you've got to be so proud of. A photocopying franchise and a guesthouse. It's not a lot to write home about.'

'Well,' he says, 'I don't suppose *you* write home at all.'

'Meaning?'

'Well. At least *my* old man can read.'

345

This really stings. None of this has ever been a problem before.

'Yeah. And you know what? I'm proud of him. Not many people get as far as he has when . . .'

'Well, you've got to ask,' says Andrew, 'how he managed it.'

'What? What do you mean?' I say, stomach lurching because we've been respectable for years now; I've never needed to let him in on things because there's plenty of cover been built up.

He shrugs. An insolent, slumping shrug. 'Nothing.'

'Well, you meant something.'

'No. Nothing. Forget about it.'

'How can I forget about it?'

'Oh, stop nagging me, willya?' he shouts. 'You and your bloody mouth. Yap yap yap yap yap!'

Firday. 3 a.m. Lord Howe Island. Milky Way Apartments. Andrew lies in bed, silent, arms folded, back turned to me. I know he's awake. After four years sharing a bed with someone, you're so attuned to the sound of them sleeping that their insomnia is, usually, catching.

He's not spoken to me for two hours. I didn't really notice while we were still with the others, but the silence since we've been alone has been oppressive, has filled my ears like white noise. The inconsequential exchanges of going to bed, shared bathrooms, finding spare pillows in a new hotel room, have been one-sided, my words dropping with thuds into the tropical night like rocks into sand.

But I'm in a good mood tonight. It's the first night of a week's R and R, and I'm just ripe to get my bubble popped. We had a good dinner at Trader Nick's, elbows on the table, shooting the breeze and sinking stubbies with Tina and her bloke-of-the-week, Dylan, and Tines's sister, Lola, and her girlfriend Rusty, a muscular, forthright type who drives one of Dad's cabs and never takes shit from anyone. Then we had a couple of sharpies on the deck of our unit, Andrew throwing jokes about, an arm lightly draped over my shoulder just like the old days, and a race in the moonlight down through the forest to Old Settlement beach, where the moon glittered so invitingly off the ocean that Tines and I were overtaken by an urge to chuck our Daks over our shoulders and go skinny-dipping, like we used to when we were fifteen, sixteen. And it was great: just like the old days. A laugh.

And then, the moment we were alone, he reverted to the silent punisher he's been for months now. That's Andrew all over: solicitous boyfriend in public, taciturn judge in private. It came as a surprise to most people when we broke up. 'But you guys got on so well,' they said. 'He was always all over you. I don't understand . . .'

I lie and listen to him breathe. Decide that I'm not going to let this night be ruined like so many recently. So I reach across the border that's been drawn down the centre of the bed, and touch his hip, run my fingers forward and down towards his doodle. Men are always harping on about women making the first move, after all.

He slaps the hand away. 'Get off,' he says.

I sit up in bed, shocked at the baldness of the rejection. 'What's eating you?'

'Just don't touch me. I don't want you pawing me tonight.'

'What's your problem this time?'

'Nothing.' The back stays firmly turned to me.

'What, nothing?'

'Well, if you really want to know, it's you,' he says. 'You give me the irrits.'

'Oh yeah? And what am I meant to have done this time?'

He sits up sharply, looks at me with an expression of loathing like I've never seen on his face before. 'Well, just look at ya,' he says.

'What?'

'It just hit me, that's all. When you and Tina were galumphing about with no clothes on. You're seriously fucking fat. You're chunderous.'

'Jesus.' Taken aback is hardly the word.

'Just look at ya,' he repeats. Jabs a finger out and rams it into my belly. 'You've let yourself go. It's like you don't care at all. Do you really expect me to fancy *that*?'

347

I'm stunned into silence.

'I'm ashamed to be seen with you,' he says.

'You disgust me,' he says.

'Just keep your hands to yourself,' he says. 'It makes me crook just thinking about it.'

Wednesday. 6 p.m. Home. I'm in a narky state anyway, because I've just got my period and I feel like my guts are about to fall out, and, believe me, the last thing you want to be doing when your hormones are all over the place is bending over someone else's bunions and listening to them grizzle. It's been a full day, driving about in forty degrees of heat, with a full complement of whingers, because, let's face it, whatever I think about the power of reflexology, the majority of the people I treat are the sort with more money than sense and too much time on their hands, and I don't really rank higher in the social order than a manicurist or a hairdresser. Even digging my trigger pointer in twice as hard as I need to doesn't seem to have had the satisfaction quotient it usually does. I've heard nothing but self-pity all day, and though I know that this is largely what people pay me for it's hard to take when your back hurts and your stomach is cramping and your tolerance levels are at practically zero. I need a shower, a long cold drink and a backrub.

What I get is a lounge full of torn-up rolling-paper packets, a floor full of takeout, a sink full of last night's washing-up and the dolie I call my fiancé fast asleep in front of the aerial pingpong, volume turned up so loud the neighbours will be over. He's been there all arvo, by the looks of it. His feet are up on my silk cushions and his mouth is open in a sluggard's snore, and he's got one hand down the front of his baggy shorts, cupping his balls. Andy, who I used to love to distraction. Andy, who when I met him was a lion – lean, strong, agile, eager – turned into a neutered tomcat, raggedy blond body hair scattered over a little pot belly. Did I do this to him, that he can have changed so much in four years? Maybe. I can be an über-bitch when I get going. Maybe that's what I do. Maybe I'm a ball-breaker. Maybe that's what I am.

I certainly act like one now. And no, the menstrual excuse is no justification. I go into the kitchen, fill a glass full of water, come back into the lounge and throw it in his face, with all the energy I can muster.

I'm not proud of this. I'm not proud of this part of my history. If I remember it, I blush with shame. How can someone have so little self-control? I knew it was ending, I desperately didn't want it to end, and this was how I went about keeping him.

If I could take it back, I would. All of it. Every little bit. I don't mean I want him back but, my God, when you know how much you are to blame, when you have so much to be guilty about, you find yourself making every bargain under the sun with God to get him to take the shame away. This was the way I behaved to someone I loved. What sort of person does that make me?

Andy rolls awake, coughing, looks up at me blearily. 'What'd you—'

'Get up!' I shout. 'Get up, you lazy bastard! What the fuck have you been doing all day?'

Andy scratches his wrist, says: 'Oh, sorry, babe, I sort of fell asleep.'

I pick up a cushion, swipe him with it.

'Ow!' he cries, puts his hand up in front of his face. Somehow this action enrages me all the more. I don't know. It was a mad time. Mad and bad, and my heart was coming apart at the seams. Suddenly, I'm whacking at him with the cushion, full-throttle, and he's curled into himself on the couch, saying nothing.

I can hear my own voice, and it doesn't sound like me. It's like an ogre has taken over my body. 'You fucker. You total pointless waste-of-space fucker. You can't even do the fucking washing-up. Sitting around on your lazy arse all day and I come back and the house is worse than when I left.'

'Melody!' his voice is muffled by his defensive arms. 'What are you doing? Stop it! Stop fucking hitting me!'

Suddenly I realise that I've dropped the pillow and am using my bare hands. I've been slapping him about the head, even got a couple of punches in on his body. The rage goes out of me as quickly as it came. My arms drop to my sides. 'Jesus,' I say.

Andy cautiously unrolls himself. His hair is all messed up and his face is red – whether as a result of my attack or from breathlessness I can't yet tell.

'Oh, Jesus, babe.' I hear the ritual cant of the wife-beater spill from my lips. I'm aware of what I'm doing, but I don't know what else to say. It all sounds so simple when you see it on the problem pages: he'll promise he's sorry. He'll say he didn't mean it. He'll say he doesn't know what happened. He'll say it'll never happen again, but don't believe it. What they don't say is this: if it's you, if you're the violent one, you probably *do* mean it. I'm all twisted up inside: confused by my rage and sickened by my behaviour. I can see myself in my mind's eye, and what I see is a monster. I am disgusting, vile, a modern leper. 'Oh Jesus,' I say again, 'I'm sorry. I don't know what came over me. Oh God, are you all right?'

Andy's nose is running. He dabs at it, obviously thinking it's bleeding, looks down at his fingers and back up at me. And the look in his eyes is so wounded, so wounded and disgusted, that I reel. I see in Andy's eyes the way I feel about myself.

I drop to my knees in front of him. Put a hand out to touch his face, attempt to offer him the comfort we used to give each other in the early days, before we started tearing each other apart. 'Let me—'

He grabs me by the wrist, pulls the hand away.

I start to cry. Crying and shouting: that's all we do these days. 'Please don't. Oh, Andy, I'm sorry. I'm so, so sorry.'

Head bowed in penitence, I look up through my eyelashes. Andy is shaking his head. His mouth turns down at the corners.

'You're sick,' he says.

He's right. How can he be wrong? Look at what I've just done.

I sob. 'I'm sorry. Andy, I'm so sorry. I swear, it'll never happen again. I'm so sorry. Let me make it up . . .'

Sharply, with contempt, he pushes me by the shoulder so I drop back on to the floor. And there's something about the gesture that is more humiliating, more enraging, than anything I've experienced before. It reminds me of Reggie Harper and her buddies back at school. It reminds me of the way he's talked to me

350

lately, the way he looks at me lately, his lip curled with a potent combination of dislike and contempt, and waits two beats before he lets go with some remark that crushes the wind out of me. And I see red: a red mist descends in front of my eyes and I lose what remaining restraint I had.

He's turned and started walking to the door by the time I'm on my feet. I belt across the room, teeth bared, and throw myself on his back, like a kid going for a piggyback, calling him a bastard, a cunt, a fucking shithead. And Andy staggers under the sudden weight, claws at the arm I've got wrapped round his throat as I batter at his head with the free hand.

'Stop it!' he chokes. 'Mel, *stop* it! Get off! Get offa me!'

'I'll fucking – I'll – I fucking *hate* you! I *hate* you! I'll fucking do for yer, you *bastard*!'

I slip down on to the ground, stand in front of him fists clenched, barely able to see him through the slits that are my eyes. And I don't know what I'm doing, really I don't, just that I hate him, and I want to hurt him, make him feel the way I'm feeling right now, hurt and humiliated and hot and stung like snakebite.

And I belt him. Pull my hand back to arm's length and clout him with all my strength, full in the face. Feel his nose give under my knuckles, feel the rush of power as his head snaps back on his neck and his shoulders roll.

And then I'm flying sidewise, air whistling past my ears, and my face comes into contact, hard, with the door-jamb and I don't know anything more.

Chapter Fifty-Three

To Think of What We've Done
for You

Even if I hadn't seen the limo coming down the drive, I would have heard their arrival if I'd been locked up in the dungeons. Well, if not their arrival, the outbreak of bellowing that follows close on its heels. She's shouting the odds, and it sounds like everyone who's in the house is shouting them back. I can hear her as I pound down the stairs to the Great Hall, her honk bouncing off the walls like cannonballs.

'I want to see my *daughter*!' she bellows. 'Let me see my bloody *daughter*!'

I burst through the fireplace door, find Mum, Mary, Beatrice and Mrs Roberts facing each other off by the door, the Bourtonites lined up, arms folded, while Mum rages impotently at them. 'Just let me see my *daughter*!' she shouts again.

Mary's voice, raised and imperious: 'No-one's trying to *stop* you seeing your daughter! I told you! If you just wait here, someone will go and *get* her!'

'Get her out of my house!' cries Beatrice. 'Mary! I will not tolerate—'

'Ahh, shyaddap!' Mum snarls. I don't understand what's got her in such a wax. Other than the fact that she must have come expecting a confrontation, like she does, so she's creating one. 'Shut yer stupid *face*!'

'Mum!' I shout. 'What are you *doing*?' I can't believe this. All that work, all the time I've spent putting up with things, holding my counsel, and she's smashing all of it, *all* of it, with one display of her explosive, vituperative, childish temper.

What sort of chance did I stand, growing up with someone who reacts to everything, *everything*, with this red-faced, stamping, swearing, fist-shaking rage? '*Stop* it!' I shout. 'What are you *doing*?'

'*You!*' she blasts at me. 'Come on!'

'What?'

Mary, Beatrice and Mrs Roberts simply stand there, drink in this example of family communication with gloating pleasure. *You see? You see? What did we say? Didn't we say it all along?*

'I've got a ticket here,' says Mum, 'and I expect you to use it.'

'*What?*'

Her voice, astonishingly, rises another notch. '*Don't* answer me back, missy! . . . Come on! We're all waiting in the limo and we're not waiting for ever!'

'*What are you talking about?*'

She blinks, slows, speaks to me as though I'm a stupid child. 'We're going back,' she says, 'and you're coming with us. You're not staying here.'

'You,' I say, 'have taken leave of your senses.'

'Don't you *dare* talk to me like that.'

'Like *what*, Ma?'

'There's no way,' she says, 'you're picking this lot over your own family.'

'I don't know what you're talking about.'

'Melody,' she says, and the threat in her voice is palpable.

I don't look in any direction at all, because I know whichever way I look, it'll undermine every intention I have. She's gone mad. Stark, staring mad. She can't seriously think I . . .

I fold my arms across my chest, look down at my feet for support and say: 'I'm sorry, Mum, but I'm not coming.'

Mary and Beatrice are far too well-bred to react to this, but I feel the *frisson* none the less.

'Bollocks,' says my mother. 'Come on. Get your stuff.'

'No,' I say. 'I'm not going anywhere.'

She looks stunned, like the idea had never entered her head. No-one gainsays Colleen Katsouris. It will literally never have occurred to her that I might say no. I never have before, after all. I've run away rather than face it.

She takes a minute to drink in this sea-change. 'Well, what are you *going* to do, then?' she asks eventually, still belligerent.

I don't know if the obtuseness is deliberate or not, but I don't want to play this out in front of the two people who hate me most in the world.

'We'll talk about it outside,' I say.

I'm careful to pull the door to as we leave the house. Hardly any point, really, as Mum's in such a rage now that her voice would pierce the walls of a nuclear bunker. I think for a moment, as she rounds on me in the courtyard, that she's going to clock me one.

'What do you mean, you're not coming?' she shouts. 'Are you going to stand for those . . . those *bitches* treating us like that?'

She's not calmed down at all. I know what she's like. She's been stewing up there at the hotel while I've been tied up with Tilly, and her rage has got worse and worse until she's worked herself into such a state of unreasonableness that everything she's doing right now seems completely logical to her. This is what I ran away from. This is how I don't want to be.

I try to speak evenly. 'Of course not. I'm sorry. I understand that that was horrible. But I don't think all the fault was on one side, and I'm not leaving my husband because you guys can't get on with his family.'

Mum looks like I've slapped her. 'What do you mean, you don't think the fault was on one side? Where do you think you get off? Are you going to side with *them* now?'

I can't stop a small snort of frustration. 'Oh, Jesus, Mum, can't you hear yourself?'

Mum's decibel level goes up another notch. At this rate, I won't need to tell Rufus what's happened in his absence, as he'll have heard it all the way over at Great Rissington. 'Oh, well. That's nice. I'm glad I've come all the way to England to get brought up by my *own daughter*!'

I give her a hopeless shrug. 'It wasn't me that decided to start shouting the odds.'

'Christ,' she says.

We reach the outer wall. I glimpse the shadowy figures of my dad and my yaya behind the limo's smoked glass windows. They've left her to it. No doubt they agree with everything she's saying, but they're leaving the fighting up to her.

'So you've decided to forget all about your family, then? Not good enough for you any more, eh?' demands Mum.

'God Almighty, Ma. Do you think you could push it a bit further with the emotional blackmail?'

This, of course, plays it right into her anti-intellectual hands. 'Emotional blackmail? Well, hark at you! What? Swallowed a dictionary now you've gone up in the world?'

A back window comes down, slightly. 'Colleen,' says Yaya reprovingly.

'Well, what?' asks Mum. 'Listen to her!'

Yaya's eyebrow knits. 'The girl's got her choices to make,' she says.

'Yeah,' says Mum, 'and it looks like she's already made them.'

I look at her, aghast. She can't seriously be offering me an either-or here, can she? 'You can't mean that, Ma! You can't! Are you seriously saying it's a choice?'

'Well, what do you think? We're your family. If you want to choose another family, then what do you expect?'

I protest. 'Are you saying,' I ask, 'that it's a choice between my family and the rest of the world?'

'You choose,' says Yaya. 'Your family. The other family. She can't make that choice. How can she make that choice, Colleen?'

'Family's family,' says my mother. 'There's nothing more important than your family, and if you haven't learned that by now, then all I can say is God help you. Your dad didn't turn his back on your yaya, and nor did I . . .'

'I don't get it, Ma. Family First, yes, but it can't be Family Or. You can't just . . . I'm not choosing another family! I'm not! I'm married, for God's sake! I have a husband!'

She carries on as though she hasn't heard a word I've said. '. . . just don't expect to come running back to us when it all goes

355

wrong. Those people. They look down on you. They despise you. You think by sucking up to them you can get them to change their minds, but it won't work. You silly, silly little girl. . .'

'You're being unreasonable! Can't you see? You're being totally unreasonable! Yaya! Tell her!'

But Yaya just says: 'They despise you. Oh, yes, they do. Don't you see that? How can you not see that?'

'. . . after everything we've done for you. After all those years, all the things we've done, the things your dad's done, and your brother, all the things we've done to protect you, all the money we've spent on you and all the worrying we've done. Well, that's fine. Have it your way. You want to get rid of us, go ahead!'

I feel like I'm being stretched on a rack of conflicting emotions. Tearfulness, anger, outrage, injustice, fear, astonishment: they're pulling me apart. 'I don't! How can you say that?'

'After everything they've done,' says Yaya.

'. . . first bloody chance you get. I suppose that's why you didn't even want us there at your wedding. Too bloody *embarrassing*, I suppose, in front of all your *grand relations* . . .'

'Is that what this is about? Mum, there was no-one there! No-one! It wasn't *you* who was excluded! It was—'

'. . . still. This is just like you. Just bloody typical. You've always thought you were too good for this family, haven't you? Right from when you were a little girl. And the funny thing is, it's always been us who's had to bail you out, hasn't it? Because you go, "Oh, I'm Melody Katsouris, I'm far too good for this family" and the first thing you do, always, is pick people who think *they're* too good for *you*. It's like, your character fault, isn't it, missy? So then who has to come in and clean up afterwards? Pick up after your cock-ups? Well?'

'Your family, that's who,' says Yaya. 'Us, that's who.'

'I'm grateful,' I say, though gratitude isn't what I feel right now. But I'm still trying to be reasonable, still clinging to the hope that somehow I can break through the barrier of my mother's self-defensive rage. 'God knows I'm grateful. I understand. I owe you an incredible debt. Like all kids do their parents. I know that,

Mum. But it's . . . don't you understand? I love him. I love him and I'm not leaving. *They've* got to understand that as much as you have to. It's not about them, or you, it's about me, and him.'

I've seen her in rages before. Every day, pretty well, that I've been with her, she's gone off on one about something. That's how it is in our family. Mum raving at the gods, Yaya echoing her like a Greek dramatic chorus and Dad, well, Dad chewing on his cigar and going off to do the business. That's the way it is, but today I'm not playing ball. I'm not doing it. It's too important. Rufus is too important.

'Yeah, yeah, yeah, *him*.' She spits the word out like wormwood. 'Always *him, him, him*. You never learn, do you? You'd've thought, wouldn't you, that you'd have learned after the last one? But oh, no. The last one thought he was too good for you too, and look where *that* got you. Jesus, Melody. Open your bloody eyes and *see*, won't you? You'll get all fucked up just like you did with the last one, and you'll only have yourself to blame. Only, this time we won't be around to sort it for you.'

I spit the dummy. 'No, *you* see! I've had about enough of this! All of you! It's not about you! None of you can get that through your heads, can you? It's not about you! The way you all go on – you and them – the only mature people in the whole bloody mess seem to be me and Rufus! It's not *about* you!'

'Yes it is! Yes it is! We've protected you, we've sorted out your problems when you were too damn pathetic to do it for yourself, we've bought your way out of stuff and fought your way out of stuff and now you're just going to pretend . . . we've done *every-thing* for you, Melody!'

'Everything,' says Yaya.

'Like what?' I scream. 'It's not – parenting's not a two-way street! It's what parents do! They look after their kids! It's not some – *repayable contract*! You have us, you raise us, and we go and live our lives! It's a debt, yes, but it's not repayable in kind!'

'Oh, get over yourself, Melody,' she sneers.

'No! You don't understand! *I love him*! I'm not giving that up!'

Mum tosses her head. Looks at me – at what I've just said – with

357

all the contempt that Mary and Beatrice have stored up, and then some.

'Well, we've heard *that* one before,' she says, 'haven't we? And look how *that* ended up. That's just what I'm talking about. You can't do *anything* without us. It always falls to us, in the end. Me, and your dad, and your brother. We do everything for you.'

'I know,' I tell her. 'I know, I made a mistake. But you can't make me pay for it for the rest of my life.'

'Everything,' she says. With a meaning that even I can't miss.

I stop dead in my tracks. She's the one with her arms folded, now: a gesture of defensive triumph.

'What are you talking about?'

Mum lets out a laugh that sends chills down my spine. 'Don't come the innocent with me, missy,' she says. 'Don't pretend you don't know what I'm talking about.'

Chapter Fifty-Four
What Did You Do . . .?

I know. Oh God, I know. Did I know all along? Have I been pretending to myself, all this time, when I knew?

She's switched off the cellphone again. It doesn't even go to voicemail. And the hotel says they checked out before they came down to Bourton, and I don't know where they are, can't go and confront them, so I call Costa because it's the only thing I can think of to do.

There's a game of footie on the idiot box in the background. I can see him in my mind's eye, my beautiful, graceful, vicious brother, sprawled out on the white leather settee with his mates, debris of man-fun scattered over the coffee table. Costa with my dad's warm brown skin and my mum's blonde curls, T-shirt hitched up over a hand that lazily scratches his six-pack. Costa who's broken my heart.

'Hey, Sis!' he says. 'How's it going? Olds behaving themselves?'

My throat is full of tears. It's the sound of his voice. I can't speak for a moment. Hear him sit up, over there on the other side of the world. Hear his voice change.

'What is it, Mel? What's wrong?'

I find my voice at last.

'You've got to tell me. You've got to tell me the truth.'

'Hold on.'

The sound of the game fades. He's walked out into the hall.

'What is it, Mel?'

'Don't lie to me Costa.'

'No. OK. What?'

'Tell me it's not true.'

'What?'

'Costa, *what happened to Andy?*'

The phone slips against his cheek. It takes a moment for him to come back on the line.

'Christ, Sis . . .' he says.

I'm shouting. My voice cracking, slipping upward. There's something inside me, gnawing and fighting to get out. My whole body hurts. My chest is so constricted I can barely breathe.

'Tell me,' I yell.

'Mel . . .'

'*TELL ME!*'

'What do you want me to say?'

'Tell me the truth!'

'Well, kiddo, we got rid of him. It was what you wanted, wasn't it?'

'What do you mean? What do you *mean*, you got rid of him?'

'I wouldn't worry about it. He's not coming back, believe me.'

'What do you mean? What did you *do*?'

He sounds so calm. Like he's talking about a walk in the park. He almost sounds like he's enjoying the memory. 'Well, we took him out fishing. You know. When you were asleep, after Ma called us.'

'What do you mean, fishing?'

'Well, Mel, you didn't think we'd let something like that just ride, did you? Come on. The bastard had it coming to him.'

'What? *What did you do?*'

'Well,' he says, 'we took him out the reef and chucked him in the water . . .'

A sob rips itself from me, huge and hot, doubling me up so all I can do is grip my chest and howl. No, God, no, no, no, *please* don't let it be true. *Please.* Tell me he's off in Tassie somewhere, living it up in the bars and never thinking of me. Tell me he went to New Zealand to get away from us, that he's running a bar at Chang Mai, that he went down to Canberra, that he ran off with someone he'd been sleeping with all along, that he's married now, with three ugly kids and a bitzer. Tell me you *paid* him to go away. Tell me he hates me. Tell me he wishes he'd never met me, that he wishes

360

me cancer, that he's been warning the world away from me. Tell me he's in jail or in hospital or in Cambodia. Anything. Just don't tell me that. Please don't tell me *that* . . .

Chapter Fifty-Five

And on Your Children's Children

I can't tell him. How can I?

Costa sat on the stairs with me, held me in his strong brown arms and told me it would be all right. He said: you never know, Sis. One day you'll be glad he's gone. One day you'll know you had a lucky escape. You've still got us. You can trust us. We'll take care of you.

He thinks that I'm devastated by my parents' departure, by the disaster of their visit, the trauma of the ultimatum, that the days I spend crying, inconsolable, the tremors, the sickness, are a reaction to the stress. How can I tell him? How can I say: 'The man I thought had left me was murdered by my family? The blood of assassins flows through my veins.'

And it's all begun again, the wound has opened up again, because before, when I grieved, I grieved for myself, for the girl abandoned, the love disdained, for all that promise come to dust. And now – now I'm grieving for Andy. I grieve for my guilt, and his loss, and the reality that he will never breathe, see, touch, screw, laugh, love, dance. I grieve for the man I loved and the knowledge that no-one will visit his grave, no-one will raise a glass on his birthday in rueful memory, that his mother-father-sister think he left them the day he left me. I grieve for the lies, and the loss, and the cold, sick shock of truth.

Tilly comes home from the hospital and brings my new goddaughter to see me and I can barely hold her for fear she will be contaminated. And Tilly, through her own exhaustion, instantly sees the desperation that drives my tears and, not understanding, comes and sits on the bed and gives me the first gentle touch I've had from anyone other than my husband since I got here. She strokes my hair and cradles me against her squashy, sloshing mummy-breasts, and all I can think is: 'I don't deserve this. I will never deserve this. It's my fault. If she knew, she would hate me. Andy's dead and it's my fault.'

I pick at the word the way you feel a bad tooth with your tongue. Dead. Oh God. Each time I say it, silently, in my head, a fresh jolt of pain snatches my breath away, makes me howl inside.

Dead. Andy's dead.

He can't be dead. I loved him.

You killed him.

I didn't mean it. I never meant it. Oh, Andy . . .

And then I remember him, alive: stupid Andy, the chiselled trapezoid jaw, the patchy blond stubble where he neglected to shave for days on end, the hair streaked with salt-bleach. Andy, singlet stained with sand and carnauba wax, smoking a blunt on the beach at Kirra, laughing fit to bust a gut. Andy fucking me, our hands over each other's mouths to stifle the noise, against the balcony wall in our resort on the same trip while several dozen people ate dinner five metres below, unaware. And worst: Andy on that last day, the last time I saw him, his face a picture of shock, remorse, disbelief, concern, apology.

The last I'll see of him.

And my mum sat with me all those nights, held my hand, stroked my hair, gave me sympathy, and all the time she knew . . .

He doesn't know what to do. He sees my desperation and doesn't know how to reach me. And every time I close my eyes, I see Andy and *crash*, the pain comes back.

What did I do? What did I *do*? It was never meant to end like this. They were never meant to hurt him.

Andy, I didn't mean it. I'm sorry. I'm so sorry.

He says: darling, it doesn't matter. None of it. They'll come round, they'll get over it, you'll find a way. You're safe with me. I'll never leave you. Nothing will ever induce me to leave you. And I kiss his hand and wipe my tears with the back of it, feel it against my eyes, and I love him, I love him so much it hurts, and if he only knew, if he only knew . . .

And he says: 'Look, if it's any consolation, I'm deeply ashamed of the way *my* family behaved, too. It's hard to believe that any of us were raised by any of them. They don't seem to have the maturity they were born with.'

I have never felt so isolated. Not when I was travelling, not when I thought that Andy had done what I deserved. I thought I knew all about grief: its searing, leaden, enervating, all-pervasive nature; the waking-to-remember and the sleep that never comes. But a grief you can't tell a soul about is murderous. I believe, for the first couple of days, that it will kill me. I am their daughter, and in their twisted way they thought they were doing the right thing, the moral thing, and I don't know what to think any more. And, yes, self-interest still drives me forward. The old *what would the in-laws think?* is still foremost in my mind. It would be the end of all hope. Even if Rufus could find it in himself to pass beyond this, his family would never, never do the same.

And besides, I know what happens if you dob on your mates. I've seen it with my own eyes.

Chapter Fifty-Six
Sorry, Sorry, Sorry

One thing you learn about pain: if it doesn't kill you, it can never remain as intense for ever. The heart – and the body – have a resilience that sees to that. And even if the pain continues, the body adjusts, gets used to it, stops complaining.

I wake up three days after New Year and realise that I've got to get out of bed. That I can't carry on here, mourning, for the rest of my life. Nothing will be the same again, I know it, but even though, for a while, I thought it had, the world hasn't come to an end.

And then I do what I've done every day on waking, and think of Andy, at the bottom of the ocean, bones and teeth and little else, and, as every morning, I get a rush of grief, a cramping stabbing grip somewhere between heart and stomach, and I run to the bathroom and throw up. And then, instead of crawling back into bed, as I have every day of the past week, and exploring the physical symptoms that assail me – the on-and-off headache, the nausea, the weird fever flushes, the aches in my joints, the dryness in my mouth – I realise that whatever happens, I have to go on. Andy's dead, and I know I will feel guilt every single day I breathe, but nothing – no illness, no retreat, no self-immolation – will change that.

I sit on the bathroom floor, splintery boards beneath my thigh through my nightie, right forearm still draped on the back of the loo seat where I was using it to rest my head, and wipe the sweat from my forehead with the left. I feel awful. Awful. I feel feeble and shaky, as though I have just emerged from a bout of flu. I am as weak as a kitten, fuzzy-headed and overwhelmed by the enervation of a three-day hangover.

I have to go. I can't carry on like this. I'm even losing muscle strength.

Another wave of nausea washes through me and I throw up once more. This is nothing. When Andy left me – even now, I can't stop myself from referring to it this way in my head – I had palpitations for a month, and shooting pains in my arm, as though my body were taking the idea of a broken heart literally. I've got to toughen up. I can't be like this. I can't let the Mummydaddy ruin my future.

It takes me a few minutes to summon the strength to get to my feet. Rufus went downstairs almost an hour ago, to do the rounds and stare mournfully at the moat, and they'll be starting breakfast any minute now.

I make my way back across the bedroom. It's only been a week, but I seem to have lost my sense of balance along with much of my muscle power: I have to use the furniture to lean against as I go. Rifle through the chest of drawers and find some jeans, a sweater, top, vest, thick socks. Sit in a chair to dress, and then sit on for ten minutes more, trying to soak up the heat from the electric fire because my fever seems to have swung to chill.

The house has reverted once again to the eerie quietness that dominated before my family's arrival. It soaks up the sound of my footfalls. I feel as though my ears are filled with cotton wool as well as my brain. I notice that a new crack has opened in the staircase wall, the one that divides the Georgian and Victorian wings, while I've been weeping. The staircase sits a full inch proud of the plaster, and I walk carefully down, hanging on to the banister and trying not to tread too heavily. It's as though the whole house is twisting, like it's been picked up and wrung out by an invisible hand.

I pause outside the breakfast-room door. Not so much to listen to what's going on in there as to try to slather some composure over my demeanour. It's daunting, the prospect of this morning ritual.

Mary is talking: by the sound of it, she's talking to Rufus. Or sort of talking generally, though I don't suppose either Beatrice or Edmund is thinking about anything other than how much longer until the sun passes over the yardarm.

'Darling,' she's saying, 'mightn't it be a good idea to talk to the doctor?'

'No, not yet,' he says. 'I think . . . no.'

'But, darling, even you must admit it's not . . . normal. Rufus, it isn't normal behaviour. We can't just close our eyes and pretend it's not happening. If she needs help, then it would be wrong of us to—'

'I don't think she does,' he says. 'She's stressed. Definitely. I don't think any of us have given her credit for all the stress she's been under. And Christmas was just awful. Worse for her than for anyone, and we've all got to take some blame for that. Not just her parents: all of us. I think she's upset, not ill.'

'Are you sure?'

'Yes,' he says resolutely.

'Because, you know, I think she's wonderful, but you have to admit we don't really know anything about her . . .'

'No, Mummy. *You* don't know anything about her.'

She pauses. 'Well, really, darling, nor do you. I mean, I hate to have to point it out, but you did get married in such a hurry, and . . . well. Are we *sure* something like this hasn't happened before?'

Rufus pauses in turn. Replies, in controlled tones: 'No, of *course* I'm not sure. But you know what? You can know someone all your *life* and not know everything about them.'

Well, that's too right, I think.

'And in the case of Mel,' he continues, 'I choose to trust what I've seen.'

Oh, my darling. Thank you. Thank you. You'll never know how relieved – how grateful – I am to hear you say that.

'Well, I don't know, darling. You know your own mind, of course . . .'

'Yes,' says Rufus, firmly. Oh, thank you, my love. You've not deserted me.

'But you know, there have been some . . . I don't know how to put it. You obviously don't want to hear it at the moment. But you know, sometimes I can't stop myself wondering.'

'Like?'

'Well, that time when she lost all her documents and they were in the car all along. And that time when she came back from London and convinced herself we'd locked her out. You can't deny there was something odd about *that*.'

'OK. So she can be a bit blonde. There are worse crimes. And as for the other thing, I can't pretend I know what happened, but I'm sure there's more than a grain of truth to her story. Sure of it.'

Mary leaves it for a moment. Hears, possibly, the element of challenge in his words. I hear the chink of china on metal. And she just can't resist starting again.

'Well, I didn't want to worry you,' she says, 'but there have been other things as well.'

Eh-eh?

Rufus sounds suspicious. 'Such as?'

'Please don't be cross, darling.'

'I'm not being cross, Mummy,' he says in a voice that suggests that the situation might not last for ever. 'What are you talking about?'

'Well, the day before, when she was in London, for instance. Hilary said she was rather odd.'

'Odd?'

'Said she came in from shopping and launched straight into some sort of attack. Accused him, straight out of the blue, of meddling, said she knew he had it in for her and something along the lines of how she wasn't standing for it. Hilary said he thought she was quite unbalanced. And I have to say, whatever complexion one tries to put on it, it *does* sound rather paranoid.'

I suck in my breath. Hold on. Hold on just one sec, here.

'Yuh, I've been meaning to have a word with you about that,' says Rufus. 'About Hilary. Believe me, that's not the way Mel's version goes.'

'Oh, yes? No, well I suppose it wouldn't be—'

'No, she said he behaved very weirdly that day, and that was why she left.' I don't suppose there was ever a chance that Rufus would talk to his mother about her friends feeling my breasts. He's

368

far too embarrassable. 'Seriously, Mummy. I know Hilary's my godfather, and I know he's an old friend and everything, but it does sound like he was very, very odd. And to be honest, I'd rather believe what Mel has to say.'

I hear a smile in her voice. 'You *are* a good, loyal boy,' she says with more than a hint of patronage. 'I'm awfully proud of you. How nice a son I've managed to produce.'

'Thanks,' he says, drily.

'But you know, your father's life was practically ruined by marrying someone who wasn't . . . well, stable, and—'

'Drop it, OK?' he interrupts.

'Of course, darling, of course. Of course you know best. It's just that I can't help—'

I open the door. She clams up. I know she knows I know, but she covers it beautifully. It's something I've come to admire about the English: their capacity to layer on the hypocrisy with charm.

She drops her serviette, leaps to her feet and advances on me, arms outstretched. 'Melody! My dear! You're up! I *am* glad! How are you feeling? Come and sit! Have a cup of tea!'

Rufus gets to his feet as well, comes and takes my arm like I'm an invalid, leads me to my seat. There's only Edmund here, buried in the *Telegraph*. No Beatrice and no Tilly.

'Where are the others?'

'Granny has a bit of a cold,' says Mary, 'so she's staying in bed for the morning.'

'And Tilly went to the new house yesterday,' says Rufus.

No-one makes a comment. Looks like he's got his way.

'Lucky –' I burst out, correct myself – 'oh good. Good for her. Maybe I'll go up and see her a bit later.'

'Good idea,' he says.

'Only if you feel up to it, darling,' says Mary.

'I'm not ill, Mary, thanks,' I say. 'I'll be fine now. I just needed a couple of days' peace and quiet.'

Now that Tilly's gone to her new house, and it's just me and Rufus, I feel even more exposed than before. I think about her, starting her day in peace, with nothing but Lucy's squawking to trouble her, and feel a surge of envy. Tilly will be warm, right now. She'll be sensing that she might have some volition over her own fate. And I've got a rock in front of me and nothing but a hard place to flee back to.

'Of course you did,' Mary says in the soothing voice of someone who's secretly dialling the emergency services. 'Are you sure we shouldn't just get the doctor to come and give you a—'

'Quite sure, thanks.'

'If you've been . . . run down . . .'

I pretend to check myself. 'Nope. Tyre marks all healed up.'

'Cup of tea, m'dear?' Edmund lowers the paper, raises his eyebrows.

'That'd be nice. Thanks.'

'You're looking a bit pale.'

'I'm fine, thank you. Just a bit short on food.'

Rufus pours me a cuppa. I help myself to toast. Spread it with butter. Reach for the Marmite. I've developed quite a taste for the stuff. It took a while to get used to, but it's almost as good as Vegemite. I take a sip of tea and make my speech. I've been trying to work out what to say on the way down, and now it seems to me that the most important thing is just that I convince everyone of my sanity.

'I'm very sorry,' I say, 'to have had such a pathetic lapse like that. It's not like me at all. Usually I'm as tough as goat leather.'

'Oh, darling, don't even think about it,' my hypocrite mother-in-law says. 'We were just worried about *you*.'

'That's very kind of you.' I muster my own hypocrisy. 'I'm very lucky to have your concern. Especially after the way my family behaved when they were here. I don't have anything I can say about that, except to offer all of you a heartfelt apology. I can promise you this, as well: it will never, ever happen again.'

I catch Rufus looking at me with something akin to admiration. I don't think he expected this of me. Like he said, you can know someone your whole life . . .

'Don't mention it,' says Mary, and she's gloating like a fly-fed toad. 'It's forgotten.'

Edmund suddenly folds up his paper. Launches into the longest speech I've ever heard from him. 'Actually, Melody, I think we all owe you an apology as well. I don't think there's a person in this room who has cause to feel proud of themselves about how Christmas went, and as no-one else seems capable of bringing themselves to do the decent thing, then I suppose it's up to me. I really am extremely sorry. I don't think we did a good job of making your family feel welcome here, and it'll be a black mark on this house for a long time. Will you accept an apology from me?'

I find myself gulping. My emotions are still uncomfortably close to the surface. It takes me a second to find my voice.

'Thank you, Edmund. I really appreciate that.'

'Good,' says Edmund. 'It was meant. I'm not having any bad atmospheres in the house. Enough to put a chap off his crossword.'

He picks up the paper, reopens it at the court and social page and returns to reading.

Chapter Fifty-Seven

Hatstand

The car's gone. I've been twenty minutes in the chemist and ten in the butcher's, and the car, in the intervening time, has vanished. In the space where it should be sits, insolent and blunt, a rusty old Fiesta in babyshit brown, its houndstooth check seats covered in a thick layer of long white dog hairs.

My stomach does a lurch. Lately it lurches without a great deal of justification.

My beautiful car. Three weeks old, and gone.

The sounds of Stow square fade into the background, replaced by the pump and slosh of blood in my ears.

It can't be gone, it can't. It was only here a minute ago . . .

I feel feverish again. I feel conspicuous, vulnerable, standing outside the back door of Scotts, by the dinky mullioned window, tourists, even in this bottom part of the off-season, swarming past me on the pavement, stopping at the estate agent's on the corner and exclaiming over the prices. I step back and lean against a green-painted junction box, scan, hopelessly, the ranks of cars parked in the square, the empty double-yellows of Digbeth Street, as though this will make my own reappear.

Maybe you didn't leave it here. Maybe you've forgotten. You park somewhere around here pretty much every day. Maybe it's your memory again . . .

I don't seem to be feeling any better. I know they say you ought to get up and get on with things, but I don't suppose the guys who say that have ever really plumbed the full depths. These days, simply moving sucks the strength out of me, leaves me weak and shaking. My legs are so heavy I feel like I'm wading through treacle.

Am I losing it? Am I? Is what they're all saying true, after all?

And I forget things. I've lost my wedding rings. As far as I remember, I took them off to wash my hands in the Great Hall loo, but when I went back for them half an hour later, they were gone, and retracing my steps through the house has done no good. And there was hell to pay because I forgot to feed the dogs one evening, but I have no recollection of anyone asking me to do it, though Mary says she reminded me twice. It's like there's a big blank space. I put books down and never find them again. I lose my house keys. The only way I seem to be able to remember anything is by writing it on the back of my hand.

I can't bring myself to tell him. What sort of wife just takes off the symbols of her marriage and forgets where she put them? I just hope they turn up before he – before anyone – notices. And the worst of it, I can see him wondering, sometimes. Clever Mary, with her poison pills coated in sugar. Cunning as a dunny rat. He doesn't want to see it, but now she's dropped the issue into the mix, you would have to have the sensibilities of a stone not to wonder, sometimes.

Sometimes, I wonder myself.

I can't see the doctor. What do you say, on your first visit to a new bloke who's doubtless heard about you through the grapevine like everyone else has? Hi, doc, I'm having a few emotional problems. Oh, yes? And what would you say has set these off? Marital difficulties? Family misunderstandings? Career crisis? Bereavement? Well, a bit of everything, really. My dad and brother fed my lover to the sharks of the Barrier Reef.

It would either be cops or loony bin, and neither prospect fills me with joy.

Steadied a little, I try looking again, but it's gone. Vanished. The square is full of Range Rovers and Volvos and Kas and Peugeots and Vauxhalls and Daihatsus. But there's no Merc. No green-black stylish chick Merc with AMG multispokes and a cherry-red interior anywhere.

'Oh God,' I say, 'this isn't happening.'

A woman who's just come out of the Co-op and paused by me

373

to light a Superking looks up. 'Are you all right, love?' she asks, because, depending on the class of people you come across, this part of the world is still one where people notice stuff.

'My car's gone,' I say.

She says the sort of useful thing people always say in these circumstances. 'Are you sure?'

I nod, gulp. *Oh God, he's going to be so angry with me.*

And then I remember I'm thinking about Rufus, not my father. I should call him. He'll know what to do.

And then I remember, say 'oh God' again.

'What?' she asks, half curiously, half kindly.

'My phone was in there,' I tell her, and burst into the sort of noisy tears that makes people nudge each other and swap looks.

She's amazing. It's incredible, the kindness people can offer, suddenly, to total strangers. She leads me – Joan's her name, though I'll never meet her again – over to the Talbot hotel and buys me something called a whisky mac, which she says will put hairs on my chest. I drink it anyway. It's good: hot and gingery and fortifying in a sticky sort of way. And then she lends me her phone to call Rufus and sits with me while I wait for him to come.

I'm still alternately cursing and bawling. This is too much. It's too bloody much.

Joan fishes in her bag and hands me a crumpled tissue. 'It's all right,' she says. 'I won't want it back.'

The joke makes me cry some more, and Joan just sits there and pats my hand while I sob and snivel and dribble and wipe my eyes.

'I can't bear it,' I say. 'I can't *bear* it.'

'I know,' says Joan. 'There, there.'

It all comes spilling out. 'It's the last bloody straw. I'm a million miles from home and my family hate me, and there are holes in the roof and water in the cellar and his family all think I'm totally hatstand, and his granny tried to pay me to go away, and now I've even lost the car and I can't *bear* it.'

'Ooh, I know,' she says, turning not a hair, as though I've just been telling her about a run-in at the supermarket. 'Still. It could be worse. At least you've got your health.'

They love that phrase. Ooh, your house is on fire. At least you've got your health. Old man banged up for defrauding the neighbours? At least you've got your health. Lost both legs in a car crash? Never mind. At least you've got your health.

'But I don't,' I protest. 'That's the thing! I wouldn't be in this state if I wasn't feeling so awful!'

'Oh, dear,' says Joan. 'Cold, is it? Or something wrong with your waterworks?'

It's funny how comfortable people seem to be with discussing their most intimate ailments with strangers when they'd blench at mentioning them to their husbands. 'I had cystitis for three weeks once,' says Joan. 'Awful. Felt like my kidneys were going to burst through my spine.'

'No,' I say, 'it's everything! I've some sort of low-running fever, and I feel sick all the time, and my concentration's blown, and I've got no energy. And the worst thing is, most of the time I can't even think straight. It's like my brain's gone to mush.'

Joan considers this for a bit. 'Never mind, love,' she says. 'It does pass. I was the same with Shelley. All that 'feeling special' stuff is nonsense, if you ask me. It was horrible while it lasted, but it does pass. You'll start feeling better.'

I backtrack. 'Eh?'

'It's just hormones,' says Joan wisely.

'Well, that would be comforting,' I say, 'if I was up the duff, but I'm not.'

Joan colours slightly. 'Oh, I'm sorry, darling. It was just the way you were talking. It did sound just like it.'

'Well, I'm not.'

'Relieved to hear it,' she says. 'I was starting to feel guilty about that whisky mac.'

I blow my nose. 'Sorry. I guess I *do* sound a bit hormonal, now you mention it.'

'Women's troubles, do you think?'

'I bloody hope not. That'd be all I need.'

'Probably just the shock,' she says. 'You don't get your car stolen in Stow-on-the-Wold every day, now, do you? Better drink that up. It'll help.'

I drain my glass. It makes me glow inside. So I go to the bar and get us a refill. At least I haven't lost my wallet.

'So you're living locally, then?' she asks as I return to the table. This, I realise, is less of a show of interest in my life than a discreet enquiry as to how long Rufus will be. I noticed her checking her watch as I waited to be served.

I sit down. 'Oh God, yes. I'm so sorry. Yes. My hubby'll be here any minute. I'm so selfish, keeping you here. Please. You've been such a heroine, but there's no need to stay.'

'Oh, no, no, no, no, no,' she says in that British fashion that means 'thank fuck for that'.

'You must have things to do. Please. I'll be fine.'

I don't know why, but something makes me want her to stay. A need for backup, for someone to look like they believe me. Something. But I know it's not fair. I can't just eat into her time like this.

'Couldn't possibly,' she says, which means 'please ask me one more time and then I'll feel able to accept'. The indirect way these people communicate can be a pain in the neck. I don't know how they ever do business. I can't imagine anyone British ever nailing down a deal.

'Seriously,' I say, 'you've been far too kind already. I'm feeling much better.' It's true, as well. The ginger in the drink has settled my stomach for the first time in weeks. 'Go on, do,' I say, willing her to stay. 'I'll be OK.'

'Well, if you're sure . . .'

'Absolutely. Seriously. I can't tell you how grateful I am.'

I've got this pommy-speak off pat now.

'Well . . .' she pretends to think while she fumbles under the table for her bags, '. . . I'd stay, of course, only Geoff'll be wondering where his dinner is if I don't get it on in the next half-hour.'

Dinner? Lunch? That's right. That's one of those words they use to tell each other apart with.

'Get going, then.'

She's on her feet and sidling towards the door. Changes her mind and pops back to down her drink in one. 'All right. I hope you don't have to wait too long. You take care of yourself.'

'Thank you, Joan. You too.'

The door clatters behind her. I light a cigarette and look around me. It's only half-eleven, but the pub is already doing brisk trade, mostly, I notice, with knots of Septics whose nationality you could tell without them ever opening their mouths just by seeing the way their backsides hang over the sides of their seats. If the United States ever fell into the sea, I swear they could carry on regardless simply by farming each other's butt-cracks.

'Say, miss!' they cry. 'Doncha got no non-dairy *Creamer*?' 'Say, miss! I asked for *half*-fat jello!'

I don't even notice Rufus until he's standing over the table, big bunch of keys dangling from his finger.

'God, darling, are you OK?'

I get to my feet, take a hug. 'No, I'm not. I'm bloody not.'

'What happened?' He's eyeing the table over my shoulder, the four empty glasses and the butts in the ashtray.

'I don't know. I just came out of the butcher's and it was gone.'

'Are you sure?'

'Yuh-*huh*.'

'Have you been drinking?' His voice is mildly accusatory.

'Yes. Yes, I have. Since it happened, yes. A nice lady bought me a drink to deal with the shock.' Why do I feel like I have to be on the defensive?

I'm glad there's no-one listening to this conversation. We sound a bit too like the long-suffering husband rescuing the dipso missus.

'I had two drinks, Rufus,' I say defensively.

'It's OK,' he says. 'It doesn't matter. Come on. We'd better go and report it, then I'll take you home. I've got the surveyor and some geologist coming at one to look at the moat.'

I follow him out of the pub. Crisp winter air hits me, makes me momentarily light-headed. I take his arm for support, cover it up as a show of affection. 'I'm sorry to drag you away. I didn't know what else to do.'

377

'It's fine, darling. I'm only sorry it's happened. Where did you park it, anyw—'

He stops, suddenly. Both talking and walking. Puts his hands on his hips and gazes in the direction of Barclays Bank. 'I thought you said it was gone.'

'It is,' I say. 'I told you. I came out of the butcher's and—'

And then I stop, too. Because my car sits, shiny and new and undamaged, ten metres down from where I thought I'd left it.

Chapter Fifty-Eight
I'm Just Saying . . .

He insists we leave the car where it's parked while he drives me home. Of course he does. I can't deny that I've been drinking, so it's inevitable that he thinks all four glasses on the table were mine. After all, if I could imagine I'd lost something as large as a car, I could just as easily have imagined myself up a Joan for company. Christ. If I'd really drunk that much this early in the day, I'd be legless. Edmund would be just starting to cheer up, but I'd be legless.

There's a telling silence between us as we traverse the green and silver countryside. Even now, in the dead of winter, this land is beautiful: great trees stretching skeletal fingers to the sky, vistas I never saw before opened up broad now the leaves have gone.

I tuck my heels up on the seat, hug my knees, say:

'Darling, I wasn't hallucinating. It was gone.'

'Mmm,' says Rufus. I know what he's thinking: *Oh God, maybe Mummy was right and I've got myself mixed up with a crazy wife. Maybe she was right: I don't know anything about her, really. Perhaps I've married the first Mrs Rochester . . .*

I hit another wall of grief. *Maybe if I'd been better, if I'd been a better person, then Andy would still be alive and we'd be living out our anonymous lives somewhere by the sea, and I'd never have known that Rufus existed.*

'It's true, Rufus,' I say, hopelessly.

He's formulating words. Turns the corner on to the Bourton village road and says: 'Darling, it's not that I don't believe you . . .'

'But,' I say.

His lips form a miserable little grimace that confirms my remark, that he tries to hide from me by turning his head slightly away. And eventually: 'Well, darling, are you *sure* you're feeling OK?'

379

'You know I'm not. I've told you. It's hardly something I've tried to hide. But Rufus, that doesn't mean I'm not the full quid.'

'Oh God, no, darling, I never said that. Did I? I'd never think it, either, but I . . .' He's having real trouble working out what to say.

As the grief subsides, I am hit instead by a wave of resentment. Damnit, Rufus. You're meant to be on my side, remember?

'Darling, are you sure you don't want to . . . maybe talk to someone?'

'No! No, I don't! Why would I? Are you trying to say there's something wrong with me?'

'I'd – sweetheart,' he picks his words with the care of a libel lawyer. I feel sick again. Sick and afraid, 'you're so unhappy, and I don't know what to do about it. I feel like I've hardly been able to reach you at all in the last few weeks. It's like you've . . . gone inside somewhere and put up a wall to stop me getting in. I don't know what to do, and it's breaking my heart.'

My eyes fill with tears.

'I'm sorry,' I say. 'I'm so, so sorry. Rufus, I don't mean to. I – I've got so much to work out, and, feeling weird as well, I just . . .'

I can't speak any more. Hang my head down and let the tears slide down my face. How did it go so wrong? What is happening to me?

Rufus pulls the car over at the top of the drive. Pulls on the parking brake.

'I know,' he says. 'That's why I'm wondering . . . you know . . . if it would be helpful . . .'

'Rufus, the car was *gone*. I'm not making it up.'

Again the resentment. *Believe me, damnit. This is* me *you're talking to.*

He sighs. Takes my hand, but not as my lover: more the way I've sometimes seen him take his grandmother's. I don't want to be like this. I don't want us to fall apart like this. 'I believe you,' he says, and for a moment my heart leaps. 'But, Melody, you must see . . . there's something missing. A link somewhere.'

'Maybe,' I start, then think: no, Mel, don't start talking about someone moving it. Don't add paranoia to the list of your eccentricities. 'Maybe it was one of those negative hallucinations. That you read about sometimes.'

He is kind in his response. I don't think he's humouring me: more that he's grasping at straws himself. 'Maybe,' he says. 'You *have* been very tired.'

'I don't sleep much.'

'I know.'

I drop my face into my hands. 'Please, Rufus. Just give me a chance, eh? I don't – please. I'm not ready for the funny farm just yet.'

Thank God, he reaches out and folds me in his arms. 'I never said that. Oh, darling.'

I realise that his face is wet as well.

'I'll do better,' he promises. 'I've been useless to you. I know, darling. I should be supporting you, and all I do is . . . I'm so wrapped up in the problems here. I'm so sorry. I swear I'll do better. I love you so much.'

We stay there, huddled together like refugee children, at the top of the drive, till the surveyor's car pulls in behind us.

Chapter Fifty-Nine
Under the Doctor

The bedroom door opens. Mary, and Edmund, and some guy I don't recognise. He looks a bit like Patrick Macnee, post *Avengers*. Sort of smooth and slightly pleased with himself; the sort of guy who'll flirt with the lay-deez and privately think them all fools for letting him do it. I don't like him: on sight, I don't like him. Don't trust him. Pull the bedclothes up to my chin.

Rufus looks up. 'Oh, thanks, Anthony. I'm so sorry to drag you away.'

'No trouble at all, dear boy. I was only downstairs, after all.'

I look at their faces. Unreadable. What's he done? Who is this guy? 'What is this?' I ask suspiciously.

Mary employs her most sugary voice. 'Melody, dear, Anthony is a doctor.'

'What?'

'And old family friend,' adds Anthony in the sort of studied Bedside Manner tones that give me the heebie-jeebies.

A chill down my spine. He's not believed me. He's pretended to, to get me back here, and all this time . . .

'I don't need a doctor.'

He gives me a white coat smile and advances on the bed. 'Your parents thought it might help if you spoke to me,' he says.

'They're not my parents.'

'Just a figure of speech, dear girl.'

Don't you *dare* Dear Girl me. I glare at Rufus. 'And you're in on this as well?'

Rufus gives a hopeless shrug. Looks down at the bedcover.

'Collecting your pieces of silver later, then?'

Rufus looks away, but not before I catch his stricken expression. But you know what? I don't care. He's betrayed me. Talked out of school. He's a Judas and he needs to know it.

The doctor is already taking my pulse. Gives me an arch, knowing little smile that makes me want to punch him. 'So what happened this morning, Melody?'

I think fast. I'm on a bit of a cleft stick here. If I refuse to talk to this man, it will only be racked up against me in the future.

'OK. I'll talk to you. But if this is going to be a consultation I don't want to have it in public.'

Mary and Edmund shift.

'I'm serious,' I say.

'Fair enough,' says Anthony.

'We'll be just outside,' says Mary indulgently.

'I'll bet,' I say aggressively.

They leave.

I look at Rufus.

'What, me too?'

'Yes, Judas, you too.'

He has the grace to look abashed. Almost says something, changes his mind. 'I'll be outside too.'

I don't even look at him as he leaves the room, I feel so betrayed.

The door closes. Anthony gives me a soothing smile. 'So,' he begins, 'how *are* you?'

I'm pretty snappish with him. 'First things first,' I say. 'If I'm going to have a consultation with you, I might as well at least know your surname.'

'Certainly,' he says calmly. 'It's McFarland.'

'And you're a doctor specialising in what, precisely?'

'Oh, just a GP. I have Mrs Wattestone under my care.'

'Right. So they've got Beatrice's tame quack in to get me carted off to the bin, then.'

He finishes with my wrist. 'Oh, I'd say that was probably a little extreme.'

'Still. Gathering data, no doubt.' Even as I say it, I realise that I probably sound disturbingly paranoid. It's the sort of thing the

Princess of Wales used to put in letters to her butlers. 'Look, I'm OK,' I say palliatively.

'But you've had. . . an incident?' It's a pointed question.

'I wouldn't say it qualified as an "incident".'

'And how long,' he continues as if I'd never spoken, 'have you been having these experiences?'

'I what?'

That's a bit like that old 'have you stopped beating your wife' question. The question itself establishes the supposition as fact, and any denials are just going to sound like attempts at evasion.

I try anyway. 'Never. Until I came to this house.'

'Interesting. So you feel it has something to do with the house, then?'

'No. But I wouldn't be surprised if it wasn't related to some of the people in it.'

Oh, boy. This isn't going my way. I can see him assuming all sorts.

'Really?' is all he says.

I heave a sigh. 'Don't try hoary old therapy tricks on me. Listen: I know perfectly well that there are people here who don't want *me* to be here, and I wouldn't put much past them.'

I have to stop. I have to stop now. I'm digging my own grave faster than David Blaine. I sound like a raving lunatic, of course I do. As long as you've already been primed to think that I probably am one.

'I see.'

'No, you don't. You don't see at all. You *think* you see, but you don't.'

I can see he's gearing up to asking me if I play with my faeces.

'Look, it's pretty easy to make someone look as though they're unbalanced,' I say. 'Seriously. All it takes is a few words in the right ear and a couple of stage-managed incidents.'

'Ah. There have been incidents?'

'Yes. Yes there have.'

'Would you like to tell me about them?'

'Not really, no.'

384

'I see. And how am I supposed to judge if you won't tell me?'

I think about that one. 'OK,' I say. And I tell him about the missing jewellery, the perambulating documents, the car and the night I came home from London. And while I speak, I can tell that I'm sounding mumblier with each passing second.

'Mmm.' He looks like he's doing some thinking. 'Mmm. Interesting.'

'So you see?'

'Yes,' he says, and I think he sees something completely other than what I've tried to show him. 'Tell me. Have you been sleeping?'

'Of course not. Would you expect me to?'

He doesn't answer that. Instead he counters with a question of his own. 'And would you like it if I could help you with that?'

The thought, I have to say, is deeply attractive. I think the chances of me sleeping tonight are pretty much zero. 'You'd do that?'

'If you like.'

'I don't know.'

'I think it would do you some good. I could write you out a prescription, if you like.'

I look at him uncertainly. 'Prescription for what?'

'I don't know,' he says, meaning that he does but wants to make me feel like it's my decision. 'I was thinking perhaps a course of diazepam might help.'

'Valium?'

'That's a brand name, yes.'

I suppress a swearword. Valium. That was the drug of choice for miserable alky housewives when I was growing up. The ones whose doctors wanted to keep them docile.

'Do you seriously think I need something like that?'

'It's up to you. But if you're having trouble sleeping . . .'

'And being a nuisance with my imaginary friends.'

'I didn't say that.'

'It's what you're thinking, though.'

The soothing smile comes back on to his face. 'You're under

stress,' he says. 'A lot of people find they help when they're stressed. You could try them for a while, and then we could review the situation.'

Chapter Sixty

A Medical Opinion

There's a tap at the door and Nessa puts her head round.

'Hi, love,' she says. 'Can I come in?'

I force myself to sit up. God, I must look a sight. I've been here crying under the covers for a good hour, and even my hair is encrusted with salt. I do a big snort, fill my mouth with snot and tears, swallow.

'Been sent to check up on me?'

'Naah. Private consultation. I'll leave you alone if you want.'

'No. Come in.'

She advances, perches on the edge of the bed. Feels my forehead. 'So what is all this?'

'Oh, Nessa,' I manage before the tears come again.

'Oh, love,' she says, her voice all nurse and her face all friend. 'Come here. You need a hug.' Feeling her solid body against mine, I'm like a child. Wail like a child while she rubs my back.

'They all think I'm mad. All of them. Even Rufus.'

'No they don't. No they don't. Shhh. Tell me what happened? Tilly's been very worried about you. We both have.'

I tell her. While she listens, she holds my wrist, looks at her watch, puts her hand on my forehead again.

'Well, your temperature's up a tad, I'd say. Mind if I stick this in your mouth?'

I lift my tongue out to receive the thermometer from her top pocket.

'Moo fink ver migh' be fumfin wrong wiv me?'

'Naah. Nothing much. Although there will be if I forgot to wash that thermometer after I took it out of Beatrice's backside.'

The thermometer shoots across the counterpane.

387

'There,' she says. 'You can still have a laugh. Not dying yet, anyway.'

I give her an experimental snuffle.

'I don't really take her temperature that way.' She picks up the thermometer and shoves it back in my mouth. 'Just fantasise about it. I like to think of ways I could torture the old bat. It stops me doing it for real. Sometimes when I'm feeding her her slop I fantasise I've laced it with Ex-lax. Yes, that's better,' she says approvingly as she watches my reaction to this statement. 'Jesus, it's cold in here. No wonder you don't sleep.'

'Rufus does.' I feel the prick of tears as I remember the look on his face when I spat the Judas accusation at him.

She seems not to notice. 'Rufus grew up this way. He's like a hamster. Goes into hibernation every night. You, in the meantime, are used to sleeping in the buff under a single sheet. You need to buy some thick jammies and a beanie hat. Not very bridal, I grant you, but he's the one who wants to live in this hellhole, and I'd say any type of bride was sexier than a dead one.'

She goes quiet for a moment, lips moving as she counts under her breath. 'Tell you what, your circulation's a tad sluggish. Not so far as to be worrying, but . . . are you sure you're not taking any sedatives or anything?'

I shake my head. 'I bought some St John's Wort at the chemist's today, but I don't suppose it will have had time to do anything at all.'

'No. Takes at least a couple of weeks for that stuff to kick in.' She takes the thermometer out, gives it a squint. 'And your temperature's up by half a degree. Again. Not such a lot, but . . .' she shrugs. 'I'll keep an eye on you. Have you been eating?'

It's my turn to shrug. 'And throwing it back up again.'

'Well, that's not much of a surprise. If I had to eat those pheasants, *I'd* throw them up.'

'I was buying a pork pie,' I tell her, 'at Lambourne's in Stow. That was why I was up there in the first place. I thought maybe I could keep it up here and eat it in secret.'

Nessa laughs. 'Well, there you go. You're way off mad yet, girl.

Those pies are ripsnorters. They're the dog's bollocks.'

'I thought they were meant to be pork.'

She laughs again, claps me about the shoulder.

'So what's the verdict?' I ask.

'You know what I think your problem is? Stickybeaks. Stickybeaks and stirry old chooks. What you need is a bit of rest and a bit of privacy and you'll be as right as rain.'

'But what about the car?'

She reflects. 'Yes. You're right there. There's no way around that one, is there? I'll call Littlemore and get them to send a van and a couple of blokes with white coats.'

'Nessa, I feel . . .' I'm hopelessly lost as to how to express it. Alternative therapist maybe, but I'm as inarticulate about my own feelings as the next guy. You still tend to stick to talking about people's holidays when you're poking them in the feet.

I get my hand taken for the second time today, but this time it's the firm, reassuring hand of friendship. 'I know you do,' she says simply. 'Don't let them win, girl. You're better than that.'

We sit for a minute, just holding hands, then she gets up, goes over to the armchair-cum-closet and throws me a robe.

'I lost Beatrice for an hour once,' she tells me. 'I thought I'd put her down for a rest in the garden when actually I'd left her on the khazi. Mind you,' she adds, 'I think it might have been one of those accidents of the Freudian persuasion.'

Chapter Sixty-One
The Fall of the House of Wattestone

Rufus is white with fear. Green about the gills. It's the only way of putting it. It's like someone's turned down the reds on his colour palate. He's got eyes like saucers and his hair is standing on end. Maybe that's from dragging his hand through it, but the effect is the same as though he'd just opened a cupboard door and found an ogre.

At least, thanks to Nessa, I'm dressed and my hair is brushed. Otherwise I'd've been sparko when the summons came, via Tilly, for everyone to gather in the library.

'What's going on?'

Tilly shrugged. 'Haven't the foggiest, but I don't think we've all been written into a comic opera.'

'Sounds more like the end of an Agatha Christie to me. Do you think he's found out where the bodies are buried?' As I said this, I got another pang, a stab of guilt for taking the mick when there's obviously something serious in the air. God, am I even going to be robbed of my flippancy? What weapons will I have left?

'More like that they've lost the venue for the hunt ball and want to have it here, I'd say. That would be a joy,' said Tilly. 'Got to go. I've left Lucy locked up in the old salt safe and I'd better get back before she turns inside out and shrivels.'

So here I am, and I've found the room full not only with Wattestones, but with the surveyor and the geologist as well. And all of them sporting that don't-care look on their faces which in England passes for concern.

'So what's up?' I ask as I take a seat by Tilly and start poking my goddaughter with an index finger. She's a nice little thing, Lucy. I don't mind what people say: I like gingas. They look like they've come pre-peeled.

'Right, well, I'm afraid I've got some bad news,' says Rufus.

'Oh, dear,' says Beatrice. 'Not another socialist government.'

'No. Worse than that, I'm afraid.'

There's an explosive sound of disbelief from Beatrice's corner.

'This is John Gregory,' says Rufus. 'He's the surveyor from English Heritage. And this is Colin Bardwell. He's a geologist from Oxford. The university,' he adds, I guess because otherwise Beatrice will be asking why they didn't get one from Fortnum and Mason.

'Uh-huh?' says Edmund. 'So what's the verdict?'

'Not very good, I'm afraid,' says Colin Bardwell.

'Not very good at all,' echoes John Gregory.

They both look expectantly at Rufus. Evidently neither of them wants to break the news himself.

'OK,' says Rufus, and his hand flies up his hair. I am surprised he's not started pulling it out, from the look of him. 'Right, well. It seems – there's no other way of putting it – that the whole place is falling down.'

You don't say. And he needed to pay these guys to tell him that?

The news takes a while to sink in. For the first time, probably ever in history, not one single member of the Wattestone family has an opinion. Finally, Tilly hoists Lucy up on to her shoulder and says: 'How, exactly, falling down?'

The geologist clears his throat. He wears thick-framed glasses and a cagoule indoors, and his curly hair looks like it's been cut by lamplight, in a tent, with the little scissors on a Swiss Army knife and no mirror. He looks, in short, exactly how I would expect a geologist to look. 'Well, it seems . . . I've been going over the old plans of the house and grounds, and I think the most likely explanation is the goldmine.'

'The goldmine?' asks Beatrice. 'But that hasn't been worked since the eighteenth century.'

'Granny,' says Rufus, 'you know that's not true.'

'Yes it is – oh,' she says.

'What?' I ask. 'What's going on?'

'Stupid, short-sighted greed, that's what,' says Rufus bitterly. 'I'm afraid the Wattestone family didn't want to pay tax like everyone else, so one of the ancestors came up with the wizard wheeze of saying the mine was dead and dealing in gold on the black market.'

I'm not quite there yet. 'Sorry?'

Rufus sighs.

'Your husband tells me,' says the surveyor, 'that the seam of gold didn't actually run out until some time soon before the Second World War.'

Rufus nods. 'That's right, isn't it, Dad?'

Edmund looks a little pink in the face. 'So I gather . . .' he hedges.

'No, not "so you gather". You were there at the time. That's how we had the money to build the Victorian wing and the Edwardian wing, and how come we managed to keep hold of an entire village when virtually every other estate in the country sold theirs off. And how come we carried on employing the same number of people for decades despite electricity and tractors and combine harvesters and machine shearing and automated milking systems and the rest of it. People in tied cottages tend to keep shtum, don't they, if the alternative is homelessness and unemployment?'

'I don't get it,' I say. 'So we've got some sort of back tax problem?'

'No,' says Rufus. 'There's a statute of limitations on those sorts of things. It's far worse than that. What we've got is a honeycomb of unmapped tunnels running under practically every square yard of the park. And it seems like they're probably running under the house as well. Because that's what happens when you're not being kept an eye on by people who know what they're doing. You dig about the place and jabber on about ancient skills and government interference, and no one has the first idea where they're actually going down there in the dark. Remember when the Greek temple collapsed back in eighty-seven, Dad?'

'That was the hurricane,' says Mary.

'We were lucky the insurance company fell for that,' says Rufus. 'But it wasn't. You know as well as I do that a bloody great hole opened up underneath it and it all fell in. If the entire country hadn't had claims in at the same time, they would probably have sent someone out to check and noticed it themselves. Anyway, the same thing's happening to Bourton Allhallows now.'

'But how come,' I ask, 'there's been no sign of it up until now? If the workings have been abandoned for over sixty years, surely . . .?'

'Trees,' says the surveyor. 'I dare say it would have shown under the house eventually, but I would say that the entire park has been held together by tree roots for the last couple of hundred years. The thing is, for the height of every tree, there's a root system at least as long under the ground. Sometimes twice as long. And you used to have excellent tree planting in this park.'

'Until Dutch elm,' says Rufus glumly.

'Europe. Stuff and nonsense. I knew no good would come of it,' says Beatrice. Everyone ignores her.

'I told you,' Mary says accusingly to Edmund, 'you should have replanted.'

'Wouldn't have made much difference,' says John Gregory. 'Even if you'd planted straight away, they wouldn't be much over thirty feet high by now. The old root systems have shrivelled up and rotted, and as a result the ground's a bit like Emmenthal. It's surprising it's held together as well as it has, to be honest. As for the house . . . well. I don't think any amount of planting could have stopped what's going on now.'

Mary's finally catching on. 'So how much,' she says, an edge of panic to her voice, 'is it going to cost to rectify?'

The surveyor shrugs. 'Hard to tell without a lot more work, I'm afraid. We'll have to get some sonic equipment in to see what the extent of the workings are. And, of course, it depends how bad the damage to the house is already and how much more there is before we can stop the rot. Though I have to say, from the look around I've had, it's pretty bad.'

'So how much?' she asks again.

Rufus clears his throat. 'Anything between fourteen and thirty million pounds,' he says.

Chapter Sixty-Two
Selling off the Silver

The surveyor and the geologist make themselves scarce in a flurry of briefcases and waterproof fabric. And the elder half of the family goes straight into denial the minute the door shuts.

'It's ridiculous,' says Beatrice. 'I'm not having it.'

'How can he stand there and tell us that?' demands Mary. 'These people . . . they think we're made of money. We can't raise that sort of cash overnight.'

'Don't be stupid, Mary,' says Tilly. I've noticed that she has started talking back a lot more since Lucy was born. I don't know if it's the hormones, or the independence of having a house of her own, or some primal motherhood protectiveness thing, but I like it. The girl's got spunk, after all. 'He's not trying to pull a fast one: he's just telling you the truth. And anyway, let's be realistic. We can't raise that sort of cash, full stop.'

Mary rounds on me. 'I'll bet your father's laughing in his boots,' she says.

I raise my hands, palms forward, at her, say: 'Don't bring *me* into it, Mary. I didn't undermine your precious house. And nor did my dad.'

Edmund simply stands up and helps himself to a large gin.

'Well, we'll just have to . . .' says Mary.

'Have to *what*?' asks Tilly.

'Well, *I* don't know. And don't speak to me like that. I won't be spoken to like that.'

'No,' says Tilly. 'Someone's got to talk some sense into you. All of you. You're behaving like schoolchildren. Sticking your fingers in your ears and thinking that if you go "la la la" loudly enough then you won't have to hear it.'

395

'We'll get a second opinion,' says Beatrice. 'We know what they're like. Just trying to get his hands on our house. Eaten up with envy, the lot of them.'

'Get a grip, Beatrice,' I hear myself saying.

Rufus raises his voice above the bedlam, shouts: 'SHADDAP!'

We all close our mouths at once, like geese when a barn door slams.

'I don't have the energy for fighting today,' says Rufus. 'Please, just stop it.'

'I'm not fighting,' says Mary.

Rufus quells her with a look. 'Sit down. Everyone,' he says.

Edmund is already sitting. Gradually, we all drift into chairs and wait for Rufus to speak.

'Mummy. Daddy. Granny. I know this is tough, and I know it's hard to get your heads round, but we have to make some plans and we have to do it now.'

'Well, obviously,' says Mary. 'We can't be here when it's swarming with builders.'

Rufus sits down himself, heavily, as though someone's kicked him in the back of the knees. Rubs the back of his neck. 'I don't think you're getting it, Mummy. I don't think there are going to be any builders.'

'Don't be silly, Rufus. You heard what the man said.'

'Yes, Mummy. I heard exactly what he said.'

'Well, then. I'm sorry. I can put up with a lot, but if you think—'

'Mummy, where do you think we're going to get this sort of money *from*?'

'The bank. Obviously,' she says as though this is the most natural thing in the world.

'No. No, Mummy. Did you hear what I said? Did you hear me at all? Did you hear anything I said? Banks aren't charities. They don't just hand out money because you want some. They need paying back. And besides: what sort of collateral are we going to offer them?'

No-one answers.

Rufus speaks softly, dejectedly. 'If this house was in good nick, it would still only be worth maybe ten million on the open market. And that would be without the loans we've already got on it. It's not going to work.'

'Well, someone can . . .' Mary sounds bewildered more than anything. 'A sheikh . . .' she says.

Rufus closes his eyes, grits his chompers. 'There is no sheikh, Mum. There's no sheikh and there's no fairy godmother and there's no benevolent banking family who want to throw money at us because of their reverence for history.'

'You are not,' says Beatrice, 'selling this house. It's unthinkable.'

'No, Granny,' Rufus says, 'you're right. We're not selling. It's too late for that. Don't you see? While we've been treating the place as a pearl beyond price, it's become completely worthless. The house, the park: all of it, worthless. The only thing it's good for now is landfill.'

'B—' begins Mary.

'Shut up, Mummy. Tilly's right. It's over. There's nothing left. We've got to make plans for how we're going to salvage what we can, and we've got to do it fast. Do you understand?'

Edmund speaks. 'I've lived here all my life.'

I glance over at him. He suddenly looks very, very old. Beaten.

He raises his glass, drains half of it in a single draught. 'My whole life. I've never been away from it for more than three months at a time. It's sat here on my shoulders and never let me go for seventy-four years. And now you're telling me it's all been for nothing.'

'We all had a duty, Edmund,' says Beatrice. 'Do you think I enjoyed it, maintaining your inheritance while your father attempted to drink it away? Keeping the barbarians from the gate?'

'I wanted to sell it in nineteen fifty-three,' he says to his mother, 'and you wouldn't let me. I wanted to be a doctor, do you remember? I wanted to help people and save lives, and you persuaded me that it was my duty to stay. And when petrol went sky-high in the seventies and the heating bill cost more than the entire estate income, and that Beatle, what's his name, wanted to buy it, and you said it would be a betrayal. You said I would be betraying you and betraying my children and no one would ever forgive me. And you –' he turns to Mary – 'you said if I gave up you'd leave me and take my son with you. You said only a weak man would betray his descendants and you would never allow Rufus to be raised by a weak man, so I stayed and passed the whole bally curse on to him instead. And now I see it was weakness that made me stay. I've spent my life keeping up appearances and it was all absolutely bloody pointless. I stayed because my son would never forgive me if I did, and now I wouldn't blame him if he never forgave me for not. Look at it. We have nothing. Rufus has *nothing*.'

'Hold on a mo, Edmund,' I say, 'I wouldn't say you were living on the streets quite yet.'

Beatrice is purple with rage. 'Your father would be turning in his grave . . .'

Edmund shouts, possibly for the first time in his life. 'MY FATHER HAS BEEN DEAD FOR FIFTY-FIVE YEARS. MY FATHER WAS A HOPELESS DRUNK AND SO WAS HIS FATHER BEFORE HIM, AND NOW I'VE FOLLOWED IN THE FAMILY TRADITION. LOOK AT ME. LOOK AT ME. I'M NOTHING. *NOTHING*. ANOTHER WORN-OUT DRUNK IN A LONG LINE OF WORN-OUT DRUNKS WHO'S WASTED HIS LIFE FOR THE SAKE OF A WHITE ELEPHANT, AND I WILL NOT LET MY SON DO THE SAME! LISTEN TO HIM! IT'S OVER! THE CALLINGTON-WARBECK-WATTESTONES ARE NOT AN EMANATION OF THE DIVINE WILL, THEY ARE A FAMILY OF BANKRUPTS, CLINGING ON TO THE RUINS OF THE HOUSE THAT DESTROYED US! I HAVE GIVEN MY LIFE UP TO A PILE OF STONES!'

Edmund's blue eyes are watery with age and distress. He finishes his drink, places the empty glass on a wine table by his left elbow. Says no more. Tilly gets up, crosses the carpet and perches on the arm of her father's chair. Lays a hand on his shoulder and kisses the top of his head.

'You're not thinking clearly,' says Beatrice.

'Stop it, Mummy. Just stop it,' he says, wearily.

I glance at Mary. I don't know what to expect: some sign of sympathy, I suppose. Some uxorial concern. Instead, she's looking at him with a face of stone. She's looking at him with the contempt of a Tory wife looking at a dero in the doorway of Harvey Nick's. And in a flash I see how Edmund's life has been; how their lives together have been. What Rufus was so desperate to avoid when he hid his world from me: a loveless bargain for the sake of bricks and mortar and the status that went with them. Heir production. The respect of the world's sad little snobs your only sense of self-worth. It makes me angry. It makes me so angry.

'I'm sorry, Daddy,' says Rufus. 'I'm really sorry that it had to end with me.'

'No,' says Edmund. 'I'm sorry. I was weak and I inflicted it all on you.' He pats his daughter's hand. 'Your mother wanted me to get out, you know,' he says. 'I let her down dreadfully.'

'Oh, Daddy,' says Tilly.

Mary has a face like an approaching tornado. She is trying to ignore this exchange, but its effect on her is all too evident. 'So what do you expect us to do?'

'I'll do what I can,' says Rufus, 'but in all honesty, I think it's too late. I don't see any way we can raise the money and, even if we did, it would be debatable whether it would be worth it.'

'You ungrateful little shit,' says Beatrice, sugar-plum surface dropping away to reveal the evil fairy beneath. 'Do you have any idea of the sacrifices that have been made on your behalf?'

Rufus colours, but he doesn't fight back.

'It always comes down to the women in the end,' continues Beatrice. 'It always has. For generations and generations. Useless, Wattestone men. Always have been. Useless and feckless and spineless. It's always come down to the women to keep it going. Me, my mother-in-law, your mother. It's we who have kept it going. We have held it all together while you whined and grizzled and chased your foxes. I thought you were different, Rufus, but you're not. Just like your father. Just like him. Always more interested in chasing skirt than facing responsibilities.'

I have to interrupt: jump to my husband's defence. 'Hold on one moment. There's responsibility,' I say, 'and reality.'

'Oh, why don't you just *go away*?' she snaps. 'It's all your fault. Selfish and irresponsible: he was never like this until you came on the scene.'

'I'm not even going to dignify that,' I say. Well, snarl. I can't believe these men just *take* it. I'm not going to be able to for much longer.

'You wouldn't even know the meaning of the word,' she snarls back.

I can't help it. I toss my hair at her. Address Rufus and Edmund and Tilly. 'It's not all over, by any means. This place is crammed with valuable stuff. Even if we lose the house, you won't be bankrupt by any stretch. God, the Caravaggio must be worth a pretty serious townhouse by itself.'

'We can't sell the Caravaggio!' cries Mary.

'Why on earth not? Is that mortgaged as well?'

'It's an asset!'

I can't stop a 'd'oh' escaping from my mouth. 'Well, sorry to burst your bubble, but what do you thing that assets are *for*?'

'It's not just *our* asset. It's an asset to the whole country. Think of the loss!'

'Yuh, I'm not suggesting you *burn* it,' I say sarcastically. 'I'm suggesting you *sell* it.'

'There we go,' says Beatrice. 'The vulture circling. You can't wait to get your hands on the cash, can you?'

'I'm just saying—'

'Oh, I know what you're saying. What do you want? Walk-in shoe wardrobe? Candy-pink leather corner sofas? Five-thousand-dollar perfume? I know your sort. I know all about you. You see people like us and all you see is dollar signs. No values. No respect. No understanding of history—'

'Granny!' barks Rufus.

A red mist descends over my vision. 'And what *are* the things that really matter, Beatrice?' I ask. 'Go on. Tell me. Let me in on the secret. Tell me what you represent that's so valuable. Go on.

What? Snobbery? Sneering at people for holding their cutlery wrong? Talking like you've had your jaw sewn up? Thinking you're a cut above a Lottery winner because you won *your* jackpot at birth? Pretty fine achievements, I must say. I can't *wait* to learn at *your* knee.'

'Melody!' barks Rufus. But I'm too far gone.

'You're a leech, Beatrice. I know you think that the word you've been hearing people say all your life is "élite", but it ain't. You're a bloodsucker. A big bundle of selfishness. You go on about the dolies and the socialists, and you don't see that someone like you is the worst kind of scrounger. People like you – you live in your own tight little world, and you maintain your belief in your own importance by making sure you never mix outside it. Wake up. Your world is over. You're nothing, just like your son said. The world's moved on around you and your precious assets are nothing in the end: nothing but bricks and stone and wood and canvas and cloth, rotting and degrading like everything in the world does in the end. Don't you see? In the end, we're born, and we reproduce, and we die, and all the stuff in the middle is just the struggle. In the long run, nothing any of us does will really change the world, but you – you're nothing but an irrelevance. An irrelevant anachronism. And you know what else?'

I know I shouldn't be saying it. I know, even as I do it, but I've exhausted my self-control. I face the evil old witch, the destructive, tyrannical old hag, and spit the words at her with all the built-up rage of my months here.

'You're still going to die. You're going to die, and you think your bloody heritage is going to buy you a ticket to heaven, but it's not. You're going to die and the only people who are going to notice are your family, so you'd better make bloody sure that they don't hate you as much as I do.'

Chapter Sixty-Three
Losing Rufus

The moat has filled up again. I'm not sure this is a good thing. What it must mean, after all, is that whatever's down there has finally filled up with water. And the house has got louder. I hear it as I lie awake beside Rufus, groaning like an animal in pain, muttering to itself like a behemoth disturbed in sleep.

I'm losing him. I know that. And I know it's my own fault. He is still angry with me for the way I spoke to Beatrice, and rightly so. I know I shouldn't have spoken that way, that Beatrice is an old woman and I hadn't the right. But it's more than that. It was that I called him a Judas. I was betrayed by him, but he feels betrayed, in turn, by me. I can feel him drifting. He doesn't come running to me at the end of the day any more, doesn't lay his head on my bosom and take comfort. And though he's still nice to me, still sweet, it's with the sweetness of a well-mannered stranger, and sometimes I catch a speculative expression on his face when he looks at me and he doesn't think I know. My fault. I know it's my fault. My bad.

Darling, darling, darling, don't leave me. Please don't leave me.

I am at a loss. Mary, of course, couldn't wait to get up to the pharmacy in Stow to fill the prescription, no doubt choosing a moment when the little shop was crowded with her acquaintances, and then making a show of protecting my privacy in her loudest undertone, but I've not been taking tablets. I tried one, once, the night she brought them home, but the hangover was worse than the lack of sleep. So we lie, wakeful, side by side, and stare at the tester in individual pools of silence. And I long to reach out to him, apologise, make it better, but I don't have the words.

No one meets my eye in the house. I've given up the pretence of family mealtimes, pick at scraps in our room while he's down there, sipping wine among the candles. They come and go, break bread without me: the neighbourhood passing through to say goodbye to Bourton Allhallows, and in the corridors they lower their eyes and scuttle past as though I were a ghost.

The house swarms, in the daytime, with technical types carrying echographs and swinging leads and things on tripods to measure the tilt of the roof beams. But the family doesn't seem to be making any efforts about leaving. They seem to be frozen in their refusal to face the inevitable. They've not even made a start on moving the furniture, getting the pictures to a place of safety – anything. I would have at the very least expected someone to get the Caravaggio out of the way of falling roof-beams, but they're acting, instead, as if it's holding the wall up. Men in hard hats and reflective jerkins scratch their ears and shake their heads as they contemplate the crumbling walls, but there have been no removals quotes, no auctioneers, no academics down from Leeds to put a value on the armour. Nessa no longer smokes behind the bush in the courtyard. Not since they discovered the mineshaft lurking inches below the leaf-mould. Sometimes I catch sight of her wheeling Beatrice around the knot garden. She raises a hand to wave at me, but we don't get to speak. Tilly's happy in her little house, never comes down to the big one if she can help it: she seems to be the only member of the family who is making any effort to disengage from the past. Mrs Roberts no longer simply ignores me. These days she treats me with open contempt. Twice now, she has barged past me, catching me with a swinging elbow or a well-aimed knee, as though she knows I won't dare to complain. I'll take a lot of pleasure from seeing the old cow on the dole.

But the wall – a glass wall has gone up between Rufus and me, and I can't get through to the other side. I don't know what to say, how to attract his attention, make him hear me. He comes in dusty and sweaty, and as low as low, but I can't make it better.

It's the house. This damn house has come between us. He knows how much I hate it, but his own emotions are far more complex: love and loathing, regret and resentment, the way you feel towards a neglectful parent. So he brushes my enquiries aside because he suspects the half-truth, that I'm anticipating with relish the day when we can leave. That I feel the house poisoning us, and I want to be free.

I'm losing him. I can no longer see my golden boy. Where his hands were rough and gentle, they're now distracted. The man who delighted in lying against me, face to face, thigh to thigh, now reclines on his back on the pillows and stares blankly at the great black nothing.

Don't leave me, Rufus. Don't leave me. It was meant to be for ever. Don't you remember? You and me against the world, protecting each other with encircling arms. And you look at me sometimes, and I see you see a stranger: you see the angry woman, the bitter one with the stinging words, the one who cries and shouts and rails against the elements. And that is what I am, but it's not all that I am, remember? I'm the girl who walked with you through the Silent City, the girl who screamed with joy at festa fireworks, who wrapped herself around you in the moonlit water at Ghar Lapsi. I kissed you deep and warm, and you told me you loved me.

Don't leave me darling. Please don't leave.

Chapter Sixty-Four

False Spring

Crocuses come. Millions of them, breaking through the soil in the park and flushing mauve and orange to the horizon. Early narcissi nod minuets in flirtatious air. The sun breaks through the clouds and stripes the hillside, brings promise of spring, and it makes me want to cry. It's so beautiful, this country: so beautiful and haughty and impenetrable.

Lucy Hunstanon-Wattestone is christened at Bourton Allhallows parish church on a Sunday morning after Matins, the congregation swelled to the power of three by the four dozen guests who come to see her rite of passage. She wears the Wattestone christening gown, two-hundred-year-old lace that pours over her mother's arms and down towards the ground like foaming water. We godparents sit in the family pew, follow her up to the font in love and pride. Tilly – I hadn't taken in how skinny the frame that has been carrying that lump about all the time I've known her – is elegant in hunting green, black button boots making her look like a Victorian governess. She gazes down at her daughter's face, and her own breaks into a glow as though someone's lit a candle. And she looks up and smiles at me, and I want, unaccountably, to weep. I want to turn my face to the sky and howl. But instead I smile back, and she interprets my tearfulness as pleasure.

Afterwards, the church party troops back to the castle for champagne from Edmund's cellar, some of the stuff the three of us rescued together. It feels like a lifetime ago.

It's a jolly party, and a young one, relatively speaking. A dozen of Tilly's old school friends have come down from London, peacocks in thigh-high, jewel-coloured suits and hats that consist of little other than dyed feathers and sequins, breasts hoist and strapped to resemble pills in blister packs, diamond earrings and clouds of Chanel, husbands and kiddies and bursts of laughter. I had no idea the English could be so stylish.

The county get into the corner as usual. Fifteen leather-faced blondes braying sourly about the other residents of manor houses, thick-necked men swapping punchlines. I avoid them. It's not hard. They, after all, are giving me a wide berth for fear that my instability might be catching.

Tilly comes over and stands with me by the window. 'How are you feeling?' she asks.

'I'm OK,' I say. 'It's good to have a happy day here, eh?'

'Are you still feeling sick?'

'No. At least *that* seems to have passed.'

'Well, that's a blessing. I'm sorry I've not been down. I've not been much of a friend.'

I flash her a quick grin. 'I'll survive, babe,' and change the subject. 'Can I hold her?'

'Of course.'

I get Lucy into my arms. She's grown. Grown and developed, heavy and warm against my breasts.

'I can't believe she's holding her head up already,' I say.

'I know. I'm already getting empty-nest syndrome and I've got another eighteen years to get ready in. I thought I'd start plugging in some extension flexes and leaving them out on the carpet for when she starts crawling.'

'Good idea,' I say. 'Save her having to go too far. Maybe a few sharp objects scattered about the place would be good too. Are you glad you've got her?'

She beams. 'I can't tell you how much. It almost makes it worth having been married to Hugo.'

'Steady.'

Tilly laughs. She laughs a lot more these days. 'No. OK. But you know what? Sometimes I wake up in the middle of the night and I get up just to go and have a look at her. Not, you know, because I'm worried or anything. Just because . . .' She looks over her shoulder to check that no one's listening. 'It's really embarrassing.

Just because I can't believe that there's anything in the world that beautiful. Don't you just want to squash her?'

'Till she leaks,' I say.

She gives her daughter a sloppy kiss on her fuzzy pate and me a shy, conspiratorial look. 'I don't suppose you . . . you know . . .'

How can I possibly say? 'Some time,' I prevaricate. And the lie makes me suddenly sweaty.

'Rufus would be a lovely father.'

'Clucky,' I accuse her.

Tilly giggles. 'I know. I'm sorry. It's just, when you've got one, suddenly you want to make everyone have one. It would be so nice, you know. If she really knew her cousins. Don't you feel at all broody?'

Lucy kicks me in the tit, footy-style. It hurts like billyo. I shift her in my arms, pinion her legs against my stomach so she can't do it again. 'Oh, you know,' I say evasively. 'I don't imagine Rufus is ready.'

'God, they never are. Mel, it would be so much fun. Imagine.'

'Jeez, you really *are* clucky.'

'Just you wait. The biological time clock will get you one day.'

'Naah. If I've got one, it's made of quartz. Never ticks. Just occasionally goes wobbly if you spill a drink on it.'

A sudden flurry of boas and kitten heels, and three of the school friends descend at once. It's like drowning in cherry pie. Each of the school friends, I've noticed, has a name ending in 'a': Christina, Louisa, Cassandra, Maria, Antonia, Arabella, Susanna, Lucinda, Tatiana, Venetia, Romina. Tilly must have seemed very exotic to them. Lucy is lifted from my arms and passed from cooing clutch to gurgling, manicured grip. 'Darling, darling, darling,' they go, 'look at her little ears, I could just eat her right up do you ever come to London did you have a maternity nurse how are your bosoms are they down to your knees yet oh darling aren't her little hands just the cutest thing you've ever seen?'

The sweaty feeling hasn't worn off. My limbs feel oddly heavy. I feel – removed. It's easy to slip away: they don't really notice me. I head for a chair and take a break. How these people manage to stay standing about hour after hour beats me. It must be early training, like the Queen and the toilet.

I snatch a Marmite sandwich from a passing plate. Stuff it whole in my mouth, because, looking at Rufus over by the fireplace, I feel a strange emptiness inside. I mean, how could I do it? Look at them: so strange and so small and so stupid. I don't seem able to look after my own self at the moment, let alone one of these little half-people.

As if on cue, one of them, a stubby blond boy, legs like sausages, belts past with his eyes shut, the way they do, runs smack into the wall. Sits down hard. Looks astonished, then offended, that the wall should have been there, that it should be so unyielding, that headbutting it should hurt, and opens his mouth to bawl.

And something weird happens. I'm on my feet and over by him in a second, and I've got my arms round him and my nose buried in the clean-feral smell of his hair, and something lurches in my stomach. Not sick, not scared: something primal. A sort of involuntary contraction, a sort of could-have-been-mine lurch. A sensation I have never felt before.

And then I'm freezing cold all over and trying to cover the fact that every one of my limbs has packed up and ceded its strength. Because I know, clear as day, what it means. What all my odd symptoms have been over the past couple of months. It means I can no longer discuss reproduction as an academic subject, think about it as a maybe-when or a maybe-if, no longer hope that one day the time might be right.

It's already way too late for that.

Chapter Sixty-Five

A Deciding Moment

Now I know why the euphemism for pregnant is the same as the one for being in prison. Banged up. That's me. Thoroughly up the duff. Bun in the oven. Knocked up. Awaiting a happy event. *Enceinte*. There's a piss-covered diagnostic stick on the bedside table to prove it. And I have never felt so trapped.

God, I want a cigarette.

My cell rings. I send it to voicemail without looking to see who it is, switch it off. I can't talk to anyone. I am a coward and I can't. Not now. Not while my head is full of cotton wool and my nasal membranes are so swollen that anyone could tell I've been crying.

How could I not have known? How could I not have worked it out? What am I, going 'ooh, no, my period'll come, it's just the stress'? A fifteen-year-old in a trailer park?

Now I know it's there, I can feel it, acutely, inside me, though it can't be bigger than a walnut. I can feel my bloated uterus, my breasts like pincushions, the pressure on my bladder. I am as obviously pregnant as paunchy Pete the potman. And it was something I always thought I'd want, be glad about; I always thought I'd be one of those serene madonna-mothers smiling secretly and cupping my tummy, but instead here I am lying on a bed in some anonymous hotel room on the Oxford ring road and crying my eyes out.

Poor little blighter. What chance does it stand? Not just the awful, chaotic circumstances I'll be bringing it into, but now I know what I know about the gene pool it's come from, I can't see a way forward. Murderous rednecks on one side, inbred snobs on the other and a slew of non-acceptance in the middle: it hasn't got a snowball's hope in hell.

409

I have to make a decision. I've been here two days, just lying on this bed, listening to the swoosh of traffic through the double glazing, watching the headlights track across the ceiling as I lie sleepless through the nights. I can't stay here for ever.

I push myself up, go into the bathroom and wash my face. I don't know why it is, but having a clean face is always the most effective first step to thinking straight. In the unforgiving striplight over the mirror, I look like a Victorian sideshow: eyes like gobstoppers, red on white on yellow, skin that's swollen and hollowed at the same time, chips of peeling skin on the underside of my nose, lips cracked and sagging. I look forty. So much for the pregnancy glow. I get out my washbag and do what I can. Slather on face cream, foundation, powder, paint my eyelids back on and charcoal in some lashes where they look stubby and thin from rubbing. Rouge my cheeks and attempt a businesslike cupid's bow on my cruddy lips. There. Now I look like someone's resprayed a car crash.

I go back to the bedroom and face the cellphone. There are six messages. Rufus: 'Mel, it's me. Where are you? This is . . . I'm . . . where are you? Can you call me?'

Tilly: 'Hi, darling. It's Tilly. I'm just a bit . . . um, well, worried. We all are. You sort of vanished in the middle of things, and, well . . . Rufus is going spare. You don't have to call me if you don't want to, but can you call him, please? Or me. Either way. It doesn't matter. Lots of love.'

Then Nessa: 'Hey, babe. Friendly neighbourhood skivvy here. Tell you what, there's a bit of a kerfuffle been going on since you went walkabout. Rufus looks like a stunned mullet. What's up? Are you OK? Can you let someone know you haven't carked it? I'll be at home most of the time if I'm not down at the house.'

Then Rufus again: 'Darling, I don't understand. I don't know what's going on. Please, call me. I've got my mobile with me. You don't need to call on the house phone. Just let me know you're all right. It isn't fair just to disappear. If I've done something, tell me what it is, but don't just . . . disappear. God. I love you. Please, darling. Just call me.'

It's like standing there while someone twists a knife in my heart. I move forward through the menu.

To my surprise, my mother. I haven't heard from any of them since they left. Just the tone of her voice is enough to let me know that her feelings haven't changed any.

'Just to let you know, he's been on the blower asking if you've turned up here, so we know all about it. I don't want to say "I told you so", but, hey. Yes, I do actually. I told you so. Just don't think you can just come back here, is all. We're done with it. You made your choices. I guess you can sell the car, eh?'

I press three to delete.

Finally, Rufus again: twenty minutes ago.

'Um . . . you don't want to speak to me. OK. I don't understand why, but I understand that much. But you've been gone forty-eight hours now, and I'm frantic with worry. Please let me know you're safe because . . . I don't know . . . I guess I'm going to have to file a missing person's report. Mel? Ring me, please? I love you.'

The sound of his voice kicks off another spasm of uncertainty. He sounds so worried, so hurt. I sit on the edge of the bed and weigh the phone in the palm of my hand. Thinking about it makes my head hurt. I find myself lying down again, hugging my knees. It's been like this since I got here: collapse, self-loathing, brief bouts of sleep, the relentless dissection of my situation; and then a brief rally, some attempt at imposing order or control over my reeling senses. And then back again: curled up, foetally, as though in empathy with my baby.

I can't go back. I can't.

You can't leave him. He loves you.

He betrayed me. He sided with them. It came down to it, and I needed him, and he didn't believe me.

He doesn't know. You have to give him a chance. You're carrying his child.

I can't. I can't do it. I can't have a baby in that place, let them take it away from me. I can't let my child grow up like them.

Rufus didn't. Tilly didn't. You didn't. Nothing is determined ahead of time. You need to be strong.

411

But I'm not. I'm not strong. I am weak. I can't fight them. I'm tired. I'm so tired.

You can. You have to. It's not just about you. It's him. It's this child of his. It's not just you any more, it's the whole world: it's the whole of life and the whole of the future. If you let them beat you now, they will beat you for ever. This is love you're letting them kill. The one, the pure, the only thing you ever believed in.

A single tear slips out of the corner of my eye and lands on my wrist. And it's that evidence of my own self-pity that finally decides me. I'm not a quitter. I'm not a leaver. I married for love and it's love that will be destroyed if I don't fight for it. If I don't stand up and be counted, then everything – the future, his, mine, the baby's – will be tainted with the brackish smack of my own frailty. I can't let it happen. I must not let it happen.

Once again I force myself to sit up, drop the phone into the side pocket of my bag, and go to find some clothes.

Chapter Sixty-Six
I Kneel Before You

I see him as I come down the hill; he's in the bottom deer paddock, hunkered down with his arms inside the engine of a tractor, a trailer carrying bales of hay parked at an oblique angle behind. I'm sure he hears my car, because he must be listening out for signs of my return, but he doesn't raise his head to look. I park up in the courtyard and go round the side of the house. New scaffolding has been erected on the Georgian wing; I have to duck and clamber to get to the garden gate.

He doesn't acknowledge my approach. Picks up a spanner and does something to the innards of the vehicle. I stand and look at him for a while before I speak: his sleeves rolled up, the slight suntan of someone who spends a lot of time outdoors, the faraway look of concentration.

'What's wrong with it?' I ask.

'I don't know,' he replies. 'I think it's something to do with the fuel feed.'

'Do you think you can fix it?'

'I don't know, Melody. I really don't know. But I'm trying.' Then he says: 'Have you come back?'

I shrug. 'I think so. If you want me.'

'More than anything,' he says simply.

I kneel down beside him in the mud, feel the wet seep through the knees of my jeans.

'I'm sorry,' I say. 'I'll be better.'

He shakes his head. 'Me too. I swear. Me too.'

Chapter Sixty-Seven
Don't You Ever Knock?

Two days later. I'm lying in bed reading *The Mysteries of Udolpho* and Rufus is getting changed out of his dusty jeans into dinner clothes. 'This is pretty sexy stuff,' I say. 'Kinky. Did you read the bit where the housekeeper swathes her in the rotting bridal veil? Do you think she realised how pussy-bumping that sounds?'

'Probably,' says Rufus. 'They were a lot more sophisticated than we give them credit for. You've got to remember, this lot bred Byron. Terrifically into rumpy-pumpy before the Victorians came along and spoiled things. Come on, darling. We've got to get downstairs. The gong went ten minutes ago.'

'Do I have to go?'

'Yes. You do.'

'I'm not looking forward to this.'

'What's the worst that can happen?'

I look at him over Mrs Radcliffe and pull a face.

'They'll be so pleased,' he says. 'Honestly. I don't understand why you're so scared.'

I put the book, face down and open, on the bedcover. 'One of two things is going to happen here,' I say. 'Either your mum is going to throw a wobbly, or I'm going to be turned overnight from sex diva into milch cow, and I don't relish the prospect of either much.'

Mary hasn't spoken to me since I came back. So there's a surprise.

Rufus comes over to the bed and puts a hand on my tummy. God, it's freaky the way everyone wants to touch your stomach the minute they know you're pregnant. 'You'll always be a sex diva to me,' he says.

414

'Give it time. I'm going to be a sex heffalump before you know it.'

'You're going to get such a great big arse. I can't wait.'

I tousle his hair and he kisses the side of my throat. And then he gets up and goes over to sit on the chair and put on his shoes. Not fair.

'I'll tell you,' I say, pulling back the bedcovers, 'it's horny stuff. Which one should I read next?'

'Oh, *The Monk*, I should think. Seriously dirty. Makes *Dracula* look like *Little Women*. There's a scene in there . . . well, I'll let you find out for yourself. Put me off my dinner, I'll tell you.'

'That wouldn't be difficult.'

'You said you wouldn't be sarky any more.'

'Sorry.'

'It's all right. Come *on*, darling. Get a move on.'

But the book and the throat-kissing have got to me. And Rufus. He always gets to me, one way or another. 'What do you say we give dinner a miss?'

Halfway to the door, he stops, turns, says: 'And just how popular do you think *that* would be?'

'A girl can't spend a little time with her husband?'

I sit forward, press my upper arms in to my sides so my breasts pop out of my top like ripe melons. In my experience, most guys will forget dinner when you do something like that. And I've got great bazookas, already. I can't think how I didn't notice them before.

The gong sounds again, echoing reproachfully through the house like a slave-bell. Rufus twitches towards the sound, havers on the carpet as I work my ancient charms. You want to see what a man caught on a cleft stick looks like? Try pulling him between his two primal urges. It's great. I feel powerful.

'Blow it,' I say. I know my NLP. 'What does it matter?'

He still looks uncertain. 'They'll notice.'

'Let 'em notice. What are you, a man or a mouse?'

He drags his feet, slowly, across the room.

'We can be a bit late, you know. We're adults.'

415

And I put my pen between my lips, give it a long slow suck just to remind him what adult entertainment is all about.

Rufus gets his half-smile, looks me right back. Strike! Did I ever tell you how dark his eyes are? Like pools of oil, pinpricks of light shining in the depths.

'How,' he asks, 'are you going to persuade me?'

I pop a button open, kneel up on the edge of the bed. 'Come here and I'll show you.'

He takes another step closer, and I get him by the belt-loops. Pull him towards me so he towers over me, arms folded, looking down.

I show him.

'Oh, God,' says Rufus, 'you're such a minx.' Then, just: 'Oh God.'

And after an interval when there's not much but silence between us, I stop for a second, look up and say: 'Do you like that?'

He says: 'Yes. Oh God.'

'Thank you,' I say. 'How much of a whore am I?'

He starts to speak, stops because I've just bent back to my task and made him breathe in, fast, says: 'You . . . are such a . . . fucking . . . *whore*.'

Which gets me happy as well as horny. So I show him just how deeply the whore in me runs, because sometimes you don't want to be anything else. I swing my legs over the edge of the bed for better purchase, and Rufus lets out the sort of long, desperate groan that only a whore deserves.

'Ah, Jesus, do that,' he says like a porn star, 'oh, yes, *aaah*,' and I have a powerful urge to smile, which is sort of impossible under the circs. He grabs, sharply, at my hair, digs his fingers into my scalp and pushes, and calls me a bitch and tells me he loves me, all in the same speeding breath. So I get my hands round his buttocks and go for it, and he's got his head thrown back and he's talking really loudly now, bitch-slut-whore-slag-harlot-go-on-then-you-fucking . . .

And there's the sound of the door handle turning and a bang as the door is thrown back against the wall, and Mary's commanding

416

voice going: 'For heaven's sake, we're all waiting to start dinner. Didn't you hear the . . .?'

Then there's a deafening silence.

I can't do a lot to dissimulate. And to be honest, I don't want to. Because it's my room, and she's the intruder, and I'm as mad as a cut snake. I sit back, slowly, with all the defiance I can find, and look at her. Rufus just stands, frozen to the spot, refusing, or unable, to turn round.

The look on her face would turn you to stone. It's a mixture of shock, faint nausea, and undisguised contempt. You'd have thought she'd just found me with her son's cock in my mouth, or something.

'Yes?' I ask. Coldly, and refusing to show any embarrassment, because I've had it with her. I've fucking had it. Standing here giving me that 'I've found you out now, missy' look when it's *her* that's just burst into my marital bedroom without so much as a tap on the door. I can hear those bitch-slut-whore-slag words racing round her brain, and I'm absolutely fucking furious. 'Yes?' I say again. 'Can we help you?'

Mary regains her composure. Addresses the back of her son's head. Not the two of us. Not me. 'Rufus,' she says, 'dinner is ready, if you're not too . . . *busy.*' She says this last word with vicious sarcasm. 'We'll see you in the dining room, if you can tear yourself away.'

He doesn't answer. I glance at his face, and it's a weird mix of rage and misery and profound embarrassment. I suppose it would be worse for him. Primal trauma works in many, many directions.

Mary turns on her heel and slams out of the room.

My blood boils over. I'm not having it. I'm not bloody having it. I'm not going to be made to feel guilty about making love with my own husband, in my own bedroom. I will *not*. She can have the run of the rest of the house, but I'm not having *this*.

Rufus realises, too late, what I'm about to do, grabs, ineffectually, at my arm, but I shake his hand off and cross the

417

room, hair flying, in two bounds. Throw the door open and storm out into the corridor. Take her by her upper arm and swing her round to face me.

'Don't you ever fucking *knock*?' I ask.

Mary blinks. '*Don't* swear at me.'

What she's not saying is: don't swear at me, whore. Don't even dare to address me, crawling doxy. She doesn't need to say it, because her tone does all the work. And I'm not bloody taking it. Though her son's just been calling me the same words, I'm absolutely not taking them from her. I've put up with months of sniping, interference, freezing out, condescension, the poisonous lies she's spread about me when she thinks I'm out of earshot, but I will not have her stand in judgement over me.

'Don't ever,' I tell her, and I'm surprised at the level of threat in my voice. Shouldn't be. I learned at the feet of masters, after all, '*ever* come into my room without knocking again. Knocking and waiting for permission to enter.'

Mary looks like she's bitten an apple and found a slug.

'Do you understand me?'

'How dare you?' she says. '*You* should be apologising to *me*.'

I don't get how she could even begin to justify a statement like that. But I don't care.

'Do. You. Understand. Me.' I repeat.

'I will not,' she says, 'be told how to live in my own house.'

'What sort of sick bitch are you? Wanting to walk in on your little darling when he's nearly thirty years old?'

'How *dare* you talk to me like that?'

I sound like a strident Strine fishwife, but I don't care. 'I'll talk to you like that, lady,' I snarl, 'because it's what you deserve. What? Did you think I was going to just sit back and let you do whatever you wanted with my life and never utter a word? We have a right to our privacy, and you're going to learn to respect that.'

'Hah,' says Mary. 'Privacy to behave like . . . like . . . *animals*.'

I fold my arms and tilt my head to one side. 'What's the matter Mary? He's not a kid any more. You've got a problem with me making love with my husband?'

418

She shrieks. Literally. Shrieks. 'You call that *making love*? That's not making love!'

'Well, what do *you* call it?'

'Revolting,' she snaps. 'I don't want to have to walk into a room and find people doing . . . especially not my son. It's disgusting. Disgusting! You behave like a . . . a . . . *guttersnipe*!'

'Well, bloody knock before you come *in*, then!'

'Get some bloody self-control!' she shouts at me. 'You're like bloody rutting pigs! You come here, and you bring the values of your bloody *funfair* existence into this house, and I won't have it!'

'It's what people do! It's what people *do*! We've got hands and mouths and cocks and tongues and pussies and tits and arses, and it's what people *do*! It's what *we* do!'

'Listen to you! Your values! They're right down there in the gutter, and you're dragging him down there with you!'

I rein it in, stand back on one heel and look her up and down with a raised eyebrow and a twisted lip. Say, triumphantly, 'Oh, don't worry about that, Mary. Believe me, he was right there when I found him. I didn't have to teach him a thing.'

And she whacks me. Right across the face. So hard my ears sing. And I think for one bally second, and then I belt her one back. And I slam the door on my way back into our bedroom.

Chapter Sixty-Eight

Cataclysm

I'm so berko I don't even notice his reaction for a minute. My head is hurting and so are my knuckles, and my breath comes like a charging bull's. 'That's it!' I shout. 'I'm out of here! I've had e-fucking-*nough*!'

I dive under the bed and retrieve my suitcase. Throw it on to the floor and start piling through the chest of drawers. 'If she thinks she can talk to me like that she can shove it. Fucking *bitch*.'

'You hit my mother,' says Rufus.

I stop what I'm doing and look at him. He is ashen-faced, grim with shock and rage, and even Blind Freddie wouldn't have trouble spotting that the rage is not directed towards Mary.

'Yeah, well, a *terrible* bloody tragedy,' I say, 'but in case you hadn't noticed, she started it.' I pick up a handful of underwear, throw it into the case.

He speaks again, louder this time and more angry. 'You *hit* my mother!'

And I'm on my feet, standing right in his face and shouting back, '*Your* mother hit *me*!'

He sounds completely at sea, talking like a man who's just banged his head on a roof-beam. 'What is it with you, Mel? What did you think you were doing? Have you *no* self-control?'

'*What?*'

'We'll never get past this. How on earth can we get past this?'

I say several s-words in a row. 'You don't get it, do you?' I ask. 'I don't give a damn. Because I'm not spending another night in the same house with her! Don't you *see* what she's like, Rufus? Are you going to stay blind to it for ever?'

Rufus collapses. Drops like a stone on to the bed and wraps his arms around his head. 'I'm in *hell*!' he shouts. 'I am in *hell*!'

Shocked, I go to sit next to him, put a hand out to touch him. His forearm comes up and pushes it away. 'Don't! *Don't!* Don't touch me!'

'Rufus!'

'No! No! Just *leave* me alone! You've done enough damage! Jesus! God! What am I supposed to *do*?'

And my calm, self-possessed husband bursts into noisy tears. Wraps his right arm around his stomach as though he has a pain and rocks, back and forth, still holding the hand nearest me out to fend me off.

'It's impossible! *Impossible!* You're tearing me apart, the two of you, and I can't do it any more!'

'Rufus, I—'

'*Don't touch me.*'

'I – darling, I – God . . .'

'It's beyond bearing. I don't know what to do. I just don't know . . . you pull one way, and she pulls the other, and you don't seem to understand, and they're refusing to listen to a word I say about the house, and I'm responsible for *all* of it . . . I've got lawyers on my back, and banks and the heritage people, and Daddy's taxes, and all the village expecting me to do something about the state of the place when there's nothing, *nothing* I can do, and you came and I thought you'd help me . . . I thought you'd at least try to understand, but you don't. You *don't* . . .'

I try, once again, to put my arms around him, to show him some comfort, but he shoves me away, hard and finally, and gets to his feet. Starts pacing, up and down, up and down the carpet, his fists clenched. I am appalled. Have I done this? Has it been me all along?

'You're such a . . . God, you say Mummy's a bitch, and you – *listen* to you. Look at the way you spoke to my grandmother. You've got such a temper, and I *can't* . . . I've tried and tried, but I'm at the end of my tether, Melody. Between you, you've . . .'

'Rufus . . .' I say lamely. 'I'm sorry.'

421

'Yeah, yeah,' he snaps bitterly. 'Sorry, sorry, *sorry*. Why don't you try thinking *before* you do something?'

'That's unfair. That's *so* unfair!'

He roars. Like a lion. No. Nothing as powerful. Like some animal that's been trapped and realises that it's about to die. It's a sound of sheer frustration, rage and – despair.

'Unfair? Don't talk to me about unfair! That's *my family*! I will *not* be . . . ripped away from my family. Not by you, not by anyone!'

I respond. 'But it's OK for *you* to do it to *me*, then?'

'What?'

There are things you look back on with shame in life, and the words that come out of me at this moment are among them. My temper. My bloody *temper*. I've not changed a bit; it's all been waiting in there to come out and sabotage everything.

'Your family saw mine off without a bloody *murmur* from you. You get rid of my family, but *yours* . . . oh, no! Your sainted bloody family comes before *everything*. You won't live your own life, you've wasted your opportunities and your talents, you stay around here doing what *Mummy* tells you and jumping through hoops not to upset *Granny*, and it's bloody *killing* me! It can't go on! I can't live with it any more! I thought I'd married a *man*, and instead I've married a . . . a . . . *Mummy's boy*. A pathetic bloody under-the-cosh *Mummy's boy*.'

I might as well have slapped him as well as his mother. His head jerks backwards and his mouth clamps shut, and he looks at me as though I have suddenly peeled off a mask to reveal a bug-eyed alien underneath.

'Is that really what you think of me?' he asks. And sits down again, this time in the chair, hands hanging loose over his knees.

I sit down myself, on the bed. The gulf between us is way more than physical. Because I should know by now that the survival of relationships – the real maintenance of the happy fantasy we call love – is as dependent on the things that are *not* said as it is on the things that are. And I should know this one fundamental truth: that words, once spoken, can never be taken back. Apologised for, forgiven: but never taken back.

'No . . . look, no. No, I don't think that.'

'But you said it.'

'Please. I'm stupid. I say things. I . . .'

He looks down at his hands. They're scraped and raw and beaten up from where he has spent the last two months labouring to mend and shore up and postpone the inevitable cataclysm.

'I'm sorry that I'm a disappointment to you,' he says eventually, reproachfully.

'No, sweetheart, I didn't mean that.'

But he's shutting down, the way people do. The way they do when they are hurt without understanding the reason.

He puts his hands back down on his knees. Hoists himself out of the chair. 'Well, I'm tired, Melody. Too tired to talk about it now.' He walks towards the door.

'Where you going?'

The voice that answers is drained of emotion, listless. 'I don't know. I'll see you tomorrow.'

I'm on my feet, trying to go to him, but the look on his face tells me to keep my distance. 'Please, Rufus. Can't we talk about it?'

'Not tonight. I'm sorry, but I can't take any more character analysis tonight. I know you're perfect and I'm full of failings, but there's only so much I can take at one time.'

'I never said . . . I never *said* that!'

'Stuff it,' he says. 'To be honest, I couldn't care less.'

'But where are you going?'

'Oh don't worry,' he replies spitefully. 'I'm not going to *Mummy*, if that's what you think. I'm just going to go and – be by myself somewhere. I know it'll come as shock to you, but even *I* need some time alone occasionally.'

I feel like all the wind has been knocked out of me. 'Don't go.'

He doesn't reply. Turns the door handle and pulls the door open.

'What will I do?' I ask pointlessly.

'Well, I'll tell you what, Melody, for once I'm not going to take responsibility for that. You can work it out for yourself.'

'Rufus, *please!*'

He pauses in the doorway, looks me up and down with the pregnant dislike I have so thoroughly earned.

'Perhaps you can take one of your pills,' he says, and leaves.

Chapter Sixty-Nine

The Unspeakable in Pursuit of the Uneatable

Andy stands over the bed, pearls that were his eyes, and he is not sneering, like I would expect, or laughing, or even angry, as far as I can see. He's just sad. Andy, who rarely sported any expression other than the dumb insolence of the unreconstructed male, has a look of such pitiful woe on his face that, if I didn't know he were dead, I would be asking if we'd lost a test match or something.

He is wearing the clothes I last saw him in, salt-bleached and tattered now, and his hair hangs down like seagrass. I seem to be welded to the bed, my arms and legs so heavy they pin me to the mattress.

'You killed me, Mel,' he says. But it's not an accusation, not a reproach: it's a simple statement.

I want to speak, but my jaw is frozen, my tongue a lifeless slab of meat in a sensationless mouth. So I lie still and look at him, and try to show him with my eyes: *I'm sorry. I'm sorry. But, see? I'm getting my reward now, ain't I? I didn't get just to walk away.*

'I never thought you did. Though there was a time there when I thought you were running rather than walking.'

I can't answer, because I know he's right.

'Don't run away this time, babe,' he says. 'Stick it out.'

Why are you being so forgiving?

Andy shakes his head. 'It wasn't your fault. You can't be blamed for what someone else did.'

I can feel the tears stream down my face. *But it was, it was. You don't understand. Andy, I'm so sorry . . .*

He stands and looks at me for a moment, says: 'I didn't come for that. I came to tell you to take care. You're not safe, babe. They're playing a higher game than you understand.'

What can I do? Tell me, Andy. How do I fight them?

'I don't know,' he says. 'But, babe: you'd better wake up. There's someone in the room with you.'

And then he's gone, and I'm awake, and even before I reach consciousness, I am crying, though I knew while it was happening that I was only dreaming. I can feel the gooseflesh rising on my arms. I'm alone in the big bed, straining to shake paralysis from my limbs. And I'm casting around with my eyes because I know that what he has just said is true.

Someone has lit a candle. Over by the window. It stands in the centre of the pedestal table and glints feebly, doing more to throw the room into shadow than illuminate it.

My heart leaps – hope, and fear, mixed together in one sick adrenal lurch. A wind has got up outside while I have been asleep; it rattles the window and makes the tiny flame dance and jitter.

'Rufus?'

A small movement, just outside my field of vision, beyond the bed-curtains. But no reply.

I struggle upright, covers heavy on my legs, head heavy with slow-clearing sleep from where I was knocked out by Nytol because I'm not letting diazepam near my baby. And then I remember that, before I took the pill, I locked the door from the inside: partly in pique, partly to stop intrusions. There's no way he can be back.

I swing my legs to the far side of the bed from where I sense the presence, try the bedside lamp. It's dead: clicks with a dullness that suggests that the electrical supply has given out again.

The candle gutters. The house shifts and groans. And a cloaked figure steps out from behind the curtain, turns its blank and hooded face towards me and laughs.

I don't scream, this time. I've learned my lesson. But I'm on my feet and across the room like a greyhound out of a trap, and fumbling with the key before my ghostly visitor has reached the foot of the bed. And in turn, it doesn't speak: just shakes a white hand from the drape of its sleeve and points a skinny finger in my direction, lets loose another peal of mocking laughter. Not funny-ha-ha laughter: the laughter of the bully watching the weakling scrabble in the mud. Laughter that contains nothing of humour and everything of violence.

The key catches, turns in my hand, and I burst out into the corridor, cold damp air on my arms and shoulders, my satin slip no protection against the wintry night.

In the bedroom, someone trips, stumbles, lets out a grunt of surprise and annoyance. There is nothing supernatural about the sound. I've been visited by someone very real and very solid. And then I hear his footsteps resume and tumble towards me, and this knowledge brings me no comfort at all. The passageway suddenly seems very long and very empty. I am half naked and alone in a house that is, to all intents and purposes, deserted. I look about me for some object — a candlestick, a doorstop, anything that's hard and would fit into the palm of the hand — but there is nothing. Wattestone ancestors gaze, glum and disapproving, at my tangled hair, my bare feet.

He appears in the doorway. I do the only thing I can think of, and run. I bolt towards the stairs, see ivy leaves thrash like storm-swept seaweed against the windowpanes. The banister is cold beneath my hand, treads slippery with varnish. I can't hear him behind me now, but I keep up my pace, pattering downward, my ears only half-registering the whispering that pursues me.

Leave. Leave. We don't want you here. Get out. Get out. GET OUT!

I don't need telling twice. I should have left last night; shouldn't have waited, hoping, stupidly hoping, that Rufus would change his mind, that he would come back for me.

I reach the first landing. Swing round the corner, screech to a halt on the very edge of the top step of the next flight. Have to grip the newel with both hands to stop myself from pitching forward into the dark.

Below me, looking up, hands tucked into heavy sleeves, empty blackness where the face should be, is my monk.

I am rooted to the spot, sound of the ocean in my ears.

He begins to climb the stairs.

I run west.

Heavy dark-wood Gothic of the Victorian wing. Stuffed animal heads watch the far distance with blank glass gazes. Wattestones in black – white bonnets and thyroid eyes – ignore me as I scutter beneath them and whisper: *We don't want you. You are not one of us*, at my retreating back.

I don't know where Rufus is. I don't know if he's even in the house. I try doors as I pass, but they either refuse to open at all, or swing back to reveal cavernous expanses devoid of occupation. I never knew a place so large could also be so claustrophobic. The house itself is watching me. I can feel it from the prickling of the hairs on the back of my neck.

The wind buffets the windows again, air pressure suddenly up, then down, as though there's been an explosion in the foundations. The house moans in protest. I make for the Victorian staircase. I still don't know what my intention is. I've no clothes, no keys: even if I can make it to the car, I can't drive away.

The descending section of the Victorian staircase has been blocked off with scaffolding. I'll have to go through the Queen Anne wing before I can go down. Glance over my shoulder before I mount the stairs. The corridor is empty.

The long gallery: gloomy light filters through uncurtained windows on to bare floorboards. The suits of armour that line the walls from one end of the room to the other, brandishing swords and battleaxes and ancient longbows, have the air of long-dead guardians awaiting the opportunity to return to life. I pause on the threshold, try to check each in turn for signs of movement, realise that I have no alternative but to pass them anyway, and set off to jog the hundred metres to the far door. I stay in the centre of the room, glance left to right as I go.

The door behind me bursts open, and a dark figure flies through, cloak hems billowing round sprinting legs.

And now I'm truly running myself: through the long gallery door, down the Jacobean corridor, tumbling, leaping down the tollbooth stair without even holding the banister.

And he's there. He's there again, coming up at me. How can he be? I must be seeing things. I must. How can he be behind me and ahead?

I can feel the scream build. Choke it down. I can't show fear. Can't show more fear than I'm showing already. Muster a voice from somewhere in the bottom of my throat and say, stupidly, lamely: 'Can I help you?'

There's no reply. What am I thinking?

I stand my ground. Search for words. Try them out in my head for signs of weakness. *What do you want? Why are you following me? Keep back, I've got a gun . . .*

'What can I do for you?'

He doesn't reply. Just raises an arm to show me the object in his hand. It's a kitchen knife. Eight inches long and pointed, for filleting. I don't need telling twice. Bound up the flight I've just come down, belt along a Persian runner into the Jacobean wing. Black wood, panelling, heavy dark furniture that squats in the moonlight like stalking trolls. I don't know my way around here well. Have only been here in daylight, passing through, following Rufus, going to the library.

Footsteps hard behind me. I step up my pace, feet slapping on polished teak, feel my face harden in a grimace. I know now what it feels like to be a fox, pursued for sport, hunted down and cornered and seeing my own mortality.

I hear him behind me. Panting more heavily than I am, heavy footfalls slapping about, as though he is beginning to flag. Perhaps there is a chance. Perhaps I can outrun him, wear him out; if I can only get far enough ahead, I can go to ground. Hide out until the danger has passed. I decide to head for the very core of the house, for the Tudor staircase, where wings, north, south, east and west, diverge from a single point and where, if I get there with time to spare, I can dive away into the darkness and lose him for good. Burst through the green baize door at the end of the corridor, rattle down the servants' staircase and hurl myself into the final straight. The passageway is lower here, more cramped, ghastly imps' faces looming from decorative plasterwork. I snatch hold of a huge pewter platter that sits on a table, frisbee it behind me. Hear it bounce from something hard, then the *oof*, receding behind, as it catches its target. Almost manage a smile of triumph – *take that, you bastard* – but lack the energy. Turn a corner, then another one, and I'm there. Turn east.

And he's right there in front of me. Hands raised like Christ blessing Rio.

Shit, shit, shit.

I try south. And he's there as well. Leaning against the wall, arms folded, like an actor waiting to play Hamlet.

And he's coming up behind. He's behind me. Behind, and to the left, and to the right.

I don't even think. Barely register that of course, it's not one, it's three, that they've been tagging me since I left the bedroom, that I'm not being hunted, I'm being *herded*. I skid round and run up the Eastern corridor, into the unused part of the house, the abandoned wing. Hear them pause and whisper. It's a dead end up here. The house comes to an end with a huge oriel window overlooking the formal gardens. I must find somewhere to hide. I have no alternative. I must find an earth somewhere and wait until they pass.

Doors: locked, locked, locked. My every muscle aches with tension. My hair sticks to the back of my neck. I tiptoe along, now, try each door in turn, feel dust on handles that haven't moved in decades.

They have started walking. Just walking, as though they know that there's no escape, that they have no need to rush.

And finally, some give. I hold my breath. Push the door open as silently as I can and enter a tiny bedroom, ugly, the proportions all wrong: long and narrow like another corridor. It's deep in fust and dust and unmoving air. A bed. A couple of chairs. Some large black screen-like object, the size of a door and thick, like it's padded in some way, leaning against the wall, pointless. And, out of place in this house of antiquities, a built-in wardrobe, floor-to-ceiling, wall-to-wall.

I close the door behind me, quietly, quietly. Tiptoe over the carpet and pull the wardrobe door open.

Weird. It's full of fur coats. Full-length fur coats, motheaten, green to the touch.

I slip inside and crouch behind them.

Chapter Seventy

Gone to Ground

Footsteps. They're here.

They enter the room, treading carefully as though nervous of falling in the dark. They don't switch on the lights. Of course they don't. There are no lights.

Then I catch a flash of torchlight through the crack in the wardrobe door. They've come equipped. Jesus.

I shrink against the back of the wardrobe, and a protrusion from the wall digs into my side. Crazy, stupid: the instinctive reaction of an animal at bay.

The door clicks shut.

'Are you sure she came in here?' Hilary's voice, muffled through the fur.

Another voice answers. It takes me a moment to recognise it. 'Of course. It's the only one that's open.'

'You don't think, while you were . . . she might have . . .?'

'No.' She sounds slightly irritated. 'No, she won't have. She'll be here.'

It's Mrs Roberts. The faithful servant, helping out in the hunt.

'Gone to ground,' says my mother-in-law, and laughs.

A moment's silence, then all three laugh together.

I close my eyes. *If you exist, God, if you exist, help me now.*

Mary raises her voice. 'You might as well come out, now, Melody dear,' she says. 'We can do it the hard way or the easy way. It's up to you.'

I don't move a muscle. Barely even breathe. I'm not going to make it easier for them. Whatever way we do it, it's going to be hard on me. A bit of me is going: *Come on, Melody, they're just trying to put the wind up you. It's another of Mary's little games. Scare me into hysterics and deny that they were ever there.*

And the rest knows that the game has stepped up another level. That I've been underestimating them all along. That the easy way is already over and now they're going to play hard.

An exaggerated social sigh: Mary's, but coming from Hilary's lungs. 'Well, it seems we have to pause to draw,' he says. 'Roberts. If you'd be kind enough to cover the door, in case she breaks covert . . .'

'Ar,' says Mrs R. Jesus. I hear her make her way back across the room, heavy-breathing as she goes. I don't know what to do. I'm cornered, like a rat in a trap. *Think, Melody.* I have nothing to defend myself with. A green silk slip and some mouldering mink. Why did I leave the bedroom? How could I have been so . . .?

Because you're stupid and you deserve to die. You should have left when you had the chance.

I feel about me as they start to search the room. It's not a big room, not by Bourton standards. It's about half the size it should be, on this floor. I've got less than a jiffy. I start to grope about the wardrobe. Maybe there's a hatpin, a brooch left in one of these stupid old-lady coats. Something – anything. I'm not going down without a fight.

They're taking their time. That's for sure certain. Enjoying themselves. They're doing things at their leisure: relishing it.

'Where, oh, where can she be?' asks Hilary. 'Could it be behind the curtains?'

A swish and a giggle as the curtains are thrown back. A bit more light, now. I can see my arm, my naked thigh.

'Could it be under the bed?' asks Mary.

'Poke about and see,' says Hilary.

There's the sound of thrusting: breathing like someone's bent over and using their muscles. Horrible. Hopelessly, I push myself further back against the wall. Feel, again, that object dig into the small of my back. Right down by the hip: something angular, something that shifts, ever so slightly, as I move against it.

'Where can she be?' asks Mary.

433

They're toying with me. They know already. It's obvious. They want to extract the max.

It moves again: more this time. Suddenly, I realise that it's not just the knobble that's moving, but a section of the wall against my back. Just a slight shift, but enough to make me realise, suddenly, what lies behind. Of course. That's why the proportions of the room are all wrong.

'Well,' says Hilary, 'there's only one place she can be.'

Torchlight plays suddenly, brightly, across the crack in the door in front of me. I hear them cross the room: neat, crisp footsteps.

Scrabbling behind me, I grasp what's been sticking into me and feel it. It's a latch. So far down the wall that no casual observer would spot it, but a latch none the less. Beneath my fingers I identify the smooth length of iron that holds the door to, and the vertical lifter, which has been what's been digging into me.

It's a priest hole. It must be. Rufus said they were here, and I've found one. Sanctuary.

The torches pause at the door. Whispers: 'Give it to me. No, let me. I want to. You promised I could . . .'

I don't waste any more time. Grasp the lifter and push upward. For one sweaty moment it resists – God knows how many decades since the last time it moved – and then with a little click it lets go of the latch and the door swings back. Carries me on its momentum, tumbling head–over–legs into a darkness so total it wraps itself around me like velvet. Darkness that's dry and musty and smells faintly of – what? Vinegar? White spirit? Rot?

Carpet beneath me. I bump against a piece of furniture, crouch, in the black. No time to close the door: the wardrobe is coming open. All my will to control my breath. If they don't hear me, maybe they won't see the aperture, will think themselves mistaken.

A giggle, again – Hilary, this time: high–pitched, like a schoolboy in the thick of some act of random cruelty.

I see a hand – bleached, fingers grotesquely long in torchlight shadows – reach out and push the coats apart. Three silhouettes move forward to fill the gap, then suddenly, with a flick of a wrist, their faces are lit from below, wide-eyed and grinning like jack-o'-lanterns.

'Boo,' says Mary.

I don't reply.

'We brought you your handbag, Melody, dear,' she says. 'We won't be needing it any more.'

'Sorry, old girl, and all that,' says Hilary, 'but family comes first.'

'They're not your family, Hilary,' I say.

'Yours neither,' he says.

He takes a step into the wardrobe, grasps the top of the dwarf door leading to my hideout. Holds out my bag at arm's length and hoicks it, disdainfully, into the void behind me. 'Goodbye,' he says. 'No hard feelings.'

'Are you crazy?'

Mary looks at me pityingly. 'You never really did understand our ways,' she tells me. 'I'd like to say it's been a pleasure, but of course, I really don't like to tell more lies than strictly necessary.'

Hilary yanks at the door and it bangs to. The darkness snatches at me, grips the back of my neck, crushes my chest. And on the far side of the wooden panel, I hear something that makes my eyes flare with fear.

I can hear sounds of strain, groans of exertion, and I hear the scrape of another panel, sliding into the place. I know what that big heavy screen was, propped up against the wall.

It was soundproofing.

Chapter Seventy-One

Priest Hole

Breath. Whooping. Frayed. In, in, in, in, my chest tight like a drum. Sounds of a wolf, snarling, hands clutched at my throat.

Black. It's black. Eyes goggling, desolate search for some tiny source of light, some pinprick of comfort. Black. The world, gone. Silence. All silence, just the sound of my breath.

All states pass. All states but death. As my awareness begins to return, I understand that I am crouched on my haunches, hands, stiff like coral, either side of my face, and that I am rocking, back and forth, back and forth, like the porcelain mandarins in the Chinese Drawing Room. My skin feels stretched from the screaming, and my teeth are dry like bones.

Panic. You're panicking.

It's dark. It's so dark. They left me in the dark. I don't know what's in here with me . . .

I can hear it. Breathing. A tiny part of my wit knows that it's only me who breathes here in the dark, that the rustling is my own scant clothing, but my mind is filled with zombies and vampires and stalking assassins. I see nothing, but I see things with red eyes, I see tall dark figures in fedora hats, I see Mary, crouched in a corner, fingernails filed to points, laughing at me.

It's cold. I think it's the cold that brings me to my senses. In the dark time has no relevance; I have no idea how long has passed. But I run my hands over my upper arms and find them covered in goosebumps, and it brings me sharply back to my mind.

I am in a sealed room, I know that. On the far side of three layers of wood, and felt, and heavy lead, fur coats hang forgotten, warm, deadening to sound. It's colder here than in the main house: this unused wing, this unused room, are permeated with the cold of decades. The cold of neglect; the cold of seclusion. It's beginning already to seep into my stomach, chill me from the inside out.

You're not dead yet. Do something.

Rufus. I want my Rufus.

He doesn't know you're here. Do something.

I can hardly bear the fear. I must explore this dark space on hands and knees, feel my way into – what? Cobwebs? Fungi? Mantraps?

All I know is that I'm pressed against something solid, and wooden. It feels warm against my back in comparison to the floor. Of course. Under the carpet is the unforgiving stone flooring of the sixteenth century.

Better hope the carpet's not fitted.

As if the cold is my only enemy.

I feel behind me. I am leaning against a desk, or a dressing table. Probably a desk: it has that solidity.

Your bag. You've got a lighter in your bag. Where did they throw it? Where did it go?

I don't want to move. It'll get me. Whatever it is, it will hear me and get me.

'Shut it, Melody,' I say, out loud, as loud as I can to vanquish the demons.

The walls soak up the sound. It's almost as though they were sucking. Nothing comes back.

I am already dead.

'Stop it,' I repeat. 'Stop it, you can't afford to do this.'

But I can't move. *It's somewhere out in front of me, waiting. I'll crawl across the floor, feel my way right towards it, and I'll put my hand out in the darkness and I'll feel its leathery skin, feel it shift as I touch it. I can't. Safest to stay here.*

'Move it, you silly bitch!' I shout at myself. 'Stay here and you're dead for sure. Come on! Just fucking move!'

Warm wood under my hands, then the yawning space where the kneehole is, then more, an arm's length further on; enough to throw me off my balance, force my hand on to the floor once more.

Giant footfalls. Stamping towards. I know they're no more than the rush of my pulse, but the noise freezes me to the spot, has me gasping again.

I want to scream.

It won't do you any good. No-one will hear you.

Let me out. Let me OUT.

I dig my fingers into the carpet, haul my soul back into my body.

I remember the bag flying somewhere over my head. For all I know, I changed position five, ten times while I panicked. All I can do is feel my way, cover every inch of the room until I find it.

There must be lights. There must be a light switch by the door.

Don't bet on it. In a priest-hole?

And I don't know where the door is.

The carpet is gritty under my fingers, as though the fabric of the building has been crumbling on to it, unswept, over the years. Something crunches under my palm – crisp going to wet – and I stifle a shriek of disgust. *I'm not up to this. I'm not. Let me die now. Just let me get it over with.*

Get a grip. You're a Katsouris. You've got more spunk than this.

Following the line of the wall, I encounter a chair – wooden, simple in design – and some sort of chest tucked into the corner. Then – strange – what feels like an old suitcase, cast roughly up against the wall. It's soft and slumped in the middle, and it takes me a moment to identify what it is. Maybe there will be clothes inside. Something I can put on.

They'll have rotted away by now, if the state of the case is anything to go by. I'm not trying anything until I can see it.

Oh God, Rufus. He thinks I've gone. He doesn't know I'm still here. He'll come back, and he'll think I've left. He'll think I've left him, like I did once before. Just like Lucy left Edmund.

I reach the next corner. Turn it and run into a small cupboard. Short legs, square, simple toggle catch on the door. A bedside cabinet. Which means – yes – that there's a bed.

My knees ache. The bag fell somewhere over by the chest. The far corner from the door. I heard it hit the wall and bounce. I turn along the bed, make my way back across the open floor. Feel instantly vulnerable again, with nothing to orient myself against, as though this room has turned into a chamber the size of the Steppes, as though it's littered with crevasses. Sweep my arms out, one by one, to the sides, as I crawl.

And then it's there, under my hand. And the leather feels like monster's skin so that I cry out in horror and then again in relief, clutching it to my chest like a baby when I realise what it is. Thank the non-existent God, fervently, wholeheartedly, like a Mullah with a new Mercedes, and tear at the zip with numb fingers.

It's chaos inside. Feels fuller than when I last held it. Someone has been through it and thrown things in on top. I feel my wallet, my keys, a jumble of credit cards, and also, not all that much to my surprise, something that feels like my passport, my driver's license, a bottle of perfume, a bra, a bunch of necklaces, a paperback, several of the plastic blister strips they put round pills. Of course. Of course they've made it look like I've taken off in the night, the way I did before.

And finally, down in the bottom, my fingertips brush against the lighter. It slips away, comes back.

'Thank you, God,' I say again. 'Thank you thank you *thank you*.'

It's a little room, my cell. Not more than four metres by five. I see, now, why my voice sounded so muffled: the walls are lined with tapestries: tattered, scotched, rotting on their hangings, but effective. Everything in here is designed to stop noise travelling: thick layers of carpet, drapes on the bed, heavy coverlet of some sort of padded damask. In the tiny light of the flame I make out what I've got available. It's as I had already mapped out with my hands. Desk, chair, suitcase from which a couple of bits of shredded cloth protrude, two bedside tables. No lamps. I rush over to the door, feel along the panelling around it, but there's no switch.

I find a candle, though, on the desk: half burnt down and thick with dust. It flares up when I put the flame to it, then fades, gutters, settles. I reckon I should get maybe four hours' burn out of it.

Plans. I've got to make plans. This can't be it. There's no way I'm going to let this be it. There must be a way out of here. You can't build a priest-hole with no internal latches. It makes no sense. It would be as though they wanted to keep people in rather than protect them . . .

And it's then that I notice that I am not, after all, alone. Because there's a figure lying, very still, under the covers of the bed.

Chapter Seventy-Two

Mummy

Her eyes, mercifully, are closed. Sunk hollow in desiccated sockets, lashes dusty on white kid skin. The nose, fleshless, like a mountain peak. Nostrils, stretched over bone, gape dark and bottomless in unsteady candlelight. Cheekbones so sharp they could have been sculpted. Jaw elegant and spare. Her mouth has fallen slightly open in death. I can glimpse neat nacre teeth between lips downturned at the corners in an expression of frozen grief.

My heart takes a good couple of minutes to slow down. For a moment, as the candle guttered under my panicking breath, I had thought I'd seen her move, and it takes some time for my sense to overcome my senses. But I can't approach the bed. Prop myself, instead, against the wall, in a corner, shivering from shock as much as cold, and stare.

The counterpane, ragged like all the other fabrics in the room, covers most of the body. A few strands of faded chestnut hair on the indented pillow. There are stains. Even by candlelight, I can see that there are stains. She's died here, and transmuted here and, I dare say, until I came along, those who were responsible for putting her here had thought that this would be the last of her. One arm lies straight by her side. The left hand lies casually on the pillow, as though she had merely fallen into a deep, narcotic sleep, was waiting to be awakened by a kiss. A diamond and emerald necklace, dangling loose where once it hugged the collarbone. Two gold bangles round the decayed remains of a pink satin fingerless evening glove. And on the third finger, a baguette-cut solitaire and a thin gold wedding band.

Edmund's wedding band.

Because I know without needing to be told that I am looking at the mortal remains of Lucinda Callington–Warbeck–Wattestone.

Chapter Seventy-Three

What Happened in Between

I wasn't thinking straight. I'd caught a serious clout against the door and my head was jangled, but even then, even at that point, I was getting my story right in my head, turning myself into the victim and him into the villain. Andy went upstairs – he was muttering something about painkillers, I remember – and I took the opportunity to make good my escape.

Like I say: I wasn't thinking straight. But the last day comes back to me in sporadic bursts. The seat burning my thighs as I chucked myself into a car that had been sitting out on the street all morning and drove off without waiting, as I usually would, on the kerb, while the aircon kicked in. The light, near-blinding without sunspecs, bouncing off the white-painted Queenslanders along the highway. Difficulty breathing because my nose seemed to be running. Stopping off at one of those stores you find in seaside towns – all white bread and animal-fat Popsicles – and picking up a pack of Longbeach because they were the only smokes they had behind the counter. Ripping the pack open there and then and sparking up with hands that shook like aspen leaves, and this chick at the register, a slack-jawed larrikin with the sort of complexion you can only get from a lifetime spent indoors serving and eating cheese toasties, taking her finger out of her nose and saying 'Hey! There's no smoking in here!' as though I was shitting on her countertop or something. And, having had the bottle knocked out of me, I couldn't find a response. Just gave her a flash of the blackening bruise around my eye, dropped the smoke on the lino, ground it out with my foot and left.

When I got back into the car I saw in the rear-view mirror that there was blood all down my front. My nose had been bleeding and I'd not noticed. My face and throat were a mass of congealing gore. I think I was still in shock, as I hadn't felt anything. No pain, no particular emotion: just a fuzzy blankness and a desire for peace.

It makes you wonder, doesn't it? That you'd see a woman covered in blood and only think to complain about her smoking?

After that I go blank again. The next thing I remember is pulling through the gates at our property and noticing that I was yawning. Big, grasping yawns, that cracked my stiffening jaw and gripped my spine. I'd driven the twenty clicks without registering a metre of it. The pain had started to kick in. A dull throb at the back of my head and the sort of ache that feels like nails on blackboard under the skin of my face. I could barely keep my eyes open. Blinked – winced – blinked again, felt tears forming as another yawn ripped itself out of me.

The house came into sight. It seemed a very, very long way away: lost among trees and more mirage than reality. I eased my foot off the gas, trickled up the hill and pulled over on the edge of the turning circle, under the fountain. They have a fountain in the front of the house, my folks. It looks a bit like Southfork. *Dallas* was the show that informed my mother's aspirations during the backroom years.

Turning off the ignition and pulling on the parking brake seemed to eat up the last of my energy. I guess the blow to the head did me more damage than I initially realised. Now the car was still, the draught from the aircon suddenly cut, a wave of nausea flooded through me. It was as though someone had unzipped my spine and my muscles had come unplugged. Slumping back against the headrest, I raised one leaden arm and dropped my hand on to the horn. Watched, as though through the thick glass windows of an aquarium, as the front door opened and my mother and Yaya emerged, crossed their arms in irritation at the disturbance, and, realising that it was me, hurried forward across the brickwork paving.

Our lounge. Mum and Yaya leaning over me, brows furrowed with concern, not a word coming out of Mum's mouth about the damage to her soft furnishings, though to be fair she did spread the wipe-clean tablecloth from the verandah beneath me before she let me lie down on the couch. Yaya had filled a plastic pudding basin with a robust solution of antiseptic and hot water and dabbed at my face with a sponge she'd fetched from the washing-up bowl in the kitchen. The effects of the one, no doubt, cancelling out the effects of the other.

It was the dabbing that brought me back to my senses. It was as much jab as dab. The combination of bruises, broken skin, astringent and my grandmother's none-too-steady hand was enough to bring Dillinger back from the dead. Djab. It was like being headbutted by a dobermann that had got itself attacked by a swarm of bees. Djab.

I grabbed her by the wrist. 'Yaya,' I said, 'if you do that again I'll have to kill you.'

'Ah, she's alive,' said Yaya. 'Alive and still got her dirty mouth.'

My mum had lit up one of her menthols, was studying me with that hard look she gets when things go wrong.

'What in'a hell happanda you?' she enquired. 'Have you got in another fight or something?'

Still groggy, I took a few seconds to remember.

Mum and Yaya, standing side by side, glaring at me like a pair of owls.

'I think I'm going to be sick,' I said, partly to stall for time.

'Well, there's a surprise,' said Yaya, reached behind the couch and produced the blue plastic bucket she uses for cleaning the kitchen floor. This has been the receptacle for family nausea since I can remember. She handed it to my mother, who held it out to me.

It's a strange thing, with lies, how often they become truths. The moment I saw the bucket, I felt my gorge rise in response. I grabbed the rim and threw up, loudly and violently, and my mum, holding it steady, stroked my hair off my forehead the way that only mums can do.

'That's it, lovey.' Her voice was soothing, with not a trace of the disgust a normal person would be feeling under these circs. 'Get it out. You'll feel better once it's over.'

Yaya left the room and came back. When I looked up, she was standing beside my mother with a glass of water in one hand and a wodge of kitchen roll in the other. Silently, she handed them to me, watched as I drained the glass and mopped the sweat from my face, then equally silently, she took them back and laid them down on the coffee table. Went and sat on the couch on the far side, hands folded in her lap.

Mum pulled the gilt and marble ashtray across the table and perched beside it on one corner.

'Did he do this? Jesus, look at the state of you. Do you want us to call a doctor?'

I shook my head. Doctors. Nuh-uh. Doctors mean reports. Doctors meant I would go down on record as the kind of sap who gets beaten up by her boyfriend.

'Are you sure?' asked Yaya. 'I think that nose might be broken.'

'No,' I said, firmly. 'It'll be OK.'

Mum stubbed out her cigarette, half-smoked. 'Can always get it fixed later, I suppose,' she said. 'Was never much of a nose, anyways. So. This door you walked into—'

'I didn't walk into a door.'

'OK. Now we're getting somewhere.'

I hate myself now. I am a liar. I am a liar and I've only just realised the full consequence of my lie. There's Lucy lying there dead in front of me, and I'm cold all over because it's made me realise the truth about myself. I killed Andy as sure as Edmund killed his first wife. The fact that neither of us knew about it makes us no less culpable.

There are moments in life that you only realise were pivotal much, much later on. This was one of them. I had a choice, in those few seconds, as to what sort of person I would be in the future. I could be the person who told the truth and took the consequences. Or I could get some sympathy, be the victim, come out the Good Guy in the eyes of the world. These were my choices and I'm damned for ever by the one I took.

Mum sparked up another menthol. 'Yaya,' she said, 'Call Don.'

'No,' I said.

'Too bloody right yes,' she said. 'Your father's going to want to know about this. What were you doing, letting him do this to you, anyway?'

I don't know what made me do it. Weakness. Pride. Revenge. Fear. None of them motivations to throw away someone's life by.

But I did it anyway. I started crying.

'That bastard,' said Mum. 'That *bastard*. It's OK, lovey. We won't let him get you. You're safe now.'

And once I'd started crying, I couldn't stop. Months of slow death, of frustration and rage and loss and self-loathing and deep, deep shame.

She lit another fag off the butt of the old one. Waited while I howled out my misery. That's my mum. Never one with the cuddles, never one with empty words of comfort. She was waiting until I'd calmed, because she's never any good until she can take action.

Yaya fiddled with her worry beads. Clickety click click.

Eventually I slowed down. My head hurt, and so did my body. And my heart was the worst of all. Betrayed and ashamed, I lay and rubbed my forehead, felt the pull on my swollen skin.

Mum spoke. 'So what do you want to do about it?' she asked. 'Do you want to talk to him? Do you want your father to talk to him? Do you want him out of the house? What do you want, Melody?'

I couldn't think of an answer. I could barely think at all.

She waited a while, looked at me with that hard, judgemental, well-get-up-and-do-something expression of hers. 'Well?' she said. 'What do you want to do?'

'I don't care,' I told her. 'I don't want to see him. I wish he was bloody dead. I wish he was in hell.'

Chapter Seventy-Four

Choices

It takes a while until I realise what I'm seeing. I don't mean Lucy. I mean what's round her neck. I mean that the diamond and emerald necklace is more of an emerald necklace with diamonds. I mean that, against the shrivelled skin, in the cavity of her collarbone, there lies an emerald the size of a pigeon's egg. The Callington Emerald.

The irony isn't hard for me to see. I've found the lost fortune and there's absolutely squat I can do about it. I've found the lost fortune and most likely lost my life in the process.

And there's something else, which takes longer to come to me, and it's this: I've been thinking it was Mary, all Mary. I've been thinking that Beatrice was just a foul-natured old harpy, but I've been underestimating her. Because the last time the emerald was seen, it was hanging round her neck. And there's only one way it can have ended up round Lucy's.

By the time the candle has burned down to two-thirds of its length, and I've cried myself hoarse and my fingernails are cracked and torn from where I have been scratching mindlessly at the tapestry-covered door, I understand that, however extreme the situation, you are always left, right up to the wire, with choices. It never gets any better. However powerless, beat up, imprisoned, humiliated, the choices never go away.

I could choose, right now, for instance, looking at Lucy, who obviously failed to extract herself from this black and stuffy tomb, to accept my fate, make my peace with God, prepare myself to die with all the dignity I can muster.

Well, fuck that for a game of soldiers. If I'm going to die, I'm going to die fighting. My baby is going to breathe real air if it kills me. Which, of course, it probably will. I may be the architect of my own misfortune, but that doesn't mean I should carry on adding wings and cornices and blind staircases until the whole edifice collapses.

By the time I have emerged from my hysteria-induced funk, I am shaking with cold instead of emotion. The first threat to my survival is hypothermia. My growing lethargy, without a doubt, is related to my body temperature. I have two choices: freeze to death or plunder Lucy's suitcase. And once I've done that, I have to find out everything I can about my prison before the light runs out.

So I plunder Lucy's suitcase. She's dead. What does she care?

But I still feel the irony of the distaste I feel for digging through the belongings of a dead person, considering that it's the entire driving force behind those who have imprisoned us. The quantity and type of belongings it took for Mary and Beatrice to convince Edmund that his wife had deserted him are slightly pathetic, bear sad testimony to the simplicity of the man. They're all party clothes. Party clothes and handbags, and just a couple of pairs of the type of shoes that fall apart if they encounter terrain rougher than shag-pile. The tawdriness of the late sixties writ large: geometric prints, empire waistlines, narrow velvet ribbons tied in bows below the bust-line. Thigh-skimming, long sleeved, bouffant-haired, pretend little-girl clothing; shiny plastic bags; square toed patent shoes, striped and Paisley tights of the sort that make your legs look like sofa arms. A jumble of jewellery – necklaces, earrings, rings – thrown in in a tangle, as though the thrower were enraged at the necessity of wasting something so valuable. Real gem stones: it must have pained Beatrice to throw away such a chunk of the family fortune for the sake of verisimilitude.

She must have been so pretty, this leggy brunette with the citified wardrobe. Pretty and petite. These clothes are sizes too small for me: not unflattering sizes-too-small, but impossible sizes too small. The delicate fabrics, already crumbling with age, rip apart as I try to stretch them over my shoulders, fall into tatters held together only by the stitching at the neck and seams. I can barely cram the ends of my feet into the toes of her shoes.

It's hopeless. All I can achieve is a sort of silk festoon affect that, even layered as I try it, is precious little protection against the February cold. I wonder briefly if she *had* any normal clothes, but of course I know the truth: these clothes are the image of Lucy that Mary and Beatrice wanted rid of. What they wanted to expunge was that part that was the greatest threat, the greatest effrontery to the dowdy grandeur that sees respectability as paramount; the part, probably, that appealed to Edmund the most: her glamour. They wanted done with her, and these clothes are a metaphor for all they hated, as my credit cards and car keys and cellphone are for what they hate about me. And besides, if you want a man to hate his ex, there is nothing like suggesting, even subliminally, that she has taken off for a life of cocktails and love affairs. Much harder to expunge her memory if he thinks she's nursing orphan kiddies in Calcutta.

There's a bottle of Chanel still sealed up and a quarter full. It smells, like all old perfume, faintly of bitter almonds.

'Oh God, Lucy,' I say to her, 'I'm sorry.'

She doesn't answer. There's a bottle of some Guerlain scent in my own bag. I noticed it when I was looking for the lighter.

'Shit,' I say suddenly. Because I've remembered the cellphone. Good grief, girl, how could you forget something as obvious as that?

I leap up, motley tatters drifting behind me, and snatch up my bag. Tip it out all over the floor, plastic and metal and glass gushing through the zipper. Sift through the pile, wishing to God I had picked something other than the high-fashion thumb-sized handset I did, because every second it takes to find it is another second I have to stay in this prison.

My pulse races again, that bitch hope playing havoc with my heart. *Of course, of course, it's so simple.* I just have to call for help and someone will come, someone will find their way behind the wardrobe and save me. I can't believe I didn't think of it before . . .

It's not there. Of course it isn't.

I sit back, heavily, feel hope rush away. The walls seem suddenly closer, the light from the candle weaker. *I will never get out. She couldn't. What hubris has convinced me that I am stronger, brighter, more resourceful than Tilly's mother was?*

Stop it. Stop it. You have so little time . . .

I wipe my eyes with the back of my hand, cast about for some new shred of hope to cling to.

There's precious little. The contents of my bag are useless: the pointless, flimsy, throwaway fripperies of life in the twenty-first century. Plastic that bends, objects designed to weigh nothing so that little old princess me doesn't have to strain her shoulder carrying them around. There's nothing resembling a tool in here, let alone a weapon. Nothing I could use to attract attention short of breaking up the furniture and setting fire to it, and I don't fancy my chances of surviving the fumes long enough for that to do any good.

They'd find the bodies, at least.

I'll save the last of the lighter. When I get to the point where the thirst is overtaking me, when I think I'm sinking into delirium, I'll put it to the tapestries. It's a faster way to die, and—

Stop it. Don't think that way. Don't you dare give up.

The only heavy object in here is the candlestick. An old-fashioned brass one made for coshing burglars. Maybe I could use it to attract attention. I know no-one uses this wing, that the chances of being heard are minimal, but if I keep it up for long enough, they've got to start a hunt for me at some point. I'll just bang away and bang away and eventually someone will hear. Or maybe I could even break through the wall. It can't be more than lath and plaster under there.

I try pulling one of the tapestries away, to see the wall behind. But it's not nailed, or hanging from rods: it's been glued in place, with some fixative that is strong enough to tear my remaining fingernails. I try the carpet, but it's the same. I am, effectively, in a padded cell. Even the ceiling, five metres up, is lined with a heavy cloth hunting scene. No amount of shouting, or banging, is going to make any difference. It would be like thumping a feather bed.

He must be waking up around now, wherever he is. Waking up and

451

thinking about coming to find me. What will he find? Will they have packed my stuff away, removed the lot, or left it scattered about the room, just a few prime objects gone, to show the hurry in which I left?

Hopelessly, I thump a couple of times on the wall anyway. Allow a couple of tears to fall. What do I do? What do I do now? I have to get out of the cold. The shivering is so exaggerated now, I can barely keep my hands still.

Choices again.

I could just let it take me. Hypothermia is a relatively kind death, or so I've read. It's more of a slide into unconsciousness and coma than anything else. It's got to be better than the cramps, the breathlessness, the slow agony of dying from thirst. But there's my baby. It's not just me. It's the two of us, facing this end together. If I let them take me now, there will be no chance at all.

I eye my only option in the fading candlelight. I don't have long now. I have to decide. The light will soon be gone, and if I'm going to do this, I would rather it were not in the dark.

I can't do it. I can't. I'd rather die . . .

I speak to myself out loud, try to drown out the voice inside.

'That's the choice, Melody. You've got to do it, or you *will* die.'

But look at her. Look at her. She's dead. *I can't touch her. What if she . . . what if she . . .*

There's not a nerve in my body that doesn't scream out against the unnatural nature of what I'm about to do. It's grave-robbing. It goes against every taboo, every disease-avoiding, dignity-in-death instinct I have. But the choice I have is no choice at all.

I cross the silent carpet, stand over the bed. Gaze down with pity and revulsion at the sunken eye sockets, the protruding teeth. How long did it take her to die, all alone in here? How long will it take me to join her, wherever she is?

Lucy is draped in a heavy coverlet, like the one on my marital bed. It's huge and thick, will wrap round me at least three times. And underneath, under the bedclothes, there is . . . oh, God, I mustn't think. I mustn't think about it.

I reach out and take the cover between my fingers.

She's dead, OK? She doesn't need it. You need it. She would

452

understand. She would be doing the same thing herself.

'Oh, God,' I repeat. 'Oh, God, Lucy, I'm sorry.'

And I lift it off. Grit my teeth as I feel it peel back, pull away from the form beneath. This is too much. It's more than anyone should have to—

And it's off. Soft and solid in my arms, my only route to salvation.

I don't even look. Turn my back and walk round the bed to the other side. Wrap the drape – my winding sheet – round my body and lie, back to the corpse, on the empty side of the mattress. Pull up my knees, tuck my hands between my thighs and try to quell the nausea. Lie for a moment like this as, gradually, the shaking slows and the weight of exhaustion drifts over me.

And then I take the final choice of all. Reach out a hand and pick up the candle.

Blow it out.

Chapter Seventy-Five

Precious Life

There are miracles. Every day there are miracles.

In the dark, there is no time. I don't sleep. But soon, I'm not awake either.

Instead I go to beautiful places inside my head. They say your life passes before your eyes when you die: mine passes in slow motion. I go home, and dive off the barrier reef. I clamber up mossy steps in Angkor Wat and watch the sun rise over a thousand gracious pinnacles. I hear the morning songs of Bali, taste the sharp dawn mist over the rice terraces, dig my fingers into the lustrous thickness of his hair and close my eyes.

The places I wanted to take him. Petra and Ephesus and Karnak and Uluru and Ubud. I wanted to feed him Moreton Bay bugs and mangosteen. I wanted us to lie together under a mosquito net, listening to the jungle symphony in the night.

Time slides past, unchanging, only the sound of my breath, the sound of my heart.

Our baby. I feel it inside me, feel it die with me. Our child. His nose, my mouth: the promise of our future; the chances that we had, the chance to get it right. No restrictions, no history, our character flaws wiped out, cancelled. I see us, stupid, stupid, all the things we will not know: the birthdays, the ponies, the skinned knees, bath-time, my husband sleeping, this cheated life clutched to his chest.

My tongue long since cleaved to the roof of my mouth, my lips, cracked, fallen open to let dry air in, ulcerate the membranes. A couple of times I dry-heave into the pillow, but it brings no relief. My head is filled with searing white light; a circular saw hacks at my skull, drills pierce my joints. My breath comes fast, periodically,

454

heart pounding as though with panic, hands, feet freezing though they are covered by the blanket. This is dehydration kicking in. Perhaps I should have let myself succumb, as I wondered, to the cold.

Instead, I take us away, to Koh Chang, to the wet heat of tropical night, and we walk along the beach to the bar strip, lie on mats on the sand beneath a million stars, drink long, cold gin and tonics, glasses frosty with ice, spicy little Bali limes crushed into the coldness. We watch the fire juggler at the tide's edge, teeth flashing in his flame-burnished face. And I look at Rufus and I am filled with peace. Love saves you, warms you. I will never leave you, darling. Wherever I am, I will always be with you.

I can no longer swallow. There's not enough spit in my mouth. To die like this: preserving energy to the very last. Holding on in the darkness because the darkness beyond is worse.

Miracles happen every day. I know that now. You were my miracle, my salvation and I will never let you go. My heart. My beating heart.

And then there are sounds, muffled, and I realise that they are no longer in my head. There is someone on the other side of the door, and they are trying to get in.

Chapter Seventy-Six

The Polyester Angels

And then there are voices. Two of them, suddenly distinct, as the barrier is moved back.

Nessa: 'Christ. Yes. There's a door back here. Good boy! *Good* boy!'

And Roly. Sounding pleased as punch with the praise: 'Well, quick. See if you can get it open.'

'*Good* boy!' she says again. 'Who's the clever, *clever* baby! Go and close the door, for God's sake. We don't want somebody finding us. Ooh, you clever, *clever* boy!'

And then the latch clicks and the door begins to swing open. Nessa calls back over her shoulder: 'You were right. There's a room back here. Strewth! We'd never have found it . . .'

I see dim light filtering through the doorway. My mouth doesn't work. I don't have enough saliva to swallow, let alone speak.

The light reduces dramatically. Roly must have come back. 'Is she in there? Pwooagh.' This latter sound is an expression of disgust.

'Well, there's *something* in there,' says Nessa.

Torchlight plays over the walls. I try to croak out some word, some indication that I'm still alive, but all I hear is the thin whistle of air in my throat. I try to turn on to my back. It takes me three goes. I'm frightened by the deterioration in my strength in the time I've been drifting.

'Something moved,' says Nessa, urgently, 'I'm sure it did. Come on. She's in here. She's got to be.'

And then there is a scrabbling, wriggling presence between them, and a body barrels across the floor. And I am lying there, dry-weeping as I feel Perkins's filthy breath, his warm wet tongue

456

slobbering deliciously over my face, my cracked lips. I extract an arm from my rank swaddlings, throw it around his neck and choke-sob into his warm silken ears.

Perkins puts his forepaws up on the bed, pants and covers me in mucus. Nothing, nothing has ever felt so good.

'I think he's found her,' says Nessa.

'Is she alive?'

'I don't know. Come on. Mel? Are you there? Are you OK? Can you answer me?'

The torchlight moves once again, hits the carpet, the far wall, the ceiling. She's climbing through. I turn my head to see her.

'She's moving!' She calls back over her shoulder. 'I don't think she can talk but she's – Jesus.'

'What?' asks Roly.

The beam has landed on Lucy's face. Stays there, wobbling, as Nessa drinks in what she sees. Then it flicks forward and she sees me, sees the whites of my eyes and says 'Jesus' again.

Roly clambers through the doorway. 'What is it?'

She's halfway to me. 'She's here. Look.'

And she's down on her knees, pushing Perkins out of the way and covering my face with her tears. Sensible Nessa, bawling against my cheek. 'It's OK. We found you. You're OK. Oh God—'

I put a finger against her miraculous face and run it along its length. It's so warm, so soft.

'Have you got the water?'

'Yuh,' he says. 'She's alive?'

'Yes, of course she's fu— yes. Yes, she is. She's pretty crook, but she's still with us.'

Roly appears over Nessa's shoulder. Hands her a plastic bottle. 'Hello, Mel,' he says, as though he were at a pheasant shoot. 'How are you?'

And I see his eyes widen as he sees past me in the dark. 'Bloody *hell*!' he barks.

Perkins bounces and wags, and Nessa twists the top off the bottle, slowly, slowly, like she's running on frame-by-frame. Holds it to my lips. I grab at it as the water touches my tongue, try to snatch it from her, but she holds firm, prises my fingers away. 'Slowly,' she says. 'You'll throw it up. Just a little. It's OK. You can have more. Oh God, Mel, I heard those bitches and I had a hard time making myself believe it, but . . . oh God, I'm so sorry. I should've looked earlier.'

'Who the hell is *that*?' asks Roly.

Nessa doesn't reply, watches me and controls the trickle of life into my body. I look up into her eyes like a small child, feel the miracle. I want to gulp, to slather it over my parched skin, to tip the bottle back and let it pour, pour, pour, but she holds it steady, pulls it back to wait to see if I've coped.

'Bloody *hell*,' Roly repeats after a few seconds' contemplation. I hear Perkins's tail slide rough against the carpet. God, that dog: I will never, ever again sneer at the Englishman's love of the canine.

'I told you,' says Roly, 'he was a good dog, didn't I?'

I try to say something, but my mouth is still dry as stones.

'Don't try and talk,' says Nessa. Tips another couple of tablespoons' worth between my lips. I close my eyes, feel it. Breathe out and let my sandpaper eyelids drop closed.

'I think it's Tilly's mother,' Nessa finally replies to Roly's question.

'Tilly's mother? The one who – oh.'

She nods.

'I didn't – but that would mean that . . .'

'I guess so,' she says.

'Poor woman. My God. What a way to die . . .'

Poor old Roly. Thinking always takes him a while, the great, wonderful life-saving galoot.

'Poor Tilly,' he says. 'This'll knock the stuffing out of her.'

Chapter Seventy-Seven
Saved by the Cell

You would have thought it would, wouldn't you? But it doesn't. If anything, after the initial explosion of tears, it has the opposite effect. Because Tilly gets so angry that I secretly wonder if I shouldn't take Lucy away in case she jiggles her to death.

One of life's great injustices: that redheads are the people least advised to cry when they have, by and large, more reason than most to do so. Tilly looks like she has been left out in the rain. She looks like she has both been bleached and gone rusty. Her eyes have that gooseberry-jam look about them and her nose, prone to colour at the best of times, would guide Santa and his reindeer through the whole of Christmas Eve and still have wattage left over to light Times Square for New Year.

But what she's not is someone whose stuffing has been knocked out. Tilly is grim with rage as she clutches the necklace with fingers so rigid that I think its pattern will be imprinted on her palms for life. Her mouth forms a single straight line from the lobe of one ear to the other, and the tendons stand out in her neck like hawsers. Looking at her, I almost pity Mary and Beatrice. Not much, though.

Tilly has been apologising pretty much her whole life for the inconvenience of her existence, for the fact that her very appearance is a constant reminder to her father of his own heartbreak. Having her need to mourn squashed by people who told her over and over how grateful she should be. Now she's found out about the source of her pain, I don't suppose either gratitude or forgiveness are high on her agenda.

She is so angry that she has stopped speaking. She sits silently on the sofa, Lucy bobbling about on her knee, and glares towards infinity, lips occasionally forming tight little words that never come out.

I'm lying on the other sofa with a drip in my arm. There are advantages to getting rescued by an SRN. I've been gone three days. I still don't know if it feels like more, or less. Both, I guess. Roly sits, legs akimbo, on an armchair, his heavenly, heavenly hunting dog grinning between his knees. Nessa is on the rug in front of the fire.

Tilly may have lost her voice, but I've found mine. 'I don't get how you worked it out,' I say.

Nessa fiddles with an unlit cigarette. Even she respects the lungs of the newborn.

'You're bloody lucky I did,' she replies.

'You don't say.'

'It was that damn cellphone. You know what? You can be grateful you got done over by a bunch of luddites. They probably thought they'd switched it off, but as you'd got the lock on, all it did was show no display. I heard it ringing. Knew it had to be yours. No-one else I can think of would have a Tom Jones tune on their mobile. Not around here, anyway. And you only put it on there in order to annoy your mother-in-law. And a lucky thing too. Everyone thinks you're gone. Your car's gone, and all your stuff. Rufus thinks you cleared, and I don't blame him. It's not like it would be the first time, would it?'

'I know,' I say. 'I'm sorry.'

'Don't apologise to me,' she says. 'I'm not the one who needs an apology. Mel, I have to say, you've not handled things well.'

'Thank you.'

'No, really. He thinks you've gone. Didn't even question it. He's furious. And those bloody harpies—'

'She's right, you know,' adds Roly. 'Tried talking to him m'self, but you know – chaps talking to chaps – not so good at it, I'm afraid. Always knew you weren't a quitter myself. 'Fraid he doesn't seem to think the same.'

'What did he say?' I ask, my heart sinking.

Roly pauses, considers. Tries to work out how to put it gently, gives up. 'Said he thought he'd made a mistake. Terrible mistake, actually. Those were his exact words. Said he should never have married you.'

'Oh, God.' I feel awful. A sick headache slams into the back of my neck, makes me close my eyes.

'Sorry,' adds Roly.

'No, no,' I manage. 'Not your fault. Mine.'

'What exactly did you say to him?' asks Nessa.

'Terrible things,' I say. 'I'm too ashamed to say. I don't blame him.'

'Don't give up just yet,' says Nessa. 'I'm sure he didn't mean it.'

'Oh, I think he did,' says Roly. Colours and adds another 'sorry'.

'I *knew* you hadn't gone,' says Tilly suddenly. 'Those – are you telling me Granny was in on this? I can't, I don't . . . oh God. My own grandmother.'

Nessa looks up at her, and her expression is a strange mix of trepidation and sympathy. 'Yeah. I'm sorry, Tilly. I think – I can't see any way she won't have been. And she's been . . . well, happy over the last few days. Sort of triumphant. I thought it was because she thought she'd seen Mel off, but then I heard the phone and I knew Mel wouldn't have gone without it. She's bloody welded to that thing.'

'She always hated my mother,' says Tilly. 'She wouldn't let me talk about her. I always thought it was because . . . and all that time, she knew. She *knew*. Oh God, Mummy. I can't bear it. It's *unbearable*.'

'It is,' says Nessa. 'I don't know. We have to think.'

'So the phone . . .?'

'Lucky coincidence. I was going along the Egyptian corridor when I heard it ringing. I wouldn't normally be there. Can't remember the last time I used it, but the Georgian staircase has come loose from the wall and I didn't trust it.'

'The whole house is falling apart,' says Tilly. 'It's coming down around their ears.'

'It was such a weird sound, I almost convinced myself I was hallucinating it. I mean: "Delilah" coming out from behind a door in an empty room. It actually took me five minutes to realise what I'd been hearing. And then I couldn't remember which room it was. I had to go and get my phone from Beatrice's room and walk up and down calling your number till I tracked it down. It was on its last legs. Another couple of hours and the battery would have run out altogether. And it was so quiet I wouldn't have heard it at all if there had been any background noise. It was in one of the wardrobes. Buried among a great heap of your other stuff. Everything: clothes, makeup, jewellery, books, pots of glop. They must have shoved it in there in a hurry. Maybe they were planning to get rid of it later. I don't know. Maybe they thought they could just leave it there to rot. It's not like anybody's used that room since I've been here. And when I found that lot, I went and found Roly.'

Rufus. I'm lying there thinking about Rufus. I can't help it. My eyes are full of tears. That in a few short months he can have changed from loving me so much, from being my champion, the one who believed in me, to this.

'Why didn't you go and find Rufus?'

'Mary and Hilary took him up to London two days ago,' says Tilly. 'They said, if you came back, it would serve you right if he was gone. I suppose they wanted him out of the house in case he went looking for you while you could still make a noise. Oh God, they did the same thing with Daddy when . . . That fucking *bitch*.'

I've never heard Tilly swear. I look over at her and she's bent over Lucy, clutching her so tightly I'm afraid she'll suffocate her.

'Oh babe,' says Nessa. Crawls across the floor and gently insinuates herself between mother and baby. Enfolds Tilly in a hug and rocks her, gesticulating with a single finger at Roly to come and get the child. And Tilly's really bawling, now, mouth open and howling at the memory of her lost mother, fingers digging into Nessa's back so viciously that it must only be granite will that stops Nessa from howling too.

'I thought she hated me.' The words spill out in a torrent. 'I thought, all this time, she'd left me, it was something I'd done. I thought, I must have been so bad, such a *bad* child, that she would leave me like that. Never look back. Never care what happened to me. And Daddy's been broken since it happened, no sort of man, no sort of father, just . . . And all the time . . . all the time she was there, lying there, and I never knew. All these years I've hated her, and it wasn't her fault. It wasn't . . . Oh God, what she must have been thinking! To die like that, my *mother*!'

Roly's chin has vanished into his neck as he goggles at Tilly over her daughter's head. Someone who never had a lot of luck with family himself, I can't think what he's thinking right now.

'Tilly,' he says, 'I don't know what to say to you. I understand that nothing – nothing – will make this better. We must do something. We can't let this . . . I think we should call the police. Do *something*.'

Tilly sits back, looks at him over Nessa's shoulder, and just like that, snap, the anger is back. Anger and something else – resolution. Her eyes are narrow and glittering, jaw hard with vengeance.

'No,' she says. 'No, not yet. I don't want her to think she can be forgiven. I don't want that. She took everything from me and she can't get away with it.'

I don't know, now, if she's talking about Mary or Beatrice. Both, it turns out: two matriarchs in one.

'Mary will get jail,' she says. 'Sure. She'll get jail and I'll laugh as I see her go there, but what are they going to do to a hundred-year-old woman? What's going to happen to *her*? She has no conscience, she has no heart, and they'll say, but look, she's too old, what can we do?'

We wait, in silence, all of us.

'They took everything,' she says. 'They took everything that mattered, and all for a house. All so they could mother the heir of Bourton Allhallows. And for what? For *what*?'

'I don't want them to get away that easily,' she says. 'They took everything from me, and she took everything from my father.'

'They took everything,' she says, 'and I want to take everything back. I want to take their sons.'

Chapter Seventy-Eight

Contact

I'm in the bath and I get a phone call from my father. It's my second bath in six hours. I can still smell my ordeal on my skin, in my hair, and I don't know if I will ever get it off. The caller display reads 'UNKNOWN', but I pick it up anyway, because, despite the fact that our making contact at this point would throw all our plans into disarray, I can't help but hope that it might be Rufus. If I'd known who it was, I wouldn't have picked up. I can't be planning a retribution for one crime and sweeping an identical one under the carpet. Even I'm not that much of a hypocrite. Or that much of a coward.

But Rufus hasn't made a single call to my phone since I vanished. I know he's washed his hands of me, given up, no longer intends to humiliate himself for the sake of our relationship. The months of game-playing have ground him down, and he's given up. I know it's my own fault.

I don't discuss this with them. But in an ironic, unintentional way, it seems that, if it wasn't for my own family, I would probably be breathing my last sometime around now. Because the only calls registered, apart from the half-dozen from Nessa when she was tracking the phone through the house, are ten unidentified-number hang-ups, the sort you get when someone's called you from abroad. One of these must have been the one that Nessa heard in the Egyptian corridor. And I can't think of anyone who would be calling me that consistently without leaving a message other than my family.

So I pick it up, say: 'Hello?' and my father, who's calling at 6 a.m. his time, says: 'Please don't hang up, Princess.'

I consider doing just that. Say, eventually: 'What do you want?'

'What do you mean, what do I want? You're my daughter.'

I don't say anything in reply to this. Listen to him breathing. It sounds as though he has a bit of a cold.

'What's going on, Melody? I don't understand.'

I continue the silent treatment.

So he says: 'Look. Your mum's got a temper. You've inherited it. You both say things you don't mean, but you've never done this before. This is crazy. You've always shouted at each other, and you've always got over it. We don't sulk in our family.'

'No,' I say. 'We do other things instead, right?'

'Oh, right,' he says, 'so you've got some other gripe?'

I bite my lip. 'Well, 'gripe' is an interesting way of putting it.'

'So do you mind telling me what it is, then?'

'You know what I'm talking about,' I say, because I'll never get used to it and saying it out loud is almost impossible to me.

'No, I don't,' says Dad. 'You women speak in code.'

'OK, I'll spell it out. I don't want anything to do with you. I don't want to talk to you and I don't want to see you and I don't want any contact with you.'

My dad's cold suddenly sounds like it's got a lot worse. 'But why, Melody?' he asks in a tremulous voice. 'I don't understand . . .'

'Ask Mum if you can't work it out.'

'Melody, I'm asking *you*.'

OK. Have it your way.

'I found out about Andy,' I tell him.

A silence. 'I thought you knew about that?'

'KNEW about it?' I feel the bile rising. 'What you *talking* about? Do you think if I'd known about it for one minute, I'd have let you . . . let you do *that* – if I'd known about it?'

'But, Melody, we were only doing what you wanted.'

'Wanted?' I slosh upright in the soapy water. 'WANTED?'

'You said you wanted to get rid of him . . .'

I practically drop the phone. 'No I didn't! No I *didn't*!'

'Well, what *did* you say, then?'

'I said . . .' I don't have an answer to this. 'I said I wished he was in hell,' I finish.

465

'Well, it was the best we could do,' says Dad.

And I'm yelling at him. 'How can you be so flippant about it? How can you behave like it's a joke? Don't you understand what you've done?'

'Of course it's not a joke,' says Dad. 'It's not to you, anyway, and we wouldn't have done it if we didn't think it was what needed to be done.'

I am practically choking on my rage. 'I don't—'

And then he chortles. Actually chortles. 'It was pretty funny, though,' he says. 'He wasn't exactly dignified, splashing about begging us to let him back on board. I would have thought you'd have found it pretty—'

'Get *away* from me! Oh my God! You're – you're *profane*! How can you talk about it like that? You're – oh – God, you disgust me!'

He starts to speak, but I cut him off by hitting the hang-up button. And then I duck under the water to wash myself clean, and I'm shaking all over. Pour half a bottle of Tilly's Crabtree and Evelyn Aloe Vera shampoo over my head and start to scrub. I feel I will never be clean again.

The phone starts to ring again. I snatch it up, snarl: 'Leave me alone! Just leave me alone! Forget you had a daughter! I'm not your daughter! I don't want to be the child of fucking *murderers*!' And hang it up so hard I nearly break the button. Hit the off switch and throw the handset over on to the pile of clothes I've left in the corner. There are tears streaming down my face. Gritting my teeth, I drop under the surface again. Barely hear the tap on the door that announces that Tilly's outside.

'Are you decent?'

'Come in,' I tell her.

She looks concerned.

'I thought I heard shouting.'

I swipe a soapy arm across my eyes. Bad mistake. Grope about for something to wipe them off with and find a soft fluffy towel being pressed into my hand.

'Yes,' I tell her, 'no . . .' I can't quite stop a sob. 'Oh God, how did we get these families? What did we do to deserve them?'

Tilly perches on the linen basket. 'I don't know. I wonder if I did something in a past life, sometimes.'

'Well, I don't believe in that bullshit,' I tell her bluntly. 'All that bloody made-up cack designed to make you say, yeah, you're right, I drew the short straw and other people drew the long one but it's all my fault. I deserve this.'

'Was that your mum?'

'My dad.'

'I don't suppose you want to—'

'No.' I massage the tension spots at the base of my skull and screw my eyes up. 'No, not right now. I'll tell you sometime, but not now. It's just – I just – I don't want to be like them. They do awful things and I don't want to be like them.'

Tilly shakes her head. A bit sadly. 'Nobody has to be like anything,' she says. 'I hope that's true. I really hope so. How are you feeling?'

'Awful. How about you?'

'I can truthfully say I've had better days. Listen, the others are downstairs and they've got the phone. Do you feel up to coming down?'

'Sure,' I say. 'Give me five minutes.'

In the kitchen, Nessa and Roly have the new phone out of its box and are programming its number into the speed-dial on Tilly's. She's going to walk Rufus along the Egyptian corridor on some pretext or another and set it ringing as they pass the door. But not until Nessa has accidentally-on-purpose left him in a room with the baby monitor.

'Rufus is back at the house,' says Nessa. 'That's the good news. At least there's no more waiting around to be done.'

I sit down. I hardly dare ask. 'How does he seem?'

'Awful. He's lost almost as much weight as you have. He's spent most of the day shut away in your room. By the looks of him, I'd say he hasn't slept much lately. Oh, and he's been crying.'

467

'Oh God.' The thought of Rufus crying makes me want to do the same.

'Don't you join in,' says Nessa.

'What have I done to him?'

'Steady on,' says Roly. 'Not you, remember? Other people. Where's your phone?'

'Here.'

'Well, sling it over.'

I hand him the phone and everyone does a quick check to make sure they're identical. I know they all think it would be best if we used the original, but where I'm going I'm not going to be parted from my lifeline, however essential the authenticity. Roly starts ploughing through the menus on the new one.

'Listen,' he says, 'don't want to put flies in ointment and all that, but isn't Rufus going to smell a rat?'

'How so?' asks Nessa.

'Well – wife gone five days, find her in a lockup and she's walking and talking?'

'Naah,' says Nessa. 'Stick her back in there overnight and she'll be wambly enough to pass.'

'*Overnight?*' I'm not happy about this. I'd sort of imagined four or five hours.

'Sorry, love,' she says. 'Got to go for a bit of authenticity.'

'I'm sorry, too,' says Tilly. 'But she's right.'

'I mean, it doesn't have to be *total* authenticity,' says Nessa. 'As long as you're looking a bit desperate and your hair's messed up and you've got no makeup on, he'll be so fired up by his own heroism the chances are he won't notice the rest of it. Simple creatures, men. Throw 'em a stick and they'll go chasing after it. Bit of misdirection, they'll believe the moon's made of cheese.'

'Thanks,' says Roly.

'Not an insult, darling, just an observation. Paul believes to this day that if they play music it means the ice-cream van's run out of stock.'

'Daddy,' says Tilly, 'believes that Mary Fulford-Ffawkes came along and rescued him when no-one else would have him.'

This sort of puts the kibosh on the joking.

'Bugger,' says Roly, 'It doesn't seem to have "Delilah".'

'No,' I say wearily. 'I downloaded it.'

'Bit of a stumbling block.'

'Honestly,' says Nessa, 'you Amish. We'll just infrared it across.'

She switches on my phone and she and Roly start aiming the two sets at each other like schoolkids playing with rayguns. Quietly, but not quietly enough, my voicemail tone bleeps.

'Oop,' says Nessa. 'Here you go.' Throws it to me.

I lay it down on the table.

'Aren't you going to get that?'

'I'll do it later.'

'Go on,' she says. 'Might be something important.'

'I very much doubt it.'

'Don't mind us,' says Roly.

I start to protest, think: oh God, might as well just do it rather than attract attention.

It's Costa. 'Shit,' he says. 'Well, you'll be glad to know the old man's actually crying. Old girl is swearing like a macaw, but Dad's blubbing away in the garden, going on about how you called him a murderer. Shit, Melody. What is your problem? Everybody does their best for you and you can't even—'

I hit three to erase the rest of the message.

'OK?' asks Tilly.

'Double glazing,' I tell her.

No-one believes me.

'Listen, are you feeling up to this?' asks Nessa.

'Yeah, yeah,' I reply. 'If you think it'll work.'

And then I burst into tears. I don't want to go back there. I don't want to be alone in the dark again. I'm so afraid.

'I'm so afraid,' I say. 'He won't want me. It won't work.'

'Ah, come on, sweetheart,' says Nessa. 'Rufus loves the spots off you.'

'Not any more. Not after everything that's happened. He hates me.'

'Bollocks,' says Roly. 'You're knackered and things look iffy.

Stiff upper lip. Always darkest before dawn. That sort of thing.'

'He doesn't hate you. He just feels awful. He's had his heart broken, but that's not the same as hating you.'

'I'm a ball-busting, foul-mouthed *bitch*. You've no idea. You've no idea the things I said . . .'

Roly hums and hahs a bit and says something about having a fair idea, actually. Oh, arse. I thought he said they didn't talk. 'Still,' he says, 'better a ball-busting bitch to the face than a sneaky assassin creeping about in the dark, what?'

'He needs,' says Nessa, 'to know you need him. They're simple that way, men.'

'But I *do*! I *do* need him!'

'And that,' she says, 'is how come you've got to go back in there.'

'I don't *want* to go back in there.'

'I don't blame you. I wouldn't want to myself.'

'Chin up,' says Roly. 'Faint heart never won fair wossname.'

'Someone get her a drink,' says Nessa. Has a feel of my pulse for good measure and says: 'Look, Melody, we're all in this together. You're just going to have to trust us, OK? Believe me. Forty-eight hours and the whole thing will be over.'

Chapter Seventy-Nine
Two Can Play at that Game

And first up, I pay a visit to Beatrice.

Roly, of course, knows where all the secret passages are. He shows me the way into our bedroom, through which the Hilary-Mary-Roberts spectre found its way the night they walled me up: a lath-lined corridor that runs the length of the Georgian corridor, parallel to it and only eighteen inches wide. He shows me how to get all the way from the Victorian wing to the Queen Anne without showing myself in the public parts of the building. And it's Roly who knows the way into Beatrice's lair.

I don't really know what to expect. I was never exactly invited in for a visit before. I wouldn't be surprised to find her tucked up in a silk-lined coffin. But, of course, it's a room like any other at Bourton Allhallows: dusty, dark, filled with the sort of furniture they use as props for the bi-annual rerecord of *A Christmas Carol*.

I step silently through the door, which is hidden, like the one in my and Rufus's room, in the shadows beyond the drape of the four-poster. I can't see Beatrice yet, propped against her pillows, but Nessa is on the other side of the room, busying herself with tidying the pots of Polyfilla and the jars of heavy-duty chalk on the dressing table. She catches sight of me in the mirror, tips me the wink. Picks up a bottle of something pink and industrial-looking and calls: 'What's this, Mrs Wattestone? I don't think I've ever seen it before.'

This, while Beatrice has her head turned away from me, is my cue to step out and stand beside the bed. Three or four feet back so that the combination of her aged eyesight and the forty-watt miser's bulb in the bedside lamp will make the hammy makeup job we put together in the Blue Bathroom look more or less authentic.

I have blue-white skin, and magenta lips. Shadows beneath my eyes and a tracery of purple veins running across my cheeks and down my throat to plunge into the *décolletage* of my nightgown. My hair is dried and coarse, hangs in knots down my back. I look, well, *dead*.

It's not so difficult to haunt an old person. There you go: I've said it. If Beatrice were younger – if she were eighty, even – my crude disguise would be unlikely to fool her for more than a moment. I am relying on her hundred-year-old senses. That, and shock tactics, and the fact that somewhere, buried deep even in that gnarly old heart, must be a conscience of some description.

So I just stand there, hands hanging down by my sides, and wait until she notices me.

It doesn't take long. Nessa directs her gaze over to where I am standing by the simple expedient of crossing the room and walking round behind me, pretending all the while that everything is as it should be. And I don't find it hard to fill my face with contempt and dislike, for that is what I feel. An evil, evil old woman: ruthlessness slathered over with the cosmetic unguents of age and aristocracy. A creature beyond my comprehension: one who would kill to maintain the *status quo*.

Beatrice's eyes follow my friend, who continues chatting about the weather and the time of year and what Beatrice might like to eat in the morning without once glancing in my direction. She is, of course, pretending that I'm not there. And as she rounds the foot of the bed, Beatrice catches sight of me out of the corner of her eye and her head jerks round to take me in in all my glory.

Nessa stops talking. Goes into the wardrobe and busies herself with organising the clothes.

'Boo,' I say.

The effect is gratifying. If eyes really had stalks, Beatrice's would be standing out a full inch from her face. The mouth, teeth removed to a tumbler at the bedside, has formed a round black O of shock and fear.

You weren't expecting that, were you?

'Lucy says hello, Beatrice,' I say.

This is the first time I've seen her without a hat. It's only now that I realise that she is almost bald. A bald, pathetic, vicious old woman. I saw the expression on Lucy's face. She didn't die well, and that's the fate Beatrice wanted for me.

The mouth attempts to form words but nothing comes.

'She says she'll be seeing you soon,' I tell her. 'Very soon. Both of us. We'll be seeing you soon.'

Nessa emerges from the wardrobe, crosses the room carrying a navy print two-piece, humming a tune. 'Cheek to Cheek'. Good choice, Nessa.

A little smile on the corner of her mouth, she drapes the clothes over the back of a chair, turns and says: 'And which shoes would you like, Mrs Wattestone? The navy courts?'

Beatrice gapes, chokes on her words.

Nessa approaches the bed. 'Are you all right there, Mrs Wattestone?'

'Gah,' says Beatrice, jabs a finger in my direction, 'gak – g-*gaah*.'

Nessa shakes her head, comes closer. 'Are you having a bit of trouble with your breathing, there, Mrs Wattestone? Want another pillow?'

Beatrice finds her voice. 'Can't you – can't you *see* it?'

Nessa looks up, stares directly into my eyes. 'See what, Mrs Wattestone? What is it? Is there a spider?'

'It's – it's *right there* . . .'

Nessa pantomimes peering into the gloom behind me. 'Nope. Sorry. What is it I'm looking for?'

I fold my arms, gaze down at Beatrice sorrowfully. '*She* can't see me, Beatrice. Why would *she* be able to see me? *She* doesn't know I'm . . .' I take a step forward. A slightly risky move, but I reckon she'll recoil, which she does.

I bend slightly at the waist, the better to show her the black around my eyes. '. . . *dead*,' I snap.

The word has the effect I've been expecting. Beatrice lets out a tiny shriek, drops back against the pillow. Nessa makes a show of

473

fussing around her, raising her up and tucking an extra pad in behind her back as she gawps wordlessly at me.

'Oh, yeah, Beatrice,' I assure her, 'I'm *dead* all right. And you know what else?' I step back into the safety of the shadows and fix her with a long, steady, triumphant gaze.

'You're going to hell, Beatrice,' I say. 'There's no going to church or dominating the county's going to save you from this one. You're going to hell for the rest of eternity, and you know what else?' I'm not entirely sure if I haven't gone too far. Beatrice's face looks like landslip.

'We're going to be right there with you,' I say. 'What do you think about that?'

'Mrs Wattestone? Are you OK?' asks Nessa.

'Don't you see it?' stutters Beatrice. '*Don't you see it?*'

'She can't see me, Beatrice,' I say. 'Why would she be able to? It's not like she *knows* what you did, is it?'

'It's . . . it's . . .' stammers Beatrice.

The struggle is delightful. What can she say? How can she tell Nessa she's seen me? Wouldn't that be tantamount to knowing I was dead?

' . . . *ghost*,' she chokes.

Nessa stands back, lets out a braying, unsympathetic laugh. 'Oh, Mrs Wattestone, you do crack me up, you really do! What would you be seeing a ghost for?'

'Gah,' says Beatrice, 'gaaah.'

'It's not like you've got anything to have a guilty conscience about, is it?' asks Nessa.

Silently as I came, I slip back behind the curtain.

Chapter Eighty
In the Dark

And lying in the dark on my nest of mink coats, under a blanket of beaver lamb brought through from the wardrobe, waiting like a princess in a fairy-tale for my prince to rescue me, I see a ghost of my own.

I suppose I should have expected it, really. Even though I know I'm only dreaming, that the unease with which I lie is as bound to give me nightmares as if I had eaten a truckle of stilton. But it seems to me that I wake up to find the room filled with an eerie green light, and Lucy Wattestone, in cocktail dress and three-inch heels, perched on the end of the bed fiddling with a diamond ear clip. Not Lucy as I have known her, but the Lucy I have seen in a silver photo frame in her daughter's drawing room. Thirtysomething, slim. False eyelashes and half a dozen rings like knuckledusters on long, slender fingers.

I struggle to sit upright. Am relieved to find that I am not, at least, subject to the paralysis that assailed me when Andy visited. But my voice sounds blurred to me, as though I have a mouthful of cotton wadding.

'Lucy,' I say.

She gives me a bright cocktail smile that matches her clothes, and says, 'Have we met?'

'No, no.' I try smacking my lips in an attempt to clear the fuzziness. 'But we've already slept together,' I try a joke.

Lucy frowns, high, pale forehead wrinkling, then dismisses the comment. 'I don't suppose,' she asks, 'you'd happen to have a cigarette, would you?'

I shake my head. 'I've had to give up. Sorry. Bad for the baby.'

'How funny. Is that the latest fad?'

'You wouldn't believe it,' I tell her.

'How long have I been dead?' she asks bluntly.

'A while. A bit over thirty years, as it goes.'

'God.' She looks appalled. 'I wasn't alive for much longer than that.'

She looks over her shoulder at the depression in the bed where her body has lain for all that time. 'I could *so* do with a cigarette.'

I give her a Gallic-style shrug. *Desolé, madame. Il n'y en a plus.*

'Don't tell me you're still getting cravings after thirty years.'

'You have no idea. How powerful nicotine is. Nobody does, until they have to give it up. Mind you, I miss most things. Sunrise. Deodorant. Bacon sandwiches.'

We take a little time to think about all the things.

'How's Edmund?' she asks.

'He's—' what do I tell her? That he's a broken man?

Don't be stupid. She's a figment of your imagination.

'He never really recovered from you,' I say.

'Oh dear,' she says. Then: 'Well, sort of – I suppose at least he didn't just forget me.'

'No, he never did that.'

'I don't know whether I'm glad or not. Life has to go on.'

I think: I'd better level with her. 'He had a son.'

She looks like I've just slapped her. 'Oh.'

'I'm sorry.'

'Can't be helped. Might have expected it really. That bloody Beatrice wouldn't have got rid of me without following the whole thing through. Are you *sure* you don't have even *one* little cig?'

I shake my head.

'And he had it – sorry, him – with that poisonous little shit Mary Fulford-Ffawkes, I suppose?'

I nod.

'Oh. I'd sort of hoped he – oh, well. I don't know. I just wish I'd realised, you know, beforehand. I just thought she was a horrible little suck-up, waiting for Edmund to divorce me. I thought she'd give up eventually. Always hanging about here with that *creepy* little poof Hilary Crawshaw.'

I quell the urge to correct her vocab. It's not an inaccurate description, in the circs.

'And Mathilda?' she asks suddenly.

Mathilda. Mathilda. Oh, right . . .

'She's great. Oh, Lucy, she's *great*. You'd be so proud of her. She's had a hard time of it, but she's grown up so – such a wonderful person. And she's had a daughter!'

'A daughter! So she got married? I'm a grandmother?'

I sort of gloss it over. 'Yes. Well, yes. And she called her after you!'

'Oh . . .'

And her face is long and tragic. 'I'm so sorry. I wish – I wish I could have seen that. I wish I could have . . . it was the last thing I thought about. Before . . . you know. I tried to send her my wishes. Beam her my . . . I couldn't be there to protect her. I wish . . . I loved her, you know . . . so much I thought it would burn me up.'

'She loved you,' I assure her. 'So, so much. There's not a day goes by she doesn't think about you. But, look. She's got Rufus. Rufus protects her. He always will. And she's got me now.'

'And Rufus is . . .?' She realises, says: 'Oh.' Then she says: 'And you're the inconvenient wife?'

I nod. Feel myself blush.

'So history repeats itself.'

And I say: 'No. Not this time. And, Lucy, we're going to get you justice too. That's why I'm here now. That's why I came back. I'm here for you as much as I am for myself. We're going to save Rufus, and we're going to save Edmund as well. By the time this is finished, they will have nothing left.'

And then she shocks me. Because instead of thanking me, instead of congratulating me on my courage, my sense of fair play, she looks grave. Leans forward and says, in a voice filled with accusation: 'You fucking hypocrite.'

I recoil. 'What?'

'You fucking little hypocrite. Do you think I don't know about you?'

I don't say anything.

'What's the difference, Melody? What's the difference? You're the same as them and you think I want to be indebted to *you*? Go on then. What's the difference between *his* family and *your* family? What gives you the right to point the finger at *them*?'

'Oh God,' I stutter.

'What?' asks Lucy. 'Oh, yes. I suppose you think that just because I'm *dead* I'm going to be grateful? You're a liar. A betrayer. A deceiver.'

She is a figment of your imagination. She's a projection of your conscience.

And Lucy Wattestone sits upright, throws her shoulders back so I see her collarbones poke through thin white skin, and opens her mouth to sing. Only the sound that emerges is high-pitched, it's grotesque, it's irritating, it's –

Electronic.

It's 'Delilah'. It's my phone. And I'm scrabbling about in the dark, cold hands feeling the dead caress of animal pelts as I grope for the handset. My hand lights on it as the tune goes into its final crescendo. I hit the yes button just as it's about to cut out.

'Nessa?' I say.

But it's not Nessa. A voice I never thought I'd hear again speaks at me out of the darkness.

'I'm not dead, you dozy mare,' it says. 'I'm running a drain clearance franchise in Hobart.'

Chapter Eighty-One
The Nearest Equivalent

My head sings. 'Andy?'

His next word is as full of sarcasm as any I've heard in my life. 'Surprise!' he shouts.

'What – what are you—'

'I knew you were dramatic, Melody, but this one really takes the biscuit, even for you. Did it never occur to you that there was something odd about the fact that my family never once asked you where I was?'

'But—'

'No,' says Andy. Like, *naouw*. 'I'm not bloody *dead*. I'm just in Tassie, which is the nearest bloody equivalent. Some bloody joke, huh?'

'But you—'

'Yeah, well,' says my not-dead ex, 'now you know, OK? But don't think that means you've got a standing invite, because there's Buckley's chance I'd be there if you even thought about coming. Matter of fact, if I ever hear you're on your way here, I'm getting the first plane out.'

I cut him off with a short, hysterical laugh. 'You're alive!'

'Well done, Einstein. Now we don't have to string this out any longer, do we? I'm alive, you're alive, how dja do, yada yada, have a nice life.'

'But why are you calling me *now*?'

Andy inhales, then exhales noisily. 'Same reason I'm in bloody Hobart, fucknuckle. Your brother told me to. Not your dad as well this time, so I suppose I'd better be grateful for small mercies.'

'But they—'

He feigns the way people talk to irritating small children. Speaks slowly and enunciates very clearly. 'No. That's what your brother wanted me to tell you. They never killed me, OK? If you weren't so fond of slamming the phone down on people, you'd have worked that out by now.'

'Andy,' I say, 'I thought you were *dead*.'

'Oh, good grief. Yes, I *know* you bloody did. And I'll tell you another thing. If I wasn't so fond of my kneecaps, I'd have let you stay that way. I wouldn't say it was more than you deserve. Have you any idea what it's *like* in Hobart? Half the population's got no teeth and the rest look at you funny if you've got all your fingers.'

I'm being a bit slow on the uptake. 'But I don't understand. If you hate it so much, why don't you go somewhere else?'

'GAAAAAH!' shouts Andy. 'Because your father and your brother put the acid on me, OK? When you went running home to Mummy? They gave me a choice, mind.'

'Which was?'

'Go to Tassie or stay in the water while they chucked buckets of chicken giblets over the side of the boat.'

'Oh.'

'Yeah, *oh*.'

'I didn't know.'

'Course you didn't, Princess. We all believe you.'

'Andy, I didn't. As far as I knew, you'd cleared out your stuff by the time I got back and that was that.'

'Yeah, right.'

'Well, you *were* always threatening to do it . . .'

'Oh right, so now it's *my* fault.'

'I didn't say that.'

'Fuck it,' says Andy. Ever the articulate.

'Would it help,' I ask, 'if I said I was sorry?'

Silence.

'Well, I am,' I say. 'I'm sorry.'

'Big whoop,' says Andy, but he doesn't sound quite so hostile.

'They always interfered,' I say. 'You know that. And you know I didn't know about it most of the time till it was too late.'

'Your ma was always a serious buttinski,' he says.

'Still is, if it makes you feel better. Well, would be if she was talking to me.'

'She's not talking to you?' he sounds amazed.

'Long story.'

'That must be a relief,' he says. And unexpectedly, we're both laughing, remembering one of the running gags we used to share back in the days when we were complicit.

'If you want,' I offer, 'I'll call them and tell them to take the curse off. You don't have to stay in Hobart, you know. I'll make sure of it. You can come back to Brissie, even, and they'll stay off your back, I swear.'

'Ah, well,' says Andy, 'I dare say I'll survive.'

'I thought—'

'Well,' he says, 'It's not *so* bad. You sort of get used to it, you know?'

'You *are* joking.'

'Well . . . and besides. I sort of got married?'

I gulp. 'Sort of?'

I can hear him scratching the back of his neck, the way he used to do, and suddenly he's standing right there in front of me, clear as daylight, Andy, shirtless in his baggy shorts, one hand cupped over his right nipple. 'Yip,' he says.

'I . . . wow. Who to? Not a local?'

'Uh-huh.'

'Christ,' I tease. 'What's her name? Charlene? Raelene?'

'Alison.'

'Alison?'

'Has she got both eyes in the right place?'

'Yeah,' he says, in that don't-go-there voice of his. 'Yeah, she has. And we've got a nipper on the way and all.'

'Snap!' I say. 'I don't believe it! You and me both!'

'No! No way!'

'Yes way, babe! Can you imagine?'

'I can't see you pregnant,' he says. 'Your tits'll get so big you'll topple right over.'

'Watch it, fella. Jee-zus. Can you credit it? You and me,

popping out twelve-toed triple-nipple babies at the same time?'

'I never thought I'd see the day,' he says. And we both fall silent, remembering.

'So what is he,' he says eventually, 'this fella of yours?'

'Rufus,' I say, and I feel a glow inside when I say it.

'What sort of show pony name is *that*, Lady Muck?'

'A family one.'

'Wow. He knows who his father is?'

'Aw, *Andy*.'

I don't believe this. We never got on this well. Not after the first couple of years. This is like we were in the early days: teasing each other, making each other laugh. It feels good. But boy, it feels distant. It's like looking through a photo album.

And he says: 'So are you doing OK, babe?'

And I can't stop myself heaving a sigh. 'Not so good for a while. It's been hard. But I think I'm getting there.'

'He treating you OK?'

'Yeah. Yeah. There's other stuff, but not him. He's great.' And I'm thinking: if only you could see where I am while we're having this conversation. If only you knew the half of it.

And he says: 'It was the fact that we never got to sort it out. Between us, you know. That was the worst thing about it.'

And I say: 'I know, kid.'

'It wasn't all bad, was it?'

And flashes of when it was good – the jokessextickling-talkingkissingholding – unfold in my brain like a film on rewind. You never forget the people you've loved. You never do.

'No, babe,' I say. 'It wasn't. Some of it was good.'

And he says: 'I'd better go, now,' and I say: 'Yes, babe you'd better had.'

'Take care of yourself,' he says.

'Yeah. Yeah, you too. Really. You enjoy that kid, won't you?'

'Bloody ankle-biters,' he says. 'It's all downhill to hip replacement from now on.'

I laugh again. 'God, you could always make me laugh,' I say.

'We screwed it up, didn't we, Mel?'

'Royally.'

'I've hated you a lot over the last couple of years . . .'

'Back atcha,' I start, and then I realise that this was only the beginning of a sentence.

'But you know what?' he continues, 'I don't know why, but now I'm talking to you, all I want to do is say sorry. I don't know what happened, but I know I hurt you a lot at the end, and I'm really, really sorry.'

And I let him this time, because not all the fault was on my side.

'It's OK. I'm sorry too. I wasn't exactly – you know.'

'We were as bad as each other.'

'We were, Andrew. We were.'

'Do you think,' he asks, 'if we hadn't, if they hadn't, you know, we would have been able to sort it out?'

'What do you think?'

'Mmm,' says Andy. 'No.'

And I shake my head in the dark. 'No.'

'I did love you, though.'

My eyes fill with tears. This was my first love, my first real love, and you never forget. You always carry a bit of them around inside you, even when you've ended as badly as we did.

'And I loved you, too. Very much.'

He sounds reluctant. 'I've got to go now, kid. I've really got to.'

'Me, too.'

'Have a good life,' says Andy. The last words he'll ever say to me.

'And you too,' I say, trying to find the right words to part with. 'You make sure you do. Be happy.'

We hang up together and I put the phone down on the coat. Bring my hand up to cover my mouth and let a couple of tears slide down my face.

I hated you.

I loved you.

I wanted you so, so much.

And I want Rufus.

483

The clock on the phone reads 10 a.m. I've been in here twelve hours, more or less, and my skin feels tight and dry.

Will he come for me?

Does he love me?

Will we last for ever, when Andrew and I failed so spectacularly?

If it's so, he'll be looking for me right now. Tilly will have tripped him over my phone, shown him the clothes and the books and the face cream, and he will be looking for me. Pounding down the corridors, banging on walls, calling out my name. He'll have Django running ahead and Tilly hustling along behind, and he won't know that the tension in her face is because she knows what she will have to see behind this door.

What is he thinking?

Let him love me.

Have we pushed it past bitterness, has it gone beyond?

Is he looking for me from love or duty, hunger or curiosity?

Let him love me.

I think of Andy, half a world away and half a lifetime, getting ready for bed and probably thinking of me. My God, is love really like this? The madness of wanting, waiting, wishing, the ache of missing someone daily, hourly, every moment, so easily replaced? There was a time when Andrew was all I could think of, the only thing I saw. I believed that that was love. Was it the same? I can't remember, now. Did I feel this raging, gnashing, immolated emptiness at the thought that I had lost him?

Let him love me.

It's cold. I crawl back under my makeshift bedding, wrap my arms around my stomach and wait.

He is everything. He is my delight and my darkness, my food and drink. He is the savour of salt and the sweetness of honey; he is colour, light, touch, taste, smell. He is my strength and my weakness, my pleasure, my pain. I have lived to be with him, waited to find him. He must want me. He *must* want me. For now that I know that he exists, my own existence is nothing without him.

Let him love me.

I close my eyes. Feel the corners of my mouth turn down as I think of him. Send him my thoughts through the crumbling house: Rufus, come to me. Find me. Love me. Please love me.

And then, as before, I hear muffled sounds beyond the door, voices, urgent and confused, the sound of the barrier being pulled back. And then his voice: calling, desperate and afraid, through the door. 'Melody! Melody! Oh my God!'

And despite myself, despite the fact that I'm supposed to stay put, lie here pale and suffering, on my deathbed, passively waiting for my prince to rescue me, I am unable to hold myself back. I scramble from the bed, hurl myself through the darkness, catch myself on the chair and stumble, heavily, against the door. Flail at it with my fists and shout his blessed name.

'Rufus! Rufus!'

And he's inside, in the dark with me, and he's saying my name over and over and over and over, hands in my hair, tears streaming down his face, and his kisses and my kisses fall upon our eyes like rain on the desert.

Chapter Eighty-Two

The Last Heir

And he passes through the house like a storm, thunder on his countenance and a hurricane in his heart. The last heir, the chosen one, going prepared for war. And the house, as though it were responding to his rage, groans and shudders as he passes, cries out in pain and age and misery: the generations who have suffered for its continuance wailing their despair. It knows he is leaving, that the last of the Wattestones is taking himself away. It knows it is over, but the end will not pass unmarked.

Down the Tudor landing, where panelling gapes, split like tinder. Through the Long Gallery, where suits of armour, shaken from their stands, slump like the fallen of Agincourt. We wheel, the three of us, away from the sagging remains of the tollbooth stair, stride together through the Chinese music room, where a beam has broken free and smashed its way through three of the grand pianos and left the spinet miraculously intact. In the game larder, glassy eyes have turned to milk and maggots spill between raddled feathers. And on we stride, the three of us: the future confronting the long-gone.

The older generation are in the big drawing room off the Great Hall, because the ceiling collapsed in the breakfast room while I was locked away. The morning is half-gone, but no-one has thought to leave. They stay on, immobile, paralysed. As though awaiting some great event.

Beatrice, querulous and suddenly aged since last night, huddles, tiny and nervous, in the corner of one of the sofas. Mary, despite the obvious futility of the activity, despite the plaster spitting in starbursts from the hammer-beam ceiling, stands, turned out for a coffee morning, in a mint green two-piece, at a pedestal table, arranging winter peonies in a blue glass vase. Edmund sits bolt upright in the night porter's chair, hands gripping the arms, staring ahead of him with sightless eyes. They have their faces turned away from us; don't notice us come in.

The past, frozen in place, unable to change itself; the future approaching on angry feet.

'They're coming,' says Beatrice

'Who's coming?' asks Mary.

'The ghosts. I feel them. The house is moving and the dead will show themselves,' says Beatrice solemnly.

'I do wish you'd stop going on about ghosts,' says Mary. 'You've turned into a pair of ghouls, you really have. It won't do.'

'I will go to hell,' says Beatrice.

'Nonsense' says Mary. 'Wattestones don't go to hell.' She says this with the certitude of one who knows without doubt that birthright passes beyond the grave.

'No,' says Edmund. 'We live in it.'

Mary lays down her scissors in a gesture of ladylike impatience. 'What on earth has got into everyone today? You sound like something out of Edgar Allan Poe.'

'It's over,' says Edmund. 'Can't you see?'

'Oh,' snaps Mary, 'pull yourself together, for heaven's sake. We've got a lot to do today.'

Somewhere in the house, the thunder and crash of falling masonry.

'We must leave,' says Edmund. 'Can't you see that? We have to leave today. Don't you see, Mary? There's no more we can do. The house is collapsing. If we don't leave today, we will *die.*'

I see her turn her head and throw him a look of unspoken contempt.

'No one,' she says, 'is going to die. Not today, not ever. Today is a good day. Today is the day when it all begins again.'

I'm not sure when the screw came loose in Mary's head. Whatever, it looks like it's dropped right out now.

Edmund shakes his head.

'It is all,' she says shrilly, 'going to be fine. Rufus is back. My boy is back, and everything will be all right from now on.'

Mary's boy steps boldly forward. Stands, with folded arms, and waits to be noticed. The three of them turn, see him, see his sister and see – gaping mouths and indrawn breath – me standing at his shoulder, and each reacts in a wildly differing manner. Beatrice is clearly terrified. Clearly still thinks I'm a ghost, thinks she's the only one who sees me. Edmund's face lights up like a Belisha beacon: a huge, beaming smile spilling across his features like sunshine. 'Why, my *dear*,' he says.

Mary looks – appalled. So many emotions register on her face: anger, astonishment, fear, loathing, disbelief. Appalled is the only word for it. And then she sees the expression on Rufus's face, and everything is overwashed by despair.

He speaks quietly, firmly, with a tone that brooks no argument. 'We've come for our father,' he says.

I step out from behind. Give everyone a sunny smile and say, because I never can resist a touch of bathos: 'Oh, and I've come for my car.'

Chapter Eighty-Three
All For You

She is distraught. Her face is wild, desperate; skin waxy, eyes wide, mouth pleading; the shiny hair tangled where she has clutched at it in her agitation. She pants between words, casts about for something – *something* – that will change his mind.

'But – but – it was for *you*, Rufus! I did it for *you*!'

Rufus doesn't move, doesn't react.

'Don't you see? It was all for you, all of it! You wouldn't even be – Beatrice! Tell him! Make him understand!'

Beatrice hasn't spoken since we came into the room. Has simply gone whiter and whiter, her hands shaking, lips moving almost at random. What must be going through her head? I don't care. I honestly don't care because she hasn't even looked at her son, at the seventy-four-year-old man softly weeping in the porter's chair.

Edmund is shattered. He looks like the earth has opened and swallowed him up. His skinny shoulders droop in his flannel shirt and his face has caved in, cheeks hollow like those of the mummy on the bed. He hasn't cried in forty years. Not publicly. Men like Edmund don't cry, not for the world to see.

And kneeling at his feet, Tilly. Weeping too, holding his hands between her own, dropping cheek-kisses on them. Shaking her head and whispering, over and over, 'Daddy, Daddy, Daddy'.

Mary lunges at her son, grabs at his arm, tries to establish some contact between them. He steps backward, raises the arm and twists it out of her grasp. Reaches out, without looking, for he knows where I am by instinct alone, and draws me into his side.

'Rufus, *Rufus*! Don't, darling, *don't*! You can't do this! You can't! It's *me*, darling! I did it for *you*!'

I know, of course, that this is true. In her own twisted way, Mary has done everything for Rufus. He was her ambition, her reason. She did the unthinkable to get him and she was prepared to do anything to keep him.

Love has a lot to answer for.

She tries again, and Rufus pulls me back, pulls me out of harm's way.

'Don't, darling! Don't! I was trying to save you! Trying to save you! Don't you see? She's not *good* enough for you! She'll destroy you. She'll destroy *everything*!'

He speaks at last. 'No, mother. Not Melody. She's the one who saved me.'

She looks like she looked when I slapped her that time.

Rufus glances over his shoulder at his father and his sister. 'Come on,' he says.

Edmund leans forward, pulls his daughter into his arms and presses his face to her scalp. They cling together like shipwrecked children, help each-other to feeble feet, prop each-other up as they pass Beatrice, then Mary, and never afford them a single glance.

We follow in their wake; head for the Great Hall, aiming for the courtyard, the drive, then freedom.

'Don't!' Mary screams. 'You can't! Don't leave me! We can make it all right! We can! We can make it all right! I'll apologise! I'll be good!'

At the top of the stairs, in the archway, Rufus stiffens, stops, turns to face her.

His voice is cold, even, unmodulated. 'You knew,' he says, 'that she was pregnant. You knew because I told you, when we were in London. I sat there and I told you, and it didn't make a moment's difference. You didn't change your mind. You didn't even think about it for one moment.'

There's an ineffable logic to her answer.

'But I couldn't *do* anything about it,' she says. 'It was too late by then. I couldn't exactly let her out, could I? How would *that* have looked?'

490

The house shifts once more. Perceptibly. Turns over and groans.

It's Rufus's turn to drain of colour. His jaw clicks shut and he swivels on his heel, marches down the steps without a backward look.

Chapter Eighty-Four

Chasm

Edmund holds himself together as we cross the courtyard. Poker back, army bearing. Looks at the sky, the wall, the trees in the distance. But when we are on the drive, have started the walk towards the village, he is unable to resist a final look back and promptly does a bit of a Lot's wife on us. Goes rigid, then abruptly loses the strength in his limbs, crumbles and plummets to the ground, on his knees and then on all fours. We're all down beside him in a flash, hands on arms, sounds of concern, trying to haul him to his feet. He waves us away.

'Don't. Don't. I'll be all right. I just need . . . a moment.'

I look back to see what can have had this effect on him. Gasp. Because Bourton Allhallows is eating itself.

A cloud of ravens shrieks and circles in the air above the house, like vultures awaiting a death. They swoop in and out of my field of vision, as a great bank of dust-fog, so thick that it obscures everything that enters it, hangs above the gables. For the house has begun to collapse in on itself, outer wings leaning drunkenly against the inner core like a house of cards. The spot where Rufus and I sat months ago and weatherproofed with plastic sheeting has vanished altogether; nothing remains but a great jagged hole open to the sky.

'Look,' I say, in wonderment as much as horror. 'Oh, *look*.'

The four of us watch as a chunk of the façade of the Victorian wings simply breaks loose and crashes into the courtyard. Another cloud of dust rises into the air, sucks itself around the house like a shroud.

I think of my enemies, still inside, still denying the end of their world. Bad, black, rotten to the core, but still human. Still people. Still capable of pain. Beatrice is too old and too crippled to walk out of there alone, and Mary, when we left, was beyond noticing, or caring, about anything.

I feel sick. I know what we have to do.

'Rufus,' I say, 'we have to get them out of there.'

We run down the hill together, force our way back through the front door. It takes the strength of both of us to get it open, for it has wedged against the floor and fights back as we push.

The Great Hall, too, is dark with dust. We pause for a moment, fight for breath, allow our eyes to adjust.

The house is still. The stillness of air before a thunderstorm. The stillness before the pounce of the predator.

Something ticks, ticks, ticks faintly in the distance. In the core of the building. Settling. Readjusting.

'Hello?' Rufus calls.

No answer.

We step forward on to spongy floorboards, which soak up the sound of our footfalls.

'Hello?' he cries again.

Faintly, through the archway, an answering voice. 'Rufus!' it calls.

We exchange a glance. 'You go get her,' I tell him. 'I can't carry her. I'll find Mary.'

He nods. Lopes away from me through the gloom. Hand over my face, I take a deep breath through my nose. Call: 'Mary?'

Tick, tick, tick.

I set off, gingerly; feel my way, step by step, around the walls. Call her name again.

Tick, tick, tick.

She could be anywhere. She could be gone already. She could be hiding, or running, or trapped, somewhere, in among the falling rooms.

'Mary?'

Something shifts in the far corner, under the Caravaggio. I peer, try to make out what it is.

'Mary?'

No reply.

I walk forward.

She is pressed against the wall, green suit gone eau-de-nil with plaster dust, face smeared with tears and grime. One elegant court shoe has fallen off, lies unnoticed on its side three feet from her sole. I look at her, at her misery, at her defeat, and my heart is torn with scorn and pity. She doesn't look at me. Her arms are wrapped around her head, covering her face.

'Mary,' I say, 'we have to get out of here.'

No response. She rocks slightly, pulls her knees closer in to her body.

'Mary. Come on. You have to get up.'

She doesn't move.

Tick, tick, tick.

I bend, reach out to touch her shoulder.

Her reaction is lightning-fast. An arm shoots out, bats me away. *'Don't touch me!'*

Rufus appears in the archway, Beatrice a bundle of fabric in his arms. She appears to be catatonic, head buried in his chest, hands hanging pendulous by his hip. He sees us, sees my predicament. Looks torn.

'Go,' I tell him.

He glances down at his grandmother, at the door, at the huddled form of his mother.

'It's OK.' I attempt to reassure him, though I am entirely unsure myself. 'Go.'

'I'll come back,' he says.

I nod. Turn back to her as his footfalls pass, head towards the open air. The house spasms once more; a cracking, howling, grating death-throe that makes my pulse surge.

'Mary! It's not safe! Can't you hear it? You have to come *now*!'

Again, the batting hand. She clings to the wall, limbs and torso rigid. I'm going to have to use force.

I squat, try to slot my hands into her armpits, uncurl her. I'll drag the bitch out of here by the hair if I have to. Get some traction, brace and haul.

Her body whips open with sudden ferocity and she throws

494

herself head-first into my stomach, winding me, knocking me backwards on to the floor. And she's on her side, legs flailing, kicking out, catching me on the thigh with her one remaining sharp-edged heel.

'Get away get away get *away*!'

'*Mary!*' I cough-shout. '*I'm trying to help you!*'

'You won't you won't you *won't*!'

She scrambles to her knees. I try to grab at her ankle but my fingers slip on ten-denier nylon, clutch uselessly for a second, feel it slide away under my fingers.

'Don't touch me don't *touch* me!'

She gains her feet, hobble-runs away across the centre of the room, a silly, half-mad ageing woman who has destroyed everything. And I think, well, at least she's running in the right direction. At least she's heading for the door.

A rush and a roar, and floor gives way. Mary remains suspended in the air for a moment, head thrown back, arms jacked in the air like a marionette. And then she drops, like a stone, through the hole.

'*MARY!*'

She's still here. Shoulders, arms, over the edge, body hanging into the chasm. Slips backwards.

And I'm crawling across the treacherous boards, keeping as low and flat as possible, spreading my weight as on quicksand.

'Hold on! I'm coming!'

Another jolt and she drops back some more; head, elbows, flat palms on splintered wood. I close the distance, spreadeagle and stretch. Look into her eyes.

'Give me your hand,' I say.

Sweat glistens on her face. Fear throws every bone into sharp focus.

'Don't touch me,' she says.

'Give me your hand.'

Inch by precious inch, her weight carries her towards the abyss.

'*Please*, Mary!'

Her jaw is resting on the floorboards, only her forearms visible now.

I snatch at a wrist. Make a last effort to save her.
The arm flies up, snatches away from me.
'*Don't*,' she says.
And she is gone.

Epilogue

A Beginning

Twanny Mifsud is growing watermelons this year. Last year it was tomatoes, the fruit fist-sized on vines so leafless and shrivelled they looked as though they couldn't support a kidney bean, but today the field is scattered with cool green gourds. We park up on the double yellows and stroll across the road to sit on the wall with a view of the chapel dome on the main road, listen to the scritch of cicadas among red-gold caper blossoms. It's my second trip here of the day, but I don't mind. I never tire of watching those big birds whizz over the stone-strewn pastures, the backdraft from the rotors throwing up great gusts of dusty air from parched red soil.

'Wow,' says Costa, but he's not talking about our surroundings.

'I suppose it is a bit,' I say.

'So did they ever find the bodies?'

I shake my head.

'Too much house on top. I suppose there's an outside chance Lucy might show up one day, though given the fact that the entire park's been ring-fenced because it's still collapsing, I don't suppose it'll happen for a good while yet. Not while Edmund's still alive, anyway, which is the main thing.'

'And how's he doing?'

'He's – sad. It was a helluva shock.'

'I'll bet. It's like the poor guy's wasted his entire life on a lie.'

'Yeah. Mind you. I don't think he felt he'd been a raging success before he found it out.'

'Mmm.'

Costa drops his sunglasses down from the top of his head over his eyes. 'Is he coming out this summer?'

'No. Hates the place. Reminds him of her. Of course, he never

497

came out while she was alive, either. I think he regarded her trips to Gozo as a bit of a holiday for him as well.'

He's studying the sky. 'What time's the heli due?'

I check my watch. 'Five more minutes.'

'OK. Hot here, isn't it?'

'This? This isn't hot. It doesn't get *hot* till August.'

'Oh, OK.'

'Take your jacket off if you think it's hot.'

'Don't mother me. I get enough of that at home.'

I look down.

'She sends greetings, by the way,' he says.

'Oh, OK.'

'You want me to send them back?'

'Would it do any good?'

A shrug. 'You never know. I guess she must be coming round a bit if she's sending greetings. You should come home for a bit, maybe. Bring Louis. You know she'll never be able to resist a grandson.'

'I'll think about it,' I say. 'A one-year-old on long-haul. It's quite an undertaking.'

'Well, don't think for too long. It doesn't do, you know. Families shouldn't be not talking to each other.'

'I know.'

I think for a bit. 'Thanks for coming yourself. It's good to see you.'

Costa reaches out and muzzes my hair. 'We're a right lot, aren't we?'

'Sure are that.'

'Maybe in the spring? Once you're done here?'

'Mmm. Rufus goes back to school in October. Going to learn to be an architect. We'd have to wait till term finished.'

'Yeah, well. You can make all the excuses you like, but the fact remains the same. You could always come by yourselves, you know.'

I don't even have to think about this one. 'No way.'

He gives me a quizzical look.

498

'I'm never, ever going to be apart from him again.'

'You're apart from him now.'

'That's three days, Costa, not three weeks. There's a difference.'

'Strewth!' he says. 'Don't tell me you've turned into a romantic in your old age?'

'No,' I lie. 'But what if I had?'

'Nothing. Just – not something I thought I'd ever see.'

'You should try it yourself sometime.'

He laughs. Sticks his hands in his pockets in a slightly obscene way. 'You're not going to catch Costa Katsouris buying flowers.'

I elbow him in the ribs. 'It'll happen.'

'Not while there's backpackers on the gold coast.' He waggles his eyebrows and gives me a flash of his pearlies. 'I like your sister-in-law. She's not bad for an oldie.'

'Don't even think about it. You're not in her league.'

'Maybe she could do with a bit of youthful vigour to wake her up.'

'Well, what would she want *you* for, then?'

We do a bit of brother-sister hand-slapping.

'I have missed you,' I tell him.

'Shaddap,' he says. 'I haven't missed *you* at all.'

The road is starting to fill up. A minibus pulls up, decants a load of pink and peeling English. They look like a bucket of prawns.

'Course,' he says, 'there's always the financial aspect.'

'Meaning?'

'Meaning if you made it up with them you'd get your allowance starting up again. Can't be easy, married to a student. Bet you didn't think *that* was going to happen.'

'We'll survive.'

'Hah!' shouts Costa. '*You*? Survive on a couple of beans and a reflexologist's income? Pull the other one! I once saw your credit card catch fire you were swiping it so fast!'

'Quite naïve for a company director, arentcha?'

'Well, *you're* quite ugly for a *Sheila*,' says my charming brother, 'but I don't say anything about it.'

I ignore him.

'Two things. One, even a derelict village is worth a few bob in the Cotswolds. As is an emerald the size of a pigeon's egg. And a slightly torn Caravaggio, anywhere in the world. And without that bottomless hole for it all to fall in to—'

'Quite literally,' he joshes.

A memory of Mary's face as she went down flashes through my mind. I dismiss it '– we're not exactly going to starve. It's certainly enough to keep Beatrice in her maximum security twilight home, anyway.'

'But I thought you said the house had fallen down?'

'Well, it did, but it didn't all fall down at once. Took several weeks before it actually did the decent thing. And you'd be amazed how many people are prepared to overlook the health and safety issues where fine art is concerned.'

'Yih. And millions and millions of dollars.'

'And millions and millions of dollars.'

He's started another game of pocket billiards.

'Maximum security twilight home, eh?'

'It's very nice,' I assure him innocently. 'Run by the council, but she's on a private basis so she only has to share with one other old lady. She's in with a second-hand car dealer's widow from Swindon at the moment. Gets to listen to stories about shopping at Primark all day.'

'That's nice.'

'Yeah. And they have a great programme of entertainments.' I'm starting to laugh. 'Bingo at three o'clock every afternoon, and once a week, the local evangelist youth group comes in and leads a rousing sing-song. "What a Friend I Have in Jesus". "There'll Be Blue Birds Over the White Cliffs of Dover". "If You're Happy And You Know It Clap Your Hands". All the old classics.'

'She must be as happy as a pig in shit,' says Costa. 'Sounds like heaven.'

'Simply,' I agree. 'It's broadening her horizons no end. And once every few weeks I pay someone to go in and serenade her with a Tom Jones medley just to keep her on her toes. We're hoping she'll last a good few years yet, she's having such a good time.'

500

'It makes me proud,' he says. 'You're so loving and forgiving.'

'I learned at the feet of masters.'

'Why, thank you. What about the rest of them, then? Mary's foot-soldiers?'

'Oh, nothing much. Like you say, I'm the loving and forgiving type. It was sad, obviously, that they had to leave their grace-and favour houses, but, you know . . . when circumstances change and everything . . .'

'Yes. Very sad,' he says.

'Poor Hilary. It's hit him hard. All he can afford is a bedsit in Surbiton, and that's done no good for his career. It's weird, I know, but no-one seems to want an art investment advisor with more than one digit in their postcode.'

'Snobbery,' says Costa. 'A terrible thing.'

'Couldn't have happened to a nicer guy.'

'So I gather.'

'Oh, look!' I say. 'It's coming!'

The big bird rises up from the Gozo channel. Dark against the sun and rushing like a flying beetle. And my heart, still and calm all afternoon, swells with excitement. I slip off the wall, boiling tarmac burning the soles of my feet, and shade my eyes to watch her. There's great romance about the approach of a helicopter. I always convince myself that if I look hard enough, I will see the faces of the passengers, staring down all lit up from the excitement of their trip along the Dingli cliffs.

'Beaut, isn't it?' I bellow over the blat and thump of the rotors. My hair is flying out behind me and I have to drop my sunglasses down to protect my eyes from the dust.

'Yeah!' he shouts back.

Like a child, I jump up and down, wave both arms in greeting.

It passes over our heads and Costa starts to walk towards the terminal.

'I'll see you in there!' I shout. 'I'm going to go up and watch them disembark!'

I jog up the road to where the airfield is visible through a high chain-link fence. He's here. Three days away from him, and I've got a heart that wants to burst with longing. I will never, ever leave you. I couldn't. I clamber up on to the low stone wall, thread my fingers through the chain-link and watch. I am three years old again, waiting for Christmas. The 'copter sets down, rotors slowing from blat-blat-blat to thock-thock-thock to schtoof-schtoof-schtoof to silence and cicadas. I scratch the back of my calf with my big toe, try to stop myself jiggling with anticipation.

Luggage van. Little bloke in overalls wheeling steps up to the door. And here they come. Bloke in a suit switching on his moby and waiting for a signal. Middle-aged couple in matching safari shirts. Tall, generously upholstered woman with wild red hair whose smile is as big as my own as she pauses on the concrete and sups the air. Three teenagers sulkily herded by a harassed blonde mother.

And he is here. Lean and quiet and gentle and mine. I grip the fence, wait for him to see me. He hooks his fingers into the tab of his jeans and offers the other hand to an old lady as she wavers on the top step. And I will him: *look at me, look at me, look at me.*

He steps out of the shade, looks up. Sees me. Bathes me in his wide blue smile and raises a hand in the air. Holds it there for one, two, three seconds. I smile back, suddenly shy, raise my own in response and press the palm against the chain-link. Watch him as he bends to pick up his haversack, starts the walk to the exit.

And then I run down the road towards the terminal, so I can touch him.

WIN A FABULOUS HOLIDAY FOR 2 ON THE ISLAND OF GOZO

SIMPLY HEAVEN: A HOLIDAY for Two on the ISLAND of GOZO

Name: _____

Address: _____

_____

_____

Phone: _____

Email: _____

Gozo is *Simply Heaven* because...

_____

_____

❏ Please send me more information about books from Random House.

❏ Please send me more information about holidays in Malta and Gozo.

Send coupon to

Simply Heaven competition, Arrow Marketing Department, Random House, 20 Vauxhall Bridge Road, London SW11 3DU or register online at **www.randomhouse.co.uk**

Terms & Conditions

1. Offer open to UK, CI and IOM residents aged 18 and over.
2. Applicants who have responded by filling in their personal details and answered the question will be automatically entered into this prize draw.
3. Your personal details will only be retained and used by Random House and/or the Malta Tourist Office and Hotel Ta'Cenc & Spa in relation to the Simply Heaven Competition unless you have ticked the box(es) below in which case your personal details will be retained in order to send you the further information you have indicated you would like to receive. Your personal details will not be passed on to any other third parties.
4. No purchase necessary.
5. Each applicant may register for the Prize Draw only once.
6. Closing date for registration is 15th August 2006. No entries will be accepted after this date.
7. The Prize Draw will take place on 1st of September 2006. The winner will be notified by email or by letter by not later than 15th September 2006.
8. The holiday is not transferable and no cash alternative will be offered.
9. Holiday must be taken within 12 months from announcement of winner. Subject to availability of airline seats and hotel rooms. Date and time restrictions may apply.
10. By accepting the holiday offer the winner gives the promoter and the Maltese Tourist Office permission to a) take photographs for publicity purposes and/or b) publish the name of the winner.
11. The promoters' decision on all matters relating to the Prize Draw is final and binding.
12. No correspondence can be entered into.

arrow books

MALTA

MALTA GOZO COMINO